THE RESURRECTOR

Praise for the Dominic Grey Series

"Relentless." —*Publishers Weekly*

"One of the top ten books of the year." —*BloodWrites Mystery Blog,* on *The Summoner*

"Layton Green is a master of intellectual suspense." —JT Ellison, *New York Times* bestselling author of EDGE OF BLACK

"*The Summoner* is one of those books that make you want to turn on all the lights in your house and lock the doors . . . [t]he settings are authentic and you can feel and smell the countryside . . . [t]his is a wonderful read for those who enjoy both suspense and action stories" —*Seattle Post-Intelligencer*

On *The Egyptian*: "Stirring and imaginative, with an engaging premise that is briskly paced. Both the characters in the story and the reader are in for a wild ride." —Steve Berry, *New York Times* bestselling author of *The King's Deception*

"I do believe Layton Green has moved into my top 5 author category - not an easy feat to attain!" —*A Novel Source*

"The confines of a page are not enough for Layton Green's writing. His work begs to be translated into 100-foot high IMAX images, rendered in 3D, and given a score by Hanz Zimmer" —*Biblioteca*

On *The Diabolist*: "A well-crafted and exciting thriller with a pair of interesting protagonists . . . and a charismatic villain who makes our skin crawl." —*Booklist*

"This is what you get when you combine Indiana Jones with Ludlum's Jason Bourne . . . A must read for all you lovers of conspiracy theories, thrillers and mysteries alike!" —*Baffled Books*

"Layton Green is an absolutely brilliant writer." —*Everything to Do With Books*

"Green's debut *The Summoner* was such a great read, I was hoping that he'd duplicate his literary excellence. In his second book, *The Egyptian*, Green exceeded my expectations." —*BookPleasures.com*

"Favorite book of the year so far." —*A Novel Source*

"A blend of action, history, anthropology, thrills, and chills, all delivered with a mature, polished voice. I am eager for more from this author." —Scott Nicholson, bestselling author

"Layton Green has written a tale with supernatural and political undertones that unravels with ever increasing suspense . . . The book is plain terrific." —Richard Marek, former president and publisher of E.P. Dutton

"An awesome read . . . . The writing is polished and evocative, the subject matter fascinating, the characters intriguing, and the pace non-stop. Spooky and occasionally metaphysical, *The Summoner* harkens back to *The Serpent and the Rainbow* in its ability to convincingly portray seemingly paranormal events in a realistic (and therefore even creepier) manner." —*BloodWrites*, Mystery Pick of the Week

"[T]his book is above and beyond in its narrative, its cohesiveness, the depth of its characters and the quality of the writing. This is one of the best books I've ever read for Odyssey Reviews." —*Odyssey Reviews*

"Green writes like a dream." —Melody Moezzi, award-winning author, *Haldol and Hyacinths*

"[C]alls to mind such series as Jason Bourne and Indiana Jones, with supernatural/religious overtones thrown in. I recommend *The Summoner* to anyone looking for a suspense-filled journey into a unique—and at times, terrifying—culture that'll keep you guessing." —*Bookhound's Den*

"Yes, I did put TWO Five Stars up there . . . giving Green's *The Summoner* Five stars and Five stars alone downplays how I felt about this book." —*1000+ Books to Read*

"Dan Brown is pretty good at what he does and I don't begrudge him his success, but when it comes to interesting characters embarking on a thrilling exploration into the dark world of cults, religions and magic Layton Green does it SO much better." —*Nylon Admiral Reviews*

"Layton Green kicks things up a notch and delivers a novel that should, if there's any justice to be found upon the shelves, make him a household name. *The Diabolist* is a dark, intelligent, spellbinding novel . . . I cannot recommend this one highly enough." —*Beauty in Ruins Reviews*

"Green's *The Summoner* proved his great talent. *The Diabolist* ensures his place at the top of crime fiction: his number 1 place. Unbelievably good, unbelievably intricate, unbelievably Green." —*The Review Broads*

On *The Diabolist*: "[A] story that will move you to the edge of your seat." —*Seattle Post-Intelligencer*

*To Ryan K. and all the
other true warriors out there*

This is a work of fiction. Names, characters, organizations, places, and events are either products of the author's imagination or are used fictitiously.

THE RESURRECTOR
Copyright © 2017, Layton Green
All rights reserved.

No part of this book may be reproduced, or stored in a retrieval system, or transmitted in any form or by any means, electronic, mechanical, photocopying, recording, or otherwise, without express written permission of the publisher.

Published by Sixth Street Press

Book cover design by Jeroen ten Berge (jeroentenberge.com)
Author Photo by Robin Shetler Photography
Ebook Interior by JW Manus

THE RESURRECTOR

LAYTON GREEN

Books by Layton Green

THE DOMINIC GREY SERIES
The Summoner
The Egyptian
The Diabolist
The Shadow Cartel
The Resurrector
The Reaper's Game (Novella)

THE GENESIS TRILOGY
Genesis
Revelation
Ascension (forthcoming)

THE BLACKWOOD SAGA
Book I: *The Brothers Three*
Book II: *The Spirit Mage*
Book III: *The Last Cleric*
Book IV: *Return of the Paladin*
Book V: *A War of Wizards*

OTHER WORKS
Written in Blood
A Shattered Lens
The Metaxy Project
The Letterbox

The world will not be destroyed by those who do evil, but by those who watch them without doing anything.

—Albert Einstein

1

KHAYALANGA TOWNSHIP
WESTERN CAPE, SOUTH AFRICA
PRESENT DAY

The light of a full moon illuminated the couple huddled around a rusty oil drum in the center of the township. The trash fire inside the barrel doubled as a source of warmth and as an oven for roasting corn.

Behind them was the storage container they called home. A good space. Unlike most of the neighboring shacks, it had a metal roof instead of tarpaper. More resistant to wind and floods.

Just beyond the township lay the gentle swells of wine country. Golden fields and sprawling manors steeped in the wealth of the old Boer families. The inequalities of life in the Western Cape used to motivate the couple, inspire nightly political discussions with their neighbors while quaffing sour *umqombothi* beer, but they no longer cared for such things. Instead they stared with sightless eyes into the fire, numb from the sudden loss of their only child, a sixteen-year-old boy who cut his leg collecting copper and, less than a month later, succumbed to a bacterial infection in the township's struggling clinic.

Shouts rose in the distance. A gang fight or a robbery. Two gunshots rang out, and then another. The grieving parents didn't flinch. These disturbances were a nightly occurrence.

Besides, what could touch them now? Their son was dead. Their souls had fled to join his.

A gust of dry wind brought a whiff of sewage. As the wife turned the sharpened sticks piercing the maize, the commotion rippled through the township, growing closer to their home. Screams. Another gunshot. The wife noticed her neighbors pointing and shouting. Someone called her by name, warning her to seek shelter.

The husband seized her wrist with startling force. She had not felt his strength since Akhona had died. Yet instead of pulling her inside, he stood motionless, a strangled cry escaping his throat. When the wife finally looked up and saw the source of the uproar, the ground wobbled beneath her, and she collapsed into her husband's arms.

Fifty feet away, a shirtless teenage boy was running towards them, followed by a group of men shouting and waving pistols. When the boy caught sight of the couple, he slowed beside a cluster of low, makeshift power lines. His smooth black skin possessed a grayish pallor. The woman thought she must have been hallucinating when she noticed that his fingertips looked like thorns from an acacia tree, and that instead of a bird-like adolescent frame, muscles rippled across his arms and torso.

Still, she knew him. She would always know him.

"Mother," the boy croaked, as if the power of speech was an unfamiliar thing.

A brick mason grabbed the boy from behind. The boy turned and tossed him ten feet away, collapsing a tin shack. Two more men rushed forward as the mother screamed at them to stop.

With a neutral expression, the boy grabbed a cluster of power lines, spasmed as electricity crackled through him, and tossed the live wires into the group of men, scattering them.

The husband took a step back, his mouth agape. "Akhona?"

The woman had no such reservations. She rushed forward, aching for her son, his touch, his smell, not caring how this impossible thing had happened. The boy, Akhona, reached for her.

Another man shouted *unclean thing* in Xhosa, the language of the township. He ran up and fired a gun into the back of the boy's head. Akhona took a few more steps, then pitched forward and lay still. Blood, bright and clean, poured from the wound.

The woman wailed and collapsed atop her dead son for the second time in a month. The father cast a fearful glance at the body, not quite as removed from reality as the grieving mother. It was their son, no doubt about it.

But how? The father had helped lower Akhona into his grave, had shoveled tired red earth onto the coffin.

Incredulous, the father lifted his gaze until it rested on the same place the rest of the crowd was staring: a halo of light spilling from the tower of a gray stone manor. Looming atop the nearest hill like a malevolent spirit trapped in granite, the manor was a place the father knew by reputation only, a place no one from the township dared approach.

A place where the Bad Things happened.

2

NEW YORK CITY

"*Hajime.*" Begin.

After announcing the last bout of the night—the finals—the tuxedoed Japanese man returned to his seat. He was not a referee. There were no referees. Only a few dozen wealthy spectators and a pair of gladiators who had weathered the storm of brutality and remained standing.

The night's arena was the courtyard of a fortified stone monastery, The Cloisters, hidden in the heart of upper Manhattan. It belonged more to medieval Europe than to New York City.

Only the clink of ice in glasses and the swish of money exchanging hands broke the silence. Hands loose at his sides, Dominic Grey pushed off the low wall ringing the courtyard. He knew the score. It was win or lose, submit or be maimed.

Across the courtyard, a Thai-American man with taped knuckles and a rubbery face clapped his hands twice as he approached. Though a few inches shorter than Grey's six feet one, the Thai fighter was fifty pounds heavier, a pit bull in comparison.

Shirtless, unwilling to give his opponent the leverage of loose clothing, Grey calmly stalked the courtyard. *What's missing*, he wondered? *There's something missing here.*

Ah, yes.

With a detached nod, Grey reached back to the illicit fights of his youth, a string of raucous underground venues from Tokyo to Marseille. The feeling of an electric current zipping through his veins was the absent sensation, the dump of adrenalized fear at the start of a fight, the dry mouth and roiling stomach and quivering hands and knees.

It wasn't adulthood, he knew, that had stripped him of the natural high that came before a battle.

It was someone he had lost.

His opponent threw a series of jabs and low kicks, testing defenses. Grey let him dance. The muay Thai expert was a bruiser, someone who relied on size and strength.

Grey had reached the finals with a series of smooth submissions that left the crowd awed but feeling cheated. The Thai boxer had pummeled his opponents into unconsciousness.

More jabs. Closer to the mark. Grey let him come, giving his opponent confidence so Grey could use his strength against him, bend when he tried to break and break when he tried to bend.

A tight snap kick. Grey bladed his body to the side and absorbed the blow. The muay Thai fighter threw an elbow combination, and Grey brush-blocked it aside.

The Thai fighter grunted and advanced, sensing weakness. Wondering how this emaciated, pale, greasy-haired deadbeat had managed to reach the finals. The thick fighter jabbed twice, throwing from so far away Grey knew it was a setup, and then attacked with a vicious roundhouse into Grey's thigh, a blow that could shatter bone even if blocked.

But Grey didn't block. Instead he pounced inside before the kick landed, so fast he could see the flash of surprise in the Thai fighter's eyes. As the shortened kick struck Grey harmlessly in the side, Grey jabbed the palm of his right hand straight under his opponent's chin, snapping his head back. At the same time, Grey swept out an ankle with the back of his heel and, keeping the ankle secured, thrust his leg high and straight back, a vicious *osoto-gari* that swept the Thai fighter off his feet. Grey wrapped the man's arm as he slammed to the ground.

The Thai fighter managed to tuck his chin and avoid thudding his head against the cobblestones. Still, he was stunned and breathless, and Grey sat atop him with an arm trapped.

In full control, breathing in the other man's sweat, Grey lifted his eyes for a quick glimpse of his surroundings. An old habit from life on the streets, and from his stints in Marine Recon and Diplomatic Security. Always be aware. Someone else could be coming at Grey from behind, with fists or knives or worse.

Instead of more attackers, Grey saw candlelit iron sconces and clusters of men in business suits, three to four per table, watching the fight with desensitized eyes. CEOs and mob bosses, arms dealers and stockbrokers. Men for whom violence was a habit.

Sorry to disappoint you, Grey thought as he jerked on the trapped arm and swung a leg over his opponent's head for an arm bar. As long as his opponent tapped out—and they always did—Grey wouldn't have to snap the elbow.

His eyes caught a glimpse of a woman seated to his left. A woman with caramel skin and a proud tilt to her chin, her hair swept into a bun. She was watching him with a cool familiar stare that left him breathless.

Nya.

Could it be?

Grey lurched to his left for a better glimpse, the manufactured focus he had summoned for the evening crashing down around him.

Nya? He thought again, whispering her name in the silence of the moonlit courtyard.

Crack.

Grey felt as if his head had just exploded. The Thai fighter reared back for another elbow strike, and Grey rolled away in desperation. His opponent followed, jumping to his feet and landing heavy kicks in Grey's side. He tried to recover but he couldn't think clearly. Head spinning, he covered his vitals and scrambled to the side, craning his neck for another look.

This time he got a better glimpse, and cackled at the absurdity of his mistake. This woman was a pale imitation of Nya. There was no curve to her lips, no depth to her gaze. Nya would never be here, sitting quietly as he participated in a sordid event like this. Not in a million years.

Another elbow smashed into Grey's face. Blood flew from his mouth and he curled into a ball.

More, Grey thought. *I deserve it. I deserve more than you could ever give.*

The Thai fighter threw a series of vicious kicks into Grey's side and back. Grey curled tighter.

Show me something. Hit me harder.

Frustrated, the Thai fighter tried to stomp on his head. Grey covered up as the blows rained down. *Better*, he murmured.

Most of the crowd had risen to their feet, sensing the end.

"Teach!"

A murmur rippled through the courtyard at the interruption.

The shout had come from a familiar voice. A voice from the living.

"Get up, Teach!"

Only his students called him Teach. After absorbing another kick, Grey shifted and saw a young African American girl standing by the doorway leading into the main building, eyes wide as she absorbed the scene.

Charlie.

One of the guards approached her while another inspected a wad of cash offered by an older man in a black suit filling the doorway.

"Viktor?" Grey said, confused.

The guard gripped Charlie's shoulder. The sight of someone laying hands on Grey's pupil incensed him, broke through his wall of depression. As the next kick came, he grabbed onto his opponent's ankle, then shot his leg out and kicked the Thai fighter in the side of his knee. His balance destroyed, the bigger fighter crashed to the ground. Grey swiftly applied an ankle lock and then jerked backwards, straightening his body and creating immense pressure on the trapped joint.

The Thai fighter bellowed and slapped the ground, a universal signal of submission.

It was over.

Grey released the hold and stood, coldly eyeing his opponent to make sure he honored the surrender. The other fighter clutched his sprained ankle and then limped out of the courtyard.

The crowd offered subdued claps at the sudden turn of events. Respectful but disappointed.

As Grey stood alone in the courtyard, sucking in oxygen and catching a whiff of expensive cologne drifting from the tables, Charlie slipped the guard's hold and ran over to him. She was a homeless teen who lived at the shelter where Grey taught jujitsu. The closest thing to a mentee Grey had ever had.

"I haven't seen you in a month, Teach."

"Yeah. I know."

"Hey, yo . . . Lurch over there told me what happened in South America." Her eyes slipped down. "I'm sorry."

Grey swallowed and didn't respond.

"He also told me you two were detectives. That you take cases all around the world. You never told me that."

"How did you think I paid the rent?"

"I dunno, you white. So what are you, some kinda superhero?"

Grey had to chuckle. "Hardly. I just watch the professor's back."

"That's not what he says."

Grey stepped over the low wall and grabbed his duffel bag. He toweled off, then shrugged into a long-sleeved black shirt. "What do you want, Charlie?"

"She's here at my request," Viktor boomed as he approached. "Since you haven't taken my calls."

The spectators had dispersed, the winners drinking and chatting in the courtyard, those who had lost bets casting irritated glances at Grey as they headed for their limousines. Grey slung his bag over his shoulder and approached one of the guards, who handed him a leather pouch stuffed with hundred dollar bills.

"Five G's, man," the guard said. "Good take."

Grey grabbed it and started walking.

"Is your salary not sufficient?" Viktor said quietly, as he and Charlie followed. The professor eyed Grey's bruised face. "Or is it not about the money?"

"You told me once I could fight in these things or study with you," Charlie added. "Not both."

"Yeah, well," Grey said, "you ever heard of 'do as I say, not as I do'?"

"Course I heard it. Didn't think you the type to say it."

Grey went through a heavy oak doorway and down a corridor of stone, past silent chapels and looming gothic vaults. A relic of the Old World slumbering amid the puzzle box of high-rise brownstones that defined Hudson Heights.

Grey had no idea who had been paid off to secure the venue or what would happen if they were caught.

Nor did he care.

As they emerged atop a hill overlooking the Hudson River, Viktor laid a hand on his arm. "I have a new case."

"You need to hire someone else."

"I don't want anyone else." Viktor folded his arms as Grey slipped on his motorcycle jacket and strapped his duffel bag onto his restored Kawasaki Avenger. "You can't live as if waiting for death, Grey. That's not a life."

"I'm not waiting for anything. Death already came."

"Not because of anything you did. You made the world a better place."

Grey snorted. "Don't."

"There are people out there who need you," Viktor said. "Wouldn't she want you to help them?" As Grey revved the bike, the professor handed him a hotel business card. "Why don't we discuss it over dinner?"

Grey glanced at Charlie and found her trying to conceal her interest in the outcome. Viktor had been smart to bring her. Grey eyed the card for a long time and sighed. "I'll come, but no promises."

And as soon as Charlie's home safe, I'm gone.

Charlie started to climb onto the back of the bike. "No," Grey said, harsher than he'd intended.

She froze, a hurt look in her eyes.

"You don't have a helmet," Grey said gruffly, masking his true reason. He couldn't be responsible for anyone's safety right now. Not someone he cared about.

"Neither do you, Teach."

Grey muttered beneath his breath and looked at Viktor. "Take her home, please."

"I ain't going to the shelter tonight," Charlie said with a grin. "I'm going to the hotel."

Grey gave Viktor a scathing look. That was a cheap ploy.

Viktor put his hands up. "It wasn't my idea."

"I made him promise," Charlie said, her grin expanding. "My payment for finding you."

Grey frowned. "How'd you know where I was?"

"What, you think you ain't a legend on the street? When Teach fight, *everybody* know."

Streetlights blurred as Grey accelerated to eighty, ninety, one hundred on the Henry Hudson Parkway, the wind screaming in his ear, Death clutching his waist like a thrill-seeking passenger.

He slowed when he entered Washington Heights. The night came alive around the homeless shelter, drunks and pushers hovering around the dilapidated brick building, the smell of piss and vomit fouling the air.

After parking his bike by the door, he nodded at the night watchman and stepped inside. Cockroaches scattered as Grey strode to the front office. The drip of water echoed down the hall.

Downstairs, single mothers and their families stayed in cubicles with plywood walls and no doors. Male teens and children resided on the first floor, girls on the second. Volunteer adult monitors provided a modicum of security. When they turned eighteen, the orphans and runaways and abandoned teens had to seek shelter elsewhere, usually at the more dangerous adult shelters.

Grey glimpsed the sign taped to the office door.

TEN THOUSAND DOLLARS NEEDED FOR
CITY-MANDATED REPAIRS.
PLEASE DONATE!

He peeled off the sign, re-taped it to the leather pouch containing the prize money, and shoved the pouch through the mail slot. Reverend Dale would be the first person inside. Grey trusted him with his life.

Outside, he sat on his rumbling bike, deciding what to do. He wanted to leave Manhattan and keep on riding, drive until city lights and the babble of crowds fell away, until civilization itself had faded, stripped to the barren desert his heart had become.

In the end, it was Charlie, not Viktor, who kept Grey from bolting. The trust in her young eyes. Again he applauded his employer—and cursed him—for his foresight.

Thunder rumbled. A raindrop splattered and ran like mercury down Grey's forehead.

He eyed the card Viktor had given him, then gunned his bike for the Lotte Palace hotel.

3

Grey outran the rain.

He ripped through the canyon-like streets of Midtown Manhattan and parked in front of an imposing Italian Renaissance façade. The beige bricks of the hotel glowed golden in the ambient light.

A recessed courtyard opened into a marble lobby with a few well-heeled guests waiting for the elevators. No sign of Viktor or Charlie. On the back of the business card, Viktor had scribbled *Rarities*.

Grey asked the concierge if Rarities was a restaurant on the property. The balding porter looked at him as if inspecting a stain on his sport coat. "It's a members-only cocktail lounge on the mezzanine level."

"Thanks."

"I assume you have an invite?"

Grey didn't bother to respond.

The doorman at the Rarities Lounge afforded him the same snooty stare. "May I help you? We closed at midnight."

"Then why are you standing here?"

The doorman looked flustered. "We have a . . . special guest."

"If it's Professor Viktor Radek, he asked me to meet him."

The doorman's haughty expression crumbled. "Ah . . . Dominic Grey? Yes, yes. I'll take you inside."

The lounge was a mélange of plush carpet, ornate wood paneling, and bottles of rare liquor displayed in glass cases. Grey found Viktor and Charlie sitting in high-backed chairs next to a stained-glass window. The somber, dark-suited professor and the street kid in secondhand clothing, a Mets sweatshirt and baggy camo pants, were as incongruous a pair as Grey could imagine. The concierge must have aged five years when Viktor bullied his way through.

Charlie looked up from a steak as thick as the professor's forearm. "What's with the beard, Teach? You look like Aragorn after a month in the forest."

Grey pulled up a chair and didn't bother to ask Viktor how he had convinced the staff to work overtime or the kitchen to serve steaks in a drinks-only lounge. Grey's employer hailed from a wealthy Czech family—minor nobility—and he tossed around money like it was free.

"You must be starving," Viktor said.

"A beer would be good," Grey said, as the waiter came over. "Whatever lager's on tap."

"We have three. Brooklyn—"

"Just pick one."

"A steak?" Viktor asked. "Burger?"

Grey waved a hand in dismissal. He drank his beer when it arrived and watched Charlie eat, enjoying her relish the meal. After polishing off a giant chocolate brownie, she got the hint and stood.

"I know you all got important business to discuss. You need some help saving the world, you let me know. I know people."

Grey gave her arm an affectionate squeeze. "It's good to see you. I'll come back to class soon."

"You better, or I might join a gang and end up in the coop. And yo, take the Prof up on that burger, unless you trying to slip through a sewer grate."

After Charlie left, Grey cupped his beer between his palms and avoided Viktor's eyes. "I'm listening."

He felt the weight of Viktor's gaze, watching before he spoke. Analyzing. The two men had saved each other's lives on numerous occasions and shared a fierce mutual respect. Their bond was an unspoken one, however, and Grey hoped it stayed that way.

Because there was nothing much to say.

"Two days ago, I received a call from Jacques."

Grey lifted his eyes. Jacques Bertrand was their Interpol contact. Viktor consulted for a variety of employers, from private individuals to police chiefs to espionage agencies. Though Interpol did not have field agents or direct jurisdiction, Viktor operated in a gray area that everyone accepted because he produced results.

That was half the equation. The other half was that Viktor was a renowned professor of religious phenomenology. His services were valued because the cases on which he consulted invariably involved religious, mysterious, or unexplainable phenomena—and no one had more experience in these matters.

The waiter brought Viktor a dusty bottle of absinthe, a Pontarlier glass, a carafe of water, and a small wooden box.

Grey nudged his head towards the glass. "Already?"

Viktor lifted the lid and extracted a slotted spoon, a cube of sugar, and a long silver lighter. "Let us say I've come to believe my recent addiction stemmed from personal issues, and not the wormwood."

Grey shrugged.

Viktor poured absinthe the color of melted emeralds into the curved well at the bottom of the glass. He used the slotted spoon to dip the sugar cube in the absinthe, then set the spoon and the sugar atop the glass. "Our assistance has been requested on an unusual matter."

"When isn't it?"

"Over the last month," Viktor continued, unperturbed, "three reports of mutations have surfaced, in three different countries: the United States, South Africa, and France."

"Mutations? Of what?"

Viktor ignited the cube of sugar with the lighter. When it flamed, he dunked the sugar into the glass and trickled cold water into the mixture, clouding it. "Of human beings."

Grey took a swallow of beer.

"An African American man in Atlanta, a South African boy, and a Muslim woman in Paris," Viktor said. "The mutations started with hair loss, an unexplainable increase in muscularity and agility, thickened skin, protruding veins, and clawed hands. By that, I mean rigidity in the fingers and expansion of the fingernails into dagger-like growths."

"It sounds like they turned into . . . monsters."

"Within roughly seventy-two hours of the appearance of the first symptom," Viktor said, "the two adults began hemorrhaging. Death followed within hours."

"Why hasn't this been on the news? Not that I would have noticed," Grey muttered.

"Autopsies are ongoing, and the various authorities are working hard to control the situation."

"Maybe they need to let it get out."

"That's not for us to decide," Viktor said. "But publicity is inevitable."

"So how does this involve you? Why aren't they using labs to figure this out?"

With a sigh of pleasure, Viktor took a sip of absinthe. "They are. The CDC in Atlanta is leading the medical investigation."

"Is there fear of more mutations? Something contagious?" When the professor nodded gravely, Grey tapped the table with his fingers. "You said *medical side* of the investigation."

"The South African victim, a sixteen-year-old boy, was found with an odd symbol tattooed in blue ink on the back of his left heel. The letter T piercing an ouroboros."

Grey knew what an ouroboros was: a depiction of a serpent eating its own tail, the eternal cycle of nature.

"The vertical portion of the T," Viktor continued, "was represented by an unalome, the horizontal portion by a double helix."

Grey had a flash of remembrance from his childhood in Japan. "An unalome . . . the Buddhist symbol of the search for enlightenment?"

"Correct. There was also a dash and the number thirteen beside the symbol. I have to say, something about it feels familiar. I'm still researching."

"Did the boy's parents not recognize it?"

"They'd never seen it before."

"Meaning he might have been part of an experiment?" Grey sat back. "That's why they called you?"

Viktor set his absinthe down and interlaced his fingers on the table. "That, plus the circumstances of the boy's death, which were unusual compared to the other two victims. Unusual for anyone, in fact."

"Those circumstances being?"

"He was already dead."

Grey paused with his glass in midair.

Viktor continued, "He died of a MRSA infection a month ago today. Both parents identified the body and attended the funeral. Two days ago, they identified it again. The boy stumbled into their township after dark, searching for his parents, exhibiting similar mutations as the other two cases. Someone shot him to death after the boy threw a grown man into a shack and ripped down a bundle of live power lines."

"Jesus."

"Numerous people saw the boy. The tabloids even picked it up, though no one really believes it happened. *I* don't believe it. Still, no one is sure what to do. There's a local officer handling the case, but Jacques wants me to go to South Africa and conduct my own investigation."

"And you want me to go with you?"

"No. If something sinister is behind these mutations, then the cases are related." Viktor picked up his glass again and eyed Grey as he took a drink. "I want you to go to Atlanta and conduct a parallel investigation."

Grey looked away, bitter that Viktor had asked so soon, thinking about actions and consequences and the darkest of tunnels to which his last case had led.

When he looked back, he found the professor still staring at him, layers of meaning in his gaze.

"Will you help me?" Viktor asked.

4

Grey woke early, before first light. He preferred mornings now. Nights were too long and empty, too full of trapped memories.

He grabbed the case dossier, stuffed a few things into a backpack, then slipped on jeans, an old black sweater, and his motorcycle jacket. Before he left his brick studio loft in Hudson Heights, he pressed his palms against the bathroom counter and gave his sleep-deprived eyes and unkempt beard a skeptical stare.

He wasn't ready for this.

He wasn't ready for anything.

Yet he had agreed to go to Atlanta, mostly because he didn't want to disappoint Charlie. She needed an anchor in her life, at least one adult whom she did not have to fear, report to, or explain herself. Someone who wouldn't treat her like a leper or a charity case, but a human being.

Someone who was not struggling more than she was.

Grey had also agreed to go because something Viktor said had rung true: there were people out there who needed the kind of help Grey could give.

Maybe he would realize he couldn't do the job any more, and this would be his last case. If so, then fine. At least he had left his apartment to find out.

It was still dark as he walked to the subway, the streets slick and quiet. By the time he arrived at Penn Station, emerging to the surface to pick up a coffee and an egg and bacon sandwich from a favorite vendor, the sun had risen and the rain had stopped and people poured through the streets like Class V rapids through a high-walled sluice.

Before re-entering the station, Grey took a long look at the city, trying to imagine the chaos a true pandemic would cause in a metropolis of this size.

On the plane, Grey pored over the dossier, cementing the details in his mind.

Five days before, local police had responded to a 911 call in Dekalb County, Georgia, just outside of Atlanta. They arrived to find a hysterical young woman,

Cora Thomas, claiming her father had returned from a fishing trip, gone insane, and was trying to kill her. She had tried to calm him, but he ran outside and attacked someone, raking him across the chest with claw-like fingernails.

By the time the police arrived, Cora's father had hemorrhaged and died. The police report chalked the mysterious symptoms up to "drug abuse and an unknown medical condition, possibly acquired from an animal bite or polluted water."

After a watchful Interpol analyst connected the three incidents, the Center for Disease Control and Prevention was contacted, and handlers sent to examine the bodies. Whatever they had discovered was not in the report.

Grey found it odd the local police had let the case go so easily.

And maybe they hadn't.

Jacques had already arranged for Grey to meet the CDC doctor in charge of the medical investigation later that night. Before that meeting occurred, Grey decided to pay a visit to Cora Thomas, the daughter of the victim.

Draw some conclusions of his own.

From above, Atlanta resembled a fishbowl of skyscrapers rising out of a flat green forest. As Grey's plane descended, he caught glimpses of the New South sprawl that housed over six million people and a bundle of Fortune 500 companies.

After renting a Jeep Cherokee at the airport, Grey swooped into town on a massive interstate that cleaved the city in two, driving past a series of billboards hawking everything from mega-churches to strip clubs, Chick-fil-A to local sports teams. He continued east on I-20 and exited twenty minutes later in a gritty suburb full of traffic lights and fast food restaurants.

Four lanes became two. Commerce morphed into farmland. After passing a rib shack, an abandoned gas station, and a clapboard church, Grey turned onto a dirt road called Carver Lane, shocked it had shown up on the GPS.

The Cherokee kicked up a cloud of dust as it rolled into a cul-de-sac that looked like something out of the Third World. A collection of clapboard houses with sheet metal roofs sprinkled an overgrown field behind the cul-de-sac. Hardwoods choked by creepers loomed over the yards.

Now Grey understood why local police hadn't put up a fight when the CDC intervened. Communities this poor didn't rate very highly on the priority scale. If at all.

Grey spotted the right mailbox, parked the car, and shooed away a skeletal cat that rubbed against his leg when he left the car.

Stillness. Dry rural air. A crisp November sky.

As Grey approached the house, he noticed an elderly African American woman eyeing him from a porch rocker next door, bundled inside a shawl and smoking a cigarette like it was the last one on planet Earth.

The creak of a screen door snapped Grey's attention back to the victim's house. A woman in her twenties, black skin carved from onyx, opened the door wearing pink jeans and a hooded white sweatshirt. Droopy eyelids gave her face a sleepy appearance.

"Are you selling something?" she asked. A headscarf swept a bundle of braids off her narrow face. "Cuz I ain't got any cash to spare."

"I'm not selling anything. My name's Dominic Grey. Are you Cora Thomas?"

"That's right."

"If you have a minute, I'd like to ask you a few questions about your father."

Her eyes narrowed. "You more police?"

"I'm someone who thinks what happened to your father was very strange."

She lit a cigarette with a shaky hand, inhaled, and pointed it at him. "Strange?" She barked a laugh. "Mister, it was unnatural. You're a reporter, I take it."

Grey didn't contradict her, since she seemed ready to talk.

"Look," she said. "I just want someone to tell me what happened. Something killed my father, and it wasn't no rabid dog or bad creek water. If it was, then every Geechee in Georgia be dead by now."

It took Grey a moment, but then he got the reference. He remembered a recent article in the national news about a land battle between the state of Georgia and a Gullah community. *Geechee* or *Gullah* referred to isolated communities of slave descendants who lived mostly in the low country of the southern Atlantic states.

He didn't realize any lived this far inland. But he didn't know much about them.

"I'll do what I can," Grey said. "And I'm sorry about your father."

"You know," she took another drag, "you the first person to come in here and say that to me."

"I'm sorry about that, too."

"Yeah, well. *That* ain't gonna change. What you want to know?"

"Just your side of the story."

She pressed her lips together and waved him into a living room just inside the door. Grey sat on a cloth sofa with an old quilt draped across the top.

"You want some tea?" Cora asked. "Coffee?"

"No thanks."

She flopped into an armchair and placed her ashtray on a coffee table. "Not much love lost between daddy and me. He only came back a year ago, after momma died, to lay claim to the house. But he was still my daddy."

Raised by an abusive father, Grey struggled with that sentiment himself. Grey had left home at sixteen, a year after his mother died of cancer. Every year he told himself he would look up his father, but every time he picked up the phone, the rose-colored lenses of time would shatter, regret would turn to rage, and another year would go by.

Cora rehashed the police report. Grey could tell she was telling the truth by the confusion and terror on her face when she described her father's condition.

She shivered. "He looked like a hairless monster, with veins like steel cords. And his fingers . . . no pill or bottle causes *that*."

"How did he drive home from his fishing trip?"

She gave a harsh laugh. "Drive? My daddy never owned a car. What he did, he walked a mile to the east and dipped his pole in the water. And probably in something else, too."

Grey realized what was missing in the cul-de-sac. Something that littered the lots of most poor rural communities. Cars. He had only seen one or two. "You don't think your father recognized you?"

"If so, he sure didn't show it. He stumbled into the house, smashed a few things, and threw a chair at me. I ran through the back door and the next thing I knew, people was screamin' and daddy was bleeding out in the street."

"So you didn't get to talk to him?"

"He wasn't in his right mind."

"The man your father attacked . . . did you know him?"

She waved the hand holding the cigarette. "That was old Brill Johnson, a drifter who made my daddy look like an upstanding citizen."

"Do you know where I can find him?"

"Try the tracks, or an empty lot." She smirked and pinched off her cigarette butt. "He don't trust no one, is crazy as a loon, and stays drunker than a sailor on shore leave."

"What about a relative?"

"None I know of."

Grey didn't hear anything else useful. He thanked Cora for her time and stepped outside. He caught a whiff of burning leaves and noticed a plume of smoke behind one of the houses.

Grey knocked on a few doors to ask about Brill Johnson, but no one had seen him since the night Seb had died.

Frustrated, he was about to leave when he remembered the old woman smoking on the porch beside Cora's house. As he approached, the woman flicked a fly off her shawl. He introduced himself. "Do you have a second?"

She mashed her lips as if chewing cud. Grey noticed she was toothless. She curled an age-spotted wrist, motioning him forward.

He squatted on the porch to make her feel more comfortable. "I was wondering if you were here the night Seb Thomas died."

A slow nod. "I seen it."

Her accent was so thick Grey could barely understand her. "Did you witness the altercation?"

She shook her head.

"What about Brill Johnson?" he asked. "Do you have any idea where I can find him?"

"He gone."

"Where?"

She cackled. "You the only person ever axed that question."

Grey rubbed the back of his neck. He was guessing the old woman sat on her porch most of the day. "Have you seen or heard anything unusual in the past week or two?"

"Sumthin," she said, without hesitation. "A truck came by the day before Seb gone fishin'. Ain't from 'round here."

"A truck—do you know what kind?"

"A white one."

"Pickup?"

"Yep."

"I don't suppose you saw the license plate?"

She took a lighter and a pack of unfiltered Lucky Strikes out of her nightgown. "Nope. But I seen the driver."

"Can you describe him?"

"Real white like you, red beard, long hair. And he big. Real big."

"Did he leave his truck?"

She shook her head. "He turn around and drove off. There was no one around but me."

"Did he see you?"

"No one ever see me."

Grey's leg started to cramp. He stood. "What do you think he was doing?"

With a deft flick of her thumb that belied her age, she lit a cigarette. "Looking for trouble."

"Why do you say that?"

"Because I old, and know trouble when I see it."

Odd, Grey thought. It was probably coincidental, but he had nothing else to go on. "How often does something like that happen? A stranger coming to this cul-de-sac?"

She coughed. "A white man? About never."

"Did you tell the police about this?" he asked.

"No one ever axed me."

A puff of smoke drifted into Grey's face. He resisted the urge to wave it away. Before he could ask another question, the old woman said, "I seen sumthin else about him. A tattoo on his arm."

Grey turned to look at the street. The edge of the cul-de-sac was only twenty feet away, but that was still a long way to see a tattoo.

She noticed his skepticism. "I'm old, but I ain't blind. He hung his arm out the window when he drove by. Like I says, it was a big arm."

"What was the tattoo?"

"Some kinda symbol."

Grey tensed. Maybe it wasn't a coincidence after all. He described the marking found on the boy in South Africa for her. "Was that it?"

"Nope," she said, then reached into the nightgown again. "Here. I drawed it."

She unfolded a piece of yellow lined paper, like the one Grey used in school as a kid, and revealed a sketch of two intersecting check marks capped by the top half of a diamond.

It wasn't the same marking, but Grey recognized it. During his time in Diplomatic Security, he had received training on the symbology of various hate groups around the world. This particular marking was known as "The Rune". Originally related to the Norse God Odin, the Odal or Othala symbol had been adopted by the Nazi party and other white supremacist movements as a symbol of Aryan heritage.

Grey grimaced and thanked her.

Realizing he was starving, Grey stopped for lunch at the rib shack he had passed. About the size of a railroad car, the restaurant had a counter window to place orders and a few picnic tables scattered around the gravel lot. While he munched on a plate of pulled pork, Grey researched white supremacist groups in the Atlanta area.

Thirty-nine active organizations at last count, according to the Southern Poverty Law Center. Names like Aryan Nations Worldwide, Supreme White Alliance, Crew 38, League of Dixie, the Blood and Honor Social Club.

Nothing sociable about blood and honor.

After absorbing a few disturbing factoids, such as the KKK rallies atop Stone Mountain and the Georgia high school that held its first integrated prom in 2014, Grey turned to the chat boards. The rhetoric was stomach turning. He didn't find a particular connection between the Odin rune and any of the hate groups in Georgia, but he did pinpoint a few local bars that seemed to be an epicenter of activity.

Grey picked at his fried okra and then pushed the plate aside. God, how he detested hate groups.

The only upside to the case was that it gave him something else to focus on. An outlet. He finished his sweet tea and considered his next steps.

The meeting with Dr. Genevieve Fischer of the CDC wasn't until eight-thirty that night. Since he had a few hours to kill, he decided it was time to ask a few questions at the white supremacist hangouts around town.

Whether the esteemed clientele liked it or not.

5

WESTERN CAPE, SOUTH AFRICA

As he flew into Cape Town International Airport, Professor Viktor Radek reminisced on his first arrival into what he considered the second most beautiful city in the world.

His hometown, of course, held the title. Nothing beat Prague on a crisp spring morning, watching the spires of Old Town emerge out of the fog. If anything truly mysterious lived in the world, then surely it kept a townhome in Prague.

The Western Cape was a stark contrast. Vast and open-skied, Viktor remembered absorbing the landscape as an impressionable teen on holiday with his parents, chewing on biltong as he marveled at fynbos-draped valleys and mythical rock formations and sunsets like supernovas.

And Cape Town itself: the dreamy fusion of land and sky and sea, nature and city, mist and earth. The city possessed an effortless cool, a supermodel since birth.

Yet appearances could be deceiving. Viktor would never forget sitting in the back of a limousine with his parents, on the way into Cape Town from the airport, eyes wide as they drove past the worst slums he had ever seen. A son of privilege seeing the harsh inequalities of the world for the first time.

South Africa, he remembered thinking, was free will in all its terrible glory.

Flash forward forty years, and Viktor was sad to be skipping Cape Town and taking the N2 straight from the airport to Bonniecombe, a small town nestled at the feet of the Langeberg Mountains. It was there, in one of the impoverished townships that provided cheap labor to the wine estates, that the Xhosa boy had returned from the grave.

Again Viktor considered the meaning of the strange tattoo. The double helix was clearly a scientific reference of some sort. An odd companion to the squiggly path and pointed tip of the unalome, a symbol of sacred geometry in the yantras of Buddhism.

Symbolic, perhaps, of the intersection of mysticism with reason? Science with faith?

The number thirteen was a wild card. Though viewed as an ominous integer by Western culture and usually linked to the betrayal and slaughter of the Knights Templar, the number had other meanings.

Older ones.

In Christian lore, the addition of Christ to the twelve apostles at the Last Supper signified ascension, resurrection, and enlightenment. Yet Judas's betrayal caused many to view the number as an ill omen. The same double meaning existed in Norse mythology, with the appearance of a thirteenth guest, Loki, at the banquet where a favorite son of Odin was killed.

The number thirteen equated to immortality in Ancient Egypt.

Romulus and the twelve shepherds, Roland and the twelve knights.

The thirteenth Tarot card is Death, signifying transition. The Illuminati and the Masons and the numerologists practically slobber all over the number.

Viktor gathered his Swaine Adeney leather suitcase and followed his valet to a black Mercedes sedan. On the seat beside him, a bottle of vintage absinthe beckoned like a siren's song.

Complete sobriety was not a state that interested Viktor. Not when his job consisted of probing the mysteries of the universe and peering into the winters of men's souls.

And Viktor had no intention of changing professions.

Using a bucket of ice and accoutrements the driver had procured, Viktor prepared his favorite drink and wondered what he would find at Bonniecombe. He assumed the Xhosa child had been buried alive, but how? A death-like state could be achieved in various ways, most notoriously in the real-life cases of zombies in Haiti, where Voodoo priests used tetrodotoxins derived from the puffer fish to sedate their victims.

Yet Voodoo was not part of South African culture, and the state of the boy had born no resemblance to Haitian zombies, emaciated figures who exhibited slow, clumsy, and purposeless mannerisms.

By all accounts, the Xhosa boy had returned with an enhanced muscularity that implied the use of powerful steroids and growth hormones. Yet even that did not explain the enlarged veins or the dagger-like fingers, anomalies for which Viktor had no answer.

Two related but separate mysteries, then. The faked death and the subsequent physical changes.

Or perhaps they weren't separate. Perhaps some bacterium or radioactive compound in the slum's water had taken hold of the boy before his death, altered his biochemical state, and literally awakened him from the grave.

How to explain the other two mutations, then? Separated by thousands of miles?

"Bonniecombe, sir," Viktor's driver called out.

The professor looked up. In the distance, a handful of white spires sat primly at the base of a russet and swamp-green mountain range that loomed over the settlement like a pile of rumpled laundry. A thick layer of mist covered the middle third of the peaks.

Viktor's last thought as he drove into Bonniecombe was of Dominic Grey. The professor knew his closest ally wasn't ready to work again. Not by a long shot.

Yet after looking into his friend's eyes, Viktor feared the consequences of leaving Grey on his own even more than asking for his help. The professor hoped the case would provide a distraction and help bring Grey back to life.

The sedan exited the N2 and rolled into a pretty town marked by well-maintained streets and elegant Cape Dutch architecture. Clusters of semi-tropical vegetation made Bonniecombe feel like a garden backed by a high stone wall. Hints of lavender and rosemary drifted through the cracked window of the sedan.

The professor's driver dropped him at a bed and breakfast with a view of the mountains and a trellis slathered in crimson bougainvilla. Viktor checked his watch. He barely had time to check in, drop his bags, and wash before meeting with the local police.

The Bonniecombe police station was tucked inside a quaint administrative building with a white, curlicue façade. A receptionist led him to a conference room overlooking a park. File cabinets, a whiteboard, and a coffee maker provided bland décor.

A female officer in her early forties greeted Viktor from behind a linoleum table. "Welcome to Bonniecombe, Professor. I'm Sergeant Linde."

Her tanned hands folded stiffly in front of her, the sergeant afforded Viktor a guarded stare. Since none of the victims was the subject of a criminal investigation yet, Jacques had given the Bonniecombe police a cover story about an investigation into local witchcraft to smooth over Viktor's involvement. A suspected tie-in between organ traffickers and indigenous religion.

She said, "I'm here to assist, though I fail to see the connection to the local religious community." Her diction sounded more like a businesswoman than a local cop. "You do realize the vast majority of Xhosa are Christian?"

"It only takes one bad actor to spoil the show," Viktor said.

She leaned back in her chair. "The Xhosa have no history of organ harvesting. So please, ya, tell me about the connection between their priests and the international cartels? Because I've never heard of one."

Viktor took a closer look at the sergeant. Wavy blond hair brushed the shoulders of her navy blue, police-issue blazer. A beige skirt, white dress shirt, and a boomerang-shaped bow tie completed the uniform. A tall and rangy woman, age and sun had tightened the skin around her eyes, though she was still fit and handsome.

"It's not uncommon," he said, "for outside religious groups to infiltrate a new territory and align with criminal elements."

She met his eyes. "We've heard nothing of the sort."

Viktor spread his hands. He didn't want to poison the relationship with lies at the beginning. The truth was, though he had seen no evidence of ritual involvement, he didn't yet *know* what was going on.

"I'm here to assist," Viktor said. "Why don't we concentrate on the facts, and save the suspicion for the criminals?"

"Ya, let's. Because someone took that boy out of his grave and did that to his hands." She gave a little shiver that did not seem faked. "And I'll bet my homestead it wasn't a Xhosa witch doctor."

"What does the coroner say?" Viktor asked. "The one who proclaimed him dead the first time?"

"She stands by her report."

After the re-appearance of Akhona Mzotho in the township, the police had investigated the gravesite and found an empty coffin beneath a pile of hard-packed dirt. Most families in the township couldn't afford funeral expenses and simply buried their dead in a hole. Akhona's parents had spent what little savings they had on a wooden coffin, which bore no scratch marks or other signs of disturbance.

Which meant someone had dug him up, returned the coffin intact, and restored the gravesite.

"I'll need to talk to her," Viktor said. "What about the case against the boy's killer?"

"The prosecutor isn't sure how to proceed. Everyone *thought* he was dead, and with the chaos in the township and the potential self-defense angle . . . it's complicated."

"Indeed."

"We haven't found any special connection between the boy and the man who shot him, if that's what you're asking. No motive for the murder other than panic and superstition and ignorance."

"It's hard to term it ignorance, when we don't even know what happened."

She gave him a sharp glance. "I meant the sort of ignorance that leads a grown man to shoot a teenage boy in the head and not wait for the police, even if the boy did return from the grave and rip down power lines with his bare hands."

Viktor tipped his head in agreement. Like many Afrikaner communities he had encountered, partly due to an insular culture and partly due to the ostracization of South Africa during Apartheid, Viktor knew that earning the trust of Sergeant Linde and the residents of Bonniecombe would be an uphill battle.

"You examined the body?" Viktor asked.

"Of course."

"I assume everything you saw made it into the report?"

She smirked.

The professor steepled his fingers. "Are there any medical research facilities nearby? Besides the local hospital?"

"No," she said, though the slight delay in her response and the shadow behind her gaze said otherwise. Sergeant Linde was not a good liar, but now was not the time to press her.

It was also a strange thing to lie about, Viktor thought. Either there were medical research facilities or there were not.

"You're wondering about the dash and the number thirteen," she said, as if to cover up her response.

Viktor gave a curt nod. "I'd like to speak to the boy's parents. Can that be arranged?"

"I've already interviewed them."

"I'd like to do so again."

"They're quite distraught, as you can imagine. And they have no idea what happened."

"I'm afraid I'll have to judge that for myself. There might be circumstances of which they are . . . unaware. Details that lie within my specialty."

Sergeant Linde tapped a pen against the desk. "I'll arrange a visit, then. Have you ever visited a township before?"

"Many."

Her brow lifted, and she seemed to consider him with new eyes.

"Before I leave," Viktor said, "I'd like to view the body."

The tapping of the pen resumed. "That will be quite difficult, I'm afraid."

"Why is that?"

"Because it disappeared from the morgue last night."

6

Grey checked into the Midtown Atlanta Hyatt, a high-rise hotel close to public transport. Viktor never questioned his expenses, and Grey never gave him a reason to. Unlike his boss, Grey felt more comfortable in beach bungalows and anonymous pensions than five star hotels. Hole-in-the-wall diners rather than restaurants with maître d's and a dress code.

After Googling the addresses of the bars with white supremacist ties he had uncovered, Grey took to the streets in the Cherokee, both to preserve his escape options and because the two-line subway barely scratched the surface of the city's sprawl. The first two places he tried were almost deserted, and five minutes with the deadbeats at the bar told him there was no information to be gained.

The third place was boarded-up and abandoned. Growing restless, Grey dug a bit deeper and found a bar called the Peach Shack advertising a rally for that very day. It was in East Atlanta, not too far away, and Grey hurried over. He wanted to catch the loose-lipped, hard-core afternoon drinkers before the Friday work crowd arrived.

Heading east on Ponce de Leon, the urban density of Midtown morphed into a four-lane road with a hodgepodge of old brick buildings, condominiums, strip malls, repurposed antebellum mansions, gas stations, and churches. An old southern street in transition to a booming new metropolis. After turning onto Moreland, he almost missed the beat-up driveway tucked between a construction site and the Dixieland Drycleaners. The long drive spilled into a gravel parking lot filled with pickup trucks and hulking motorcycles. A shamrock-green building made of wood and stucco, the aging watering hole had blacked-out windows and a long angled roof, like a Swiss chalet.

Next to a marquee announcing the Peach Shack in bright orange letters, a trio of flags hung limply from iron poles: the thirteen stars of the confederacy, a black and white POW*MIA flag, and a frayed Bikers for Kids emblem. A wooden fence topped by baseball pennants enclosed the rear lot, and Grey heard the blare of country rock from outdoor speakers.

So much for beating the crowd.

Grey passed two older men sitting on Harleys, stubbing out cigarettes and pulling on leathers. They eyed Grey's rental Jeep but didn't comment.

Inside, he paused to absorb the scene. The bar stretched along the back wall, fronted by communal wooden tables. High ceiling, brown tiled floor, walls covered with old beer and cigarette signs. A digital jukebox in the corner blared a rockabilly tune that drowned the outside speakers, and the place smelled of greasy bar food.

It was standing room only. Though Grey saw a handful of young professionals sprinkled throughout the crowd, next-door neighbor types who gave him chills, most of the crowd fulfilled the Neo-Nazi cliché: prominent tattoos, clothing with racist slogans, shaved heads and goatees.

See me, world. You may have never noticed me before I started to hate, but you will now.

The sticky residue of bigotry oozed out of the walls. Grey felt soiled just stepping inside. He eyed the bar and found space next to a goateed man in his thirties with a Swastika baseball cap and a T-shirt that read *The Original Boys in the Hoods*.

Grey sidled up next to him and ordered a Coors. After a few minutes, the goateed man nudged his head at Grey. "New around here?"

"Yeah," Grey said, without looking over.

"Thought so. Seen you looking around when you came in. Lots of new faces here for the rally."

Above the bar, Grey had noticed a banner with the day's date printed beneath the slogan.

HERITAGE RALLY: ONE WHITE NATION, UNDER GOD

The man had close-cropped hair and mushy hands. His weight sat heavy in the middle. "Who you with?" he asked. "NSM? Aryan Nation?"

"No one," Grey said.

The man looked surprised. "You're not here for the rally?"

"Just seeing what it's all about."

The man sized him up again. A nervous look entered his eyes. "Not a Zog, are you?"

Zog stood for Zionist Occupied Government. Far-right slang for a federal agent or informant.

"Do I look like one?" Grey asked.

He shrugged and pointed his bottle at Grey. "You ain't with no one, you don't got no tats."

Grey gave the man a flat stare, did a half-turn on the stool, and lifted his shirt. The man chortled when he saw the mixture of scars and cigarette burns covering Grey's back. Relics from combat and street fights, plus his father's handiwork.

"Prison?" the man guessed. "Or you been fighting the mud people in the desert?"

Grey concealed his revulsion with a snort, implying he couldn't or wouldn't talk about it.

The man stuck out his hand. "Walter Briggs. League of Dixie. Though that don't matter no more, does it? We're all coming together now. We live in embattled times, my brother."

"You got that right," Grey murmured.

"Hell, I don't need to tell you, do I?" Walter said, almost shyly now. He ordered another round for them both. "You ask me, the New White Order can't come soon enough. Our country won't last like this much longer. The coons ain't even the biggest problem any more. We got the berry pickers crossing the border in droves and breeding like minks, the rice niggers taking over our schools, the Jesus Killers richer than ever. Say, you know how many Jews can fit in a VW?"

Grey took a swallow of beer.

"Depends on the size of the ashtray." Walter slapped the bar, then clinked glasses with a woman in a tight-fitting white shirt sitting next to him.

"I need the john," Grey mumbled, and stepped away. If he heard any more, he was going to slam the guy's head onto the bar, and that wouldn't help his cause.

Or maybe it would, he mused. He could ingratiate himself with the crowd by telling them Walter was the Zog, after knocking him senseless. He gave the idea close consideration and then discarded it as too risky. People at the bar knew Walter, and Grey was an outsider.

That said, he really wanted to slam Walter's head onto the bar.

Grey stepped into a hallway, ignored the restroom, and continued to a set of double doors leading outside. He pushed through and found himself in a sprawling biergarten filled with people and surrounded by a fence covered in scraggly vegetation.

A blond bartender in a biker's jacket was slinging drinks out of a Tiki bar set up on the right side of courtyard, between a horseshoe pit and a whole pig roasting on a smoker. Another banner announcing the rally, printed on a black background and depicting a grinning skull with two crossed rifles, hung from the rear portion of the fence. Beneath the banner was a temporary stage with a podium.

Grey tried not to look obvious as he ambled through the crowd. Nothing caught his eye until he saw a beast of a man looming above a group of hard-eyed types. A mass of curly red hair spilled past the larger man's shoulders. His full beard and metal jewelry added to the Viking look, but what really caught Grey's eye was the distinctive tattoo stretching along his left forearm.

The Odin rune.

Is this the guy the old woman saw?

With a rally this size, Grey was not surprised someone involved in the local white supremacist scene was in attendance. Yet the giant's stylish attire—designer jeans and a green V-neck shirt—didn't fit with the crowd. He was deep in conversation with a dapper blond man who had a suntanned and hawkish face, late-twenties, wearing an orange silk Polo shirt and a watch that looked as if it cost more than Grey's yearly salary.

He moved closer. He wanted an ear on this conversation. After grabbing one of the Styrofoam plates of smoked pork, he made his way towards the podium, exchanging nods as he went. Eyes slid right past Grey's motorcycle jacket, black boots, and unkempt appearance.

Twenty feet from the redhead and his companion, the crowd of men around them, mostly skinheads and bikers riddled with prison tats, began to eye Grey.

Despite the fall weather, some of the men were shirtless, flaunting engorged muscles and body art.

The group hovering around the two men were not just part of the crowd, Grey realized.

They were a bodyguard unit.

Grey decided he didn't care. It was the middle of the day in a public space. He moved closer. Ten feet from the Viking, one of the men stepped in front of Grey, cutting off his path. He was a lean skinhead with a nose ring, the number 88 tattooed on his chest, and a dog collar wrapped around his neck. "Where you headed, buddy?"

"The podium," Grey said.

"What for?"

Grey needed one good look at the big redhead. His eyes, his hands, the brand of his shoes. Details that might matter. "It's a free country, last time I checked."

He tried to slip around the skinhead, but a thick-necked man wearing overalls and combat boots stepped forward and jabbed Grey in the chest. "Nothing free in this world except love and hate. Now get your ass outta here, boy. This corner of the bar ain't for you."

"I thought this rally was supposed to bring us all together?"

The skinhead snorted, exchanged a glance with the other man, and stepped toe-to-toe with Grey. The smell of cheap beer leaked from his pores. "What are you, some kinda retard?"

"Just a paying customer."

The man gritted his teeth. "Listen. I know you ain't a Zog, cuz they ain't that dumb. There's generals in every war, and that's one of 'em right behind me. He needs his space. Now *get*."

The word *general* brought a surge of tightness to Grey's chest. An image of Nya perched on the edge of a precipice filled his vision, held tight in the grasp of the kind of man who gave orders and took what he wanted from life.

The General. An ex-CIA agent turned international crime lord who had taken Nya as insurance once Viktor and Grey started closing in on his jungle hideout in Peru. At the end, instead of admitting defeat, the General had stepped backwards off a cliff, sending himself and the love of Grey's life to their deaths. Grey had watched it happen, lunging a second too late.

Rage filled his vision, both for the past and for the animal blocking his way. Grey dropped his plate of pork and shoved the skinhead's chest at the same time he wrapped a leg behind his ankle, taking away his balance and tipping him backwards.

The man's beer bottle shattered as he fell. Grey stomped on his face and kept walking. Guns and knives flashed. A bevy of men swarmed Grey, but not before the redheaded man spun with raised hands, revealing a glimpse of a flat-faced ring that snapped Grey back to the present.

The man in overalls grabbed Grey by the neck at the same time a booted foot slammed into his gut. Grey doubled over as blows rained from all sides. He tried to crawl away, but there were too many men and he couldn't get free. The only choice was to curl into a ball and take the beating.

"Enough!" a voice called out, in an odd accent.

Grey lifted his head and saw the redhead staring right at him, a cunning intelligence glittering behind pale blue eyes. Beside him, the man in the polo shirt looked down his nose as if Grey were a piece of hair stuck in his food.

Two men stood Grey up by the arms. They looked at the Viking for orders.

"Let's not ruin the festivities with petty squabbles," he said. "It's a great day to be alive." A charming, wolfish smile split his red beard. "Greater than most of you realize."

He nudged his head towards the parking lot. The two men holding Grey dragged him across the biergarten. Grey saw the gleam of a handgun sticking out of a waistband, inches away. Sloppy. An escape plan sprang into his mind: a quick manipulation of his wrists to free his hands, a grab for the gun as he twisted away, a shot to the kneecaps and then holding one of the men in a chokehold as he backed through the bar.

Grey let them drag him. Too many tempers and weapons were involved. A fight would get him shot, force him to take out a dozen people, or both. Even if he escaped, a man with Grey's training did not have a green light to take out civilians in a bar fight, no matter what kind of scum they were.

Walter's eyes popped as they hustled Grey through the bar. "I knew you was a rat! Filthy Zog!"

"That hat and shirt make you feel like a big man?" Grey said. "Get some empathy training, you bigot."

Walter flew off his seat, full of courage now that Grey was subdued, but someone held him back. The two men tossed Grey in the street and kicked him in the ribs for good measure.

Grey staggered to his feet and wiped blood off his mouth, feeling to see if anything was broken. Just bruises and a few cuts. He knew he would have to keep his temper under control if he wanted to stay on the case, then wondered if he cared enough to try.

He also wondered what a bunch of racists from Georgia had to do with a trio of strange murders on three different continents. Most of all, he wondered about the enormous ring he had glimpsed on the redheaded Viking's right hand, a sapphire blue stone carved with a double helix and an unalome in the shape of a T piercing a circle.

7

The morning after Viktor's arrival, dressed in his customary bespoke black suit with tie and cufflinks, the professor joined Sergeant Linde outside the Bonniecombe police station. They were meeting to interview the parents of Akhona Mzotho.

The story still fueled local news, fanning flames of witchcraft and superstition, though the national media had moved on after blaming gangs and drugs and, more subtly, the parents. Viktor supposed the angle was one to consider.

The morning mist smelled of sod and fresh roses. Sergeant Linde had added a pair of silver-framed sunglasses to her uniform. A tall woman, just above six feet, Viktor had watched the sergeant's shoulders drop a fraction when she greeted him, as if relieved not to be the larger person.

"You met with the parents?" Viktor asked.

"I did."

"What do you know about them?"

"They're both qualified as teachers and worked at the same secondary school in Cape Town. They lost their jobs during budget cuts. The wife tutors when she can, and the husband works part-time as a maintenance man."

"Criminal record?"

"Before their marriage, the wife was arrested for disorderly conduct in a public place. A political rally."

"Any substance abuse?" Viktor asked.

"They live in a poverty-stricken township, and their son just died. I'd imagine they abuse a substance of some sort."

In the patrol car, Viktor glanced over at her tight mouth and stern jawline, wondering at the sergeant's stance on racial matters.

In a community this small, where de facto segregation was woven into the fabric of society, there was bound to be tension. Choices. The night before, a guest at the bed and breakfast had warned Viktor not to walk at night, because "the *blicks* take over after dark."

All those pretty churches, Viktor thought, and they couldn't follow the one Golden Rule.

"But nothing," he said, "that would lead you to believe they might have helped disguise the body of their own son?"

She was looking straight ahead. "One can never tell."

The mountains glowered overhead as Sergeant Linde drove through the center of town, awash with quaint-looking shops and cafés and pubs. After passing a string of period homes with wrought iron railings, rotunda porches, and lawns like putting greens, she took a local highway due west.

"The body disappeared from the morgue two nights ago," Viktor said. "Why didn't you contact Interpol?"

"I wanted to ensure it wasn't a mistake on our part," she said. "Before we cry wolf."

Viktor frowned. "Corpses do not tend to get lost in the bureaucratic shuffle."

"This is South Africa, hey?" She gave him a wry look. "A precinct delivered the wrong body to a funeral home in Jo'burg last year, and no one caught it until the viewing. Talk about a shock at the end."

She chuckled, but Viktor wasn't convinced. Bonniecombe was too small a jurisdiction to misplace a body. Even if it wasn't, Sergeant Linde didn't seem the type to let it happen.

As with her shifty answer to his question about the medical facility, Viktor got the sense that Sergeant Linde knew something about the disappearing body, too.

Was he dealing with a corrupt cop? If so, how did it relate to the case at large?

After a brief glimpse of wine country, a parfait layered with vineyards and orchards and olive groves, groups of workers in blue overalls bent like triangles in the sun, the patrol car rolled into the outskirts of a slum sprawled across a dusty, weed-filled plain. Sergeant Linde parked beside a dirt soccer field.

"By the way," she said, "I did report the missing body this morning. Just before you arrived."

Viktor paused with his hand on the door handle, then afforded her a curt nod.

He would check and see.

The air in Khayalanga Township reeked of dung and burning ash. Sergeant Linde kept her hand on her gun as she led Viktor through a maze of claustrophobic dirt paths lined with shacks cobbled together out of wooden planks, cardboard, and corrugated iron. The slum reminded Viktor of a collection of crumbling children's forts.

As sobering as the poverty was, he kept his focus on his profession, on the signs of Christianity dotting the settlement. Crosses nailed onto doorways, statuettes of angels and saints perched on windowsills.

He looked closer. Saw the fetishes of indigenous religion, tokens of charm and protection. Colored glass beads and dried plants and leather braids that shouted far louder than Viktor had expected in a township in the industrialized Western Cape.

Far more, in fact, than he had seen in many years, even in villages hidden deep within the bushveld.

Emaciated dogs slunk between the houses, wary Xhosa faces watched from sheeted windows and cracked doorways. "The amount of religious iconography," Viktor said in a low voice. "Is it common here?"

"I don't suppose. I'm not sure I would have noticed."

An emotion had shadowed the sergeant's eyes since they had entered the slum. A distant sadness, he thought. Not for the condition of the slum but for a memory evoked. "Do you investigate here often?"

She gave him a sharp look, her eyes neutral once again. "Of course. Poverty breeds crime, as I'm sure you're aware."

"And institutionalized inequality breeds poverty."

She didn't take the bait, still leaving Viktor in the dark as to where her sympathies stood. Instead she led him across a wooden plank spanning a sewage-filled canal running through the middle of the township. Thickets of reeds with yellow flowers resembling corncobs flanked the canal. The stench of fetid water rocked Viktor.

"Almost there," Sergeant Linde murmured.

They passed beneath a pair of dolls with faces covered in white paste, sightless eyes watching the road, hanging by shoestrings from a low-lying power line. Viktor grimaced as he ducked the ward. The village was rife with superstition. Reeking of it.

Near the end of the path, Sergeant Linde approached a rusting storage container painted green and sprayed with fresh graffiti. It did not take an anthropologist to interpret the lurid images.

A middle-aged woman, once attractive but saddled with malnutrition and a world-weary expression, answered the sergeant's knock. The woman crossed her arms over her gray sweater with a shiver that belied the sunny, mild weather. "Is there news?" she asked, in a thick but educated accent.

The woman spoke directly to Sergeant Linde and didn't seem to notice Viktor. Which was odd. People noticed Viktor.

"There is," the sergeant said, "but I'm afraid it's not good. Is your husband home?"

"No."

"Would you like to call him?"

The woman waved a hand in dismissal. "If you haven't come to tell me who did this, what is there to say?"

Sergeant Linde pressed her lips together. "I'm sorry to report that someone has taken your son's body."

At first the woman seemed not to have heard her, standing still and gazing dully at the ground. Then she put her hands against the sides of her head and wailed.

Viktor flinched.

"When will this stop! Who is doing this to my boy? He'll come back again, won't he?" She fell to her knees and cried out again, then began speaking in rapid Xhosa, as if praying. Neighbors stared from windows with distrustful eyes.

Not at Viktor and the sergeant, but at the woman.

Sergeant Linde started to put a hand on the woman's shoulder, then withdrew it. "I'll do everything I can to apprehend the culprit."

The woman rose and jabbed an accusatory finger at the sergeant. "You'll do everything you can?" she mocked. "The body was stolen from the *morgue*. At the *police station*. You probably opened the door for them."

Sergeant Linde pressed her lips together. "Who did this to your home? It wasn't here the last time."

The woman's eyes flicked to the graffiti, and she rasped a chuckle. "Some of my neighbors blame us. *Us.* They think we summoned a *tokoloshe.*"

"A what?"

"A tokoloshe," Viktor repeated. "An evil spirit or undead being, a sort of zombie or gremlin, that does the bidding of its master."

The woman raised her eyes to Viktor for the first time.

"I don't understand," the sergeant said. "They think Akhona was one of these?"

Viktor grimaced. "A tokoloshe is a domestic servant summoned by witchcraft, often to do harm. Many who believe in such a thing believe the price of creating this abomination is extracted from the living. More specifically, the sacrifice of a relative within one year."

The sergeant struggled to conceal her disgust, and Viktor saw a struggle he recognized in the mother's tortured eyes, an intelligent person dealing with something she could not explain.

"As if I would harm my son," she said, yelling as she turned in a slow circle. "*My only child!*"

Sergeant Linde was silent. The woman pointed a finger at her again. "You know who did this. We all know." She flung her finger toward a line of undulating hills, awash in the soft light of wine country that seemed to last forever, backed in the distance by the mist-covered Langebergs.

Akhona's mother appeared to be singling out a fortress-like manor surrounded by a high stone wall, straddling a hill not far from the township. She snarled. "*He* did it."

"There's no need to accuse innocent citizens."

The woman threw back her head and guffawed. "*Innocent?* Go!" she screamed. "Away from my house! He took my son and you're protecting him! Again! Why did you even come here? To mock me? *Go!*"

Viktor heard muttered curses from a crowd that had started to form behind Viktor and the sergeant. Someone threw a rock that clanged off the side of the storage container.

The sergeant whirled. "Who threw that?"

No one responded. More people gathered as Akhona's mother continued to shout at them to leave. Some of the men held sticks and broken bottles in their hands.

"Best if we leave," the sergeant said in a low voice to Viktor.

"I have more questions."

"Good luck asking them."

Viktor found the eyes of Akhona's mother and saw nothing but grief and anger and confusion. She glanced at the manor on the hill again and spat on the ground, then entered her home and slammed the door behind her.

Head high, wishing Grey were with him, the professor's long stride quickly caught up with the sergeant's. A crowd of people strangled the road ahead, forcing them to shoulder their way through. He wondered why Naomi didn't pull her gun and realized that could backfire. Someone tossed a handful of something on Viktor's suit, a white substance. Salt. A ward against evil.

A gunshot sounded from somewhere behind them. The sergeant gripped the hilt of her baton, whirled and saw nothing, then kept walking. For a few tense moments, Viktor worried their lives were in danger, but the crowd thinned once they crossed the canal. Gunshots continued off and on in the background all the way until they reached the sergeant's car.

The sergeant's knuckles gripped the wheel as she pulled onto the highway. Viktor stared into the rearview, not at the township but at the secluded manor on the hill. "You let them shoot around police officers?" he asked.

"Emotions are high these days. They're just releasing tension. Unless you'd like to spend the rest of the day conducting pointless interviews?"

"Who was she talking about? The man she thinks took her son?"

The sergeant paused a beat before she spoke. "Jans van Draker. A retired neurosurgeon. His family has occupied the manor on the hill above the township for generations."

Viktor waited for a further explanation that never came.

"I see," he said finally. "I assume you have no idea why she might blame him for what happened to her son?"

"Superstitious nonsense," she said. "That is all."

"Deriving from what?"

She sighed. "Over the years, the township has experienced an unusual number of . . . oddities. Tragedies. Stillborn children with gross deformities. Wild animals and fish that resemble crossbreeds."

"How have these been explained?"

She frowned. "You saw the canal. Contaminants, bacteria, the ravages of disease."

"The people in the township believe otherwise."

"They're looking for someone to blame."

As they entered the town, Viktor decided to push. "Yesterday, when you said you had no knowledge of a nearby medical facility, I noticed hesitation in your answer."

"And?"

"Could Akhona's disappearance involve Jans van Draker?"

Naomi compressed her lips. "A rumor persists in the township that he still practices medicine, in an illicit laboratory in the manor. Forbidden knowledge and arcane secrets, of course. Worthy of Dr. Frankenstein himself."

"You don't believe the rumors."

"To be honest, I almost wish they were true. It's a harsh and mysterious world, Professor. Nature is a cruel mother. I sometimes wish there were better explanations."

"You could have told me."

"What could van Draker possibly have to do with the other two victims?"

"I have no idea."

"I don't engage in rumors and hearsay about our citizens," she said.

"Have you ever been inside the manor?"

"No."

As she pulled into the police station, Viktor drummed his fingers on his thigh. "I'd like to meet Jans van Draker. Will you arrange an interview?"

"Ach. On what grounds?"

"Did Akhona approach the village from the direction of the manor?"

"I believe so, yes. But he could have come from anywhere."

Viktor smiled without showing any teeth. "Exactly."

8

Sergeant Linde watched Professor Radek step into a hired sedan outside the police station, wondering what sort of professor chauffeured around in a top-of-the-line Mercedes. For that matter, what kind of professor traveled the world investigating crimes?

Not only that, Viktor had looked less nervous than she had—a seasoned police officer—when the township crowd had closed on them.

There was obviously more to his involvement than he was letting on. So what was he doing in her town?

At first, she berated herself for not telling him the true history of Jans van Draker. Or at least the one that was common knowledge.

Then again, let the professor do his own legwork. If he wanted to play coy, then she felt no duty to aid his investigation. This was her home, and the rural Western Cape was not a place easily penetrated or understood by outsiders.

Naomi finished up her duties and stepped into her personal vehicle: a battered, beige, three-door 1984 Land Cruiser J70 closing in on four hundred thousand kilometers. Her baby. Before driving off, she spent a moment in contemplation with her hands on the wheel, staring at the front of the police station.

The fact that Professor Radek was an outsider wasn't the issue. He seemed a decent enough man, if a little haughty.

The problem was the investigation.

The potential subject of it.

She drove to a bakery-café on the eastern edge of town and strolled into the lush back garden. After inhaling the aroma of baked cinnamon, she spotted a slim Xhosa woman waiting at a secluded table beneath a trellis wrapped in hibiscus.

Thato, the sergeant's oldest friend in Bonniecombe, greeted her with a warm smile. Thato had come of age in the township, a rare success story, and both she and Naomi had been surprised when, after meeting in a study group at the

University of Cape Town, they realized they had both grown up in the same small town, though in very different circumstances.

Not that Naomi was privileged—far from it. She came from a family of liberal educators with very little land and a strong sense of social justice, all of which rendered them virtual lepers among the Boers.

Still, even the poorest white communities were much better off than the townships during Apartheid. Naomi had gone where she pleased and had access to the best schools and doctors.

During that first meeting, Thato had leveled a challenging stare at Naomi, expecting awkward questions of class and privilege, but Naomi had simply hugged her and asked if she had wanted to escape the small-minded confines of Bonniecombe as much as she had. Thato invited her to a progressive café in the Bo-Kaap, Naomi went, and they had been best friends ever since.

After spending the decade after college pursuing very different lives—Thato had married and divorced an accountant, and Naomi had worked two jobs in the city to pay off her student debt—they both returned to their hometown, appreciating its quiet beauty with new eyes and for new reasons.

Thato fidgeted. "So? You're not going to say a thing?"

Naomi swirled her wine. Thato was the lead journalist at the local paper, the Bonniecombe Herald. The two shared information freely. "About what?"

"Really?" Thato waited until Naomi met her gaze. "About the tall one you escorted to the township this morning?"

"How'd you know?"

"Come, Nae. It's a small town."

Thato looked hurt, and Naomi gave her a distracted smile. "I just haven't had time to catch you up. The last twenty-four hours have been a little . . . strange." She told her about the disappearance of the body from the morgue.

Thato's eyes widened. "Can I go with that?"

"Yes. But not yet."

"Why not?" She leaned forward. "There's something bigger?"

Naomi crossed her legs and smoothed her pants. "The man I was with is Professor Viktor Radek," she said quietly, glancing around to ensure no one else was within earshot. Van Draker had many eyes and ears. "He's not a typical professor. He works with police around the world and has been in the news on a few high profile cases—weird ones, to be honest. He's some sort of expert on religion and mysterious phenomena."

"And seven feet tall with broad shoulders?"

Naomi rolled her eyes. "He's got to be nearing sixty."

"So? You've rejected every eligible male in the district, hey?"

"You mean the Boertjies who want me to quit my job and make *potjie* all day?"

"If you don't want an outsider, or anyone around here, then who *do* you want?"

Naomi leaned forward. "I need you to focus. Something's happening, something serious enough that Interpol sent him down here. I have no idea what that is, but you and I both know who's involved."

Thato's grin faded. "How can I help?"

The Bonniecombe police department did not have the most modern resources, and Sergeant Linde was not very Internet savvy. She often relied on Thato for research projects that would benefit them both.

"First, I want you to find out what Professor Radek is doing here. Then learn as much as you can about van Draker's movements over the last few weeks."

Thato made a face. "You know he never leaves the manor."

"Still. Just check."

The reporter shrugged. "Okay."

Naomi's blue eyes burned into those of her old friend. As did most blacks in town, Thato hated Jans van Draker, though not as much as Naomi did.

No one hated him like she did.

"And then," the sergeant said, leaning over her wine, "we'll go from there."

Naomi drove home deep in thought, turning off the highway a few kilometers outside of town and taking a dirt road twelve more kilometers to her home, a flat-topped bungalow on a half-acre of scrub and windblown fynbos. Along with other reasons, she had kept the house for its solitude. Naomi was an amateur astrophotographer, and the clear Western Cape skies provided some of the best stargazing in the world.

On edge from the day's events, she greeted Max, her boisterous Rhodesian Ridgeback, and then poured herself another glass of wine. She was eager for her rooftop patio and the velvet arms of the South African night, sipping her pinotage as she marveled at the constellations.

First things first. She stepped into her study, a small room off the kitchen filled with a sad collection of brown seventies furniture inherited from her parents. The room resembled a war room more than an office. Photos and newspaper clippings covered the walls, stacks of papers and handwritten notes littered the desk and bulletin boards.

At a glance, the office appeared to belong to an ambitious detective, someone who couldn't leave her work at the office.

On closer inspection, all of the photos and notes and clippings, everything in the entire room, pertained to one man alone.

Jans van Draker.

Naomi didn't trust home computers. She had seen too many stolen or hacked. Everything of importance, she wrote down by hand.

She sat at her desk and made a note of the day's events. Just before she rose, her eyes fell on the middle desk drawer. A drawer that contained a triangular silver ear tag a ten-year-old boy had found attached to a dead cane rat floating in the filthy township canal over a year ago.

A cane rat with two heads, each bearing a set of curved incisors as long as those of a jackal, in absurd proportion to the size of the craniums.

Horrified, the boy's mother informed the police. At the morning meeting the next day, the captain had presented the call as a joke, laughing off the event and wondering how many township families a two-headed rat would feed. On a hunch, Naomi had gone to the township herself, off-duty, and taken a look at the abomination.

The rat, kept by the parents under a bucket outside their shack, had horrified the sergeant. But the ear tag—not reported in the call—had intrigued her.

A bit of quick research told her that the tag, made of a nickel-copper alloy with excellent strength and ductility, was typical of those used for lab research on mice and other small animals.

Even more intriguing, and unseen by the boy or his parents because they were too superstitious of the two-headed monstrosity to peer closer, was the odd marking the sergeant found engraved onto the back of the metal ear tag. A circle pierced by a T, formed by a double helix and a symbol the sergeant had discovered was called an unalome.

Enlightenment. As if.

Snapping back to the present, Naomi clenched her fists as she strode out of the room. She could, of course, have denied Viktor's request to interview Jans van Draker, or at least impeded the process.

But she had waited a long time for a reason to peer behind those walls.

9

The worldwide headquarters of the Center for Disease Control and Prevention was a sprawling campus of glass, steel, and trees in a semi-residential neighborhood adjacent to Emory University, just a few miles from the center of Atlanta. Except for the giant fence and the guards and the specter of hazmat suits and zombie-inducing pandemics stored inside, it could have been any other semi-urban office park in the South.

Grey's visit to the Peach Shack earlier in the day was still fresh on his mind, a sharp contrast to this paragon of medicine and progress. *All the advances in the modern world, and places like the Peach Shack still exist.*

The nation's first line of defense against deadly pathogens, the CDC was one of a handful of Biosafety Level 4 facilities in the world, and one of only two places where smallpox was stored. Grey was not surprised to find one of the center's leading epidemiologists, Dr. Hannah Varela, spearheading the charge to investigate the mutations.

Jacques Bertrand had asked Viktor to attend the briefing, but since Grey was in Atlanta, Viktor had sent him. Jacques trusted Grey, and approved the arrangement.

After passing through security so tight they checked under the hood of his Jeep, a guard led Grey on foot down a winding concrete path that led through the miniature cityscape to an office building accented by a reflecting pool. Grey signed in. A different guard led him to Dr. Varela's office. The modest space was decorated with a slew of professional certifications, photos and knick-knacks from countries around the world, and a quilt that covered half of one wall. Below the quilt, a handwritten note accompanied a photo of Dr. Varela and an African woman hugging on the bank of a muddy river. The note thanked Dr. Varela for curing the woman's daughter.

Willowy and pale, Dr. Varela had a warm smile and the hint of a Spanish accent, enough for Grey to peg her as Argentinian. He had learned Spanish for his Bogotá posting and was familiar with the major dialects. He also knew Dr.

Varela's thin nose and blond hair were not uncommon among the privileged families of Latin America, many of whom traced their heritage directly to European colonial powers.

Generals. Latin America. It seemed like every stray thought, every chance encounter, was designed to force Grey to confront the ghost of Nya, wailing a soundless scream inside his head.

As if he needed a reminder.

When Dr. Varela greeted him, Grey saw hints of surprise and disappointment, even pity, in her turquoise eyes. She was probably wondering why Interpol had sent someone covered in bruises and who resembled an out-of-work hipster on a three-day coffee bender.

"Please," she said, motioning for him to take a seat.

Grey slipped into the armchair in front of her desk and regarded her with stony silence. If Viktor and Jacques had wanted an ambassador of charm, they should have sent someone else.

"I was expecting you an hour ago," she said.

Grey checked his watch. She was right. "I got caught up."

"Visitor hours end at eight. Even for a case like this, it takes time to procure an after-hours pass."

He didn't respond.

"All right, then," she said, after a long moment. "We'll get through what we can."

Grey leaned forward. "To be honest, I don't really get this meeting. If a deadly pathogen caused the mutations, then this would be over my head. You wouldn't have the time to meet with me. Not unless and until there was a more direct link to Viktor's specialty."

Dr. Varela gave him a sharp look. "*I* requested this meeting, after I learned of Interpol's involvement."

"Why?" Grey asked bluntly.

"Because everyone else denied my request."

That caught him off-guard. "I don't understand. Are we dealing with a communicable pathogen, or not?"

"It's not that simple."

"Enlighten me."

Dr. Varela glanced at a manila folder on her desk. "I've read your CV. You seem like a smart guy. Is there any medical training not listed?"

"Just basic emergency."

She looked through him as if making a calculation in her head, then slipped into a white lab coat. "Come with me."

The lights from the high-rise gleamed golden in the reflecting pool. After walking across campus to a domed building, Grey followed Dr. Varela through more security, down a set of concrete hallways, and into a second-story interior room full of computers and whiteboards and file cabinets. A large window overlooked a futuristic stainless-steel laboratory on the level below.

"That's BSL4 down there. I can't take you in, but we view our slide images from here."

Bio-safety Level Four, Grey knew, was for agents that cause severe-to-fatal disease and for which no known vaccine existed. The worst of the worst.

"That's a lot of ductwork," he said, staring down at the lab.

"Powerful air filters. We can't exactly have particles escaping."

"I suppose not."

Dr. Varela sat in front of a monitor and brought up an image of a three-foot-tall microscope that looked like a mini space rocket attached to a computer.

"An electron transmission microscope," Dr. Varela said. "The only tool powerful enough to see a virus particle, which are one-millionth of an inch long. One hundred times smaller than bacteria."

"So a virus caused the mutations?"

"Most likely, yes."

"You don't know for sure?"

"Scientific proof, especially in epidemiology, is far more elusive than people imagine. I'll explain after a brief overview. Stop me if I'm giving you stale information."

"That shouldn't be a problem."

Dr. Varela clasped her hands behind her back and paced the room. She had a habit of biting the left side of her bottom lip during a pause. "Viruses are the most common biological unit on earth. In fact, they outnumber all the other types put together. The human immune system is incredibly adept at fighting viruses, but given the sheer number and adaptability, there are always ones that slip through."

"Do you think we'll ever eradicate them?"

"No."

Her answer was swift and decisive. Grey took her at her word. "How do they . . . work?"

"Unlike cells," she said, "which are self-sustaining, viruses need a host to survive. When they enter an organism, they hijack a cell's replication apparatus, make copies, then burst out of the cell and destroy it. This will continue until—*unless*, I should say—the immune system puts a stop to it."

"So they travel from host to host to survive?"

"That's right. Different viruses—there are more than five thousand known species—have different survival rates outside the host."

"So how did they start?"

She stopped pacing. "Clever question. We're not quite sure. Maybe evolved from plasmids, or bacteria. Viruses occupy an evolutionary grey area, somewhere between the living and the dead."

The morbid choice of words reminded Grey of the South African teenager stumbling into his village a month after his own funeral.

Dr. Varela waved a hand at the electron microscope. "Take a look."

She changed the slide, and Grey saw an organism that resembled a set of spindly spider legs, connected via a metal screw, to a multifaceted gem with spikes sticking out of it. It looked, he thought, like an evil lunar lander.

"That's our guy?" he said.

"That's a virus we found in samples from the victims. I'm calling it PX-1 for now. Phage for eater, X-1 for the unknown."

"Eater?"

"Have you heard of a bacteriophage?"

"No."

"It's a virus that infects and replicates within bacterium. Eats it, in cruder language. A phage. The structure of our virus resembles a bacteriophage, but we don't yet know what it uses to replicate. We assume a bacterium of some type."

"Why don't you know?"

"We've only examined dead tissue. A live specimen is essential to further the research."

"Gotcha."

She pointed at the screen. "Normally, bacteriophages are our friends. They're even used to target superbugs. But they can also turn normally harmless organisms lethal."

After a detailed description of virus substructures that made his head start to spin, Grey put a hand up. "Let's relate this to the victims, so I can get a footing. I assume you found the same virus in two of the victims, which caused the deformities?"

"I didn't say that."

"Okay."

"I said *most likely*. Given the problem of control, not to mention the lack of a live virus, it's impossible to be one hundred percent certain that a particular condition is linked to a particular virus."

"Since you'd have to experiment on human beings."

"Yes. That's why controversy still exists over Zika causing infant encephalitis. We can't prove that. But demonstrable evidence and the use of reason tells us there's a link. You're a detective. Imagine a body is found in a locked cell with a gunshot wound to the head and no gun. It can't possibility be a suicide, right?"

"Bad example."

"Why?"

"Let's just say you don't live in my world. But I'll accept your reasoning and assume the virus is causing the deformities. Any theories there? Why do the victims mutate and then die?"

"Scientifically speaking, the engorged muscles and the dagger-like growths on the fingers, which are formed of keratin, are termed hypertrophic myopathy and keratinopathy."

Grey frowned. "The victims change so quickly."

"A good hard anaerobic workout can engorge the targeted muscles, not to mention steroids and growth hormones. Add in gene editing, CRISPR or another technique, and the science is there. Our virus simply causes an overproduction of certain cells, producing viral proteins to perpetuate its life cycle. Rapid cellular expansion can result in hemorrhaging and a cerebral edema. And *that* is what killed our victims."

He shuddered. In the span of forty-eight to seventy-two hours, each victim had swelled like a piece of overripe fruit and then burst.

"How deadly of a virus are we talking?" he asked, again wondering why she was telling him all of this, and not a roomful of federal agents.

She said, "We have no evidence yet that our mystery virus is highly contagious—but we don't know that it isn't. It's too early to tell. I hate to phrase it like this, but we'd need more victims to judge."

Grey saw hidden knowledge in her eyes. "But you have a guess, don't you?"

She bit her lip longer than usual. The suspicion looked awkward on her, not part of her scientific universe. "In terms of mortality rate, I'd say somewhere north of small pox, maybe as bad as Ebola. We're talking eighty, ninety per cent."

He put his hands to his temples. "So back to the original question. Why am I standing here?"

She regarded him with an unreadable expression, glanced at the camera in the far left corner of the ceiling, and then checked her watch. "Our time's up."

After they left the lab and started walking across the grassy space leading to her office, she said quietly, "I eat dinner at Café Magnolia most nights after work. I have a few things to wrap up, but would you care to join me in an hour?"

Unsure what had spooked the epidemiologist, but curious, Grey gave no reaction other than a murmured acceptance.

Later that evening, Grey settled into a quiet corner of an upscale vegetarian restaurant a few miles from the CDC. Located in a strip mall on a busy artery leading to the suburbs, it did not seem like the type of place that would be popular on a Friday night. Dr. Varela arrived ten minutes later, wrapped in a sapphire shawl that matched her eyes.

"Did you know," she said after they ordered, "that rabies has a mortality rate of nearly one hundred per cent in unvaccinated patients?"

"So why aren't we all dying of rabies?"

"The better question is, before the vaccine, why was there never a rabies *pandemic*? Mortality rate isn't the whole story. The Spanish flu had a 2.5% kill rate but claimed more lives in one year than the Black Plague did in four, more than the entire number of casualties in World War I. The difference between rabies and the Spanish flu? Transmission rates. Rabies lives in the saliva of an infected host. The flu is airborne."

Grey rubbed his beard. "Okay."

"All viruses are infectious by nature, but Ebola and other hemorrhagic fevers are so deadly because they combine an extremely high mortality rate with facile transmission. A viral nuclear bomb."

"So no one is panicking right now because the virus that killed our victims is hard to transmit?"

"It's too early to pinpoint a vector. But as of yet, there's no evidence of human to human transmission."

"So how did they get it?"

She met his eyes over her wine glass. "Precisely. We can hardly declare a pandemic before evidence of transmission surfaces. But they got it *somewhere*. And the rapid onset and mortality rate—one hundred per cent thus far—is highly disturbing."

"I'd think that would be enough."

"Again, rabies. And we haven't established a causal link between the deformities and the virus. But this is something so new, so *bizarre*, that one would think I'd get the resources I've requested. Instead I'm getting pushback."

He thought about it. "Is it the victims? Poor and not white?"

"That certainly makes it easier to ignore, or to blame on a variable like water source or radioactive exposure." She gave the room a nervous glance, then lowered her voice. "Nature is strange. Stranger than you could ever imagine. But this . . . it doesn't feel right."

The food arrived, a green curry for Grey and a beet and goat cheese salad for Hannah. Grey took a few disinterested bites as he waited for her to continue.

"One example in particular: instead of hair loss, one would expect hypertrichosis, or abnormal hair growth, to accompany the myopathy and overproduction of keratin. The lethal structure of this virus, the bizarre effects that almost feel pieced together . . . it makes me think that it was manufactured."

Grey's eyebrows shot up. "Manufactured? By whom?"

She lifted a palm, as if to say, *I'm just a scientist.*

But her eyes, the nervous glances around the restaurant, told a different story. Whoever the culprit was, Dr. Varela obviously suspected they might have eyes on the lab.

On her.

"Whatever the nature of this virus," she said, "it's going to take some time to get a handle on it, especially if there are roadblocks. I'm worried the transmission could be latent or the virus could mutate into a more mobile form." She took a breath and looked at him. "If it truly is natural, there's not much you can do to help. But if it's not . . ."

She finished her meal in silence. Grey heard her loud and clear.

When the check arrived, Grey paid in cash and asked Hannah if she had pen and paper. She took a pen and a green notepad from her purse, and he scribbled his email and cell number down.

"If I find something I think you should know," he said, "I'll call you."

She brushed a nervous hand through her hair, then flashed a smile that almost broke the tension. "Keep the pen. There's a rabies vaccine inside."

Grey chuckled.

Her phone rang, and she looked down. "That's my pager. Listen, thanks for meeting me."

"Sure."

"Good luck."

"You, too."

The parking lot was located behind the storefront. Hannah left via the back door, the phone cradled to her ear. Grey started to hit the restroom on the way out when he stopped and cocked his ear towards the parking lot. A car door had just slammed shut.

He and Hannah were the last two patrons. No one had left the restaurant in the last ten minutes. The other shops in the strip mall were all retail, closed for the night.

Grey reached into his pocket and gripped the pen.

Knowing there was probably a good explanation, an argument between teens making out in a car or a night cleanup crew, Grey stepped outside to be sure. As the door opened, exposing his ears to insect chatter accented by the low hum of a fluorescent light, he scanned the rectangle of blacktop walled in by dying kudzu.

And saw four men he had never seen before, one of them with a hand clamped over Dr. Varela's mouth, forcing her away from her silver Jetta.

10

The day following his visit to the township, Viktor decided to travel thirty minutes afield, alone and without prying eyes, to the forensic pathology lab servicing Bonniecombe. The tiny but gleaming medical facility, which shared space with a cattle embryo transfer center, sparkled under an azure sky.

The medical examiner in charge of Akhona's body, a heavyset woman with solemn eyes and freckled brown skin, greeted Viktor with all the enthusiasm of a scout reporting to his general that the opposing army had just snuck through the mountain pass in the fog. Once Viktor assured her that he was not there to railroad her, but to help solve the crime, she opened up.

No, she said, she had no idea how this could have happened. The body disappeared between midnight and six a.m., when she had arrived for her shift. The only people with the key to the morgue were herself, the Director, and a janitor who had worked there for twenty years and who everyone held in the highest regard. Moreover, her preliminary notes on Akhona had been stolen, and the janitor was illiterate and couldn't possibly have known what to take.

No, she continued, she had never seen Akhona's tattoo before and had no idea what it meant.

No, she had not had time to adequately examine the body. What little she had seen defied logic, especially the clawed hands and the engorged muscles and the lack of tissue damage from the live wires—unless, she muttered with an uneasy glance at a crocheted cross on her desk, that tissue was already dead.

And no, she said after Viktor had thanked her and was reaching for the door, she had no idea what God was trying to say by sending that poor boy back to his parents in such a state, whether dead or alive or in some limbo which no one understood.

Viktor believed her, on all accounts. Before he left the facility, he secured an audience with the Director. The theft of the body and the medical records was an important development that needed to be explored. A risky maneuver that told Viktor that Akhona's case was no freak of nature or environmental accident.

No. He couldn't say that yet. A company who knew they had poisoned the canal water might resort to similar tactics to cover up their crime. He had seen it before, in remote locales. Blame the mutations on local legend or the witch doctor. Frighten the investigators away.

The area around Bonniecombe, however, had no major industrial site. The stream that fed the sewage canal in Khayalanga ran clear as glass until it reached the township.

Viktor filed away his thoughts and moved on.

The director of the facility turned out to be an ebullient, highly educated family man with an infectious smile and an alibi: he had just returned from a weeklong vacation to Mauritius. After showing Viktor pictures of the vacation on his cell phone, the director walked him down the hall to meet the janitor.

Once the professor saw the expression that crawled onto the seventy-year-old janitor's face at the mention of the disappearing corpse, a look of atavistic horror at the thought of a dead body rising on its own or being stolen by someone who dealt in such abominations, a look Viktor knew all too well and trusted more than a lie detector test, he knew the man was innocent.

Alibi by superstition, he thought wryly.

Before he left, Viktor asked the director and the janitor how they thought Akhona's body had managed to leave the facility. Both had no idea, unless someone had unlocked the front door from the inside or somehow breached the keypad lock.

On the drive back to Bonniecombe, the beauty of the red-gold hills felt muted to Viktor as he stared out the window. Though the police had reported no unusual fingerprints or evidence of a break-in at the facility, access codes could be stolen.

And, of course, the police could be lying.

It frustrated the professor to no end, but at this stage, he had no choice but to trust the department's findings.

Which meant trusting Sergeant Linde.

Viktor had made inquiries. Naomi was forty-three years old, the only child of an essayist and a marine biologist. Her mother, the writer, had died of a heart attack a decade earlier, a year to the day after Naomi's father perished in a car accident.

After attending local Bonniecombe schools as a child, Naomi had studied photography at the University of Cape Town, then taught high school art in the city. Soon after her father's death, she returned to Bonniecombe to join the police force.

A most curious decision, Viktor thought. An artist turned detective? Perhaps her parents had stunted her true desires.

Naomi's record as a police officer was as clean as polished silver. As far as Viktor could tell, she had toed the line her entire career, made no obvious enemies.

A team player, then.

But who, he wondered as Bonniecombe came into view, was team captain?

Something about the picturesque little town felt off. Viktor was used to gathering stares due to his height, and he knew the rural Western Cape was quite insular, but the attention paid to him in Bonniecombe was different. It was nothing overt, no challenging looks or violent confrontations. Just a sense that he was unwelcome. A hush when he entered a café, mothers gripping children tighter when he passed on the street, stares prickling his back at every turn. Viktor realized he had seen no other tourists or foreigners, no hotels other than the bed and breakfast in which he was staying. The only other guest was a local accountant going through a divorce.

What did this town have to hide?

Once he started researching Jans van Draker the next morning, over cappuccino and eggs benedict and a delectable chocolate croissant, Viktor began to formulate an answer to that question.

A brilliant neurosurgeon, schooled at Cambridge and Johns Hopkins, Doctor Draker worked at hospitals in London and New York before returning to South Africa to serve his country during the final years of Apartheid. More specifically, van Draker worked as a medical advisor for the government, a nebulous position that Viktor couldn't quite pin down.

Yet it was the timing, not the job, that screamed for attention. Viktor remembered that dark period in the country's history. He had traveled to South Africa on a number of occasions for research, and he had read and heard things that did not reach the outside media. He remembered the rising cries for freedom, from both blacks and whites, competing with the hard-liner Afrikaners who fought like cornered lions to keep their state-sponsored segregation.

The world remembered Nelson Mandela's release from prison. Viktor remembered reports of policemen flaying black villagers alive and barbecuing them in the bush.

The hard-liners clamored for even stricter measures against blacks than were already in place, using genocide as their rallying cry. Not genocide of the black population, but the potential genocide of the whites, outnumbered more than ten to one. Lose your grip on power, the Apartheid supporters avowed, and you will be slaughtered by those you once oppressed.

It was not, Viktor remembered thinking, an unreasonable assumption.

Thanks to peace accords that left the wealth of the whites intact, a remarkably calm transfer of power occurred. Yet, as with the final hours of a diseased and dying emperor, willing to destroy heaven and earth to cling to a spark of life, the Apartheid hard-liners worked diligently behind the scenes. In the years before the fall, rumors of planned massacres and worse surfaced, grotesque experiments to prove that blacks were a subhuman race that did not deserve equality. Van Draker's name had appeared in connection with these reports, stemming from one incident in particular.

The year was 1989. A guerrilla fighter named Solomon Nyembezi, clad in a hospital gown and with his head wrapped in a bandage, feet bare and bloody from walking across thorny scrub and urban detritus, showed up emaciated and half-dead on a doorstep in Soweto, one of the most infamous townships in Johannesburg. He claimed to have just escaped from a secret medical facility where the government performed illicit experiments on black prisoners.

A lengthy incision on his scalp seemed to confirm Solomon's story. Raving about vivisection and electric shock and amputation, cells with no windows and doctors with their faces covered by ghoulish masks, Solomon's story was suppressed by the government-controlled media but inflamed by the underground press. A journalist investigated the building in which Solomon claimed to have been held, and found an abandoned school with bloodstained floors and evidence of recent occupation.

Public outcry grew. Whether due to shoddy investigation or government crackdown, only one charge was ever filed. Solomon had drawn a single face for the sketch artists, the only person he could identify from his captivity. A doctor who Solomon claimed had once removed his surgical mask in Solomon's presence, when he thought the patient was unconscious.

Dr. Jans van Draker.

Forced to investigate, the local authorities found enough evidence to prosecute, but dropped the case when the key witness—Solomon Nyembezi—fell asleep at the wheel and ran into an eighteen-wheeler.

Apartheid ended. Jans van Draker never saw a jail cell.

But the public never forgot. The new government forced van Draker out, no hospital would hire him, and the neurosurgeon moved across the country to live out his retirement in obscurity at his family's ancestral home, a small town in the Western Cape nestled amid vineyards and streams and mountains.

A town called Bonniecombe.

Viktor drummed his fingers on the table, ordered another cappuccino to wash away the bad taste in his mouth, and thought about what he had read. He also thought about the questions he would ask at six p.m. the next day, at a secluded manor on a hill, when he was scheduled to meet the man the South African press had once dubbed the Surgeon of Soweto.

"Thank you for arranging this," Viktor said the following evening, as he stepped into the passenger seat of Sergeant Linde's beige Land Cruiser. The wind had picked up, charcoal clouds heralding a rare thunderstorm.

Naomi grunted in reply. Viktor eyed the cracks in the dashboard, the tea and coffee stains worn into the leather. "Is there a reason we're taking your personal vehicle?"

She coaxed the engine to life. "Doctor van Draker is a respected citizen. I prefer not to cause him any distress."

"Respected. I see." Viktor decided to be blunt. "Why didn't you tell me about his past?"

He wasn't sure what he expected, perhaps an angry rebuke, but Naomi focused on the road and said, "I'm not sure what you mean."

"Come now," Viktor scoffed. "The Surgeon of Soweto? The allegations of experiments? Surely that bears examining, in light of recent events?"

"How so?"

Viktor worked hard to control his temper. "A township boy was found with terrible deformities and a strange marking that looked suspiciously like a research tag. Van Draker's past in this regard speaks for itself."

"There are legions of tattoo artists, especially in Cape Town, capable of such work. Van Draker was never convicted of a crime, and there is no evidence whatsoever suggesting he had anything to do with Akhona's death."

The professor waited a long moment to speak. "At least I know where you stand," he said quietly.

"What does that mean?"

"Did you mourn the fall of Apartheid, sergeant?"

She gripped the wheel. "May I remind you," she said coldly, "that you are a *guest* in this town."

"I'm starting to feel like a prisoner."

"You have no jurisdiction except that which the Bonniecombe police department affords you. You would do well to remember that."

"Would you risk your regional commissioner's wrath by disregarding an Interpol request?"

"The request was for an exchange of information, not to watch you harass my citizenry. You're lucky I'm allowing this interview."

"We'll see what an upstanding citizen Jans van Draker turns out to be," Viktor said.

They topped a rise, and van Draker's manor came into view. A square of granite topped by a sloping red-tiled Bavarian roof, the three-story chateau looked as if it had materialized from the roiling gray sky, belonging more in a dreary English heath than the sun-soaked Western Cape.

Double rows of angular windows lined both the lower and upper stories, all protected by iron bars. Ivy climbed the walls of a conical tower topped by a weathervane jutting upward from the left side of the manor.

Sergeant Linde pressed a buzzer on the intercom, beneath a pair of video cameras.

The iron gates swung open.

The grounds of the manor were much larger than they appeared from below.

A hundred yards of lawn separated the house from an encircling stone wall. Behind the wall, thickets of eucalyptus smothered the hillside.

Viktor saw no one on the grounds or in the windows, but he had the sensation of being watched as they parked in the circular drive and approached the front door. He noticed that Sergeant Linde's jawline had firmed, the ring finger on her left hand twitching as she rapped the wolf's head doorknocker on the eight-foot tall door.

The wind had calmed, and the heavy air felt oppressive as Viktor turned to view the smudge of township in the distance. To his left, a stream ran from the mountains to the slum, trickling beneath a decorative stone bridge at the base of the manor hill like a trail of saliva seeping from the mouth of a dragon.

After a brief wait that made Viktor feel uneasy, as if he were a specimen under a microscope being catalogued and examined by unseen eyes, the door to the great house swung open.

11

Heads turned as Grey stepped into the parking lot of the vegetarian restaurant. He didn't recognize any of the men, but all four could have been transplanted from the Peach Shack. Not the creepy suburbanites with reptilian smiles, but the rough, ex-con crowd.

The medium-size man holding Dr. Varela had a craggy face, an SS double lightning bolt tattooed on each cheek, and forearms as hard as tire irons. He ignored Grey and said, in a gravelly voice, "Get in the truck, bitch!"

Another man, hulking and bald with pierced eyebrows, stood beside the driver's side door of Dr. Varela's Jetta. Ten feet away, in the shadows of the secluded lot, the two remaining men hovered next to a forest green Chevy Tahoe with tinted windows. One of them must have weighed four hundred pounds, and two braided goatees hung off his chin like horses' tails. "This ain't none of your concern, boy," he said, with a step towards Grey. "Now go on back inside."

Dr. Varela tried to pull away from her captor. "Let me go!"

The man holding her snarled and gripped her harder, forcing her towards the Tahoe. "Don't make me ask again. *Get in the truck.*"

"Don't do it, Hannah," Grey said evenly, stepping towards Dr. Varela.

For a moment, the assailants seemed confused by Grey's calm demeanor. Then the huge man took another step towards him, blocking Grey's path, and the fourth, a skinhead in his twenties wearing black jeans tucked into combat boots, pulled a hunting knife out of his camo jacket.

Scenarios of how this could play out flashed like paparazzi cameras in Grey's mind. He noticed a gun sticking out of the back of the craggy-faced man's jeans. The two larger men had baggy shirts and could be armed as well. Grey knew he could sprint into the darkness before they got off a good shot, but that wasn't an option. And Dr. Varela's hostage status narrowed his choices.

How far, Grey wondered, were these men willing to go in a public place? That was always the question in a situation like this.

Because if they got her in the truck, Grey knew how it would end.

The bald man was rummaging through the backseat of Dr. Varela's car. Hannah tried to scream but her captor covered her mouth. Grey slipped his hand into his pocket and grabbed his phone.

"Hands up, boy!" the obese man roared.

Grey eased his phone out and dialed 911, right in front of them. He hoped someone would rush him and give him access to a weapon, but the huge man held his ground while Craggy Face drew his gun and pointed it at Dr. Varela's head. "Last chance," he said, with quiet menace. "Get in the truck."

When the 911 operator answered, Grey barked, "Café Magnolia, back parking lot, kidnapping situation. Send help *now*." He hung up and slipped the phone back in his pocket.

"Oh, you'll pay for that," the fat man said. He quivered with rage but kept backing towards the Tahoe. A smart move that made Grey's hopes sink. Whoever had sent these men had given strict orders.

Now it was a race against the clock, and a deadly game of will.

The bald man emerged from Hannah's car with a briefcase and a stack of manila folders. Cringing from the gun pressed against her temple, Dr. Varela took a hesitant step towards the Tahoe.

"If you get in the truck," Grey said, speaking directly to Hannah, "you might never see sunlight again. The cops are on the way."

"Shut up!" Craggy Face shouted. "I'll waste her right here!"

"If they wanted you dead," Grey said to Hannah, "you'd be dead."

She looked ready to faint from fear. Grey needed her awake and fighting. He walked slowly towards them, hands up, hoping they'd let him get close enough to do damage.

The kid in the camo jacket was standing beside the hood. He pulled a gun and aimed it at Grey. As the fat man jumped into the driver's seat of the Tahoe, Craggy Face man shoved Hannah towards the open rear door. At the last moment, she straight-armed the roof.

"No!" she screamed, bucking wildly.

The bald man ran over to help shove her in. If Grey tried to help, the kid with the gun would probably shoot. He was twenty feet away and might get lucky. Instead, Grey took another step towards Hannah with his hands up. The obese man started shouting, and the kid shot into the gravel at Grey's feet. The back door of the restaurant opened and then slammed shut.

"They're out of time," Grey said to Hannah. Anything to stall, keep her out of that truck. "Help will be here any second. Someone inside just saw their faces. Keep fighting."

The kid shouted and shook his gun at Grey. Dr. Varela redoubled her efforts to escape, but Craggy Face tired of the games and cracked her in the head with the gun.

Hannah slumped to the pavement.

Sirens sounded in the distance.

"*Get her in!*" the obese man roared.

The bald man bent to pick up their captive, and Craggy Face swung his gun towards Grey. Ten feet separated them. Too far away to go for the gun. He also had the kid to worry about.

But Grey had no choice. Before anyone could shoot, he dove at Dr. Varela and managed to grasp one of her ankles, putting himself at their mercy. The bald man cursed and tried to yank Hannah away. Grey held tight. He fought for a better grip as the leader kicked him hard in the side. The kid ran over to take aim at Grey as the bald man finally pulled Hannah away and forced her towards the truck.

Before he could stuff her inside, Dr. Varela came to life and bit him on the arm.

Her attacker roared and dropped her. Grey was as surprised as everyone else. The sirens blared closer, accompanied by a flash of light strobing the night sky. Hannah tried to run but the obese man reached a hand out of the window and grabbed her by the neck.

"Blue lights!" the kid shouted. "C'mon, Johnny!"

Grey was lying flat on his stomach, two guns pointed at his head. Craggy Face stepped on the back of Grey's hand with the sole of his boot, leaning into it. Grey stiffened in pain as the man leaned down and cocked his gun. "You're dead, boy."

"Do it, then," Grey said.

"We have to go!" the kid screamed. "*Right goddamn now!*"

Hannah kept trying to twist out of her attacker's grasp. He finally shoved her away in frustration. Craggy Face pressed his gun against Grey's cheek so hard he thought his jaw might crack. "Soon. That's a promise."

As Grey breathed hard on the ground, the men clambered into the truck and sped off, moments ahead of the first cruiser.

Hours later, hovering over stale coffees, Grey and Hannah found themselves alone in a conference room at the Dekalb County police station. Dr. Varela's head was bandaged, and Grey had accepted an ice pack for his hand. Nothing was broken but it hurt like hell.

Hannah looked shell-shocked. Grey was still annoyed that the Chevy Tahoe had managed to elude the police. He shook it off and focused on the present. "What'd they get from your car?"

"A few notes and papers," she said. "Nothing important. It's all at the lab."

He thought about what had happened. No one had followed him to the restaurant, he was sure of it. "How often do you eat there?"

"Three to four nights a week."

"Time to find a new restaurant. And your pager? Who called you?"

"When I called back, it rang and rang."

Grey grimaced. "Do you live alone?"

"Yes."

"Is your house secure?"

"I have an alarm and live in a gated community."

"That's probably why they jumped you at the restaurant."

Dr. Varela drew her arms across her chest and rubbed her arms. "What does this mean?"

"It means your instincts were right."

She swallowed as the implication of that knowledge set in. "What do I do now?"

"Tell the police and your boss everything you know, and let them sort it out. You've been doing the right thing by being cautious. Just keep your head down and focus on your work."

"What if those men come back?"

"I think they're after the research, not you. Be careful and tell your coworkers to stay aware. Can the CDC assign a security detail?"

"It's not unprecedented. I'll ask." She pressed her lips together, took a deep breath, and let it out slowly through her nose. "I'm not cut out for the James Bond stuff," she said, then surprised him by laying a hand over his.

At first he thought she was hitting on him, and it made him resentful because she wasn't Nya. Then he remembered how beautiful Hannah was and how strung out he looked, and realized that it was pity, not attraction, he saw swimming in her eyes.

"Thank you for saving me," she said.

"Yeah."

She withdrew her hand. "I know I barely know you, and we just got assaulted, but . . . is everything okay?"

"Of course not," he snapped, jumping to his feet and pacing. "You just got attacked, I've barely slept in three days, and we've got three dead bodies and a virus no one understands."

Barely slept in three months, he corrected silently.

After Grey and Hannah gave their statements, a lean officer with short gray hair and a gold bar on his sleeve entered the conference room. He identified himself as Lieutenant Palmer, and asked Grey to stick around.

No surprise. Eyebrows had lifted when Grey handed over his Interpol ID. It was a liaison badge, nothing more—Interpol didn't put agents in the field—but it did what it was designed to do. Command respect and open doors.

Grey agreed to stay after making sure the police gave Dr. Varela an escort home. Soon after she left, an African American man with two gold bars on his sleeve entered the room. He looked about the same age as the lieutenant. "I'm Captain Gregory. We appreciate your statement." After Grey tipped his head in response, the captain said, "Now why don't you tell us what the hell really went down?"

"Who are you with, son?" the lieutenant added, as they both took a seat. "DEA? FBI?"

"You'd know by now if I was."

"He's right," said Captain Gregory. "I called Interpol, and they said the guy we need to speak with, Jacques Bertrand, should be in soon. I guess it's four a.m. or something in Paris." He leaned forward, causing his stomach to push over his belt. He had white hair at the temples, thick hands, and the shoulders of a bison. "So do you want to tell us what's going on, or do we sit here until Jacques calls us back?"

Grey saw no reason to hide his assignment from the local police, but that wasn't his call. He told them as much, and they didn't protest. Cops understood chain of command. Grey also told them he didn't care if they held him for four minutes or four hours or four weeks, which caused them to look at him blankly.

While they decided what to do, Grey ran through the database with them and found three of the four men who had tried to snatch Dr. Varela. Everyone except the kid. The others belonged to the League of Dixie.

"A Neo-Confederate hate group," the captain explained to Grey. "You said you're from New York? Before you get all high and mighty about the South, the NSM—outta Detroit—just held a membership rally in Rome, Georgia."

"That's a thing now, see," the lieutenant said. "Used to be the hate groups spent more time fighting amongst themselves than burning crosses, but that's changing. ISIS and immigration and the economy, the world's a powder keg for white supremacists right now. Activity is through the roof. There's even a new group from Europe recruiting around here."

"Christ," the captain muttered, "even the neo-Nazis are globalizing."

"This new group," Grey said. "What's it called?"

"W.A.R. The Wodan Aryan Republic."

"Wodan?"

"German version of Odin. You know, chief of the old Norse Gods? King Whitey himself?"

"What do you know about them?" Grey asked.

"They seem smarter and better organized than the klukkers. But that ain't saying much, to be honest."

"Your typical Confederate flag wavers don't give us much trouble," the captain said. "The worst of the bunch are the Aryan Brotherhood and the profit-driven gangs, but that's different. Dollar bills are colorblind."

"Are they?" Grey asked.

"I'm not saying they're not a bunch of racist assholes. But their agenda's more about getting paid than saluting a flag."

They might be under new leadership, Grey thought. He hadn't seen either the redheaded Viking or his dapper companion's photos in the mug shots, and he described them.

The two cops exchanged a glance. "The big guy with the accent doesn't sound familiar," the captain said slowly, as the lieutenant shook his head, "but the other guy—describe him again?"

Grey did. The captain opened a laptop, started typing, and waved Grey over. He found himself staring at a photo of the same well-groomed man he had seen at the Peach Shack rally, suntanned and sharp-featured, waving from the back of a yacht like a Kennedy. "That's him. Who is he?"

The captain grimaced. "Eric Winter. The new face of hate in America, though you won't catch him dead with a hate tattoo or burning a cross."

"Wait—Winter, as in Nate Winter?"

Nathan Lowell Winter III was a former congressman from Alabama, as well as a Holocaust denier and a reputed Imperial Wizard of the KKK.

"His son. Ivy League educated, trust fund baby, real well-spoken. Just announced a Senate run. Claims he's a white nationalist but not a racist. Huh. Those domestic abusers always love their wives, too."

Lieutenant Palmer added, "The apple never falls far from the tree."

Grey had always hated that saying, because it whispered in every kid's ear with a terrible father that, no matter how much he thought otherwise, he was destined for the same fate.

"Is he involved with W.A.R.?" Grey asked.

"Not that we know of."

Grey made a mental note to have Jacques coordinate with the feds and immigration. "Did you know Winter was in Atlanta?"

"No, but he's probably stumping. Plenty of wallets around here who'd like to see him elected, even if it's in another state."

"What about the other guy? Is it possible he's been seen with him before?"

The captain looked annoyed, as if just realizing he'd let Grey take the lead in the interrogation. "Like I said, he doesn't sound familiar. And a guy like that, I'd remember. See the sketch artist before you leave and we'll look into it."

The captain afforded Grey a long stare and crossed his arms. "Listen, I've seen enough of your background to know you're probably pissed about what happened tonight, and might decide to do something about it. You got a conceal/carry permit valid in Georgia?"

"No."

"Keep it that way. No Lone Ranger stunts, you hear?"

Grey took a sip of coffee.

12

According to Sergeant Linde, Jans van Draker lived alone. Still, accustomed to the habits of the wealthy, Viktor expected to find a domestic helper or a younger relative greeting them as the door to the ancestral manor opened.

But he was wrong. Dressed in loafers and clean-pressed slacks and a beige sweater, well-preserved for a man in his mid-sixties, Jans van Draker answered the door himself.

Viktor recognized him from the photos. A short man of unassuming build, barely reaching Viktor's chest, he had a puckish mouth and the same trim, rust-colored beard he had sported twenty-five years before. A purple birthmark splotched his forehead above his left eye. Viktor thought he looked a bit like, well, the family physician.

A distracted smile creased the former doctor's lips. "Welcome." His eyes took in Sergeant Linde with a curious glance, then lingered on Viktor.

"Thank you," Sergeant Linde said. Her voice was calm and businesslike, a cop performing a routine duty. Though as soon as van Draker's gaze left her face, Viktor noticed her eyes darting towards the interior of the house.

Jans stepped aside and held the door. "Please, come in."

Viktor noticed that he walked with a limp as they stepped into a towering stone foyer decorated with hanging rugs, heraldic emblems, and medieval weaponry. High above the floor, a knight in full armor stood at attention in a nook recessed into the wall. A stone staircase curved upward to the second story.

"German, if I'm not mistaken," Viktor said, staring at a pair of gryphons facing each other on a coat of arms.

"Very astute. My father's side of the family is Dutch, my mother's German. Not uncommon among Afrikaners. Come."

He led them down a hallway and into a sitting room overlooking a slope of the hill covered in a tangle of untended grapevines. The lounge was a cozy medley of wood and polished granite that stretched towards a hearth at the far end. A collection of old war memorabilia adorned the walls, Viktor guessed from the Boer Wars. Vintage field maps, rifles, medals, binoculars, framed black and white photos of soldiers.

Jans chuckled. "Not as grand as your own familial estate, I'm sure," he said to Viktor.

Interesting, Viktor thought. It would take some digging to uncover that his family still owned a castle in southern Bohemia. Sergeant Linde looked surprised at the comment.

"Grandness is a relative term," Viktor replied. "Quite unrelated to wealth."

"Bah," Jans scoffed. "We must have objective standards. Otherwise all is nonsense."

"A hermit's cave of solitude is grand to him or her, a child's tree house more opulent than the Taj Majal," Viktor countered.

"Perhaps, but those are not apt comparisons. Does even the hermit not seek a cave with a superior view, the better to ponder the questions of existence? And what child would not prefer a tree house with a trap door, a slide, sugar-coated walls?" He flashed a shrewd smile. "It is a fact, professor, that some things in life are superior to others."

"Some people, too?" Viktor asked.

"But of course. Would you argue otherwise? The saint over the sinner, the murderer beneath the nun?"

"I would argue that applying objective standards to people is a very dangerous thing."

Sergeant Linde had grown increasingly stiff during the innuendo. "Doctor van Draker," she interrupted, "we appreciate your time, and I apologize for the intrusion. As I informed you yesterday, we're investigating the death of Akhona Mzotho, and would like to ask you a few questions."

Jans took a seat in a high-backed armchair. After waving his guests into similar seats, he said, "You mean the professor would like my medical opinion on how the boy returned from the grave."

Naomi's chuckle sounded hollow. "We don't think Akhona returned from the grave."

Jans blinked. "Did he not? From where, then, did he return?"

"I believe you know what I mean."

"I believe that I do not."

Naomi looked flustered, and Viktor said, "Why would we seek your medical opinion? I was under the impression that you no longer practiced. Or am I mistaken?"

"Oh," Jans said with a nonchalant wave, "I like to keep abreast of the journals, poke my nose into the research now and again. In fact, I have a particular area of interest these days. Something which has grown into quite the hobby."

"Oh?" Viktor said. "What might that be?"

The corners of his lips curled upward. "Resurrection. Life after death. A preservation of species."

Tension thickened like swamp humidity around the two men. After a prolonged stare during which neither Viktor nor van Draker turned away, the physician blinked and crossed his legs. "I'm speaking of taxidermy, of course."

"Of course."

"What else did you think, professor? Dear God, what a morbid mind you must have, after all the dark places to which your cases must have taken you. If you have time after the interview, I'd love to show you the game room. I have a recent acquisition, a single-horned gerenuk. A deformity to some, a quite literal unicorn to a collector like myself."

Naomi had grown still during the exchange, and Viktor wondered why she allowed it to go on. Perhaps she was afraid of interrupting van Draker.

"I'm sure it's a professional job," Viktor said. "Though taxidermy is not to my taste."

"Perhaps I can change your mind. My work is . . . quite extraordinary. Now, where were we? My medical opinion on the boy's return? A miracle or a hoax, of course. I don't believe there's a middle ground to be had."

"I do," Viktor said. "Pharmaceuticals that lower respiration to an undetectable degree, autosuggestion, nerve agents. There are multiple ways to feign a death. As for his physical condition, I suppose a poisoned well or radioactive waste could be the culprit, but I believe a human hand is to blame. Experiments of an unknown nature."

Van Draker looked amused. "Why would anyone do such a thing?"

"That's what I came here to ask you."

Jans's smile was more forced.

"From your past experience with illicit experiments," Viktor said, "would you care to hypothesize why someone might have snatched Akhona from the grave and altered his physicality in such a way? An insight into motive?"

Jans turned towards Sergeant Linde with an accusing stare.

"We *came*," Naomi said, glaring at Viktor before turning back to van Draker, "because Akhona was seen walking from the direction of your manor. We just wanted to know whether you'd seen or heard anything unusual that night."

Jans smoothed his shirt and folded his hands in his lap. "I'm afraid not."

"Thank you," she said. "And my apologies."

"No no," Jans said. "History is history, after all. I was indeed once accused. Tell me though, sergeant, why bring a religious phenomenologist with you today? You could have asked these questions yourself."

Viktor thought the question would catch her off-guard, but Naomi was quick to answer.

"Professor Radek is an expert in many types of bizarre occurrences. Due to the strange nature of the case, we've requested his assistance. He's here to observe and provide input on the investigation, nothing more."

"Ah," van Draker murmured, with a lift of his head. "But of course."

She said, "I'm afraid I have to ask: was anyone else here that evening?"

"Just Kristof. My butler."

Naomi looked stunned. "I thought . . ."

Jans blinked. "You thought what?"

"Nothing," she mumbled.

"I'm quite certain he saw no one either, but shall I call him?"

She swallowed. "If you don't mind."

Jans rose to pull a cord inside a nook by the arched entranceway. A bell chimed in the distance, and Viktor felt as if they had traveled back to the seventeenth century. Everything about the manor felt archaic, from the decor in the foyer to the ash-stained hearth to the thick, gnarled grapevines tangled like snakes in the overgrown vineyard.

Curious as to what had spooked Naomi, Viktor waited in silence until an elderly white man entered the room who made a chill inch down the professor's spine. Dressed in woolen pants and a well-worn tuxedo jacket that sagged off his spindly frame, Kristof ignored the guests and looked to van Draker for instruction. His movements looked oddly jerky, though that could have been due to his age or a medical condition. What caused Viktor's unease was the pallor of the butler's face and hands, skin so gray and lifeless it looked more akin to the flesh of a corpse than a human being. Viktor could tell that heavy makeup had been applied in various places on his cheeks and neck and ears, smooth patches that almost, but not quite, matched his skin tone.

Out of the corner of his eye, Viktor saw Sergeant Linde's fingers tighten at her side. She asked Kristof if he had seen anything unusual the night of Akhona's return.

"Not a thing," he said, in guttural Afrikaans. His voice had a roughness to it beyond that of a smoker's rasp, as if his vocal cords had once been damaged.

"Doctor van Draker was present with you in the manor?"

"The entire night."

"Do you live here?" she asked.

"Of course," the butler said, as if the question had surprised him.

Naomi asked a few more questions that provided no further insight.

"Would that be all, then?" van Draker said.

Sergeant Linde glanced at Viktor, and the professor let his stare linger on the owner of the ancestral estate. "I believe we've satisfied our inquiries," Viktor said. "For today."

Van Draker gave an amused smile and spread his hands. Before he could see his visitors to the front door, a scream erupted from deep inside the house.

13

Grey signaled to the bartender for another rum. Zaya 12 year, neat. *And keep the cocktail napkin.*

Modern décor, warm lighting, floor to ceiling windows with long elegant drapes. A couple of late-night businessmen at a cocktail table pattering about bonds and luxury cars and the most effective forms of digital marketing, a cacophony of white noise.

Grey knocked his first one back.

Ordered another.

Earlier that same night, on the way to the hotel from the police station, Grey had had a long conversation with Viktor. They exchanged notes on the case, and the professor relayed that Jacques had briefed Captain Gregory on the case.

Then Viktor told Grey about W.A.R.

Contrary to Captain Gregory's belief, W.A.R. was not a new group. Or at least Interpol didn't think so. They really didn't know much about it, which scared them, but the suspicion was that the group had been around for some time and was just starting to emerge from the shadows. No one was sure when or how the group had arisen, or where it was based. What little they did know came from rumor and internet chatter.

The group had cells popping up all over the globe. Law enforcement groups from various nations had managed to plant informants, but no one had penetrated the leadership. W.A.R.'s nerve center remained shrouded in secrecy, its objectives disturbingly opaque.

Nor did Interpol have any idea who the red-headed man at the rally was.

That accent, Grey wondered. What was that accent?

If even half the rumors were true, then W.A.R. was hard-core even for hate groups. There were reports of torture, beheadings, crucifixions. On the fringes of Europe, witnesses had linked them to mass killings in refugee camps, then later recanted. Authorities in the States were working hard to pin down cells, suspecting the group's hand in violent attacks against mosques and border communities.

The truly frightening part, as Captain Gregory had mentioned, was the inclusive nature of the group. Most hate groups argued about everything from the number of stars on their flag to who really killed Martin Luther King. Somehow, sweeping aside past differences, W.A.R. sucked in disgruntled whites like a vacuum cleaner of hate.

After hanging up with Viktor, Grey had not bothered going to his room for a shower. He went straight to the bar and started drinking.

Muslims killing whites killing blacks killing browns. Crucifixions. Targeted rape.

God, it was a vile world.

Even Grey's father had not been a racist. Not from any moral stance, or at least not one communicated to Grey, but because his father respected something else more than the color of one's skin.

Power.

Might makes right was his father's favorite credo. Big Stick diplomacy.

Never forget about power, his father used to say to Grey after a beating. *Like it or not, power makes the world go round. What do you think happens if I don't rule my own roost? I'll have a wife who talks back. A son who walks all over me. That's small scale, son. What do you think happens if our country doesn't police its borders, stockpile the most nukes? We'll be speaking Chinese or Russian. The world is ready to tear your throat out, right after you turn the other cheek.*

Grey hated that argument. Hated it even more because his father's words bore some truth, both about the world and about human nature.

Grey had studied racism, and he knew it all went back to power, from some group in history who wanted to keep what they had from others, or who wanted what the other had, or who wanted to use another group for profit.

He had also studied pacifism. And learned that amid the unspeakable atrocities of World War II, prominent pacifists across the globe had been forced to adjust their belief systems.

A swallow of rum went down with a vengeance. He couldn't take it anymore. Couldn't handle the world. The amount of pain and suffering had always depressed him, but the senseless tragedy of Nya's death had sent him hurtling off a bridge, limbs flailing, the ground rushing up to meet him.

She was gone, he knew that. He didn't need to pine over her or smash things or talk about her death with anyone.

He just wanted to hurt. Disappear.

Dr. Varela seemed like a nice woman and Grey was sorry she was in trouble. He really was.

But he couldn't dance anymore.

His cell buzzed, and he looked down. Captain Gregory wanted him to ride along with the lieutenant tomorrow, see if they could find Big Red.

Grey ran a hand through his hair and left it cupping the back of his neck. Charlie and her knowing young eyes were a long, long way away. Tomorrow he would go with the lieutenant, wallow in the world of these disgusting neo-Nazis, and find out what he could before the trail got too cold.

Then he would step away. Pack his bags and find some forgotten corner of the world until he could breathe again. Viktor might not like it, but Grey had told him at the beginning to find someone else.

The bartender gave him an inquiring look. Grey pointed at his glass.

The next morning, Grey felt as if a heavy bag was wobbling inside his skull. He dragged himself out of bed and splashed cold water on his face until his eyelids were no longer gummy. Threw on some clothes without looking at them. Tripped on the entrance to the elevator. Mainlined coffee in the hotel lobby.

Lieutenant Palmer texted that he was waiting by the curb. The sun flared like Armageddon as Grey stepped outside. He squinted and eased into the unmarked police car.

"You go on a bender last night?"

Grey mumbled a reply.

"Listen, we appreciate your help. Both the captain and Jacques think Big Red might be important to getting inside this group. You're the only one who's seen him up close."

"Why isn't the F.B.I. involved?"

"They're watching from on high, believe me. They'll swoop down like harpies once we do the dirty work."

Grey gave a careless wave. "Drive on."

After a stare, the lieutenant pulled into traffic. "What do you think they wanted from that CDC doctor?"

"Her files, obviously."

The lieutenant snorted. "Let me ask it better, smartass: what do a bunch of backwoods rednecks have to do with the CDC and whatever happened to that Gullah?"

"No idea."

"If it's really some kind of virus, that's some nerve-racking shit," the lieutenant said. "You know they got Muslims working in the CDC, right?"

The interstate split and they headed north on I-75. Just past Buckhead, the trees thickened for a few minutes, before another urban cluster came into view.

"I saw your background," the lieutenant said. "Hand-to-hand Recon instructor, Diplomatic Security, three languages. Pretty impressive stuff. Why'd you give up gov work? Better pay?"

"The State Department fired me." Grey looked at the lieutenant. "For asking too many questions."

"Yeah, okay, we don't have to be friends."

Grey leaned back against the headrest, shutting his eyes to block out the sun.

They spent the day wading through the muck of the poor white underbelly of metropolitan Atlanta, mostly in the northern towns and neighborhoods where the lieutenant said the far right elements were concentrated. Marietta and Kennesaw and Acworth, Roswell and Powder Springs Road. At a glance, the scenery was pleasant, tree-lined streets and stately old homes and graceful front porches, but as soon as they scratched the surface, got behind the historic districts and the swim-club communities, they entered a whole new America. Strip mall after strip mall after strip mall, pawn shops and dollar stores and fast food restaurants, block after block of cheap duplexes and mobile home parks, pit bulls straining on leashes, everyone in sight covered in ink. Endless stoplights and cracked pavement and a barrage of banal commerce that sucked every ounce of charm out of the world.

The tragedy of poor white America, Grey theorized, was that their poverty would forever be overshadowed by the blight of the ghettoes. As heartbreaking as the class-based, institutionalized poverty in certain white communities was, the legacy of slavery was worse. Shoeless children in Appalachia with cola-stained teeth didn't get the news cameras or affirmative action. The general consensus was *buck up, trailer trash. You don't even have slavery to blame*.

Grey was shocked by the extent of the Atlanta underclass. The blighted areas went on for miles and miles, cutting across counties, as pervasive and depressing as the desiccated kudzu that smothered the light poles and chain link fences.

The white ghettoes did share one thing in common with impoverished communities of color: they didn't like cops.

Grey and Lieutenant Palmer stirred the hornet's nest all day long and had nothing to show for it except lies and curses. They even went door-to-door in certain hotspots, showing a sketch of Big Red, offering a five hundred dollar reward and then threatening a crackdown.

Nothing worked. No one knew a thing.

As they left a notoriously xenophobic Irish Pub near the historic Marietta Square, someone shouted "Take off, pigs," and threw a half-eaten chicken wing at Lieutenant Palmer's back. Furious, the lieutenant forced the bartender to wipe the wing sauce off his shirt, threatened to lock up the whole pub, and stormed out spewing curses. Grey absorbed it all with hooded eyes.

With daylight on the wane, the lieutenant returned downtown, muttering about his stained shirt and the decline of the middle-class. As they passed beneath the Seventeenth Street Bridge, the police radio chirped.

The lieutenant pushed a button. "Palmer."

"Where are you?" Captain Gregory asked.

"Connector. Almost in."

"Keep going. You must have ruffled some feathers today, because we just got a tip on the hotline. Some pipehead wants the five hundred bucks you offered. Said he doesn't know Big Red personally, but heard about a super secret Wodan rally at midnight, led by some big shot out of towner."

"What's the rally about? Same old?"

"He said it was a leadership initiation. Something about getting a ring."

Grey and Lieutenant Palmer locked gazes.

"Yeah," the captain said, breaking the silence. "My thoughts as well."

"Where's this going down?"

"Piedmont Park. The trail near the dog run."

"Are you serious? Right in the middle of town?"

"That's the intel."

The lieutenant tightened his grip on the wheel. "What do you want us to do?"

"Scope it out and get a team in place. Then take those fuckers down."

By eleven p.m., Grey and Lieutenant Palmer had camped out in an unmarked police car on a road lined with graceful old homes, most of them restored Craftsman bungalows, near the eastern entrance to Piedmont Park. Set on nearly two hundred acres in Midtown, the park was the city's premier green space.

Field officers disguised as vagrants had been inside since dusk. After midnight came and went with no suspicious activity, the lieutenant sent off a few texts. He frowned when he saw the replies.

"Not a peep," he said to Grey.

"False advertising?"

"Probably."

After another half hour, the lieutenant got on the walkie-talkie. "We're coming in."

"10-4."

Disappointed, Grey and the lieutenant strode into the park on a paved bridge arcing over a lower-lying section of greenery. The skyscrapers of Midtown glowed in the distance like giant neon rockets waiting to lift off. After crossing the bridge, the lieutenant led Grey down a set of stairs to a footpath that ran alongside a dog run. The cityscape was no longer visible and the narrow, low-lying portion of the park felt cut off from the rest.

The officer in charge of the SWAT team, a slope-shouldered gorilla of a man named Robert Swanson, removed a filthy blanket and rose off a bench to greet them. "A little strange," he said.

The lieutenant peered through the chain link fence, into the darkness of the dog run. "What?"

"There's no one around. Down here, hidden from view like this, it's usually a refugee camp at night."

During the day, Grey and the lieutenant had walked the area and decided to post sentries on either end of the dog run. To their left, between the footpath and the steep hillside leading to the upper portion of the park, a wetlands trail wound through a marshy area for a few hundred yards.

Grey shone his flashlight onto the gravel footpath leading into the wetlands. "Anyone check in there?"

"Nothing inside but marsh," Bob said, "and we've been watching both access points."

"What about the hillside?"

"Really? A bunch of white supremacists are going to climb down an overgrown hill and hold a meeting in a swamp?"

Grey pursed his lips. Bob had a point.

"Might as well walk it," the lieutenant said. "You guys stay on the entrances, and call the others down."

The lieutenant curled a finger at Grey. They started down the paved wetlands trail. Off the path, their flashlights illuminated a nest of spindly branches and a stagnant creek that shone with the dull gleam of an oil stain. Except for the hum of distant traffic, they could have been traipsing through a swamp a hundred miles deep into the wilderness.

They almost missed the tiny trail. Littered on both sides with discarded wrappers and plastic bottles, the footpath led down a muddy slope and into the thick of the swamp. They might not have bothered to explore except for a new smell, one of death and rot, that overpowered the stench of the fen.

After radioing for backup and waiting for the other officers to arrive, Lieutenant Palmer drew his gun and took the lead. "Probably an OD," he muttered.

Grey stayed right behind him. Branches whipped into their faces as they crunched on dead leaves and brambly overgrowth, and an owl startled them both by taking flight off a stump ten feet away from Grey.

The trail led to a squatter's camp in a hidden hollow on the bank of a broad section of the creek. Bits of clothing and debris clung to bare branches, broken bottles littered the ground, and the odor of urine and feces would have assaulted Grey's nostrils if not for the worse stench of a headless corpse lying beneath a pile of rocks. Off to the side, a stake impaled the brown-skinned man's severed head, pinning it to the ground.

The other officers cursed as they gathered in behind them. Moving as if underwater, the lieutenant called out, "Hey Bob, did that informant leave his name?"

"Anonymous tip, and he insisted on a drop before he talked."

Grey, along with everyone else, was still staring at the insect-covered corpse. The decapitated head looked Middle Eastern, mid-thirties.

"And you paid him?" the lieutenant asked in disbelief.

"He knew about W.A.R., and you said any info was real important."

"Did he sound drunk? Like a vagrant?"

"I guess. Why?"

The lieutenant grimaced, took out his cell, and made a call. "Captain? The informant was right, there was an initiation. Only it happened last night."

14

The scream cut off as abruptly as it had arisen, as if silenced by someone or something. Viktor thought the voice sounded muffled, coming from beneath a sheet or a blanket.

Sergeant Linde jumped to her feet. "What was that?"

"We have a number of cats," Jans said smoothly. "I'm afraid they fight at times."

"That didn't sound like a cat."

Viktor watched the conversation with interest. He was surprised the sergeant had stood up to van Draker.

"Unnerving, isn't it?" their host said. "Feline cries sound surprisingly human when in heat." He pulled the butler's rope again. "If it will ease your mind, we'll ask Kristof."

"Who else is in the house right now?" Naomi asked.

"No one."

Kristof appeared in the doorway half a minute later, a damp white cloth draped over his arm. Chloroform, Viktor wondered? He kept an eye on both men. Neither seemed perturbed by the scream, though Viktor would bet his absinthe collection that it was not feline.

"Are the cats at war again?" van Draker asked with a chuckle.

Kristof paused a beat before he spoke. "Ah, yes. Sir Francis will not leave Sir Leopold alone this week."

Sergeant Linde looked as if she were gathering her courage, torn between duty and some other force. Or perhaps she was saving face in front of Viktor.

"If you don't mind," she said, "I'd like to walk the premises."

Van Draker opened a palm in consent, but his eyes were cold. "By all means. I'm glad to know our town is well looked after." He met his butler's gaze, and something unspoken passed between them.

"Would you care for tea or coffee?" van Draker asked.

"Neither, thank you," the sergeant said. Viktor declined as well.

"Kristof? If you don't mind?"

"I'd prefer if he stays with us," Naomi said, again surprising the professor. "I won't be long," she added. "I'm sure everything's in order."

"It doesn't solve the problem of my tea," van Draker said. "Unless you object to a stop in the dining room?"

"Of course not."

Kristof led them down the hallway to a dining room with a crystal chandelier sparkling beneath a wood-beamed ceiling. As Kristof crossed the room to the tea service, passing gold-framed paintings depicting spectacular vistas of the Western Cape, Viktor's eyes lasered onto a full-size mannequin hanging on the wall. The effigy was encased in a leather body suit covered head-to-toe with one inch-long spikes.

Viktor walked over to the macabre figure, which resembled a human blowfish. "I've never seen this torture device before. Was it something used to punish slaves during colonization?"

Van Draker gave him an amused glance. "That is an original nineteenth century Siberian bear-hunting outfit. Rather striking, isn't it?"

"It gives the room just the right accent," Viktor said drily. He wasn't quite sure what van Draker's game was, but one thing was certain: Jans wasn't intimidated by the presence of either Viktor or Sergeant Linde.

Shambling along with his shaky gait, Kristof led them on a tour of the high-ceilinged, two-story manor. Van Draker calmly sipped his tea as they walked, and Viktor noticed Sergeant Linde absorbing every detail.

This was no simple sweep, he realized with a start. She wanted this to happen.

But why? Was it all an act?

Whose side was she on?

The layout of the house was much more confusing than it appeared from the outside. Instead of the wide hallways and simple linear structure Viktor had expected, the mansion abounded with shortened corridors, staircases in unexpected places, and irregularly-shaped rooms. Though tidy and free of cobwebs, aristocratic furnishings from centuries past filled the manor, heavy velvet drapes and faded rugs and antique chairs. Family portraits lined the hallways, most of the van Draker clan dressed in hunting clothes or military attire. The manor also possessed a gloom, a pallor that went beyond the lack of natural light. As if the collective spirits of the Cape settlers depicted in the photos, lives steeped in violence and war and subjugation, had congealed inside the house.

Where was the science? Viktor wondered. The evidence of Jans's profession? Except for a few medical journals on the nightstand, Viktor saw nothing that spoke of a man accused of performing surgeries on the cutting edge of technology.

In the library, an amber-hued room stuffed with leather armchairs and floor-to-ceiling bookshelves, Kristof's eyes flicked to a particular shelf in the rear left corner.

Was the glance indicative of an important book, Viktor wondered? A lever to a secret passage?

When they left the room, the professor took the opportunity to move next to Kristof. The butler's skin looked even worse from up close, ashen and plasticine. Almost artificial. The only odor emanating from the man was a cheap, overpowering cologne that smelled more like disinfectant than a fragrance.

Another incongruity was that most of the bedrooms on the second story—Viktor counted eight—looked recently occupied. Rumpled bed spreads and streaks on the mirrors. Papers in the wastebasket. The doctor apologized with a wave, explaining Kristof did not clean the upper story very often.

But Viktor wondered.

They heard no more screams and saw no one else in the manor. From the maze-like design of the architecture, it was impossible to tell if they had searched the entire house, though van Draker accommodated every request to enter a room or try a new staircase or corridor.

As they entered a lushly carpeted billiards parlor at the end of a first floor hallway, van Draker opened a palm towards Viktor. "As promised."

A legion of mounted animal heads, so well-preserved they looked alive, hung from the paneled walls of the room. The taxidermy presented a startling variety of species: rhino, wild boar, all the big cats. He saw the exquisite gerenuk their host had mentioned, a sable-toned antelope with an elongated neck and legs. Viktor looked closer and noticed the creature's bizarre single horn was in fact two horns fused together above the scalp.

Viktor stepped to a pair of French doors overlooking a family cemetery. A ways past that was a low-lying outbuilding made of stacked stone, perhaps a wine cellar. Too far away for the scream they had heard.

Van Draker folded his arms. "I'm afraid the tour is finished. You've seen the entire house."

"Is there a basement?" Naomi asked.

"In a house this old, the proper term would be *dungeon*. Thank God we don't have one. We can barely manage the upkeep as it is."

"Then I suppose," the sergeant said, "I've seen enough."

Van Draker turned to Viktor. "What do you think of my taxidermy?"

"As impressive as you said. I'm wondering, though, about a different collection."

"Oh?"

Viktor stepped aside, revealing a section of the wall covered with horrific framed photos displaying groups of people, many of them children, so emaciated that Viktor could count the ribs. More living skeletons than human beings, they lay listless in hospital beds or slumped in piles at the base of barbwire fences. Viktor had seen countless photos like these before, though usually in the somber halls of holocaust museums.

"More remembrances from the past?" Viktor asked.

"Ya," van Draker said. "Concentration camps, you must be thinking? World War II, the Germans? An evil the world had never before witnessed?"

Viktor noticed Sergeant Linde staring at the floor.

"You're correct," van Draker said softly, "except the Germans are not to blame. Those are my people in those photos. Stuffed into camps like garbage by the British, during the second Boer war. Hitler was far too banal to have invented such a thing," he said bitterly. "The British made him the man he was."

Though Viktor was no longer surprised by the cruelty of his fellow man, he had not known that particular piece of history.

Van Draker began to pace in agitation. "At least the Germans killed for ideology. The British killed for pure profit."

"Ideology?" Viktor said. "Is that what you would call it?"

"Wasn't it? Personal preferences aside? What would you term it, professor?"

"Mass disgrace stemming from the Treaty of Versailles, a bout of collective insanity, and the conditioning of a vulnerable and dangerously nationalistic public by a once-in-a-generation leader gifted with the sort of charisma that panders to the lowest common denominator."

Van Draker flung his hands at the photos. "Savagery. Pure savagery."

"Then why display them?"

"Glossing over the past merely dooms us to repeat our mistakes."

Viktor knew it was more than that. Though the professor did not disagree with the sentiment, there was a time and a place for certain things, and the casual displays of barbarism scattered throughout the house screamed more to the monster lying beneath the surface than a warning about the pitfalls of ignoring history.

On their way out, van Draker all but ignored Sergeant Linde, and gave Viktor's hand a hearty shake. "I enjoyed meeting you, professor. You should return for tea one day. I sense we'd have much to discuss. Both of us, I suspect, enjoy pondering the mysteries of our strange and glorious universe."

"I look forward to it," Viktor murmured, with a final glance at the clam-colored face of the butler.

On the drive back to the police station, dusk wormed its way into the sky, throwing purple shadows against the mountains. "I've met Kristof at least three times before," Naomi said, looking straight ahead as she spoke.

Viktor cocked his head. "He acted as if he'd never met you."

"He had a massive heart attack a while back, in a local café. After he stabilized, van Draker drove him to his preferred hospital in Cape Town. When Kristof never appeared in town again—he ate breakfast every day at that same café—everyone assumed he had returned to his family's homestead in the Eastern Cape. Either to recover by the sea or in a casket."

"Why did everyone have to assume? No one asked van Draker?"

"He never mingles with the masses. Kristof was standoffish, too. He was often seen around but didn't have any friends. At least not in town."

"When did this happen?"

Naomi glanced at Viktor. "Six years ago."

Viktor felt as if the night chill had seeped through the windshield and wormed its way underneath his suit coat. "How many white butlers are there in South Africa?"

"More than you might think. Some of the hard-line families refuse to have a 'colored' in their home."

"In my estimation," Viktor said after a moment, "the scream in that house was not feline."

"No."

"It possessed a muffled ring. Perhaps coming from underneath a sheet or a blanket. Or through the walls of a basement."

"He said there was no basement."

"There's *always* a basement."

Naomi gave him a sideways look, as if once again wondering what sort of professor she was dealing with.

"I believe there are parts of the house we did not see," Viktor said, "and I'm convinced of van Draker's involvement in the matter. We need a closer look. One without the master of the house present."

"What do you propose?"

"What are the odds of a search warrant?"

"Without evidence, nil. I don't think you understand. He *owns* this town."

"Then we start with a stakeout. At night. Observe the comings and goings."

They pulled into the station, and she let the engine idle in the parking lot, tapping her fingers on the gearshift as if weighing not just the decision, but whether or not to work with Viktor. "When do you propose we go?"

"He'll be wary after our conversation, on the lookout for my involvement."

"Agreed."

"But he might not expect us tonight."

15

NEW YORK CITY

"Hey kid."

Charlie emerged from the alley and turned towards the sound of the voice. To her left, a few feet down the street, a burly white man in jeans, a Yankees skullcap, and a creased leather jacket beckoned to her from beside a van with no rear windows.

The man held up a fistful of cash. "Want to make a few bucks? I've got a job for you. Legit. Easy money."

Charlie glanced both ways down the street. No one else in sight.

She had wandered down to East Harlem earlier that day, plying her cup-and-golf balls routine at a street festival known for drawing kids and fresh-faced tourists. Not kids like her, but kids with parents and real bedrooms and money to spend. The golf ball trick was her latest sleight of hand scheme. So far it had worked like gangbusters, whatever that meant. She had earned twenty dollars, enough to buy a few meals at McDonald's.

But she wasn't about to spend that money on the subway, and the long day in Harlem meant the buses had stopped and she had to risk the streets going home. She was working her way over to Broadway, the safest route back to Washington Heights, but at the moment she was in No-Man's Land, sticking to the shadows and praying no one from a gang caught sight of her.

Though right now, it wasn't a gang member that had her worried. A large white man standing beside a van near a deserted alley in Harlem, thrusting cash her way?

Never a good thing.

"Come on," he said, taking a step towards the mouth of the alley, misreading her hesitation for indecision. "Like I said, easy money."

Charlie wasn't confused. She was deciding which way to run.

The muscles bulging at the sleeves of the man's jacket and his testosterone-laced baritone reminded Charlie of her seventh-grade gym teacher. She hadn't trusted him, either, even before he got her best friend pregnant. But this goon with the smashed face and combat boots was worse. His eyes hadn't left her face for one moment, which meant he wasn't interested in sex and was watching in case she ran.

Nope. She wasn't buying it. No one, especially no whitey, was stupid enough to encroach on drug territory in East Harlem—the only reason she could fathom that someone might want to pay her to do something.

Stupid girl, she berated herself. She should have ponied up and spent a few bucks on the subway. Palms slick with sweat, she took a step back on the sidewalk, her heels butting against the edge of the curb. The man moved closer, a lopsided grin creeping onto his face.

Charlie turned and ran.

Back into the alley, away from the light. Into the gaping maw of the city.

The man cursed, shouted for someone named Jared, and pounded the pavement behind her. She heard a sliding van door screech open.

The man almost caught her before she reached the end of the alley. She scrambled to her left, turned over a trashcan, and turned left again, into another alley. He was faster than she was on the straightaways, but she was more nimble. Unfortunately, this part of the city was not a maze of small streets and alleys like Soho or the Village. Her best bet was reaching the intersection of MLK and Malcolm X Boulevard, less than five blocks away. A busy area known as White Castle because it was one of the few areas of Harlem with big box stores and white people.

She could disappear there. Slip into a corner store or the subway. And if the men chasing her were crazy enough to grab her in public, the cops or the local thugs would take care of them.

She glanced back. He was twenty feet behind her and breathing hard as he ran, fists balled. Another man was right behind him, carrying some type of black garment.

What the hell is that? Charlie thought in a panic. *Who are these people?*

Just before she reached the end of the alley, her pulse spiked further when a third man stepped into view. Dressed similar to the first man but wearing a

Mets hoodie instead of a skullcap, he clutched a set of car keys in one hand and a handgun in the other.

The gun was pointed down, at the ground. He pocketed the keys and held out a hand as she ran towards him. "C'mon," he said, "we just want to talk."

Charlie slowed.

He smiled. "I promise."

She nodded and heard the other two closing in behind her. She kept walking towards the third man, hands up, a look of defeat on her face. "Yeah?" she said. "What do you want?"

As he opened his mouth to respond, she kicked him in the groin as hard as she could, curling her toes as Grey had taught her, trying to catch the testicles. The man bellowed and dropped to the ground. Charlie sprinted past him, sticking to the darkest part of the street. She weaved as she ran, also as Grey had taught her, in case someone shot at her from behind.

No shots came. She didn't think any would. A gunshot would alert every cop and gangbanger in a three-mile radius, and whatever these men were up to, they sure as hell didn't want company.

Charlie ran like she never had before, knowing her life was at stake, attuned to the labored breaths of the men behind her, all too aware of the silence in the streets. A window opened and Charlie screamed for help, only to catch a glimpse of an old woman in a nightgown right before she slammed the glass shut.

Somewhere behind Charlie, an engine rumbled to life. A glance back told her it was the van. Two of the men were right behind her. She ran in a dead sprint, her breath rasping like sandpaper across rough wood. Nostrils flared as she sucked in oxygen, and behind the street garbage she caught the distant smell of barbecued chicken. A desperate hiccup of laughter escaped her. For a split-second, her hunger had almost overpowered her fear.

Malcolm X was too far. She wasn't going to make it. As the tires of the van squealed behind her, Charlie veered to her left, darting across a parking lot and through a nest of prickly bushes that tore at her skin. She leapt onto an iron fence and scrambled up it, aiming to disappear into the fortress-like housing complex on the other side.

Voices emanated from a nearby courtyard. As dangerous as those voices might be, they couldn't belong to anyone worse than the men chasing her.

It was an eight-foot spiked fence. She jumped and clutched the horizontal bar near the top, scrambling to pull herself up, prepared to twist, flail, fling her body over the fence. Whatever it took.

Muscles quivering, she got a foot on the bar. Just before she pulled her other foot up and tumbled over, a hand grabbed her by the ankle.

"Get off me!" she screamed, lashing out with her leg. The grip held. She swung her other leg down and tried to kick her attacker in the face. The man in the Yankees skullcap caught her leg in midair and yanked her off the fence. After wrapping her in his arms from behind, he dragged her towards the street, towards the idling van.

Her panic spiked and then settled. She forced herself to concentrate. *Bear hug from behind. I know this escape. I can do this.* Charlie stomped on top of the man's foot at the same time she bucked her hips and tried to create distance.

Neither move worked. The top of his boot felt like iron, and he was simply too powerful. She knew if she had Grey's technique and training she could pull it off, but she didn't. In desperation, she leaned her head back and tried to bite the man's shoulder. He slammed her to the ground, dazing her, then gripped her by the upper arms so hard she moaned in pain.

Arms straight in front of him to keep her from biting him again, he half-pushed, half-carried Charlie towards the open rear doors of the van. Another man handcuffed her and tied a hood over her face, then shoved her inside.

16

Viktor's bones and joints creaked as he waded through the morass of old-growth grapevines gone to seed. Swathed in darkness, he and Naomi had entered the grounds of van Draker's estate via an old game trail that wound through the forest on the southwest side of the manor. After helping each other struggle over the old stone wall, Sergeant Linde managing much better than the professor, they scurried down what remained of the dirt paths separating the rows of gnarled trunks. A canopy of vines masked their progress, though at times they had to cut their way through with a pair of garden shears Naomi had brought.

Viktor grunted as he stooped underneath a chest-high cluster of branches. "My partner," he whispered, "is much better suited to this."

"Your partner?"

"A good man," Viktor said, as he caught his breath, "who battles some demons."

"Don't we all," she murmured.

"He recently suffered a loss. A tragic one."

"I'm sorry to hear that," she said, and when Viktor glanced over, he could tell that she meant it.

A moldy, sickly sweet odor permeated the air. They stopped moving a few minutes later, safely ensconced within a dome of vines. Viktor had the sudden worry a dog could sniff them out, though they had seen no evidence of an animal.

Why the lax security, he wondered, if the doctor had something to hide? Were they following a false trail after all?

As the night deepened to expose a mature canopy of stars, Viktor checked his watch. Ten past midnight. He was facing the tower and, in the darkness, he could just make out the manor grounds with the naked eye. No visible lights except for a wrought-iron gas lamp by the front door. To his left, past a stretch of lawn sprinkled with avocado trees, the stippled tops of the cemetery glowered in the moonlight.

Naomi sat cross-legged beside him, adjusting the eyepiece on her night goggles. "I looked into Kristof's transfer today. From the local hospital to Cape Town."

"Yes?"

"There was no record of it. I went further afield and checked every metropolitan area in the country. No hospital in South Africa has a record of admission for Kristof Heuvel within a year of his heart attack."

Viktor was quiet for a moment. "Then I suppose he recovered on his own."

"I suppose so."

After a longer, more uncomfortable silence, Viktor said, "Van Draker is a physician. There is also the possibility he took Kristof's care into his own hands."

Sergeant Linde didn't respond. Viktor could almost feel the tension radiating out of her.

"I think it's time we had a discussion," he said.

"About what?" she asked, though the strain in her voice implied she already knew.

"About your confusing involvement in this case."

"I'm unsure what you mean." She sounded as if she had to force the words out.

"You've been keeping things from me from the beginning. Van Draker's past, the possible existence of a lab. Contrast that with your willingness to search his house, and the fact that you're trespassing right now to get a better look at his property."

"How do you know I don't have a warrant?" she muttered.

"Police officers with warrants generally do not climb eight-foot walls to access the property." When she didn't respond, he said, "Let me be more clear. You mentioned that van Draker owns this town. Does he own you?"

When he looked at her, there was just enough light to see the rigid clench of her jaw.

"No one owns me," she said. "Especially not *him*."

"Then why not be more forthcoming? If there's a classified or undercover investigation going on, I need to know."

Her silence stretched for days.

"Sergeant Linde, are you keeping facts from me?"

She lowered the goggles and looked him in the eye. "The Interpol request," she said evenly, "only compels me to disclose anything I have learned during a *professional* inquiry."

That took Viktor aback.

She did, then, have an agenda—a *private* one.

She hadn't been shielding van Draker. She'd been keeping Viktor at arm's length so he wouldn't step on her own investigation.

Viktor decided not to press the issue. He needed to know what she knew, but first would have to gain her trust. After seeing her reactions inside the manor, he was satisfied she was not working for van Draker.

Two hours passed. During the wait, Viktor pondered Grey's recent report, the assault on the CDC doctor, and the mutilation of the body in Piedmont Park. He combined it all with the progress of his own research. Disturbing progress.

Earlier that day, he had finally realized why the symbol found on Akhona, the letter T piercing a circle, looked familiar.

At first the professor speculated the T represented a stylized version of the cross. Long before the birth and death of Jesus Christ, the cross was a sacred symbol of nature worship to a plethora of pagan cultures across the globe. The true origin of the cross was a mystery for another day, but what got Viktor thinking was an article theorizing that the cross had in fact derived from an even more ancient, pan-cultural symbol: the tree of life.

Alarm bells had started ringing in Viktor's head, though at first he wasn't sure why. Then he thought about the case and realized what it was.

One of the more developed tree of life mythologies was Yggdrasil, or the world tree, from Norse religion. Viktor was familiar with Yggdrasil because another cultural group, in a much more modern era, had appropriated the symbol for their own designs.

The Nazis.

More specifically, the Ahnenerbe.

Spearheaded by Heinrich Himmler in 1935, the Ahnenerbe was the occult arm of the Third Reich. The one no one wanted to believe was real. Over the years, a myriad of theories had arisen concerning the Ahnenerbe, and the organization had even been popularized in popular media, such as the Indiana Jones films. Viktor knew some of the rumors concerning the Ahnenerbe were pure fantasy—but he also knew much of it was true. In fact, many of the organization's beliefs, experiments, and expeditions were so horrific and fantastical they *defied* belief.

At its core, the Ahnenerbe was dedicated to researching the history of the Aryan race. In an obsessive attempt to prove the superiority and purity of the Germanic people, Himmler sent people around the world on archaeological and fact-finding expeditions that often delved into occult and pseudoscientific arenas. An expedition was sent to Finland to photograph pagan sorcerers at work. Linguists studied runes and petroglyphs in an attempt to gather evidence of an ancient Nordic language that preceded all others. Multiple voyages to Tibet, launched to collect scientific data establishing that the Aryans had conquered most of Asia, also sought contact with black-magic adepts and the mythical kingdom of Shambhala.

Even Viktor was unsure where the real truth lay. What he did know was that the symbol for the Ahnenerbe was a circle—a stylized version of the Swastika—pierced by a T.

It was almost a replica of the symbol on Akhona's leg, with an ouroboros replacing the swastika and the tree of life supplanted by a double helix and the unalome.

Science supplanting myth, perhaps?

Grey's report of the gruesome initiation at Piedmont Park bore an ominous parallel to the Death's Head Ring used by the SS. Designed by Himmler and depicting a skull surrounded by an array of Germanic symbols and runes, the ring embodied the Nazi fascination with Aryan mysticism.

Add to that the signs that W.A.R. practiced Odinism, an ancient Norse religion not uncommon among harmless neo-pagans, but which had been adopted by white supremacists eager to flee a religion—Christianity—they saw as too weak and inclusive of non-whites.

Viktor took a deep breath. He did not at all like the direction this case was taking. Was there a revival of the Ahnenerbe afoot, or a remnant that had evolved into a modern incarnation? One using the ideology of Odinism to unite the hate groups?

He had to dig deeper.

"Viktor," Naomi whispered.

He snapped to attention. She held up a finger as she peered intently through the night goggles. He checked his watch. Just after three a.m. The witching hour.

"Two people," she said, after a moment. "By the door to that outbuilding."

Twenty yards past the cemetery, almost at the edge of the forest, loomed the stacked stone structure Viktor remembered from their earlier visit. Little more than a wooden doorway and a roof that sloped almost to the ground, he had guessed the building housed a wine cellar.

He hadn't seen anyone crossing the lawn from the manor. "Where did they come from?"

"Inside the cellar. They came out for a smoke."

"Intriguing."

"Take a look," she said, sounding a little uneven.

Viktor strapped on the goggles. As he honed in on the cellar, Naomi put her hands on his broad shoulders and leaned forward. The intimacy of the gesture surprised him.

The smoker, a bespectacled man with a Roman nose jutting over a weak chin, jabbed at a younger woman with a finger as he spoke. Viktor didn't recognize either the man or the woman, who wore her whitish-blond hair in a bun and had a mouth too thin for the cherubic roundness of her face.

It wasn't the physical features of the two people that had produced the tension in Sergeant Linde's voice, Viktor knew.

It was the blue hospital scrubs they were wearing.

"Ever seen them before?" she asked.

"No," Viktor said. "You?"

"Never."

After the man pinched out his cigarette, the two disappeared through the doorway. From his vantage point, Viktor couldn't see inside the cellar. He lowered the goggles. "We need to see what's behind that door. If the lab is there, we can figure out a reason to pursue a warrant."

"I don't disagree." Naomi pursed her lips and scanned the lawn. "The cemetery's probably the best location."

He ran his eyes over the orderly square of stone vaults and sepulchers, some as big as a small garage. Impressive for a family graveyard.

"I hate to say this," Naomi said, "but I don't think I should be the one to go."

"Understood," Viktor said. He was an outsider and would suffer fewer repercussions if caught creeping through van Draker's cemetery.

"Are you game?" she asked.

"Of course."

She offered a hand to help pull him up. He accepted, hoping she didn't hear the creaking of his knees.

"Be careful," she said. "If you can't see inside the cellar the next time someone leaves, then come back. We'll try something else."

After ensuring no one was watching, lulled by a soft chorus of crickets, the professor crept across the lawn as best as a seven-foot tall man can creep. Pausing behind a yellowwood twisting up from the earth like a petrified crone, he scanned the grounds of the manor and saw nothing stirring. Viktor hunched when he resumed walking, feeling as if ten pairs of eyes were watching from behind the shuttered windows. When he neared the cemetery, the smell of musty earth wafted in, as if the disintegrating bones had seeped through the dirt and caused the air to stale.

It's just another cemetery, Viktor thought to himself. *You've been in thousands.*

Searching for a good angle, he spied a ribbed vault with an angel perched on top, right in the middle of the cemetery. The vault afforded an unobstructed view of the wine cellar, with only a few small tombstones in between. Viktor hurried forward. He climbed over the low stone wall and cringed as his foot sank into a pile of loose dirt. The unnerving sensation of stepping into a fresh grave caused him to look behind him, just in time to reveal a spectral figure gliding out of a closet-sized crypt that Viktor had just passed.

17

Just before Lieutenant Palmer dropped Grey off at his hotel, they got word that a wallet left in the pocket of the decapitated corpse identified the victim as Naseem Raja, a green card holder from Yemen. Naseem had two young children, a DUI conviction, and sometimes performed the call for prayer at a local mosque.

A quick search on Google revealed that an impaled head was a common form of execution during the Crusades. A horrific practice meant to send a message to the infidels.

Grey stopped at the hotel bar and drank until they kicked him out. He stumbled to his room, took an airplane bottle of vodka out of the minibar, sloshed the contents into a glass, and carried it to the balcony. Cold air seared his lungs as the noise and lights of downtown dazzled like a monstrous pinball game.

After the horror of the night's events, he was finished. Sick of the world and its disgusting injustices and depraved actors who never seemed to change.

He put his elbows on the railing and looked down, at the blacktop looming a hundred feet below. The siren song of vertigo lured him forward, urged him to let his body go free, embrace the timeless pull of gravity.

Suicide had never been an option for Grey. He wasn't sure why not, because he had certainly crawled along the bottom before, inch by terrifying inch. Yet nothing had hurt like losing Nya. He couldn't deny the feeling of peace he felt at the thought of shutting it all down, flushing away the final glimpse of her falling into that green-walled chasm, eyes full of love as she merged into the mist.

It was his fault she had died. The General had taken her to get to Grey.

And there was nothing, ever, he could do to change that fact.

As he stumbled inside and reached for his phone, ready to call Viktor and announce his resignation, he tripped over his suitcase and fell. The carpet felt soft and warm against his cheek, and he decided not to get back up.

The morning rushed at Grey like an oncoming train. Head throbbing, he splashed water on his face, fixed a double-strength coffee in his room, and stepped onto the balcony for some fresh air while the caffeine kicked in. After he woke up, he could make that call to Viktor with a clear head.

His cell phone chimed. Strange. It was the number for the shelter in Washington Heights.

"Hello?"

"Grey?" Reverend Dale's restrained, pleasant voice sounded more tense than usual. "Do you have a moment?"

"Sure. What is it?"

"It's about Charlie."

Grey's hand tightened against his coffee mug. "What do you mean?"

A pause. "I . . . I don't know how to say this, but someone took her."

"You mean social services? Did she finally decide to—"

"It wasn't social services."

Grey grew as still as the surface of a pond on a windless day. "Who was it, then?"

"We're not sure who they were. Three men in a van, that's about all we—"

"A van? *Wait.* How do you know it was her? Charlie disappears all the time. Who told you this? What do you mean?"

"Grey—someone saw it happen. Another homeless teen, from a shelter in Harlem. He was watching from a playground and recognized Charlie from the street."

Grey held the phone against his ear for a long moment, fighting not to choke on the rage bubbling forth. "These men—what did they look like?"

"All we know is they were white and big. Dressed in street clothing. The other child wasn't close enough to see their faces, but she thinks she saw tattoos."

White. Big. Street clothing. Took her. Someone saw it happen. Three men in a van. Took her. White. Took her. Tattoos.

Took her took her took her took her took her

Grey dropped the phone and hurled his coffee mug against the wall. Dizzy with fury, he stumbled to the TV, yanked it off the dresser, and put his fist through the drywall. He roared and fell to his knees, palms pressed against the sides of his head. He roared and he roared and he roared, until his voice grew hoarse and his vision blurred and men with badges burst through the door.

A few hours later, Grey sat in a coffee shop down the street, hovering over a green tea. Detoxing as he struggled to order his thoughts. Thank God the two hotel security guards had not been armed, or Grey might be sitting in a jail cell instead of a coffee shop. Or a morgue. The guards had seen the look in his eyes and backed away, asking if he needed help as Grey screamed at them to leave.

By the time the cops arrived, Grey had calmed down enough to give them Lieutenant Palmer's card and mumble an apology. After agreeing to pay for the damages to the room, they let him go with a warning, and an order to find a new hotel.

A useless admonition, Grey thought grimly. He would be in New York before nightfall.

Taking Charlie was a warning, of course. For Grey to back off.

Which meant whoever took her had something to hide. An endgame. It pained him to think about it, but he knew if they were going to kill her, they would have already.

Right now, she was leverage. More valuable alive than dead.

But he also knew that in the vast majority of these situations, once the bad guys got what they wanted, the victim was expendable. Especially a victim like Charlie, who didn't have a parent or a guardian to look after her, not to mention a hostage-trained FBI unit ready to come swooping in like a Hollywood cast.

No, there was no knight in shining armor looking out for Charleene Desiree Watkins. No relatives, no friends, no teachers.

No one except Grey.

So yeah, he knew what they wanted him to do. Back off and pray they let her live. Leave her precious young life at the mercy of those bastards.

He knew what they wanted, he knew the odds of her going free, and he knew what he had to do.

Ten a.m.

As he drove down Peachtree Street, Grey called and booked a flight to New York for later that afternoon. He had already sent Viktor a curt email explaining the situation. Grey didn't want to talk. He had nothing to say.

A shiver coursed through him. It had happened again. They had taken someone he loved.

He turned east onto Ponce de Leon, relentlessly watching the road, his eyes a blazing signpost at the entrance to the gates of hell. He no longer cared about the tide of dirty dishwater flooding the earth, wondering whether his own violent nature was part of the problem. Agonizing over it, as he used to do. Reading philosophy about it late at night. Should we all lay down arms like Gandhi, he used to wonder? Protest with love and empathy? In his heart, he wanted that so much. Knew it was the better path.

What, then, he would ponder, do we do about Nazis and ISIS and the slave ships? What do you do when the Devil himself comes to your door?

He knew that if humanity gave in to the monsters, the world would live under a reign of terror. He also believed that turning the other cheek was the only path to salvation for the human race.

How those two coexisted was the question. Maybe they couldn't, not in the world as it was.

None of it mattered anymore. The moment Charlie was taken, Grey had known he was done with moral dilemmas. He had a new credo, one flapping like a panicked bird in Grey's head as he lay immobile on the floor of his hotel room with fists clenched and a lump the size of Texas in his throat.

To the person who took Charlie, he vowed, to anyone harming innocents for his own gain, lining his greedy pockets with a few extra dollars, ruining a child's life to satisfy his perversions, thinking of you you you you you you you you

To you, I have only this to say.

I no longer care whether it's right.

I no longer care about the state of my soul. I will drown in violence if I must.

The one thing I know for sure?

I am coming for you.

Grey parked his Jeep and noted with satisfaction the handful of pickup trucks already in the parking lot. One of the trucks had a bumper sticker depicting a confederate flag and a gun, along with a slogan that said COME AND TAKE IT.

Employees, Grey was guessing. Just the people he wanted to talk to.

If talking was what one could call it.

After wrapping a length of heavy chain he had bought at a hardware store on the way over around his hand, three feet of tempered steel dangling loose to the ground, Grey left his vehicle, checked to make sure no one was watching, and rapped on the door to the Peach Shack.

18

The figure creeping behind Viktor was no ghost, but a lean, six-foot tall man dressed entirely in black. His strong-jawed face glowed pale in the moonlight, and a long scar curved across the bottom of his throat like a mock turtleneck. Similar to Kristof, his skin possessed a plastic or rubbery quality, as if not quite real.

Alarmed by the sudden appearance of the man, Viktor stumbled backwards, almost tripping over a headstone. Another glance told him the man's dark clothing was in fact black-and-green combat fatigues, and that his hand was resting on the grip of a handgun strapped to his belt.

"Professor Radek!" Sergeant Linde said, beaming a flashlight across the lawn as she stepped out of the grapevines.

At the sound of her voice, the man stopped advancing on Viktor and froze near the doorway of the crypt.

Naomi walked quickly towards them, her eyes trained on the man in camo. "You're on private property, professor."

After an economical glance at Viktor, as if assessing a threat, the man turned towards Naomi and stepped into the beam of light. The sight of him caused her to gasp.

To his right, Viktor heard a door open. A set of floodlights popped on, and Jans van Draker stepped out of the doorway to the wine cellar, dressed in the same clothes from earlier. "What an unexpected surprise," he called from across the lawn.

Naomi lowered her flashlight as she turned to face van Draker. Viktor glanced back at the man in camo, and did a double take. There was still a lean man in fatigues standing by the closed doorway to the crypt, arms folded across his chest and a stern expression on his face—but it was a different man.

Viktor was sure of it. Though similar at a glance, the newcomer was a few inches taller, his features less defined. Most of all, his face bore no trace of a scar or the eerie plasticity of the other man's skin.

"I noticed Professor Radek trespassing on your property," Naomi said to van Draker. "I decided to intervene."

"Ya? And why were you watching my property at night?"

"For this very reason," Naomi shot back. "I feared the professor wasn't satisfied by our walkthrough today."

There was a hard edge to van Draker's voice. "Why not?"

"You'll have to ask him."

Viktor turned towards the guard standing by the crypt. "What happened to the other man?"

The guard's face was as expressive as a brick wall. "Who?"

"You know who."

"I see you've found my guardhouse," van Draker said, waving a hand as he strode towards the cemetery. "A bit morbid, I'm afraid."

"Your guardhouse?" Viktor said incredulously.

Van Draker waved a hand. "Show him, Pieter. It's fine."

The man in fatigues opened the door to the crypt. Wary of a trick, Viktor cautiously peered inside, Naomi right behind him. Instead of a cobwebbed mausoleum, he saw a metal desk built into the side of the vault, a high-tech switchboard, and a small bank of monitors overseeing the grounds.

Viktor blinked. There was no sign of the other man.

"Where is he?" Viktor asked the guard again.

"Who?" Jans asked, as he approached.

"A different guard approached me first. I'm sure of it."

Van Draker's look turned quizzical. "You must be mistaken. Pieter is the only man on duty tonight. It was dark and you must be tired, after such a long day worrying about my affairs."

Viktor noticed Sergeant Linde, too, eyeing the guard in confusion. For whatever reason, she chose to remain silent. "Well, professor?" Naomi said. "Would you care to explain?"

"I stepped out for a midnight stroll, and am afraid I got a bit lost."

Van Draker smirked. "And then stumbled over an eight-foot wall?"

Naomi took Viktor by the arm. "I'll deal with Professor Radek. I apologize for the intrusion."

"Tsk tsk. The professor is only curious. Ya, I believe he thinks I am some kind of Dr. Frankenstein." He gave a light-hearted chuckle. "Isn't that true, professor?"

His comment caused Naomi to pale.

"Are you?" Viktor asked.

Van Draker's head wove slowly back and forth. "Perhaps, as a younger man, in another life. But are not all true scientists? I confess: 'it was the secrets of heaven and earth I desired to learn, the inner spirit of nature and the mysterious soul of man.' "

"Quoting the great work itself," Viktor said. "You left out the parts about combining human body parts and bringing them to life."

"Is the concept so strange? Did Jesus not commit the first necromantic act by raising Lazarus from the dead? Followed by Christ's own resurrection? God gave us the precedent Himself!"

"I believe there was a slightly different context."

"Was there? Or did He employ imagery we could envision at the time, the shroud of the grave instead of an operating table? I am not one who believes that faith is a concept distinct from reason. What is God but the ultimate expression of science? Quantum physics, black holes, the miracle of the human brain? We are searching for kernels of truth in the mill of the universe, a place of unimaginable size and complexity. Are we not entitled to answers from our creator? Are we ourselves not like the Frankenstein monster, stumbling through the village of our reality, confused and frightened?"

"So you're still searching?"

"Who isn't? I read all the new journals, I ponder my existence every night with my journal and my glass of wine, a toast to the heavens by the dying embers of the fire."

"I see."

Van Draker's face turned wistful. "To be honest, I wish I were still practicing. There is so much work to be done. Let me quote again: 'What glory would attend the discovery if I could banish disease from the human frame and render man invulnerable to any but a violent death!' "

"Were your motives so pure when you experimented on unwilling victims during Apartheid?"

Van Draker's eyes flashed. "Choices for the greater good are always made, by governments and individuals alike. It is an inevitable fact of human progress."

"Then perhaps we should not progress so rapidly," Viktor said quietly.

"I'm confused, professor. I'm familiar with your life's work. You seek the truth, the answers to life and death, as much as anyone."

"Not at the expense of others."

Van Draker gave a slow, knowing smile. "Men of greatness *always* make sacrifices along the way."

Sergeant Linde gripped Viktor's arm and shone her flashlight towards the long driveway. "I apologize again for the intrusion. I'll deal with this in an appropriate manner."

"Ya, of course," van Draker said. "Thank you for your service, officer. Shall I have Pieter take you to your car?"

"That won't be necessary," she said, with a hitch in her voice.

"What about a glass of wine to settle the nerves? We've all had an eventful evening, and you must be wondering why I emerged from the cellar. I confess I'm subject to bouts of insomnia, and had just opened a nice vintage."

Naomi and Viktor exchanged a glance.

"Come," van Draker said. "Earlier today, you sought my opinion on the matter of the boy, and I've given it some thought."

What is his game? Viktor wondered, as Sergeant Linde hesitated. Still, the professor didn't want to waste an opportunity to gain valuable information. He tipped his head. "I'd be obliged."

After another moment, Naomi gave her assent as well. With a magnanimous sweep of his palm, van Draker walked across the lawn and opened the old wooden door to the cellar, exposing the murky interior.

19

Grey had knocked instead of kicking in the door to the Peach Shack so he could catch his first opponent by surprise. As soon as the familiar, scrawny skinhead with a nose ring, spiked dog collar, and 88 tattooed across his chest opened the door, Grey snapped a front kick straight into his solar plexus, caving his torso and sending him flying backwards.

Chairs scraped across the floor as "Sweet Home Alabama" played in the background. Bodies rose. Grey scanned the room like a hawk eyeing a panicked group of squirrels.

Four men were scattered around the room, including the one he had kicked. Grey recognized them all. The same bartender from the rally, a sandy-haired man built like a former college linebacker, was closest to Grey. He was holding a mop near the front door, ten feet away. The obese man with the twin goatees who had helped abduct Dr. Varela was standing above a half-eaten plate of eggs. The fourth, the craggy-faced man who had led the assault, appeared the calmest. He broke off half of his beer bottle as he eyed the length of chain Grey had brought in.

No guns in hand, as Grey doubted there would be. No one except cops and drug dealers stayed strapped indoors, in their own place of business.

As he had also guessed would happen, no one ran or reached for their cell phones.

They came at him.

The bartender switched his grip on the mop and thrust the handle at Grey's midsection. Grey sidestepped the attack and whipped him in the face with the chain. Bone crunched and skin split and blood sprayed out of the bartender's mouth like a burst packet of ketchup. He screamed and fell away, his mouth a broken jigsaw puzzle.

The skinhead was still on the floor, gasping for breath. The other two men leapt forward, trying to get to Grey before he could use the chain again. The fat man whipped a butterfly knife out of his pocket, slicing diagonally at Grey as

Craggy Face raised the bottle. Grey let the chain dangle and stepped smoothly to the left, brush blocking the knife thrust and putting the larger man between Grey and his other attacker. The obese man turned and jabbed the knife at Grey's stomach.

Instead of dodging, Grey took half a step back and swung down on the back of the knife hand as hard as he could, tipping his fist downward and using his base set of knuckles, the ones connecting the fingers to the hand, as a hammer. It was not an easy move, but the goateed fat man was slow and Grey was lightning fast. He scored a direct hit and felt his opponent's weak metacarpal bones cave beneath the blow.

The butterfly knife fell from numb fingers. It took a moment for the pain to register, but when the fat man's neurons lit up, he stood there and screamed.

Grey stepped backwards, just in time to avoid a swing of the beer bottle. Behind the craggy-faced man, the skinhead with the nose ring lurched to his feet, struggling to breathe and looking for something to use as a weapon. "You can't do this," he gasped. "You're a cop."

"Think again," Grey said, lowering to lash Craggy Face across the knees with the chain.

Not expecting the low blow, the man staggered but kept his feet. He snarled and threw the bottle at Grey's head, then rushed him, trying to get inside the length of chain. He had fists like granite and threw tight punches. A trained boxer. Grey whirled to the side, out of his reach, and lashed him once, twice, three times with the chain. He fell and tried to cover his head as Grey lashed him again until he lay still, a bloody mess on the floor.

Grey gripped the chain and looked around the room. The bartender was leaning against a chair for support, moaning with pain. "There's a gun under the register," he croaked to the skinhead. "Third drawer."

The skinny man dove over the bar and scrambled through the drawers. Grey strode to the bartender, smacked him when he tried to get away, and grabbed him by the scruff of the neck. Pinching against the sensitive bilateral occiput insertions, where the neck muscles attach to the base of the skull, Grey walked the bartender behind the bar as the skinhead fumbled with the gun.

"Shoot him!" the bartender screamed.

The skinhead raised the gun, hands shaking as he tried to find a place to aim. "I ain't got a shot!"

Ten feet separated them. Grey kept walking, using the large bartender as a shield, knowing it was an impossible shot without going through him. Grey could tell by looking at the skinhead's panicked face that he wasn't ready to shoot his friend. Even so, the tiny handgun looked like a .22 that wouldn't make it through.

The bartender bucked and tried to get free. Grey squeezed his neck and kneed him in the base of the spine, causing him to shriek in pain.

"Do it, Dale!"

The skinhead let loose a string of curses as he waved the gun in the air and backed away, towards the closed end of the bar. Grey kept advancing. The skinhead gave up and tried to dive over the counter. Grey lashed him with the chain, causing him to drop the gun. Grey flung the bartender to the ground, picked up the gun, and hopped over the bar, pulling the skinhead the rest of the way over by his dog collar.

Grey rounded all four men up on the floor in the center of the room. Craggy Face was barely conscious, but the obese man was sitting up, holding his ruined hand and flaying Grey with his eyes. Grey checked to make sure the gun was loaded, then pointed it at the group. Someone else was bound to show up before long, so he had to hurry.

"You!" he said to Dale, the skinhead. He debated interrogating the bartender, but Dale had been standing right next to Big Red at the rally. "Get over here."

"Nah, man, hey, I—"

"Now!"

Like a kicked dog, Dale skulked over to Grey. He was wearing low-slung jeans and a ribbed white tank top with the edges of the 88 tattoo peeking out. Grey knew the number stood for the eighth letter of the alphabet, H, twice over. Short for *Heil Hitler*.

Even if Grey hadn't been teetering on the edge of madness due to Charlie's kidnapping, he would have shown little mercy.

Grey lifted the bottom of Dale's chin with the gun. The skinhead cringed.

"Who is he?" Grey asked. "The big redhead at the rally. Funny accent."

Recognition flashed in the man's eyes. "I got no idea—"

Grey elbowed him in the side of the face. The blow spun him around and caused him to whimper and start babbling for Grey to stop. The man was a straight-up coward.

Grey pointed the gun. "I won't ask again."

"Don't tell him nothing!" the bartender shouted.

Grey pressed the gun against the skinhead's eye.

"All right!" Dale screamed. "Dag. That's what we call him."

"Last name?"

"Dunno, man. I ain't his mom."

Grey let that slide. "Where's he from?"

"Somewhere in Europe. Germany, I think."

Grey knew the accent wasn't German, but Dale wouldn't know a German accent from a Chinese one, so he pushed forward. "Where is he now?"

"I got no idea."

"You don't *know*?"

"Nah man, I swear! He's been in town a few weeks, drumming up support. I only seen him that one time, at the rally. Swear to God."

"Then why were you standing right next to him?"

He looked away. Grey nudged him with the gun.

"Don't say it," the bartender man said, his voice low and threatening.

The skinhead looked ready to cry. "I can't, man."

Grey grabbed him by the back of the head and pressed the gun even tighter. "Choose."

The skinhead cursed under his breath and mumbled, "Winter, man. Winter's people paid a bunch of us to make sure nothing happened."

"Eric Winter?"

"Yeah."

"Shit, Dale," the bartender said. "You gotta shut up."

From outside, Grey heard tires crunching on gravel. The bartender rose, and Grey swung the gun around. "Sit!"

The bartender complied, but a smug expression crept onto his face. "What are you gonna do, shoot us all?"

"Maybe," Grey said, with quiet conviction.

The bartender's smirk evaporated.

Grey reached up and grabbed the skinhead by his nose ring, bending him double. "Last question. If you don't tell me the truth, fast, I'm taking this ring with me."

"Don't do that, man."

"There's a black girl named Charlie, sixteen years old. Someone took her last night in New York."

Confusion flooded the skinhead's eyes, and Grey's heart sank. *Damn.* Whatever had happened, it was above Dale's pay grade.

"I got no idea about that," Dale said. "Swear to God."

Grey looked the group over. Even the bartender looked puzzled.

A car door opened outside. The bartender opened his mouth as if to yell, and Grey pointed the gun at him. "Shut up, and you might live."

He closed his mouth.

Grey pulled harder on Dale's nose ring, until it started to tear through the skin. "You got to the count of three to tell me where she is. One, two—"

"Don't! I swear I swear I swear! I got *no idea* what you're talking about!"

"Who would know?" Grey said.

"What?"

"Who's the next man up in Atlanta? Who would know something?"

"Don't say a word!" the bartender screamed.

The skinhead looked to the side, avoiding Grey's eyes. Grey pulled on the nose ring harder, yanking it half way out, at the same time he swept the back of Dale's legs out and sent him crashing to the floor. Grey leaned on his chest with a knee and jammed the gun against his forehead. "I'll shoot you right here, right now, if you don't give me a name."

"He won't do it!" the bartender said.

The footsteps neared the door.

Grey pressed the gun harder, looked Dale in the eye, and made him a believer. "Last chance."

"Ronnie," he whispered. "Ronnie Lemieux."

"Where can I find him?"

"He owns a tire garage in East Atlanta."

Grey rose as two people burst through the door, one of them the blond woman from the Tiki bar at the rally, the other a tall man with a moustache. The man was holding a gun, but Grey was already aiming at his chest.

"Lose it," Grey said.

The man complied, and Grey picked up the second gun, a Beretta nine-millimeter, on his way out. He walked backwards to the Jeep Cherokee, eyeing the door of the Peach Shack the entire way.

After placing the Beretta in his lap and stuffing the .22 under the seat, Grey Googled *Lemieux* and *East Atlanta tires* as he drove off, knowing the men inside the Peach Shack were already on their phones.

20

Darkness.

Hunger.

Fear.

Charlie had no idea how long she had been locked in the back of the van. A day, at least. Where were they taking her? Alaska?

No, little girls didn't disappear in Alaska. They disappeared in New York City.

So why move her?

Charlie had tried hard not to cry, she really had. She was a homeless teen on the streets of New York, and life didn't get much rougher than that. She was tough. *Hard.*

But this was no good. No good at all. She knew that some people, pimps and some kinds of gangs, snatched girls off the streets and forced them to work as drug mules and sex slaves. That was how Charlie had ended up homeless. After her mother died of a drug overdose, leaving Charlie orphaned, the court had sent her to live with an aunt in the Bronx. Her aunt's new husband, a man whose grease-stained shirts and sleepy eyes Charlie hadn't trusted from the start, took her to a hotel in the South Bronx one night and said she had to start earning money for the family.

It'll be easy, he had said. *We'll have ice cream when it's done.*

At the time, Charlie was eleven years old. One of the many tragedies was that she had known exactly what he was talking about. She had cried and demanded to talk to Aunt Desiree. Her new uncle handed her the phone with a smile, and Charlie called.

Aunt Desiree told her to be a good girl and do what her uncle wanted.

When Charlie started to cry, her aunt said she did it sometimes, too.

Forcing back the horror and panic rising like bile in her throat, Charlie had given her uncle the phone back and said she needed a minute in the bathroom for girl things. He let her go. Charlie crawled out a window and hid in a dumpster until sure her uncle was gone.

And she never went back.

The memory made her hug her knees and rock in the darkness. "Stay strong, Charlie," she whispered to herself.

Unlike most of the homeless girls she knew, Charlie had never used drugs or turned to prostitution. Her mother always made her promise not to make the same mistakes she had. Said that if Charlie stayed clean and worked hard, she could do anything she wanted. Be a doctor one day. Even though Charlie knew the world didn't work like that, that homeless black teens became doctors about as often as paraplegic Vietnam vets won the New York City marathon, she clung to her mother's words like a life raft on a heaving sea. It gave her hope, those words. And on the streets, no commodity was more precious.

Every now and then, Grey would teach a class on Chee-Gung, or something like that. He said it was an internal martial art, and that it was just as important to be strong on the inside as the outside. The kids in class had laughed at the strange breathing exercises. Grey always smiled and let them poke fun, then made them lay still and quiet for the last ten minutes of class, asking them to pretend their minds were hourglasses that would slowly empty.

The first time was a surreal experience for Charlie. New York was not a quiet place. Hers was not a quiet mind. But eventually, after the giggling stopped and she tried to follow Grey's soft commands, her mind drifted to unexpected places. Out of her body, out of the streets of Washington Heights that comprised her world, out of New York, out of everywhere. She went to someplace dreamy and vast, where race and money didn't matter and the world did not revolve around where to get her next meal.

In the black van, after she tried without success to force the door open, she had regulated her breathing and gone to that place again. It had worked for a while. But the clock kept ticking and her hunger pangs grew worse, and she couldn't stop thinking about where they were taking her. Shit, it would take some kind of Buddhist monk sitting in the snow with no clothes on to have the kind of discipline to get through this. Not thirty minutes of slow breathing on a dirty mat in a homeless shelter.

That's fine, she muttered to herself. Grey had taught them lots of stuff. Not just fighting, but what to do in bad situations. How to keep their wits and not panic.

Charlie was a survivor. She was alone now, but she had been alone for years.

But you're not enough, that persistent voice in the back of her head whispered. *You never have been. That's why you're still on the streets, dummy.*

The van rolled to a stop. Someone on the outside fumbled with the lock, and Charlie sat up straight. Instead of scrambling to the back of the van, she positioned herself by the door and balled her fists. Her handcuffs, secured in front of her body, were not that tight. She would have one shot at this. If she was lucky and they had taken her to another city, she might be able to stun her kidnapper and disappear into the streets.

The back of the van opened. Someone untied her hood and yanked it off.

Sunlight flared.

Charlie had not counted on the effect of prolonged darkness. She was blinded by the light.

Didn't matter. She had to take a chance.

After leaping out of the van, she swung upward with her bound fists, striking at empty air. Her pupils adjusted in time to see a red-bearded man, as cartoonishly big as a professional wrestler, take her by the arm with a grin. Charlie tried to shake free, but it was like trying to pry her arm out of a cement block.

The man was not alone. A group of scary-looking whiteys were smoking cigarettes and taking crates out of a huge barn and loading them into a pair of semis. Behind them was a scraggly field peppered with mobile homes and Harleys. Behind that, the skyline of a city she had never seen before.

The big man's eyes roved over her as if inspecting chattel. His gaze made her feel smaller and more helpless than she had ever felt in her life. Like a slave who had just stepped onto the shores of America and met her new owner.

They didn't bother to hood her again. The redheaded man gave a curt nod, then shoved her into the arms of another man. "She'll be flying out with me."

21

Van Draker disappeared into the wine cellar. As the guard, Pieter, slipped back inside the crypt and closed the door, it unsettled Viktor further, as if he and Naomi had been left alone on purpose in the cemetery, helpless prey for some foul thing lurking inside one of the tombs.

Naomi's face looked drawn. "The first guard that disappeared? I recognized him. His name was Robey Joubert."

"Was?"

"Robey was three years ahead of me in school. During the end of Apartheid, he was a commando for the South African military. He hunted down militant members of the ANC and PAC. After that, he joined the Cape Town police force."

"And?" Viktor said, when she didn't continue.

Naomi finally tore her eyes away from the tomb. "Three years ago, he was killed in action. I have friends who attended the funeral."

At first Viktor was stunned, and then he scoffed. "It's dark. You were far away."

"I'll show you a picture. You can judge for yourself."

"I'll do that."

Viktor started walking towards the wine cellar, shoulders hunched in determination.

"You're sure about this?" she asked.

"I thought you wanted to find out more about him."

"I do," she said, hurrying to keep up with his long stride. "I just . . ." She glanced back at the crypt one more time, but before she could speak, van Draker stepped into the doorway, wine glass in hand.

Jans gave a lopsided smile. "Coming?"

Naomi slowed as she fumbled with her phone. "Just texting the station." She forced confidence into her voice. "Reporting the break-in."

"Ah," van Draker said faintly. "Of course."

Smart woman, Viktor thought.

Unless van Draker controlled the entire police station except for Sergeant Linde, and they were walking right into a trap.

As Viktor ducked the thick wooden beam topping the door frame, his eyes were everywhere, taking in the brick-walled tasting room and the two passages of rough-hewn stone that curved deeper into the earth.

The furnishings in the old tasting room consisted of an oblong wooden table surrounded by chairs, a pair of ledgers hanging from pegs on the wall, dusty oak barrels with the vintage written in pink chalk, an old map of the Cape Province, and a fading black and white photo of the ancestral van Drakers. The air was a touch cooler than outside and smelled of musty stone.

As far as Viktor could tell, the wine cellar was typical for an old estate. No sign of medical equipment or the two people in scrubs they had seen. Then again, from having visited similar cellars, he knew those stone corridors could lead to a maze of tunnels and storage rooms.

Naomi declined the offer of a drink, but Viktor accepted a pour from a bottle bearing the van Draker name. The professor sniffed. Still a little rough. Under their host's watchful eye, Viktor swirled for longer than usual, examining the color by lifting the glass towards the light bulb hanging above their heads.

"Very nice," Viktor murmured, after taking a sip. "Quite smoky, tannins not too strong, just the right touch of acidity. A Pinotage-Syrah blend?"

Van Draker tipped his head in approval. "You know your wine. Shall we sit?"

"I've an affinity for old wine cellars," Viktor said. "Perhaps we could tour yours?"

The professor thought Jans would decline, but instead he beamed with pleasure, took a handheld kerosene lantern out of a cabinet, and led them down the passage to the right.

Rows and rows of wine bottles lying on their sides, tips white with dust, honeycombed the plaster-covered walls. The group's footsteps slapped on the stone floor, and the dusty barrels looked as if they hadn't been touched for a century. Viktor often had to duck beneath the cobwebs clinging to the low, rounded ceiling.

Naomi walked beside van Draker as he related the history of the wine cellar, first built in 1697 and expanded at the turn of the eighteenth century. They learned the cellar had shielded guerrilla fighters during the second Boer War, and even served as a makeshift hospital.

When he paused the narrative, she said, "You mentioned your thoughts on Akhona's disappearance."

Van Draker stroked his beard. "Ya, it's a curious one. I assume you've made a full forensic examination?"

Naomi walked a few steps before answering. "I'm afraid that will be difficult. This is not public knowledge, and please see that it stays that way, but the body has disappeared from the morgue."

"Oh my." Van Draker gave a dramatic pause. "Then I'm afraid my speculation is on the mark. The only person of whom I can conceive taking an interest in a dead body is a witch doctor." His tone soured. "I hear the market for certain body parts is quite a lucrative one, in the townships. A disgusting practice which I find hard to believe has survived into the modern age."

He's toying with us, Viktor thought. *But why bring us down here?*

"I find it hard to believe that rape, murder, and sexual abuse have survived into the modern age," Naomi said. "Crimes that occur infinitely more often than stolen body parts. In fact, I've never worked such a crime."

"I have," Viktor said. "Many times. Though I must disagree with our host's conclusions. I'm well aware of the . . . interest . . . certain practitioners of a few indigenous religions have in such matters, but nothing about Akhona's disappearance—or his *re*-appearance, I should say, implies such involvement. Akhona was tagged and studied. Altered. Not by a witch doctor, but by a scientist."

"You might be surprised by what the witch doctors can accomplish with their roots and potions," van Draker said. "With enough time, anyone can stumble onto science."

"Surprised?" Viktor said, amused. "I've known witch doctors who could redefine your concept of reality, not to mention pharmacology. Thousands of years of practice and refinement are hardly *stumbling onto*."

Van Draker spread his hands in surrender. "I'm afraid I can't be of more help."

As they spoke, he led them deeper and deeper into the structure, past a dozen storage rooms and a host of dank, unlit passages with cobwebs stained black from decades of grime and debris. There was no sign of medical equipment, or anything other than a semi-abandoned wine cellar. Viktor managed to keep the route in his head, wondering if van Draker was leading them into a trap somewhere deep beneath the earth.

"How would *you* accomplish the task?" Viktor said suddenly, deciding to appeal to their host's vanity. "The thickening of muscle, the growths on the fingers, the imperviousness to electricity?"

"Oh," van Draker said, with a careless wave of the hand, "I wouldn't know where to begin."

"You're a brilliant doctor," Viktor said. "Why don't you speculate? Are we dealing with a virus, an anomaly of nature?"

"Bah," Jans said, though a sudden shrewd look brightened his eyes. "Was the boy not absent for weeks? Steroids and growth hormones could easily account for the increased muscle mass. VO2 and adrenaline can be manipulated, taken to extremes. Keratin can be grown in culture. As for the superhuman response to electricity, the makeshift wires in the townships are far from full strength, and there are pharmaceuticals and nerve agents, even medical conditions, that can dull or suspend the body's response to pain. This is without account for the advances in molecular biophysics, gene editing, modulation of ion channels, and recombinant DNA. Today's scientists can hack genetic codes like a computer program."

Viktor lifted a palm. "It sounds simple. A project for a homemade lab."

Jans stopped walking and turned to Viktor. "It is in fact easy, compared to the portion of the boy's story which, if true, stands out as a medical impossibility. I'm a brain surgeon, professor. Manipulation of human physiology pales in comparison to the sort of scientific advance it would take to create a true Frankenstein monster, to breach the boundary between life and death, to dig Akhona out of his grave and breathe life into him once again. Restore a *consciousness*. Ya, it would take a true genius to accomplish such a feat, and mark a transition in our understanding of what it means to be human." His eyes gleamed. "Let me know."

Sergeant Linde started. "I'm sorry?"

"If Akhona did in fact return from the dead, please do let me know. I'd be highly intrigued to know how the feat was accomplished."

They resumed walking. Just as Viktor began to suspect Jans was ready to spring a trap, they emerged into the tasting room from a different passage by which they had arrived.

Van Draker spread his hands. "You've seen it all, I'm afraid, except for a few storage halls which haven't been used in fifty years. I warned you it was modest."

With a sinking heart, Viktor realized why van Draker had brought them inside and agreed to the tour. Whatever he had wanted to conceal from them was still hidden. If Viktor and Naomi tried to obtain a warrant, they would now have a hard time overcoming the fact that they had seen inside the wine cellar and found nothing of interest.

On the walk back to Sergeant Linde's Land Cruiser, cutting across the hill by the light of the crescent moon, Viktor couldn't stop thinking about the conversation with van Draker and the appearance of Robey Joubert, the man Naomi claimed was a deceased classmate. Viktor felt exposed on the hill, subject to the watchful eye of the manor, and he dispelled his tension with a long breath.

"Thank you for stepping out in the cemetery," he said. "You didn't have to do that."

"He had his hand on a weapon. I would hardly be doing my duty if I didn't intervene."

"Will there be repercussions?"

"I don't know. I don't know what to make of any of this, professor." She folded her arms across her chest and shuddered.

"Call me Viktor," he said absently, glancing back at the manor. What manner of thing, what dark creation of van Draker's, was incubating inside? When the Land Rover finally appeared, he wiped his brow with relief. "I believe the time has come for a full exchange of information."

Naomi bit her lip and surprised him by saying, "Well, I can hardly sleep after *that*. I know it's late, but would you care for a nightcap?"

"You're willing to discuss what you know about van Draker?"

Her eyes grew distant as she nodded.

22

On the way to Ronnie Lemieux's tire shop, guided by GPS, eyes skittering back and forth between the rearview and the road, Grey thought about canceling his plane ticket to New York. He decided to call Sergeant Palmer instead, then changed his mind and dialed 411 to get the number for the NYPD.

Unable to make a decision, he set the phone down and gripped the wheel. He couldn't think straight. He didn't know what to do.

Deep breaths, Grey. You have to hold it together.

With a shudder so deep it scooped him out and left him hollow, Grey forced his rage and grief to the background and tried to think it all through. The first forty-eight hours were critical to a missing persons investigation. Scratch that. A *kidnapping*.

Revered Dale had notified the police, but an investigation would take too long. Even if Grey went solo, he would have to scour the streets and work backwards, or start wading into the white supremacist community. He would go that route if he must, but he had the gut feeling the order to kidnap Charlie had come from Dag—who was right here in Atlanta.

Grey had to find him. Now. Before they took her too far away.

And the alternative, a little devil in the back of his mind whispered? *The one where she hasn't gone anywhere at all, and never will again?*

No, whispered back. *They need her alive. They do. They do.*

Grey called Lieutenant Palmer and got his voicemail. He left the address of the tire shop and said a man named Ronnie Lemieux had evidence crucial to the investigation.

Oh, and that he was on his way there himself. That should get the lieutenant moving.

In the blink of an eye, Moreland Avenue transitioned from a bourgeois neighborhood to the narrow streets and grungy strip malls of East Atlanta. Grey noticed he had messages from Viktor and Dr. Varela. He didn't bother to listen. No distractions. As the tire shop drew closer on the GPS, Grey's left hand slipped to the grip of the Beretta, and he pressed the accelerator.

Soon after he passed an old drive-in movie theater, he whipped into a lot full of rusted cars and lurched the transmission into park. His eyes flew across the parking lot of the garage. It looked deserted.

Was everyone at lunch? Or had they heard about the Peach Shack and decided to take a day off?

As he stepped out of the car, a side door to the garage burst open and the snout of a hunting rifle poked out, gripped with two hands by another member of the group who had attacked Dr. Varela, the thick-necked man in overalls and black combat boots. The only addition to his wardrobe was a nametag and a worn baseball cap bearing the name of his shop. *Ronnie's Tire and Auto.*

"Like I said before," Ronnie growled. "Get your ass outta here, boy."

Grey pulled the Berretta up to nose height, both hands on the grip, and aimed at center mass. He estimated they were fifty feet apart. "How's your aim?"

Ronnie chuckled and held the gun steady. "I been hunting the Georgia woods since the day I could walk. My daddy and uncles taught me."

"I hunt men. A Force Recon sniper with an Olympic medal taught me."

The tip of Ronnie's gun wavered. "What do you want?"

"I want to know where she is. The girl Dag took."

"The little negress you asked about earlier?"

Grey fired into the garage wall, a few inches above Ronnie's head. The bullet ricocheted off the concrete and shattered the window of a parked Ford F-150.

Ronnie stumbled backwards, away from the door. "Goddamn, boy!" He realized he had exposed his position and tried to duck into the garage. Grey cut him off with another shot. Ronnie stilled like a deer in the forest.

"Hands high!" Grey ordered.

Ronnie set down the rifle with a string of curses. "You're making a big mistake." He turned out his forearm to expose a large tattoo, a red stylized A surrounded by a circle. "You know who I'm with?"

Grey recognized the symbol of the Aryan Brotherhood. He stalked forward, keeping the gun trained. "Where is she?"

"I wouldn't tell you if I knew."

"Where's Dag?"

He grinned through tobacco-stained teeth. "Who?"

Grey waved the gun at the garage door. "Inside."

The conviction in Ronnie's voice faltered. "Why's that, now?"

"Go!"

As Ronnie took a reluctant step towards the door, knowing what was in store, Grey heard brakes screeching to a stop behind him. He whirled in time to see the doors opening on three pickup trucks and a van. A dozen armed men, ex-con types, spilled out of the vehicles and fanned out around Grey.

"I told ya," Ronnie crowed from behind, "you done stepped into the wrong pile."

Grey scanned the crowd of newcomers, assessing the situation. A public road with traffic was steps away, and he was going to call their bluff. He had no choice. If he was taken, Charlie's hopes disappeared.

Instead of dropping the gun, Grey lowered it and started walking back to his car.

"I said *drop it!*" Ronnie screamed.

"You going to shoot me in full view of the street?" Grey asked, without bothering to turn.

"He's right about that, boys," Ronnie said. "Take him inside."

A barrel-chested man in a flannel cap took the first step, and Grey leveled the gun at him. "So you're first?"

The man stopped moving. The others seemed confused. Grey reached the Cherokee as someone shot out his tires. Grey got in the car anyway, holding the men at bay with the gun pointed out the window. He started the car, prepared to drive back into town on ruined wheels.

They were all pointing guns at him and screaming, and Grey wondered if anyone had the guts to shoot. Just as he started to pull away and find out, a pair of cop cars whipped into the lot, sirens whirring.

At first it looked like there might be a gun battle, but one of the policemen ordered the men to stand down with a megaphone, and said that more police were on the way.

After a muttered exchange, Ronnie and his men laid down their weapons and put their hands behind their heads. Car doors flew open, and a quartet of policemen jumped out, led by Sergeant Palmer.

"You're all coming with me," he said, and then pointed at Grey. "Including you."

"What were you thinking?" Lieutenant Palmer said to Grey, as soon as they were alone in a conference room.

Grey told him about Charlie.

The lieutenant sank into a chair. "Jesus."

"You know how it is with kidnappings. The trail goes cold," Grey snapped his fingers, "like that."

The lieutenant shook his head and drummed his fingers on the table. "I'm sorry about the girl, real sorry, but that doesn't mean you can run around the city like Charles Bronson." The lieutenant sighed and rose to pour a cup of coffee from a thermos. "Who's Ronnie Lemieux?"

"Aryan Brotherhood."

"Yeah. I know. How'd you find him?"

Grey told him about the conversation at the Peach Shack.

"And they told you about him because you asked them to?"

"I might have asked firmly."

"Yeah, I bet," the lieutenant said. "You know I can't use any of that as evidence."

"You can use it to help me find Charlie."

The lieutenant threw his hands up. "What, you gonna take on the whole white supremacist movement in Atlanta in one night?"

"If I have to."

"Do you know how big it is here?"

"I know I just have to find one girl." Grey leaned forward. "Will you help me? We both know it involves whatever's going on with the mutilated bodies and the CDC."

"No, you *think* that. And you're lucky I'm not locking you up for possession of two hot pieces and whatever it is you did at the Peach Shack."

Grey's face tightened. He stood to leave.

The lieutenant pointed. "Sit."

Every muscle in Grey's body twitched, and he could feel the blood rushing to his face. Still, he knew it would only hurt Charlie if he got arrested. Even if Jacques bailed him out, Interpol couldn't order the APD to let Grey run around Atlanta. With an effort of will that felt like wading through wet cement, he returned to his seat.

"Now wait," the lieutenant said.

He disappeared, leaving Grey seething at the delay, pacing the room and running through scenarios in his mind. Twice he started for the door, then told himself he had to hear the lieutenant out.

Nearly an hour later, the lieutenant returned with Captain Gregory. The captain had donned a pair of reading glasses, and he folded his massive arms and looked down his nose at Grey. "You have friends in high places. You can stay in the city, but I'm putting you on a short leash. No investigating without the lieutenant. You get him for two days."

Grey swallowed his disappointment. Two days. "Thanks," he muttered.

The muscles in the captain's arms tightened as he pointed at Grey. "I won't tolerate the vigilante stuff. I mean it. One more strike and you're out."

Grey pressed his lips together, did his best to look sincere, and nodded.

For the next twenty-four hours, eating and sleeping became disposable functions. Grey sat in while Lieutenant Palmer interviewed Ronnie and the other men who had stormed the tire shop. Other than a few unregistered weapons charges, they didn't have a good reason to hold them. Since Grey had entered the property carrying a weapon, Ronnie was perfectly within his rights to brandish a rifle. The other men should have called the police instead of gang-rushing Grey, but they had backed down from the lieutenant, and Georgia had gun laws as loose as a two-legged stool.

A search into Ronnie's background revealed two stints at Jessup, a federal prison in South Georgia where he had become a full-fledged member of the Aryan Brotherhood. Meaning he had killed a black or a Latino to make his bones.

The tire shop was obviously a front, Ronnie was really bad news, and none of that helped get them closer to Charlie. No one would breathe a word about Dag, and while Ronnie was a player on the local scene, he was a small-time thug compared to this mysterious parent organization about which Grey was starting to get a very bad feeling. He didn't think Ronnie knew where Dag was staying, though if nothing else panned out in the next two days, Grey was going to go back and ask him again.

They tried the FBI, the DEA, and any other federal agencies that might have a bead on Dag. Still nothing. The man was a ghost.

In desperation, Grey asked the lieutenant to visit the penitentiary in Atlanta and talk to the highest-ranking white supremacists in residence, hoping for a lead from a rival gang.

Surprisingly, the lieutenant agreed.

They went.

Nothing but flat stares and silence.

Lieutenant Palmer headed home for the night. Grey shoved down some takeout Japanese and returned to his hotel. Despondent, he hunkered down in his room with coffee and his smartphone, spending the night researching hate groups and human trafficking. Maybe they were keeping Charlie in a known stash house.

Sickened by what he read, the extent of the trafficking crisis in America and the likelihood of hundreds of stash houses hidden around Atlanta alone, he knew he was grasping. Charlie was slipping away. Her life was sand pouring through an hourglass in which he was trapped, the grains spilling over his fingers, and he couldn't stop the flow.

A molten sun crept above the tree-lined horizon. Grey splashed water on his face and drove to the station. He hovered over a coffee in the conference room until Lieutenant Palmer walked in.

"Don't you sleep?" the lieutenant asked.

"How did he get in the country?"

"Huh? You mean Big Red?"

"He's got a very distinct look. Thick accent."

"You thinking immigration records? Airport cameras?"

Grey nodded. "Maybe we could trace him backwards, find out where he's going next."

"That would take forever, even if we got permission."

Grey scratched at his beard. He should have taken a shower; he could smell his own stink. "We could try Hartsfield, at least," he muttered.

"You know that's the busiest airport in the world, even if he did come through." The lieutenant gave Grey a pointed look. "Which we both know he didn't."

Grey slumped in the chair and put his fingertips to his forehead.

The lieutenant laid a hand on his shoulder. "I'll put in a request."

Working through Jacques again, the lieutenant got permission to scour immigration records at Hartsfield over the last several weeks. It took them the rest of the day to pore through the computer records, but none of the passport photos resembled Dag.

By late afternoon, Grey was a sleep-deprived zombie. After they had exhausted all the short-term avenues they could think of, the lieutenant pulled into The Varsity, a famous Midtown diner. "When's the last time you ate?" he asked Grey.

"Last night," Grey muttered.

"Enough is enough. We're taking a break."

As the lieutenant ordered, Grey watched a few homeless men shuffle down the street outside the window, which made him think of Charlie. The first time he had met her, she had strutted into his jujitsu class and tugged on her dreads and declared she already knew how to fight and wasn't sure what Grey could teach her. A grin escaped him at the memory.

Something else had stuck with him. He would never forget the look on her face the first time he had asked her to teach a wrist lock to the rest of the class. Not just a look of pride, but of shock. A deep and profound disbelief that anyone would find her worthy of something, even as small as a class demonstration.

Charlie, he whispered to himself, *I'm so sorry.*

As the lieutenant grabbed straws and napkins, Grey heard his cell buzz. He glanced down, annoyed at the interruption. Couldn't Viktor get the hint?

Grey berated himself. It wasn't the professor's fault. Then again, if he hadn't talked Grey into leaving New York in the first place . . . .

Disgusted, furious at himself and the world, Grey read the text, which to his surprise had come from an unlisted number.

And then he stopped breathing.

-Want to see your muffin head again? You got something we want, too. Climb to the top of Stone Mountain tonight. Alone. Zero two hundred. No cops or guns. If you don't know how to listen, she dies.-

Another text came in showing Charlie sitting on a filthy linoleum floor, holding a copy of the *New York Times*. With trembling fingers, Grey Googled the *Times* and clicked on the PDF of the front page of the day's edition. It was the same photo.

The lieutenant slid two trays laden with greasy goodness onto the table. "Chili cheese dog and rings. Best in the South. Hey, you okay?"

"Yeah," Grey said, sliding the phone into his pocket as he reached for a chilidog. He was going to need the fuel. "I'm good."

One a.m.

Grey shrugged on his motorcycle jacket and left his Jeep parked behind a church near the west entrance to Stone Mountain Park. With no hesitation, he skirted the gatehouse, jogged down Robert E. Lee Boulevard to the walking trail entrance, and started hiking up the isolated dome of granite that in daytime resembled a giant thimble rising out of the forest.

Fifteen miles from downtown, visible from the higher reaches of every east-facing building in Atlanta, Stone Mountain was a six hundred acre park that Grey's research told him served many roles: popular campground and hiking destination, theme park, cultural attraction.

Stone Mountain was also a Confederate landmark, and sometimes served as a meeting spot for pro-white rallies. An enormous carving on the north face, the largest bas-relief in the world, memorialized a trio of Confederate heroes. The second iteration of the Ku Klux Klan had been founded at Stone Mountain in 1915.

After dinner, claiming exhaustion, Grey had parted ways with the lieutenant and scouted the mountain before dark, climbing up the thousand-foot outcropping with a legion of hikers from all around the world. After that, he caught a few hours of sleep to restore his wits and reflexes, then paced his hotel room until it was time to return.

At night, the moderately steep trail was as isolated as he expected it to be. Grey followed the rules. He didn't tell the cops or even Viktor, and he didn't bring a gun. He wasn't about to play dice with Charlie's life, and he was going to have to trust his own instincts and experience. A gift had been given, he felt, a chance to trade himself for Charlie or at least find out where she was.

He kept a steady pace up the trail to loosen his muscles. The aroma of pine needles infused the air. After a time, the gravel walking path merged into the natural granite surface of the mountain, pockmarked by erosion and slippery as polished concrete.

Grey made sure he reached the edge of the gently rounded summit right at two a.m. The ridged surface reminded him of overlapping tortoise shells. His breath fogged the air as he scanned the darkness. Nothing. From his earlier visit, he knew the summit spanned a few hundred feet and included clusters of stunted pine. On the far side, a cable car provided an alternate route to the summit. He guessed Dag and his men had somehow commandeered it.

Grey walked slowly across the granite, hands above his head. A cold wind seared his face. He was sure he was being watched. After fifteen paces, the darkness in front of him materialized into a group of shadowy figures, at least a dozen strong, clutching weapons and spread out on the summit.

One of the men stepped forward. Despite the charcoal darkness blurring his features, Grey recognized the long hair and powerful bearing from the rally at the Peach Shack.

"I hear you've been looking for me," Dag said.

23

Viktor rattled in his seat as the Land Cruiser bounced over the rutted dirt road leading to Naomi's house. At times the headlights would illuminate a small creature, a Cape mouse or a rock rabbit, slinking into the bush.

Naomi glanced over and grinned, enjoying the drive. It caught Viktor by surprise. He realized, not for the first time, what a handsome woman she was.

He thought she was going to speak, but her expression faded and she returned to watching the road. It was easy, he thought, to mistake reserved behavior for arrogance or close-mindedness. Though he still wasn't sure what to make of Naomi.

Viktor did not think he was in danger, but just to be sure, he tried to text his whereabouts to Grey. No signal. Naomi must use a different carrier.

He had the feeling he was about to find out where her true interests lay.

The dirt road dead-ended at a modest, L-shaped bungalow surrounded by knee-high fynbos that in the darkness resembled a shadowy ocean bottom, full of bulbous coral beds and stalks of floating kelp.

A motion-sensor light flicked on as they pulled into the gravel drive, illuminating a giant tan dog that bounded alongside the Land Cruiser, barking furiously.

"It's just Max," Naomi said. When she parked, the dog ran over and sniffed Viktor's leg, and the professor gave him a pat on the head. He had not owned a pet since childhood.

As they walked to the front door, the raucous nighttime chorus of insects and animals on the prowl startled Viktor.

"Three percent of the world's plant species are found in the Western Cape fynbos," Naomi said. "With the added advantage that it's impossible to drive through."

"A beautiful and secure backyard."

She led him down a short hallway and into a cozy if cramped kitchen with canary yellow walls. A few stunning photos of the cosmos, streaking stars and glowing clouds of nebula riven by psychedelic swirls of color, hung in glass frames about the room.

"Wine?" she asked, reaching for a bottle of Shiraz as she undid a barrette. Her tawny hair fell past her shoulders, softening the angles of her face.

What Viktor really, desperately wanted was to sink into a glass of absinthe and ponder everything he had seen and heard that evening, the mysteries hovering around van Draker and the disappearance of Akhona's body. The professor even had an emergency flask hidden in the breast pocket of his suit. For some reason, however—Viktor told himself it was not to please Naomi—he accepted his host's offer of wine and then obliged her as she beckoned for him to follow.

The kitchen opened onto a covered outdoor terrace. When she led him up a short flight of steps to the flat-topped roof, he was surprised to find an enormous telescope enclosed in a thick waterproof tarp.

"My hobby," she said shyly. "Astrophotography."

"I admit I've never encountered an astrophotographer."

"Look up."

He did, and was so awed by the glittering awning of stars that for a moment he stood with his mouth hanging open, transfixed by the beauty. All night long he had been vaguely aware of the brilliant night sky, but with the chaos he had not taken the time to stop and absorb it. Not only that, but Naomi had switched off the lights behind them, and not a speck of artificial light disturbed the celestial expanse.

This, Viktor thought, is why we search. To wade deeper into the mystery of that miracle, cradle the starlight in our hands and never let it go.

He noticed that Naomi, too, was staring rapturously above, as if she were a child gazing at the night sky in the country for the first time.

"You took the photos in the kitchen?"

She nodded.

"Stunning."

The hint of a smile lifted her lips. Viktor had the sudden urge to walk up and take her in his arms, which he attributed to the wine and lingering adrenaline from the night's adventure. Earlier that day he was convinced that she thought him her enemy. Maybe she still did.

She broke off her gaze and took a swallow of wine. "The other mutations . . . has a connection been found? Among the victims?"

"The only thing we can determine so far," Viktor rubbed his chin and gave a helpless shrug, "is that they're all people of color."

Naomi's eyes flashed. "Van Draker's a racist. Of the very worst kind."

Viktor told her about Grey's discoveries and the suspected link between the victim in Atlanta and the white supremacist organization. She remained silent when he finished, peering into her glass with a disgusted expression.

"Come," she said finally, taking him by the arm. When they reached the kitchen, she peered up at him. "Who do you really work for?"

He sensed his answer to her question would determine what happened next. "Myself."

"As an officer of the law, I don't appreciate someone who plays outside the rules."

He didn't respond, thinking he had misjudged her intent.

"Except when it comes to Jans van Draker," she said coldly.

"Why?"

She held a finger up. "I want to show you something. It's something that, if it came to light, would reflect very poorly on my decisions as a police officer."

"Whatever it is," he said, "you want it to stay between us."

She closed her eyes, holding them shut as she took a long breath that seemed to stretch back a decade. "I don't know you very well," she said, when she opened them, "and I think you're a man, at the very least, who has complicated motives for what he does. I'm not even sure yet if you're a good man. But I do sense that you're a man who keeps his word."

Viktor held her gaze. She took his arm again and led him down another hallway, through a closed door, and into a paneled study furnished with an old wooden desk, a pair of rifles hanging on the wall, and the sort of drab cloth sofa common in the Seventies.

It was not the furnishings that commanded the professor's attention, but the contents of the photos, handwritten notes, and newspaper articles littering the walls and blanketing the desk.

The story they told about Jans van Draker.

As he walked around the room, eyeing the photos taken over the years from surreptitious angles, Naomi pulled up a photo on her smartphone. "Is this who you saw tonight?"

He stepped closer and saw a lean white man wearing a South African policeman's uniform. He had the bearing and sinewy musculature of a soldier. Viktor scrolled down to read the caption. *Local policeman killed in gang shootout.* The first few lines told him that the policeman's name was Robey Joubert, and that he had been killed in the line of duty three years ago in the Cape Flats.

Viktor felt his skin prickle as he stared at the familiar face. There was no sign of a scar or the plasticized skin, but it was the same face he had seen earlier that night. The first guard who disappeared. He was sure of it.

"That's him," Viktor said grimly. "Unless he has a twin brother."

"He doesn't."

The professor paced back and forth, disturbed. He swept a hand around the room. "Explain."

Naomi clasped her hands on the desk and spoke in a quiet, resigned voice. "Unlike most Afrikaners, especially outside the cities, my family were never farmers. They were scholars. Activists. This homestead—it was my parents'—is extremely modest by white standards. Uncleared, unworked land. My parents refused to employ domestic servants who they could not afford without exploiting them. Our political views," she said wryly, "were not very popular.

"I studied art history in college, and taught high school in the Bo-Kaap for a decade. I was sickened by the inequalities, but it felt good to help someone, kids, on a daily basis. Anyway, as you know, van Draker moved to our town after the scandal in Johannesburg. He moved here because it was his family's homestead, but also for privacy. Most people in town welcomed him. From the start, he used his family's money to give liberally to the local community—the white community—doling out loans to those in need and providing jobs for his family's businesses. They were bankers, you know. Farmers in the beginning, but Jans owns the banks and half the prime real estate in town. My point is that, because he helped them financially, no one blinked an eye when this depraved relic of Apartheid, this *torturer*, moved into town. No one except my father."

Viktor could only imagine how her family's activism must have gone over in small town South Africa.

"He demonstrated against Jans from the start. Organized protests, wrote op-eds in the local paper, hosted liberal journalists from Cape Town. He and van Draker hated each other, and they made it public. Of course, the rest of the town sided with their patron saint," she said bitterly. "I told my father it would get him killed, and one day—" her top lip pressed down hard over her bottom—"it did."

Viktor's eyebrows lifted.

"My father had gone on one of his bird watching trips to the Langebergs. He was an avid birder and knew the roads as well as the park rangers. It was a clear day, bright and sunny, and somehow he drove his car off a thousand-foot cliff."

"Dear God," Viktor said. And you think—"

"I don't think. I *know*. Except there's no proof of the accident, and I doubt there ever will be."

"That's why you became a policewoman?"

"I made my decision to move back home the day after it happened. All these years, I've been nothing but cordial to Jans. I want him off his guard. Which is not hard, since the whole town thinks he walks on water." She shrugged. "And I can see why. To those he cares about, his *people*, he's a model citizen. A benefactor."

"They often are," Viktor murmured.

"There have been plenty of suspicious deaths since his arrival. Deformed children and animals in the township, rumors of even worse. Yet he's extremely careful, and as I've said, the town is in his thrall." She swept a hand across the room. "Even with all of this, I've got nothing to show for it." Her eyes glittered with excitement and barely controlled rage as she opened a desk drawer and withdrew a small silver item that resembled a triangular dog tag. "Nothing except this."

Viktor moved to study the item. Engraved into the back of the tag was the familiar unalome and double helix piercing a circle. His eyes flew up. "Where did you get this?"

"A woman in the township found it attached to a two-headed cane rat her son found floating in the canal."

"When?"

"A year ago."

Viktor put his palms on the desk. "You should have told us. I asked you about evidence of a lab."

She glanced away. "I'm telling you now."

He set the silver tag on the desk, clasped his hands behind his back, and paced the room. "You didn't want anyone to ask uncomfortable questions. Even though it might have affected the investigation."

"It's a case to you. It's my *life*."

After a moment, Viktor said, "What's done is done. Let's move forward."

"Thank you," Naomi said quietly, her voice saturated with relief.

Viktor continued to pace, thinking through what they knew. "I'm going to consult a few people in Cape Town tomorrow, one of whom is van Draker's old colleague. A former neurosurgeon. I also want to speak to someone who knew Robey."

"Should I go with you?"

"I'd prefer if you stayed here. We know there's a lab on that property, but we have no reason to conduct another search. Find a way to get us inside."

"I noticed the monitors only displayed the grounds. Nothing inside the house or the wine cellar."

"There might be multiple entrances. People coming and going who require anonymity. He doesn't want evidence on video."

"But it gives us an advantage," she said, "if we can get inside."

He gave a slow nod of agreement, and she gave him a rundown of van Draker's suspicious activities over the years, including a list of people she had photographed visiting the manor. After brainstorming for another hour, Viktor yawned.

"Call it a night?" she asked.

"I believe so. Naomi, after what we saw, would you prefer if I . . . stayed here?" He blushed. "In the guest room, of course."

As soon as he said it, he saw the look of annoyance on her face and regretted his words. She was not annoyed, he knew, at his bumbling apology or any perceived advance, but because his offer to stay was a chauvinistic comment from another era. Naomi was a seasoned policewoman who lived by herself, owned at least two firearms, and kept an enormous dog on the property. If anyone needed protection, it was Viktor.

Or both of them.

Before he could apologize, the annoyance in her eyes softened, and she laid a hand on his arm. "I'm fine, but thank you for the offer. You're welcome to stay."

Her fingertips lingered on his arm, and Viktor felt a prickle of heat flowing from her touch. He caught a mischievous glint in the corner of her eye as she said, "In the guest room, of course."

Viktor straightened his tie; his neck had suddenly grown hot. He checked his watch. It was too late to call his driver, and it would be supremely rude to ask Naomi to take him home. Still, ever the gentlemen, he couldn't quite bring himself to accept her offer, so she took him by the arm and made the decision for him, showing him to the guest room and asking what else he might need.

"Nothing," he said. "Nothing at all."

She stood on her tiptoes and kissed him on the cheek. "Thank you," she whispered close to his ear, before backing away. It caused another hot flush to spread across his skin.

"For what?" he said, his voice huskier than he intended.

"For not being a man like Jans van Draker. For understanding why I didn't come forward with that evidence."

Viktor wasn't quite sure what to say, and his brain seemed muddled by the closeness of her scent and the warmth of her lips on his cheek. She was still standing there, and just as he began to realize that the attraction might be mutual, his cell rang in his pocket, breaking the spell.

The sudden noise startled him, and he reached for his phone. The caller was Jacques, and after Viktor listened to what he had to say, he slowly closed the phone and looked at Naomi.

"Nine more victims have been reported. All with similar mutations, in the same two communities as before. Atlanta and Paris."

She covered her mouth with her hand.

"Whatever this is," he said, "it's spreading."

24

A cold night wind whisked across the top of Stone Mountain, darkness pressing all around. Grey barely noticed the elements. He stopped advancing ten feet from Dag, far enough away to preserve his options, and focused all of his attention on the W.A.R. leader. "Where is she?"

Dag folded his massive arms and returned Grey's probing stare. "Close."

"She's alive?"

"More than most," Dag said wryly.

Another man had stepped out of the crowd of men behind the W.A.R. leader: a handsome blond man in a vintage Nazi uniform who was almost as tall as Dag, though not as thick. The blond man looked a few years younger than Grey, and his short, precise haircut, the cowlick trimmed back in a tight wave, was reminiscent of a look from the 1940s. Grey noticed a Swastika emblem pinned to the right breast.

As far as Grey could tell, neither Dag nor the blond man were armed. The rest of the crowd had black assault rifles trained on Grey. He held his palms up. "Like you said. No weapons, no cops."

Dag gave an eerily prescient smile. "I know."

"What do you want?"

Dag chuckled. "Not one for formalities?"

Grey wanted to say he reserved his formalities for people who deserved respect, not for kidnappers of children. But he had to keep his cool. "Where are you from? I don't recognize your accent."

Dag's smile widened. "I'm a citizen of the world, shall we say. The New World."

It was a fifty-fifty chance that Grey could reach Dag without getting shot, and he debated taking him hostage. Though both men looked formidable, Grey thought he could incapacitate the blond man quickly, and then subdue Dag.

The problem was, Grey didn't have anywhere to go, or a viable threat to use. He couldn't kill Dag. Not before Charlie was safe. And these men knew it.

He didn't see an option other than to play their game. He wasn't even sure what the game was, because Dag was studying him in a bizarre manner, as if evaluating him for some unknown purpose. The blond Nazi had a stare both vacant and intense, a cunning predator trained to await orders.

Dag sniffed the cold air and swiped a knuckle across his nose. "I hear you know how to handle yourself."

"I didn't come here to fight," Grey said quietly. "I came for Charlie."

"It's a commendable trait, loyalty to a cause."

"Is it?"

"Loyalty is honor. The heritage, the hallmark, of our people. *Your* people."

"Charlie is my people."

Dag lowered his head and shook it. "She's quite spirited, your young charge. Black as, how do they say here, a cast-iron skillet?"

Darkness seeped into the corners of Grey's vision.

"She speaks of you often, you know. I believe she looks up to you." Dag cracked his knuckles and started to pace. "Let me pose a question. Do you believe in family? In protecting your own?"

"Doesn't everyone?"

Dag wagged a finger. "Yes, yes. We all do. It's the highest calling. So why," he asked, with a genuinely puzzled expression, "risk your life for someone not of your own blood? Someone not even of the same species?"

The darkness, the rage, threatened to cloud not just Grey's vision but his judgment, and he bit down on his lip until he gained control.

"Leave the girl and come with us. Join the cause. A soldier like you would be invaluable. In return, I'll teach you how to restore your honor and value your heritage." Dag stopped pacing. "I'm quite serious. Past sins will be forgiven. You'll be one of us, a brother in arms, fighting the disease the modern world has become. Poverty, class inequalities, the lie of globalism, the rampant injustice inherent to the system: we want to put a stop to it all."

"For those who look like you."

"Tribal boundaries have always been formed, from the beginning of mankind. It's a necessary state of existence. Americans take great pride in their nationalism, Western Europeans in their starry-eyed humanism, Muslims in their religious identity. Who is right? Where is the line drawn? We don't hate anyone, we just believe that we must protect our own kind."

"World War II is over," Grey said. "Or didn't you hear?"

With an amused expression, Dag turned to his blond companion. "What do you think, Klaus? Is he right?"

"Quite," Klaus said, in a thick German accent.

Dag turned back to Grey. "Yes, that battle was lost. But it was one skirmish, a stone in the river of history. The greater conflict is far from over." He cocked his head in self-reflection. "And we have learned much from our mistakes."

"That wouldn't be hard."

Dag gave him a sharp look, and Grey regretted the snipe. The big man clasped his hands behind his back and continued to pace. "An example, then. Of what a focused family can accomplish, the superiority and ingenuity of the Aryan mind. I have a proposition for you. Best Klaus in single unarmed combat, force him to submit, and I will release the girl into your custody. No questions asked. You both walk away. Tonight."

Grey stared at him in disbelief.

"I give you my word, in front of all my men."

Grey looked at Dag's face and saw no sign of deceit. In fact, he saw a man who truly believed what he preached, consumed by his convictions.

Someone who would keep his word.

Grey glanced at the men in the shadows, none of whom had moved, and then to Klaus, who was watching Grey with an emotionless expression.

Who in the hell was this guy, and why was he dressed up like a Nazi from eighty years ago?

"If I don't fight?" Grey asked.

Dag cocked his head. "Then I doubt your options will be to your liking. Or to Charlie's."

"Let me see her."

Without turning, Klaus gave an imperious wave, and one of his men hustled out of the crowd holding a cell phone with a generic black casing. The man held up the phone. Grey leaned in and saw a video showing Charlie sitting on the same filthy linoleum floor as before. The date on top was the day's date, the time an hour earlier. *She's close,* Grey thought.

The man pressed play and Grey watched Charlie, who looked bedraggled but unharmed, stare at the camera in sullen silence. After she blinked a few times, the man turned off the video and returned to the crowd.

Grey's voice was thick. "I want to talk to her."

"Of course you do," Dag said. "I assure you her condition is unchanged. What happens next depends on you."

Grey gritted his teeth. While he believed Charlie was alive and nearby, he didn't trust Dag, and knew something was wrong with the scenario. He hated to walk away and lose his only link to Charlie, but he decided to hurry down the hill and sneak around to the base of the cable car, then try to follow one of the men.

"Maybe another time," Grey said, backing away slowly. "When you bring her with you."

Dag lifted a finger, and the men behind them started to fan out in a wide circle, guns trained on Grey. "I'm afraid there never was an option not to fight," Dag said, with a cold smile. "Though my offer was sincere."

Grey's adrenaline spiked as Klaus stepped in front of Dag. He expected the blond man to pick up a gun or pull a knife, but instead Klaus removed his jacket and raised his fists in a classic boxing stance, leading with his left foot. It was almost comical. He even fought like someone from the 1940s.

With no choice but to fight or let the blond man pummel him, Grey circled as Klaus led with straightforward jabs and tried to land his bigger punches. This was child's play to Grey, or any jujitsu expert. He should be able to track the punches in and get close enough to quickly end the fight. Lock in a choke or strike the throat or sweep Klaus off his feet.

The problem was, Klaus was fast. Far faster than Grey expected. Faster than anyone Grey had ever fought. As fast as Grey himself.

A right hook almost caught Grey on the chin. He ducked, sidestepped, and regained his stance. Footwork was everything in a fight. So was initiative and having a killer instinct. Grey could tell from Klaus's flat, focused eyes that timid fighting would not be an issue.

They exchanged a few more punches, absorbing minor blows. Grey knew Klaus was much stronger than he was. This did not alarm him; Grey almost never fought opponents his own size. Jujitsu thrived on exploiting weakness, utilizing leverage and skill.

But Klaus was so strong Grey's forearms and obliques ached just from blocking his blows. Klaus hit like a fighter twice his size. A four hundred pound bruiser. Good God, the man was powerful!

After another flurry of lightning-fast uppercuts by Klaus, Grey sidestepped and snapped a low roundhouse into the side of his leg. Grey's lips parted in a grim smile. A solid connection. The biggest downside to boxing versus other martial arts was the limited range of a kick versus a punch. Grey had won entire fights by throwing low kicks until his opponent's calf or thigh collapsed.

Yet when the kick connected, Klaus didn't so much as wince. He even managed to land a quick uppercut. Grey staggered back, blinking away the blow and feeling blood drip from his nose.

He couldn't believe that kick had failed to slow his opponent's counterattack. A large part of martial arts prowess, and especially jujitsu, was knowing how the human body reacts to pain. Klaus should have faltered, at the very least.

Grey had seen enough. He had wanted to quietly end the fight with a standing submission—a choke or a shoulder lock—but Klaus was proving too formidable. Nor could Grey risk a throat chop that might crush the trachea. He didn't know how Dag would react to the death of his friend.

Another problem with the skillset of a boxer was the absence of training on the ground, a place where a jujitsu expert excelled. Grey timed Klaus's rhythm and, after his next swing, dove into him, planning to wrap him around the waist and take him down.

Somehow Klaus threw his hips back in time to avoid the tackle, and landed a hard elbow on Grey's back. Aching from the crushing blow, Grey managed to snatch an ankle. He rolled to the side to avoid another blow, then put a foot on Klaus's knee and pushed it backwards at the same time he jerked on the ankle.

The crowd of men murmured as Klaus crashed to the ground beside Grey. The blond man tried to regain his feet, but Grey put a hand on his face and shoved him down while he scrambled atop him. Knees straddling Klaus's chest, Grey assumed the dominant mount position, and didn't waste time. He rocked

Klaus with a series of elbows to the head, his legs tucked under his opponent's thighs to keep him in place.

Klaus bled. He spat out a tooth.

But he didn't submit.

Grey couldn't believe his opponent was still conscious. No one could withstand the damage Grey had just dealt. He was going to have to break a bone or put him to sleep to end this fight.

Klaus struggled to get off his back, but Grey was too skilled. He countered every maneuver and set himself up for a choke, crossing his hands and grabbing Klaus by the shirt on both sides of his neck, deep into the collar. The military uniform was made of stiff material and Grey planned to use it to strangle Klaus with a blood choke.

He leaned over Klaus to increase his leverage. When the blond man tried to buck free, Grey head-butted him. The final disadvantage to a boxers' arsenal, the main one in Grey's view, was that boxing was a sport and not a street fight. Head-butts and groin shots and eye gouges did not exist in the ring, and always threw boxers off their game.

Grey locked the choke into place, turned his wrists to increase the pressure, and squeezed.

Klaus's eyes bugged. Grey had a perfect choke in place and his opponent should succumb in seconds. Because both of Grey's hands were occupied, he knew he was vulnerable to being rolled by a jujitsu opponent of equal skill, but Klaus had shown no knowledge of ground fighting.

Two seconds went by. Klaus fought like a cornered animal but couldn't get free. Somewhere in the back of his mind, Grey heard mutters from behind, but he couldn't worry about what happened next. He was fighting for his life. For Charlie's.

Klaus's face turned blue. The veins on his neck popped like steel cables. Grey knew he had won. His choke was locked in. Klaus was about to see stars.

And then he did something impossible.

The blond man wormed his palms into a position underneath Grey's chest, his elbows bent double, and pushed. From flat on his back, with Grey's entire body weight pressed down on him, Klaus shouldn't have been able to move

Grey an inch. Yet with the strength of his hands alone, he managed to push Grey a foot off him, and then two, and then roll him to the side once his elbows were extended.

Grey was stunned. No human being was that strong. It defied physics. Yet he didn't have time to marvel. He kept the chokehold and let Klaus assume the superior position. Unless the man didn't require oxygen to breathe, the choke would still work.

Klaus tried to escape by throwing punches, but Grey knew how to absorb the blows. His consciousness fading, Klaus did something else unexpected. He grabbed Grey by the forearms and tried to pry the choke loose.

Again, this was a desperate move that simply should not have worked. Grey's forearms were crossed and locked in, his entire body focused on keeping that hold. Yet somehow, with superhuman effort, Klaus relieved enough pressure to breathe, and he sucked in oxygen with huge gasps of air.

By this point, Grey was fatigued. He had lost the chokehold. Klaus picked him up by the collar and slammed him into the ground. Growing desperate, Grey pushed a thumb into Klaus's eye. It didn't faze the man. He slammed Grey again, then punched him in the face faster than Grey could react. The world started to go black. Grey tried to wedge his hips and roll Klaus off him but he didn't have the strength. Klaus hit him again and again—

"Enough!"

The blows stopped. Grey collapsed on his side and lay gasping on the ground.

Except for his labored breathing, Klaus betrayed no sign of having been in a fight. He didn't rub his battered neck or hold his injured eye. He simply retreated behind Dag and stood in place.

Dag squatted next to Grey on the balls of his feet. The big man's expensive cologne, combined with the head blows, induced a bout of nausea in Grey.

"I'm impressed," Dag said. "No one has lasted half this long against Klaus, nor injured him. You are truly a remarkable man."

"What is he?" Grey managed to gasp. "He's not normal."

Dag's soft, mysterious smile chilled Grey. "Charlie and I are going on a trip tonight. Somewhere far, far away."

Grey struggled to a knee, his head spinning so badly he had to stop moving.

Dag offered him a bottle of water. Grey refused, though he needed it desperately.

"I understand," Dag said. "You're a proud warrior. This was not an attempt to embarrass or dishonor you, just a demonstration of who we are. Of what we will accomplish. Of what you could be. I said that I wanted something from you. You and your associate, Professor Radek, are at the forefront of an investigation that is contrary to our interests. I understand that Interpol and other police agencies are involved, that matters have progressed, and I also understand that you cannot simply call it off. But," he wagged a finger, "you can derail it from the inside."

Grey's vision wouldn't clear, and he knew he had a concussion. He wiped sweat and blood from his eyes and tried to concentrate.

"I took Charlie knowing you and I would have this very conversation. I waited long enough to impart the futility of trying to locate me. I am leaving you both alive to ensure you take steps to impact the investigation." Dag pushed to his feet. "So. You will do whatever it takes. If you fail, I'm afraid you know what will happen."

"If I agree to this," Grey said, fighting back nausea as the night sky continued to revolve, "when do I get her back? How?"

"You'll know," Dag said, his voice low and chilling, "when we have won. And you have my word she'll be returned."

"They won't listen to me," Grey said. "I need more time."

Dag waved a hand. One of the soldiers ran over, brandishing a syringe bearing a long needle. He jabbed before Grey could react. The pain of the injection felt distant, muted.

The big leader leaned down and gave Grey an affectionate squeeze on his shoulder. "Think about my other offer. It will stand. Imagine Klaus with the benefit of your training, and you with Klaus's . . . enhancements." He straightened. "I know how your mind will work. What you will want to do. Trust me when I say that you will *never* find her on your own."

As Dag and his men retreated, fading into the darkness of the mountain, a feeling of gooey warmth poured through Grey's veins and into his limbs. The sky seemed to lighten for an instant, as if the night had caught fire, and then despite his best efforts, Grey's eyes fluttered shut.

Voices murmuring nearby. Light searing Grey's eyes as they opened. A chill had seeped into his bones and left him shaking on the cold ground.

When he blinked and sat up, groaning at the pounding in his head, he noticed a small crowd of hikers gathered around him. A family of five with a dog. The dog was calm, but the father had his arms out, backing his children away from Grey.

It took Grey a moment to remember, and then it all came crashing back. "I'm okay," he said, pushing to his feet and feeling for his phone. They had taken it but left his wallet. "I'm fine."

"Do you need help?" the father asked, clearly thinking Grey was a homeless person who had, for some unknown reason, collapsed atop Stone Mountain. "Should I call an ambulance?"

"Your phone," Grey muttered, stumbling towards the father as the dog bared its teeth. "I need your phone."

Later that morning, Grey hovered over a coffee at a diner on the way back to Atlanta. Little by little, aided by large doses of caffeine and Ibuprofen, his strength had returned. He guessed Dag's men had given him a strong sedative, enough to knock him out for a few hours.

Which meant they were confident in their escape.

The first thing Grey did was call Lieutenant Palmer to tell him exactly what had happened. "Keep it quiet," Grey said, "but send men to every airport in the area. I think they're leaving the country."

The lieutenant had agreed, but he had informed Grey that Atlanta was surrounded by millions of acres of forest that concealed dozens of illegal airstrips for human traffickers and drug dealers.

In his heart, Grey knew the lieutenant was right, and that they had almost no chance of thwarting Dag's escape. In fact, Grey was so convinced of the futility of this effort that he didn't bother following up himself.

Instead he ordered his fourth cup of coffee and finished his eggs, bacon, and hash browns, all while he thought about Charlie.

Grey, too, had been homeless at sixteen. He had never inquired about Charlie's particular circumstances, because it didn't matter. A homeless child was a failure of family and community, of humanity itself. Grey knew all too well what a despondent existence it was, and how afraid she must be. How alone.

There was no one coming for her, and she knew that.

No one but him.

Grey wasn't going to sabotage the Interpol investigation. He didn't trust Dag, and as much as he loved Charlie, he would never imperil one innocent life to save another. He wasn't an ends justify the means kind of guy.

But what he *was* going to do was go after her.

He knew Dag was right. Grey would never find Charlie on his own. He needed help, but not the kind of assistance the law could provide. Not phone calls from Interpol or visits from FBI agents with playbooks of rules to follow.

No, Grey didn't want the police. Dag was going dark, Grey could feel it. On to his next recruitment or back to wherever he had come from. Disappearing into a netherworld of international crime and forged documents and twisted ideologies. Maybe Grey could find him with enough time and investigative prowess—but not in time to help Charlie.

No, what Grey needed was a particular kind of help. Someone who lived and worked off the grid. Someone with his hands in the dirt and contacts in all the wrong places.

What Grey needed was help without a conscience.

And he knew just the man.

25

Viktor woke to a spray of sunbeams muscling through the blinds. It took him a moment to realize where he was, and then the chaos of the night before came crashing home. The bed sagged under his weight as he sat, causing him to remember his very unusual decision not to stay at his bed and breakfast.

For some reason, the lumpy pillow and short bed and lack of five-star amenities hadn't bothered him at all.

As if on cue, there was a knock at the door, and Naomi called out, "Coffee and toast."

He dressed and found Naomi studying a calendar of the Greek Islands in the kitchen, wearing a high-waisted pantsuit that accentuated the long lines of her body. She indicated two mugs near the coffeepot. "Sugar and cream?"

"If you have them, yes."

Her sleep-filled eyes, the color of a stormy sea, took in his appearance. "Do you always wear your tie and cufflinks to breakfast?"

Viktor glanced down. "Ah, yes. I suppose I do."

"I appreciate a man of habit."

"You do?"

She smiled and prepared his coffee.

They dined on the rooftop patio as birdsong filled the morning air and the vast fields of crinkly fynbos, pink and green and yellow, glowed neon in the sun. Despite the grim mood, they kept the conversation light, and Naomi squeezed Viktor's hand just before he left. A wordless admonition to watch his back.

Viktor's head swam with questions on the drive to the Cape Peninsula, the claw-shaped spit of land stretching from Table Mountain to the Cape of Good Hope. Near Stellenbosch, instead of veering towards Cape Town, his driver took the coast road towards the home of Dr. Ehlers, the retired neurosurgeon Viktor had contacted.

Along False Bay, beneath a range of granite peaks sloping to the sea, a succession of seaside towns dotted the shoreline like a string of pastel pearls. Outside

Viktor's window, the shimmery blue sky and high dunes trapped in mist felt dreamlike, ephemeral. Though the beauty of the drive stunned him, Viktor's mind was elsewhere. That morning, four new cities had reported cases of the virus: London, Johannesburg, Berlin, Detroit. No one knew how it was spreading. The symptoms progressed incredibly fast and resulted in death in a matter of days. The concurrent onset of mental confusion made it impossible to question the infected.

So far, none of the victims was white. A pharmacist from Mumbai died from the disease on a London subway, injuring four people before hemorrhaging to death on the floor. A Detroit bus driver attacked a group of children at an inner city playground, before an onlooker gunned him down.

The CDC held a news conference and confirmed a virus was to blame. While they had not discussed the possibility of a manufactured agent in public, the symptoms were so unusual it seemed to Viktor the only plausible explanation.

If it is manmade, Jacques had said, *then the fastest way to a vaccine is to find the prototype.*

Get inside the manor, Viktor.

Find the lab we know is there.

Easier said than done. There was still no evidence tying Jans van Draker to a crime, and Interpol could not strong-arm the South African police, especially with van Draker's political connections. Apartheid might be over, but the country's wealth remained in the hands of the old regime. Jans possessed powerful friends.

Instead of marching into the van Draker manor, Viktor found himself watching the road behind his private car for signs of suspicious vehicles.

A glimpse at the world news on his smartphone revealed the beginnings of panic. What if thousands were already infected? Why did the mysterious disease, which the press had dubbed the gargoyle virus, only target people of certain phenotypes? Could it spread to other groups? Even if not, could it mutate? Should certain communities be segregated?

The questions—the fears—had polarized the public. White supremacists referred to the virus as the new Black Plague, calling it the work of God. The

NAACP wondered why the government had waited so long to go public. More than one municipality was considering segregated restrooms and drinking fountains until more was known.

Viktor could only imagine what would happen if someone proved the virus *was* manufactured. It could spark a race war. Internment camps. Vigilante action on both sides.

He shuddered and wished the drive were shorter. He could have made phone calls but he wanted to conduct the interview in person. Witnesses, he knew, might be leery of discussing a man such as van Draker over the phone.

Doctor Ehlers lived in a sleepy seaside village marked by steep cobblestone roads and a line of cottages fronting a tidal pool. As the Mercedes pulled alongside a lemon-yellow bungalow just steps from the sea, Viktor got a text from Grey that caused a cold lump of unease to settle in his gut. The text was a seemingly innocuous message about a client invoice, but imbedded within the words was a code they had developed in times of distress. They had a number of codes, but this particular one had never been used before.

Grey's message meant he was compromised but unable to discuss why, and that Viktor could not let on that he knew. Under any circumstance.

Viktor stared at the phone. Coming on the back of Nya's death, he knew the news about Charlie must have sent Grey into a tailspin.

It also meant Charlie's captors had something to fear from their investigation.

The professor didn't know for sure what Grey's message meant, but knowing his friend, he would not take the kidnapping lying down. After blowing out a long breath, Viktor straightened his tie and stepped onto the pebbled path. There was nothing to do but move forward.

The cries of seagulls filled the sky and the chimerical mist had lifted, the sky as sharp as cut glass. Viktor had told Dr. Ehlers only that he wanted to consult with her on a current case. He had chosen her because of her ties to van Draker, as well as her documented work with victims of "medical kidnapping," the controversial practice of remanding children into government care for various reasons, usually involving child abuse or the parents' failure to follow a doctor's order.

According to Ehlers, the government and pharmaceutical companies used these children as subjects for medical trials for which they would not otherwise get approval. Even more sinister were the reports of homeless or severely disadvantaged children who disappeared while in state care.

Someone who cared about such causes, Viktor was hoping, would talk more freely.

Dr. Ehlers opened the front door with a pleasant but reserved greeting. She had short, coiffed auburn hair and age lines framing her mouth, which added to her stern demeanor. Viktor declined her offer of refreshments, and she led him into a sitting room with a grand piano and a view of the rocky shoreline.

"I assume the investigative matter on which you're seeking my opinion," she began, with a formal accent full of strong *r*'s and *t*'s, "involves medical kidnapping?"

"Actually, no," Viktor said, causing her eyebrows to arch. "It involves your employment with the South African Medical Commission alongside Jans van Draker."

Her tea paused halfway to her mouth.

"I realize it was only a short time," Viktor said. "A year, if my research serves, before you were transferred to Cape Town."

"I wasn't transferred."

"No?"

"I demanded that I be moved. And that an investigation be opened."

"An investigation into what?"

Dr. Ehlers blinked twice. "My dear professor, you just said this matter does not involve medical kidnapping. Yet you wish to probe my time with Dr. van Draker?"

"And?"

"Why do you think I began my crusade?"

Viktor leaned back in his chair.

"Jans van Draker," she continued methodically, as if discussing the chance of rain in the afternoon, "under the auspice of the medical commission, regularly took children out of their homes and performed tests on them while in government care. Tests for experimental drug trials and vaccine controls and a host of other unconscionable practices."

"Why wasn't he arrested?"

"Because it was legal. It still is, in many cases. It's not just South Africa, either. The problem exists from America to Andorra to Australia. It's often worse in developing countries, but not always."

"Did children . . . disappear . . . under his care?"

"I suspect that they did. Of that I have no proof. Who did you say you were with?"

Viktor let out a deep breath and displayed his Interpol badge. "I assume you've heard the recent news? About the virus?"

"How could I not?" She set her tea down, her face draining of color. "You suspect he's involved. That's it's manufactured."

Viktor let a prolonged silence speak for itself. "I'm not in a position to divulge details."

She looked dazed. "I'll provide what I can, though we weren't exactly social. What I can tell you is that he's brilliant. Possibly the most brilliant medical mind I have ever encountered."

"That's high praise, coming from a neurosurgeon."

"Unfortunately, his empathy was not so advanced. His pro-Apartheid stance is well-documented. And he was hardly alone," she said bitterly.

"What about your own views? The government didn't mind?"

"I was a doctor. No one ever asked me." She wagged a finger. "Far more people opposed Apartheid than you might think. It's easy to assume a majority view as an outsider."

"Indeed."

She looked down and smoothed the front of her blouse. "What is it you wish to know?"

Viktor thought about what he wanted to say, and what he was allowed to say, then chose his words carefully. "When you worked for the government, did you ever come across evidence of a virus or medical condition similar to what we're seeing?"

"No," she said slowly. "Though during that period, there were numerous studies that sought to . . . substantiate . . . the tenets of Apartheid."

"You mean to establish the superiority of the white race."

"Bunk science, of course. Modern genetics has taught us that nearly all living humans descended from a common group of ancestors in primitive Africa. But back then . . . many of the initiatives stemmed directly from experiments performed by the Nazis. Which, of course, were inspired by eugenics legislation passed in the United States."

Viktor tensed at the mention of the Nazis. A potential connection between van Draker and the Ahnenerbe.

"Many of the Nazi experiments were carried out by doctors with no ethical restrictions. The testing might not have led to proof of racial uniqueness, but—and I can only speculate here—they might have led to an advanced understanding of genetics and structural biology in certain phenotypes."

Viktor digested her words. "Are you implying that the Nazi experiments were studied and improved upon by Apartheid doctors?"

"I'm saying that a similar . . . medical mindset . . . was in place during Apartheid. Especially during the latter years, when the regime felt threatened. I also heard talk of a cabal of doctors working on a top secret project."

"Why keep it secret if it was government-sponsored? Because of backlash from the international community?"

"As I said, support for Apartheid was far from universal. It was known within the medical community who was supportive of such barbarisms, and the rest of us were kept in the dark. I don't know much of anything about this project, except two rumors that cropped up about it. The first was that our most brilliant physician was the mastermind."

"Van Draker."

"The second," she said, after a long sip of tea, "was that it involved biological warfare. Don't bother asking for details, because that's all I know. Whether it actually existed, how far it got or when it was discontinued, I've no idea." Her face darkened. "But I have no doubt—I *know*—that victims of medical kidnappings were used as guinea pigs during this time."

"Are there any doctors who might know more about this?" Viktor asked.

"No one who would talk to you. And it would be dangerous to ask."

"An investigative journalist?"

"There were two close to the story. Both killed in house explosions."

Viktor whistled out a long breath and thought about what he had learned. One thing he still didn't understand was the relationship between the virus and Akhona's alleged return from the grave.

"Let us speak in the abstract for a moment," he said, thinking also of the bizarre appearance of van Draker's butler, and the guard Naomi claimed had died years ago. "Let us imagine that a doctor wished to reanimate a human corpse."

Her hand twitched against the chenille sofa. "I'm sorry?"

"I understand how it sounds. A tale of Gothic horror. I can't go into specifics, but I'm sure you heard the news of the Xhosa boy's return from the dead."

She gave a curt nod.

"Is such a thing . . . possible?" he asked. "Theoretically?"

Dr. Ehlers wrinkled her face, as if physically dispelling her distaste of the topic. "Brain injury is the chief impediment to recovery after what physicians call clinical death. With modern advances in resuscitation techniques and recombinant DNA, limbs can be reattached, organs regrown. But the ischemic damage to the brain cells that results from loss of blood flow—that is irreversible. It depends, then, on what you are asking. Do you mean reanimation of a corpse shortly after death? Or recombining body parts in order to manufacture some type of life?"

"Both, I suppose."

She forced a grin that fell flat. "Are you asking, professor, if the tale of Dr. Frankenstein might be plausible with today's medical advances?"

Viktor crossed his arms. "I suppose I am."

Dr. Ehlers's gaze drifted out to the ocean. "Let me tell you a dirty little secret. Neuroscience teaches that the brain gives rise to consciousness, a computer spitting out complex bits of data. But that's guesswork. We don't really understand consciousness, the exact boundary between life and death. What if one day we could map the entire connectome of the human brain at a fixed point and regrow it in a lab? Is that consciousness? Could we do that over and over and live forever? I personally believe scientific thought has become myopic in its refusal to consider alternate theories of consciousness and self-awareness. We don't know why love and long walks in nature can heal the brain. We don't know why some NDEs—near death experiences—occur without a functioning neocortex. Quantum physics implies that reality is, at its deepest level, a vast number of impossibly small, impossibly complex, interconnected vibrations of energy. What if consciousness, rather than a byproduct of physical existence, is the *source*? Or even a medium: a way to bridge the gap between the spiritual plane and the natural world?"

"I'm beginning to think we have the same job," Viktor said.

Dr. Ehlers shook her head. "Don't mistake my intent. I've given my life to science. Yet just because questions concerning the soul and consciousness have proven elusive—perhaps impossible—to answer does not make them go away. To return to your question, our bodies are an energy field swimming in a universe of energy. While I don't see how it's possible to restore life after brain death has occurred," she shrugged, "I suppose if one could reboot the ion channels, create a spark of energy that could jolt the brain back to life without destroying it, then it might be possible to reanimate a corpse."

"I imagine ethical considerations would prohibit most studies," Viktor said drily.

"Plenty of requests for research have been filed. Have there been explorations in China and other places with less rigorous oversight? I'd say without a doubt. As for your other question—recombining body parts—a cephalosomatic linkage was achieved between two monkeys in 1970."

"Cephalosomatic?"

"Sorry—the head of a live monkey was severed and surgically attached to another."

"And the monkey lived?" Viktor said, incredulous. It seemed like science fiction. "For how long?"

"Eight days. They didn't have the ability to link the spinal cords, but, professor—1970 was almost fifty years ago. In technological terms, that's *eons* in the past."

Viktor felt a prickle on the back of his neck. He checked his watch and took a few moments to find his next words. "Assuming the science was possible, would a re-animated person be . . . normal? When they came back?"

"Ya, that is the question. How a delay in consciousness, in life as we know it, would affect the neurological structure. Or, in case of a cephalosomatic linkage, would the personality survive the transplant? Will it be the same human being, or will a completely new awareness be imparted? Another entity plucked from the well of souls?"

"And?" Viktor asked, when Dr. Ehlers seemed to lose her train of thought.

She shrugged and returned her gaze to the silver-tipped waves thumping against the rocks with a steady, languorous rhythm. "No one knows."

26

CARACAS, VENEZUELA

Fabiana screamed her orgasm as she raked her nails down Jax's chest. "*Asi, mi amor, asi!*" After she finished, the former national beauty queen collapsed beside the mercenary, her light brown hair a halo on the silk sheets.

God, Jax loved Venezuelan women. Feminine beauty was more prized than oil in the South American country, and those rare few women who actually won the competitions?

Royalty. Fawned upon by the entire country. Possessed of a finely honed spirit of entitlement that made conquest all the sweeter.

It wasn't just the women or the staggering beauty of the landscape that drew the mercenary to the South American capital. In terms of plying his trade, Venezuela might be the most lawless country in the world, outside of a war zone. Right up there with the Horn of Africa.

Who was he kidding? Venezuela *was* a war zone. It was just a different kind of war. One waged by the hordes of drug lords, urban gang leaders, illegal exporters, oil barons, and other criminal despots who ran roughshod over the country in the waning years of Chavez's regime, and who had blossomed like monstrous Chia pets under the dictator's successor, a halfwit sycophant who ruled the country with the effectiveness of a discarded banana peel.

Fabiana stroked his clean-shaven cheek. "Again?" she asked, in that lilting Spanish accent that stirred his blood.

Jax sat with his back against the headboard and lit a cigarette. "Sure, love. Just give a man a moment to indulge."

Fabiana was the mistress of one of the most powerful crime lords in Caracas, Diego Cabrera. Off to Maracaibo to oversee an oil deal, unable to trust his own people, Diego had hired Jax to protect his most precious possession. Jax had been in the country for months and developed a reputation as a rare hired gun who would keep his word and not flip sides.

Still, he thought, as his eyes roamed the horizon of Fabiana's bare legs, every man had his limits.

And what kind of moron hired someone like Jax to watch his *mistress*?

He resisted the urge to light another cigarette. He was in his mid-thirties now, and had to watch his health. Forget that live fast and die young bullshit. Jax planned to live fast and *smart*, then die at ninety-five in perfect health, surrounded by women and good Scotch and a palatial estate with a view of the Aegean.

Which meant a few sacrifices here and there. This was the twenty-first century. Sustainable mercenary living.

Fabiana traced a finger across Jax's lips and moved slowly down to his crotch. She took him in her hand as his cell buzzed. He swore and reached for his phone.

It was just a text, but the number had not been re-routed from one of his burners. It had come straight to his phone, from one of the few people in the world who knew his private number.

Dominic Grey.

The very name caused a flood of conflicting feelings. Annoyance. Respect. Fascination. Unease.

The message had said to call Grey immediately. Fabiana sensed Jax's tension and removed her hand. "Who is it?"

Jax's thoughts were elsewhere, to a dusty jeep flying across the Egyptian desert, an insane adventure with one of the few men alive Jax wouldn't want to meet alone in a dark alley. "An old acquaintance."

Her pillowy lips curled into a frown. "Your next conquest?"

"It's a *he*, love. Not my vintage."

"So you don't have to call him back?"

Jax's eyes drank in her curves. The Venezuelan ideal of feminine beauty did not include women who looked like ironing boards with legs. "Not in the next half hour."

She stretched out on the bed, teasing. "Is he a man like you? A handsome, lone wolf *mercenario*?"

"He doesn't think he is."

"*Que?* What does that mean?"

"I do what I do for money. He does the same things for principle. It's all a matter of justification."

She thought about it, gave a faint smile he couldn't quite decipher, and slid on top of him. "Where did you meet him?"

"Now that's a long story."

"Maybe you should introduce him to Diego, once you leave me."

Jax gave a mock smile. "Leave you? Who would ever do a ridiculous thing like that?"

"Isn't that the attraction of the lone wolf? That we know you'll leave one day? Where would be the fire if you stayed?"

Jax wondered who was playing whom in this relationship. "I don't think a meeting between Grey and Diego would go over too well. You know how there's an Alpha male in every wolf pack?"

"*Si*. So he's the dominant type?" she asked, her voice turning husky.

"No, love. He's the reason the Alpha males need the rest of the pack behind them."

She slid onto him and slowly began to rock. "Then he *must* come for dinner."

A while later, Fabiana fell asleep, and Jax slipped outside to call Grey back. After hearing him out, Jax decided to make a trip to the States. Diego was due back the next day. He had already hinted that he had more jobs for Jax, but the mercenary knew he was pushing his luck with Fabiana. If Diego ever found out about the affair, and they always did, then he would send his men to emasculate the cheating *gringo* with a rusty pocketknife.

While Jax loved taking risks, especially where beautiful women were involved, he loved staying alive even more. He didn't trust Fabiana not to slip up when Diego returned and let her eyes linger on Jax a moment too long, or seek his bedroom when a guard was watching.

The call from Grey had served as a wake-up call. It was best, Jax thought, to leave Venezuela tomorrow, while he still could.

Right after he said his goodbyes.

27

Charlie's captors kept her locked in a mobile home with ten other African American children, ranging in ages from eight to nineteen. She had learned the skyline in the distance was Atlanta, and that the other children were from all over the South.

Charlie was the lone New Yorker. In fact, the more she thought about it, it seemed as if her captors had gone to an awful lot of trouble to bring her here.

Armed guards patrolled the perimeter of the clearing. Outside the grimy windows, she counted twelve trailers. Some of them, she knew, held more children.

Every morning and night, a gray-haired woman with lips like cracked leather shoved trays of chicken nuggets and boiled spinach into the trailer, as well as milk jugs full of cloudy water. Frost rimed the windows in the morning, and the guards ignored the children's pleas to bring them a heater.

Charlie tried to stay calm and in control. She could take the cold and the awful food. She had endured worse. Though not the oldest, the other children looked to her as their leader. She was from the Big City and knew jujitsu and didn't panic like the others. In the confines of the cramped and squalid trailer, Charlie did her best to impart self-defense tips, and plan an escape for when the opportunity arose. She hadn't realized it, but helping Grey teach class had made her something of a leader.

The sliver of hope gave way to despair when the guards herded them onto a small plane that made her want to throw up when it lurched into the sky. A *plane*? Where were they taking them? Who were these people?

An hour later, the plane landed on a raised and narrow runway surrounded by cleared swampland. Charlie had never seen a more desolate place. The younger children wailed in fear. At first she thought they planned to kill them and dump them in the marsh, but that didn't make sense, and the guard herded them onto the blacktop and made them stand in line while the plane returned to the sky. A few minutes later, a larger plane with a snub face landed on the airstrip. The guards forced all of the children except Charlie into a cavernous holding area at the rear of the new plane. Even more children crowded the back of the bigger plane. All dark skinned. All terrified.

When the plane took off, leaving Charlie by herself on the runway with a dozen guards, she had never felt so alone.

She looked back and forth, searching in vain for an escape route. The trees had been cleared for a hundred yards in every direction, providing visibility for the rifles. Beyond that lay nothing but fetid gray marsh.

The kidnapping. The plane. Now Charlie knew the score. She had heard about gangs who took kids to other countries around the world and sold them as slaves to rich people. Sometimes even kings and sultans and shit. Those countries didn't even have laws against it. It was just bad luck if you ended up there—and no one was coming to get you.

But why had they left her behind?

An hour or so later, a smaller cargo plane landed. After the big red-headed man boarded with a group of men, one of the guards stuck Charlie by herself in the hold and slammed the door. As the plane took off, she felt long fingernails of panic digging into her skin.

The cargo door stayed locked the entire flight. A long time later, hours and hours, the door lowered and Charlie stepped warily down the ramp.

When she saw the world outside, she thought the pilot of the plane must be a wizard who had taken them through space and time to another dimension, because the landscape looked like the cover of one of those fantasy novels the librarian at her old school used to read.

Surrounding the airstrip was a jumble of green mounds that resembled giant heads of broccoli, unlike anything she had ever seen. A range of jagged, snow-topped peaks riddled with waterfalls surrounded them. It didn't even look real. Even more startling, on the other side of the giant sponge field, she saw the glassy surface of a humongous blue-white thing that snaked into the mountains like a twisty playground slide.

She thought she knew what the blue-white thing was, again from the books in the library.

A glacier.

The freezing weather reinforced her conclusion. A laugh hiccupped out of her, despite the gravity of the situation. Maybe they *had* taken her to Alaska.

What the hell? she thought. *Does Santa Claus need sex slaves?*

Armed men poured out of the cargo plane. Charlie looked around in panic. To her left, she saw a paved road and a cluster of wooden buildings.

She had to get away. Now. During the transit. Before they took her to some cold place she would never get out of. Made her do things she couldn't forget.

For whatever reason, the guards hadn't tied her up. Probably because they thought she would never try to escape in such a remote place. The guards might be right about most kids, but Charlie would take her chances. Find a way to survive. Just like she always had.

And if she didn't, then that was okay.

It was better than wherever they were going.

A guard loomed right beside her, but he was barely paying attention. The next closest was twenty feet away. Charlie took a deep breath and punched the guard in the solar plexus, as hard as she could.

He gasped and doubled over. Charlie darted past him, knowing the moment she had gained by silencing his voice would give her a chance to escape. Without a sound, moving as quietly and swiftly as if she was sneaking through gang territory, Charlie darted for the cover of the green mounds. Another guard noticed her, but he was too far away to catch her before she reached cover. Now it was a matter of how fast and far Charlie could run, and how bad they wanted her.

The mazelike landscape enveloped her. Most of the spongy mounds rose higher than her head. She guessed they were boulders covered by moss or fungus. Whatever it was, it was the best hiding place ever.

She had no idea where she was going, but for the moment, she was free. If she was lucky, the location wasn't as remote as she thought. Maybe it was New Hampshire. She had a chance!

Just as she wondered why no one had bothered to raise the alarm, the side of one of the green mounds hinged open, scaring Charlie so bad she tripped on a rock and fell.

A man stepped out of the mound who scared her even more. A man with a weird face that looked like hardened wax, and a fur-lined jacket with a silver symbol, some kind of T, attached to the front. He took Charlie by the arm with a grip that felt like pliers, even firmer than the big red-headed man.

Charlie debated trying to choke him but decided against it. It was hard to choke a grown man in a fight. Real hard. Especially one this strong. And he was holding a gun and would just shoot her.

She opted for the solar plexus again. The man didn't react when she hit him. Not even a change of expression. Instead he dragged her by the arm back to the landing strip, expressionless, as Charlie bounced along the ground at his side.

28

NEW YORK CITY

During the evening rush, Grey watched a debonair man with sandy hair and a strong cleft chin navigate the crowd at the Grand Central Station food court.

Earlier in the day, Grey had taken the first flight to New York he could find, visited a Harlem homeless shelter for a fruitless conversation with the teenage boy who had witnessed Charlie's abduction, and then hurried to meet Jax at his requested destination.

Though the mercenary appeared nonchalant as he strolled through the masses, smiling at the pretty women and eyeing the array of food vendors, Grey knew Jax was watching the crowd as keenly as Grey, a wolf among sheep.

"Midtown," Jax said in disgust, when he arrived at Grey's table. "Is there anything besides Starbucks and pharmacies around here?"

"Not really," Grey agreed.

He didn't rise to greet Jax, or even offer his hand. Grey didn't like mercenaries. He had a history with Jax—they had saved one another's lives—but a grudging mutual respect was as far as the relationship went. Or would ever go.

Beside them, a dreadlocked man was sitting by himself, waving his hands and cursing at invisible people. Grey had chosen his seat on purpose. Their unbalanced neighbor kept everyone else away.

"You look like hell," Jax said. "Is your shower broken?"

Grey took a sip of coffee. "Thanks for coming."

"It was time for a change of scenery." Jax spread his hands and grinned. "Your money's good with me."

"I meant, thanks for skipping your protocols and meeting me in person right away."

Jax rolled his eyes. "It's not like I didn't scout this place beforehand. And watch you come in before I doubled back."

Grey ran a hand through his hair in agitation. "I don't have time to argue."

He had already filled Jax in on the gist of what had happened, enough to get him involved. They had yet to discuss next steps. Not until they met in person.

Jax bobbed a hand. "Whoa, cuz. I'm here to save the day. You bought me for a whole week."

Grey had been shocked—and relieved—to discover the credit card Viktor had given him had a sixty thousand dollar limit, with no withdrawal restrictions. As agreed, Grey had paid Jax half up front.

He wanted to think Viktor would have approved, but Charlie's life was at stake. Better to ask forgiveness than permission.

"A week is too long," Grey said. "We need to find her before the investigation progresses. Today. Now."

"Listen, whoever took her has to give you time to impact the investigation. At least a few days."

"You don't know these people."

Jax leaned forward, the glint in his deep blue eyes belying the easy grin. "My brother. Know your audience."

Grey waved a hand. "There are things I haven't told you about."

"Like what?"

"Like the dead Nazi who kicked my ass."

Jax stared at him, then started to chuckle. "Is that some kind of tenth degree black belt humor?"

"I wish. You said over the phone you had something in mind. Someone who can help us get started."

Jax settled back in his seat, probing Grey's eyes and then glancing around the busy dining hall. "Hungry?"

"Yeah."

The mercenary wrinkled his nose. "We can do better than the food court."

They hailed a cab to the West Village. After telling the driver to drop them at Sheridan Square, Jax led Grey a few blocks deeper into the neighborhood, to a cramped street with a few ethnic restaurants wedged among grimy apartment buildings.

Grey almost missed the faint green lettering marked *Ceviche* on a dirt-streaked awning. He was further distracted by a bare-chested obese man in a wheelchair leering at passersby as he ate a bagel out of a paper bag. Crumbs covered his hairy chest, and a sign asking for money was taped to the chair. "You got something for me?" he asked.

Jax made eye contact. "Just here for the grub."

The grotesque man winked and kept chewing. Grey had the feeling they had just passed a test.

As Jax opened the door, Grey realized *restaurant* was somewhat of a misnomer. If someone looked up *hole in the wall* in the dictionary, surely a picture of this place would appear.

The entire dining area consisted of a wooden bar counter, half the length of a bowling lane, that began just inside the door and ended at the rear wall. A barebones kitchen lay on the other side of the counter, tended by a gruff hipster and a man of Latino-Asian descent, fussing over a saucepan.

Their backs brushing against the crumbling brick wall, Grey and Jax squeezed past a trio of patrons near the door and grabbed a pair of stools at the far end. Despite the humble environs, the smell of fresh lime and caramelized garlic made Grey's mouth water. The hipster slapped down a menu, then stood with his hand on his hips and waited for them to order.

Jax pushed the menus back. "We'll take whatever the chef wants to give us. And two Cusqueñas."

Without a word, the goateed hipster collected the menus and grabbed two bottles of beer out of a mini fridge. Grey noticed that Cusqueña was the only beverage on offer.

Jax took a swallow of beer. "You're not gonna believe the food in this place. The guy fussing over the pan like he's performing surgery on Baby Jesus is a genius. Best damn ceviche this side of Lima."

Though he ached to take action, Grey didn't bother asking what was going on. He knew Jax had not taken him to a random restaurant. They sipped their beers in silence, until Jax wiped his mouth and said, "I heard about Nya."

Grey stilled.

"I've been there, too. I know how you must be feeling."

"You don't know anything," Grey whispered. He stared straight ahead and gripped his beer bottle. He couldn't let himself think about Nya right now. She was dead. Charlie was alive.

"All right, then," Jax said, after a moment. He clinked his bottle against Grey's motionless one. "To fallen companions," he said quietly.

The food arrived, slim wooden platters artfully stacked with raw fish soaked in lime juice. Slivers of pickled onion and cubed sweet potato accentuated the dish. Grey's eyes widened with the first bite. Jax was right. The food was the truth.

The other customers left. When Jax finished eating, he set his beer down and flicked his eyes toward the rear door. "Why don't you have another? I'll be back in a few."

"I'm going, too," Grey said quietly.

"I can't take you in."

"Then I'll take myself. I might need to be there for whatever happens."

"You really want to get your hands dirty?"

"You don't know me as well as you think you do," Grey said.

Jax pushed away from the counter. "Look, why don't you just trust me?"

"It's not that. I know this case."

"Are we going to do this with every decision?"

Grey stepped down off the stool.

"Jesus," Jax said. "Fine. I'll take you if they'll let me." He turned and addressed the chef in decent Spanish, asking whether he needed a *llave maestra* for the restroom.

Strange turn of phrase, Grey thought to himself. *Llave maestra. Skeleton key.*

For the first time since they had entered, the chef stopped working and looked up. He was wearing black earlobe stretchers and a sleeveless vest. After hearing Jax's request, the chef lifted a hinged wooden section at the end of the bar, unlocked the rear door, and disappeared.

He returned a few minutes later and said, "The Sensei is not available."

"I told you," Jax muttered to Grey. Then, to the chef, he said, "Should I come back later?"

The chef gave Grey a disapproving glance before he returned behind the counter. "No."

"Look," Jax said. "I'll vouch for him. And you know what that means."

The chef shook his head.

Feeling desperate, Grey said, in much better Spanish than Jax, "I'm looking for a little girl. She's been kidnapped, probably trafficked. *Please*. We need your help."

The chef pointed at the door.

"C'mon," Jax said to Grey. "We'll find another way."

Grey could see in Jax's eyes that this was a major lost opportunity. As Grey stood with his fists clenched atop the bar, unwilling to leave, the chef stopped chopping and cocked his head, as if listening to an invisible microphone. Grey wondered if his earlobe stretchers contained tiny radios.

The chef gave a curt nod, then returned to slicing fish. The hipster set down his dish towel, ushered Jax and Grey through the rear door, and closed it behind them.

The door opened onto an elevator that looked as ancient as the rest of the building. It started moving of its own accord.

"The whole building is theirs," Jax whispered, looking surprised by the turn of events.

"Who's they?" Grey asked.

"I don't really know. Information brokers. It's the new black market."

"You've been here before? In person?"

Jax nodded.

The elevator stopped on the fourth floor. Grey tensed as he stepped into a waiting room with a finished cement floor and glass walls he assumed were one-way mirrors. He and Jax allowed two men in street clothes and ear pieces, both armed with semi-automatics, to check them for weapons. Jax handed over his utility belt, Grey his boot knife.

After the pat down, the men herded Grey and Jax through a keypad door and into a room with a green marble floor and a crystal chandelier. Against the far wall, a staircase with ornate iron railing led both up and down, and the walls were painted in purple swirls and covered in martial arts movie posters and memorabilia.

A large stainless steel computer station dominated the center of the room, with an even larger white man sitting behind it. Younger than Grey, the man had a waist-length ponytail and a bushy black beard that spilled onto his hooded velour tracksuit. He also sported a red-and-white *rising sun* headband, rings on each finger, and a pair of horn-rimmed glasses as thick as Grey's pinkie.

The room reminded Grey of a vintage hotel lobby redecorated by, well, an underground hacker obsessed with the martial arts. An aficionado himself, Grey recognized almost all of the posters, from *Fists of Fury* to *Come Drink With Me* to *Iron Monkey*. The memorabilia consisted mostly of ancient weapons hanging on pegs or preserved in glass, including a pair of crossed samurai swords that looked genuine.

The two guards were lean but muscular. They had the economy of movement of trained soldiers. Grey doubted he could make a move before they shot him, but he canvased the weapons on the walls and decided his best play would be to grab one of the samurai swords.

"Sensei," Jax said.

The man in the tracksuit tipped his head.

Eyeing the array of computer equipment sprawled on the desk, as well as the gut spilling over the man's waistband, Grey took a wild guess that the man's honorific referred to his tech skills and not his martial arts prowess.

"We're in need of your inestimable services," Jax said.

"You know the deal."

The man's accent sounded suburban to Grey. A Jersey kid.

"Charge it to my account." Jax said, then winked at Grey. "I'll bill you later."

Grey didn't respond. He didn't even want to know how much this was going to cost.

The ponytailed man shifted to regard Grey, then eyed Jax. "If he talks, we'll come for you."

"Sure thing, champ."

The man gave a supercilious smile and opened a palm. Jax gave a rundown of Charlie's abduction and the men they were seeking. Grey passed them a photo of Charlie and an array of mug shots he had copied from the police station.

After examining the photos, the man looked to Jax. "I need you to wait outside."

"Me?" Jax said.

The man folded his thick arms. With a shrug, Jax locked gazes with Grey and backed towards the door. One of the armed guards followed him out. When the door closed behind them, the man behind the desk said, "She wants to see you in person."

"Who does?"

Part of the wall near the staircase slid open, a cleverly concealed pocket door. The man held up another palm, and Grey stepped through the opening, curious but wary.

The door slid shut behind him. Grey found himself in a boxy, dimly lit room filled with computer equipment and wires running into the walls. A young, lissome Asian woman sat with crossed legs in a futuristic, lime green office chair that hovered over her like a praying mantis.

She was wearing black leather shorts and a matching halter-top, and her straight dark hair almost touched the floor. Black eyeliner and heavy white face paint, similar to a Geisha, obscured the exact curve of her eyes. Red lipstick puckered her mouth. Grey knew other Asian cultures painted their faces, so he couldn't peg her as Japanese.

Nor would a true Geisha cover her body in fierce tattoos and piercings like this woman had, as if mocking the image of a demure courtesan. Her body art was more invasive than anything Grey had ever seen, spikes and barbs and pins that turned her body into a living weapon. He also noticed scuffed knuckles, a black belt hanging on a hook by the door, and tattoos depicting judo throws.

"You're the real Sensei," Grey said.

She bent at the waist, a half-bow from her chair.

"A judoka," he added, though he wondered how she trained with all of her piercings. Some of it looked embedded into her skin.

"And you're Zen-Zekai."

Her voice sounded hollow, metallic. Had it been damaged at some time? Modified by a throat implant?

"Trained by Hanshi Mizushima," she continued. "A living legend."

Grey was stunned. "How did you know that?"

"Your tattoos also tell a story."

At first he was confused, since his shirt hid his own body art on his back, but then he remembered the one-way glass in the foyer.

They had scanned him somehow. Seen the tattoos covering his back, as well as the scars from his father's abuse.

"It's why I let you in," she said. "That and your mission."

"I'm just trying to find a girl."

"And you're not seeking to find her for your own . . . gain?"

"She's my student. My friend."

She stared at him for a long moment. Maybe it was the illusion of layers created by the white paint, but her eyes seemed to possess a secret depth, as if a different person was peering out from behind the mask.

"I'm not sure I can help," she said finally. "But I will try."

A wave of hope crashed over him. "We can search for these men in the photos, but I doubt we'll get anywhere. I need to find Dag."

"The one with red hair your friend mentioned. Tell me more."

Grey told her everything he knew, about Dag's strange accent and the white supremacist ties and even the connection to the virus. Still, he knew it wasn't much to go on.

"There is no photo?"

"No."

"Describe him further. As detailed as you can." After Grey finished, she mulled it over and said, "He has physical characteristics helpful to a search. Without a photo, though . . . we need to limit the search. Can you narrow down the time frame?"

"I believe he left the country within the last twenty-four hours."

"And his next location? Are there any clues?"

Grey paced. "I'm convinced he left in a private plane. I think his accent is a European blend of some sort, maybe Nordic. Given the white supremacist ties . . . I think we should concentrate on Western and Northern Europe."

"That will help limit the vector, though it's still quite large. Anything else?"

"Add South Africa to the list. And he's urbane, a city guy. He could be going anywhere, but I'd try the major cities first. Maybe even the capitals. Then work our way down. Is that possible?"

"The definition of possible changes every day."

Grey's eyes flicked to the glowing laptops, monitors, modems, and who-knew-what-other technology was in the room. He believed her.

"Without a photo, I cannot run a facial scan. That will limit my search."

"I understand."

"Would you like to stay?"

"Please."

"You don't want to know how long it will take?" The question felt droll to Grey, though her expression or intonation never changed.

Grey shrugged. "Do you have coffee?"

She pointed to a corner of the room. Grey realized the tangle of machinery included a sink and a small steel fridge built into the wall. He stepped closer and saw a machine that looked like a spiked silver ball on a tripod, with a row of buttons on the base. Grey noticed a line of delicate ceramic cups on a shelf, took one and placed it beneath the spiked ball, and pressed *brew*.

The machine purred to life. Grey got his caffeine.

And then he waited.

The coffee helped him stay alert, but it only increased the sweat on his palms and the nervous pounding of his heart as he waited on the Sensei to finish.

What if she couldn't help? Dag could be anywhere in the world, and to have any chance at helping Charlie, they needed something to jumpstart the investigation. Something immediate.

The Sensei worked in silence, fingers whirring across the keyboard. At times, she slid between monitors in her mechanized chair, or stood and walked to and from a different beverage machine, returning with a cup of steaming liquid that gave off an aroma of jasmine.

Grey wasn't sure how long he had been there, two hours, maybe three, when a printer spun out a piece of paper like a spider releasing silk. The Sensei plucked it off the machine and curled a finger at Grey. He walked over.

"Is this the man?"

Grey looked down and found himself staring at the right half of a face he would never forget, a man entering a bar at nighttime in a city with an oddly shaped tower behind him. It resembled a concrete obelisk with indented sides, like steps.

Grey tensed as he took the photo. "That's him. When was this taken?"

"Last night, at one-thirty-three a.m. Eight-thirty-three New York time."

"Five hours . . . London? Dublin?"

"Wait."

She returned to her computer. Grey paced in agitation. Finally the printer whirred again, and she swiveled in her chair. "Facial scanning produced no other recent hits. His name, at least the one on the passport associated with the photo, is Dagna Argmundsson."

"Dag," Grey said grimly.

"He's an Icelandic national. The photo was taken on a cellphone by someone in Rekyjavik. Probably a tourist snapping a photo of the church tower."

Grey snapped his fingers. "Iceland. *That's* the accent. You can access private phone photos?" he said incredulously.

"It was posted on Snapchat. We pulled the deleted file."

Grey whistled and looked closer at the photo. The name of the bar Dag was entering was not quite visible.

"He has no criminal record," she said, "but there are past associations with militant white supremacists groups. On the printer, you'll find five of his known associates."

Grey darted to the printer. "Thank you."

Her eyes found his, a look of unnerving intensity. "Thank me by taking him off the street."

He pressed his lips and nodded.

"We can't be sure of his real name," she said, "but whoever he is, he's a member of the Iceland Heritage Society and a patron of the Rekyjavik symphony. In the past, he's competed in both chess and strongman competitions, and has won all-terrain races in various Nordic countries, both on foot and in vehicles."

"A Renaissance man," Grey murmured.

She held his gaze for long moments. "You can never speak of me. Of this place."

Grey clasped his hands, prayer-style, in front of his chest. "You have my word. On my Hanshi's honor."

She gave a curt nod and pushed a button. The door swooshed open.

Grey found Jax waiting downstairs in the restaurant, drinking a beer. When he saw Grey, the mercenary jumped to his feet, slapped down a bill, and followed Grey out the door. Darkness had fallen.

"What the hell did you do in there? Dictate your autobiography?"

"We're going to Iceland," Grey said, as soon as they hit the street. "Right now."

"Iceland?" he said in surprise, then, "I'm not going anywhere with you."

Grey stopped. "What?"

"Not until you take a shower."

29

After Professor Radek left in his private car to visit Dr. Ehlers, Naomi's gaze lingered on the empty road.

Was Viktor a crusader for justice, a rare person who would risk his life for others? Or was he gripped by the provocative nature of van Draker's research?

A mixture of both, she guessed.

It was her day off, but she had received a call from the station asking her to come in. She didn't have to ask what it was about. Van Draker had probably filed a complaint, and Captain Bakker had long been a puppet of the town's benefactor.

The events of the night before flashed through Naomi's mind as she washed dishes, straightened the bedrooms, tended to Max and her houseplants. The smell of Viktor's aftershave, rosewood and expensive leather, lingered on the sheets in the guest bedroom and helped take her mind off the disturbing visit to van Draker's mansion.

Even now, her hand trembled as she documented the encounter in her private files. Three men—Akhona, Kristof, and Robey—all supposed to be dead.

Had Jans faked their deaths? Hired actors to imitate their appearances?

Neither of those options made much sense. But the alternative was even more unacceptable.

Naomi shuddered and closed the journal. It was time to get moving. She had a number of stops to make.

The first port of call was the local Deed Registry. Located right next to the town's clock tower, which rose elegantly above the town center like the bride and groom stick on a wedding cake, the Registry kept property records for the town dating back several hundred years. Not just ownership records, which she could access from the police station, but all cadastral surveys and diagrams documenting land surveys approved by the government.

Evidence that, at some point in time, a laboratory had been built. Or at least the infrastructure to support one.

Naomi would have heard about any large-scale construction at the van Draker estate during her lifetime. Her guess was an underground bunker of some sort had been erected, perhaps during a war, and retrofitted into a lab. If she could get her hands on the plans . . . .

As soon as she entered the stately Cape Colonial building in the center of town that housed the local government offices, she knew something was wrong. The clerk near the front door saw her enter and looked away. A group of people in line gave her glances ranging from annoyed to scathing. Despite her plain clothes, the Bonniecombe police force was tiny. Everyone in town knew her.

She glimpsed the front-page headline of the local paper, tucked under the arm of a restaurant owner.

TRESPASS ON VAN DRAKER PROPERTY

Lovely, she thought. Not only did Jans file a complaint against her, he smeared her name in the paper.

She broke through the line and strode right up to the Clerk of Property Records, an elderly man she had known her entire life.

"Good morning, Martin," she said.

The angular man with a rim of white hair looked nervous at her approach. "Officer Linde."

She assumed a voice of authority. "I need a set of property records from you."

"What about the station?" he said, perplexed.

"I need land surveys, permits, annexes—everything in the file."

Martin swallowed and shuffled his feet, as if he knew what was coming. "I, um, yes, which records do you need?"

"The van Draker mansion. I assume you know the address."

"Ach," he muttered. "I'm afraid that won't be possible."

"I'm sorry? Why not?"

"Because they were, ah, stolen."

"Stolen? When?"

"Some time ago."

Naomi clenched her jaw. "*When?*"

With an ill expression, Martin disappeared into the back. The people in line behind Naomi muttered as they waited. Naomi's face grew hot, but she didn't turn around.

Martin returned and said, "Yes, ah, the records were reported missing on December thirteenth, nineteen ninety-four."

Naomi stared back at him, so intensely the poor clerk looked away. In disgust, she shoved away from the counter and stormed out.

1994, when Apartheid had officially ended, was a year no one in South Africa would ever forget.

It was also the year Jans van Draker had returned to Bonniecombe.

Naomi swung by the police station to see the captain, file her report on the night before, and research the records theft. Since Captain Bakker was on the phone when she entered, she jumped on her computer and logged into the system.

Just as Martin had said, a theft in the Office of Deed Registry had been reported in December of 1994. Someone had stolen a handful of property records, a purse left overnight by an employee, and the contents of the petty cash drawer.

No arrest was ever made. No documents recovered. Whoever had written the report hadn't cared to speculate why anyone would bother swiping a few sets of random property records.

Naomi looked up the other stolen files. As far as she could tell, none of them had anything to do with van Draker. A couple of homesteads near the N2, a defunct waste water treatment plant, and a trio of city houses. Random thefts, she knew. Stolen to cover up the real crime.

More damningly, as far as she could tell, the break-in had not been reported in the local paper. Bonniecombe was small enough that a theft in the middle of town was big news.

Which meant Van Draker had paid someone to keep it out.

"Naomi."

She jumped at the voice. When she turned, Captain Bakker was standing at the entrance to her cubicle, chewing a piece of biltong and squinting at her computer screen.

The captain was an old-school Boer. A bald, hard-drinking ex-athlete who liked to shoot guns in the bush on the weekends with his mates, throw a few steaks and boerewors on the braai, and watch rugby in the pub while his wife took care of the kids. He broke his gaze away from the computer and stared down his sunburnt nose at Naomi. "What are you doing?"

"Sorry?" she said, trying to think of an excuse.

"A petty theft from a quarter century ago? I called you in to discuss that stunt you pulled at the van Draker residence."

"I haven't even written my report."

"Ya? And why not? It should have been written last night!"

Naomi worked hard to control her temper. "It was a minor trespass at three a.m. I was off duty. I accompanied Professor Radek to his residence and thought the report could wait until morning."

"Jans van Draker didn't think it was minor."

Naomi stiffened.

"He says the professor is harassing him. And that you're helping him. Something about the township boy."

"His name is Akhona."

"What?"

"The Xhosa teenager. His name is Akhona."

"Jesus Christ, Naomi, we're not the fucking ANC. And you know as well as I—" He broke off whatever he was about to say, shook away a look of apprehension, and replaced it with one of righteous anger.

Go ahead and say it, Naomi wanted to say. *Tell me how van Draker runs this town and keeps you in that captain's chair. Tell me how you're terrified of crossing him.*

Instead, not wanting to impact the investigation, she looked down in mock submission. "I'll file the report right away."

The captain planted a meaty forearm on the ledge of the cubicle. "I don't care what some bureaucrat in Paris says, you keep that professor away from van Draker. You know what outsiders think about South Africans. Always ready to point the finger. They have no idea what life is like here."

Naomi mumbled a response and bent over her desk.

She couldn't agree more.

On her way out of the station, Naomi found a copy of the local paper and took a minute to read the article. She grew more disgusted with every word. There was a photo of her and Professor Radek talking outside the police station, and the article painted her as an accomplice in the harassment of Jans van Draker.

Naomi started to wad up the paper and throw it away, then tucked it in her purse and decided to ask Thato about it.

As a breeze chased away the morning mist, Naomi jumped into the Land Cruiser and drove northwest out of town, along the spine of the Langebergs, towards the red-and-gold fields and gentle hills of the Robertson Wine Valley.

Halfway to Worcester, she turned onto a switchback drive leading to a white manor with tidy mahogany trim, sitting atop a manicured slope. A vineyard surrounded the manor, undulating towards a line of peaks that resembled squatting vultures.

One of Naomi's ex-flames, an architect named Daniel de Swart, had grown up on the property. Their breakup had been amicable, a fling that ran its course, and Naomi stopped by from time to time to say hello.

She walked into the tasting room, more modern than most of the villas in the valley, full of stainless steel and polished oak. The Robertson Wine Valley was one of the Western Cape's best-kept secrets. Too far from Cape Town to be on the tourist map, but with scenery and wine just as exquisite as Stellenbosch or Franschhoek, Naomi loved to drive the wine route on a sunny day with Thato and visit the dusty cellars. More often than not, the owners would pour the wine themselves and ply Naomi and Thato with free glasses.

A woman in her twenties with cheekbones that looked stuffed with wads of tobacco greeted Naomi from behind the bar. Naomi didn't recognize her.

"Here for a pour?"

Naomi glanced towards a side door she knew led to Daniel's office. "Is he around?"

The question caused the bartender to look Naomi up and down. "Hold on."

After the woman knocked on the office door, a well-built man in his fifties with glasses and an aquiline nose stepped out. His wavy brown hair showed gray at the edges.

The man's face lit up. "Naomi!"

"Hi, Daniel."

"Just stopping by?"

Naomi hesitated. "I know you're working, but can we talk for a minute?"

He checked his watch. "Lisa and I were about to break for lunch. Why don't you join us?"

"I'm afraid it's private."

"It's fine," Lisa said curtly. "I'll join you later. I had a late brekkie."

Daniel studied Naomi's face, apologized to Lisa after formally introducing the two women, then led Naomi to a dining room in the main house. Lunch had already been laid on a long wooden table, platters of olives and cheese and cured meats.

One of Daniel's domestic workers, a Zulu woman named Rose who had raised him from infancy, refilled glasses as they talked. Domestic workers, paid very little but given room and board, were a normal part of South African life, for wealthy blacks as well as whites. As unfortunate as Naomi found the arrangement, it employed a lot of families who would otherwise go hungry. Until the country solved some of its poverty issues, she didn't have a better solution, except better pay.

Still, she made it a point to treat everyone as a social equal, and had grown close to Rose over the years.

"Are you and Lisa . . ."

Daniel looked embarrassed. "No. She's the daughter of a family friend. Halfway through a doctorate at Stellenbosch in sustainable agriculture."

Naomi nodded, too distracted for small talk and not believing his story. Daniel was charming and intelligent and a good man overall, but he had a weakness for his employees of the opposite sex.

Naomi waited long enough to be polite, plucking a few olives and taking a few sips of Chenin Blanc, then told him what she needed: old plans for the van Draker place. She gave him just enough details about the records theft to enlist his help.

While she trusted Daniel, she didn't want to involve him any more than she had to. He shared her distaste of van Draker, though she had never told him about her private crusade.

He frowned. "That's going to be a problem. The only people who might have a copy are the architect and the home owner. The estate is so old I'm doubting the architect is even on record."

"Correct," she said.

"I assume the home owner isn't going to comply?"

She smirked.

As he considered the problem, Daniel paired a slice of local Camembert with a piece of charcuterie. "In the days before stainless steel, farmers used to dig out storage chambers underground to cool their wine. They used stones from the Breede river to cast concrete cisterns, rubbed them with hot beeswax to stave off any cracks and prevent the wine from coming into contact with the cement. My winery is fairly small, but some of the larger ones have entire tunnel complexes below ground."

"Van Draker has one, too. I've been inside his cellar."

Daniel's eyebrows rose. "And? You didn't see what you were looking for?"

"I think he's either sealed a section off, or expanded. My guess is there's an entrance, probably more than one, which he didn't let us see."

"And you want another way to access it." She nodded, and his face darkened. "That's dangerous, Naomi."

"I know," she said quietly.

Daniel took a swig of wine and drummed his fingertips on the table. "If you want, I can look into this for you."

"How?"

"I'll ask around with the vineyard owners. It's a small community. While van Draker doesn't produce anymore, his family used to."

Naomi shook her head. "I can't ask you to do that. As you said, it's dangerous."

"I'm not one who believes the safeguarding of our community should fall entirely on the police. If we as citizens don't act on occasion . . . who will?"

"Is that you talking, or Afrikaner pride?"

"I'm not proposing I go undercover. I'll just ask around discreetly, with people I trust. Come to think of it, I'll ask my architect circle, too."

Naomi stared at a vintage billhook hanging on the wall, then sighed. "Be careful. I mean it."

Daniel wiped his mouth and took a long sip of wine. "Something else comes to mind. I don't even like discussing it, but how much do you know about the AWB?"

Naomi's hand tightened against her glass. The *Afrikaner Weerstandsbeweging* or AWB was a white supremacist movement that gained notoriety for claiming the tenets of Apartheid were too liberal. The extremist group garnered far more support than Naomi cared to think about, and had bolstered its cause by delivering meals to poor Afrikaner families.

As generous to their constituents as they were vicious to their enemies.

"Too much," Naomi said. "There's been a resurgence lately."

"I've seen their signs around here, and in parts of Cape Town. The group goes further back than people think."

"All the way to the Greyshirts," Naomi said.

The Greyshirts were an infamous paramilitary organization that arose during the 1930s. South Africa's first pro-Nazi movement. South Africa had officially sided with the Allies, but plenty of Boers had been sympathetic to the German white nationalist cause. Also, the Afrikaners had never forgiven the British for the Boer Wars, and opposed entering the war on the side of Britain.

"During World War II," Daniel said, "Nazi propagandists came to South Africa to establish a foothold. Many of them were given shelter in the rural areas, including around here." He grimaced. "Wine cellars made natural hiding places. A few of the estate owners retrofitted or expanded to conceal the Nazis."

Naomi's eyes widened in understanding. "Your family?"

"We didn't build out, but we were sympathetic. My grandfather kept records."

Daniel had started speaking in monotone, and she put a hand over his. "You weren't even born yet."

He compressed his lips and looked past her. "I don't know if any of that matters," he said. "But knowing the reputation of the van Drakers, my guess is it might."

At the end of the day, her mind spinning, Naomi met Thato for a brandy and coke at their favorite watering hole: a French-inspired café with red walls and booths, a lush patio, great local wine, and none of the *rah-rah* Afrikaner nostalgia bullshit most of the local pubs catered to.

Naomi arrived first and did her best to enjoy the calming effect of the alcohol and the beautiful foliage. Tall aloe plants rose around her, joined by banana palms and orange trees and hydrangeas as big as basketballs.

A few angry stares, cast her way by the other patrons, soured her mood. This was supposed to be her safe haven. She wanted to stand up and scream at them, tell them exactly who Jans van Draker was.

The problem was, she thought they already knew.

A quarter after eight, Thato walked in, still dressed in her work clothes. The journalist gave Naomi a hug and said, "I'm sorry about the article."

"Yeah."

"I wasn't even told."

"Which says something," Naomi said.

"I guess it does." Thato looked around, noticed the sidelong glances and said, "You want to get out of here?"

"No," Naomi said. "Let them stare."

She waited for Thato's drink to arrive, then lowered her voice and told her most of what she knew. As much as Thato wanted to break a story, she wouldn't go public until Naomi gave the okay.

"It must have taken a lot to confide in him," Thato said. "The professor."

"I need him. And, yes, I trust him."

Something must have crept onto Naomi's face, because Thato's eyes widened and she said, "You slept with him!"

"No, actually."

Thato grinned. "But you're keen to, hey?"

"He's very . . . confident. At least in most things." She waved a hand in exasperation, made sure no one was listening, then leaned forward and said, "Listen. This is our chance, Thato. To take him down."

"You really think so?"

"I just need a glimpse of that lab. Once I have evidence, I'll go straight to the commissioner and get a warrant. We'll see what's inside with our own eyes, and you'll run the story."

Thato chewed her lip as she considered the plan. "You know what happens if we slip up."

"We've known from the beginning."

"That man's got political connections to the moon."

"Then make sure the story you run severs them," Naomi said.

After a deep breath, Thato stirred her drink. "So what's next?"

"I have to get inside that house, without anyone knowing. That's your territory. Can you help?"

"That might be hard." Thato was silent for a few minutes, then wagged a finger. "Unless you'd consider letting someone else go?"

"Why? And who?"

Thato grinned. "What about your new fling?"

Naomi leaned back. "I don't know about that."

"What if it was the only way?"

Naomi took a long drink, fidgeted, and ran a hand down her cheek. "I'll think about it, if it's the only thing you can think of. And Viktor would have to agree."

Thato downed the rest of her brandy, a hard glint in her eyes. "If he wants van Draker, then he will."

30

As the plane neared Rekyjavik, Grey went to the restroom and stared at his new face in the mirror.

Or rather, an old face, resurrected and disguised for a sojourn to the land of the midnight sun, a country known for its ties to Vikings and the ancient Norse pantheon. A country prized by genetic researchers for its well-kept ancestral records and, most of all, the homogeneity of its white population.

Jax had supplied them both with fake passports before they left New York, and Grey put his hands on his smooth cheeks. They felt alien. No beard. No stubble. He had cropped his hair short and donned a shoulder-length blond wig, applied a bronzer to his face and hands, bought a pair of sport sunglasses that covered half his face, and planned to hide behind a scarf and hooded parka wherever he went. Since no one in Dag's organization knew Jax was involved, the mercenary's only addition was a sporty winter jacket.

Just a couple of snow bums coming to Iceland for some adrenaline-fueled adventure.

Grey returned to his seat and gazed out the window as a landscape of unearthly beauty unfolded, snow-covered massifs overlooking porcelain blue fjords, volcanoes and glaciers looming on the horizon, a prismatic and constantly changing terrain forged by eons of fire and ice.

The redeye flight touched down at eight a.m. Grey was relieved by the polished wood floors, modern finishes, and toy-like charm of the airport. Even if an alert customs official on Dag's payroll recognized Grey, he did not expect to be dragged into a back room and tortured.

Still, one could never be sure. He and Jax hoisted their backpacks and scurried outside, hailing the first taxi they saw and planning to disappear into the city.

The ride to the center took forty minutes. On the way in, Grey glimpsed slopes of moss-covered lava rocks rippling into the distance, swells of crashing green waves frozen in time.

Rekyjavik felt more like a town than a city to Grey. Traffic was light and they quickly penetrated the outer suburbs, cruising through a downtown that resembled a mix between an Ikea and a Brothers Grimm tale. Tidy and quirky, full of playful street art and sloping streets of boxlike houses with colorful pitched roofs, Reykjavik's charm was balanced only by the biting cold and the feeling of insignificance induced by the stark beauty of its surroundings. Grey had never been in a place where the footprint of mankind felt so fleeting. As if he could close his eyes and, when he opened them, the people and buildings would disappear and he would be an explorer from centuries past, alone with the elements, trudging across the frozen basalt on the shore of a windswept sea.

Jax knew the city and had the taxi drop them at the public plaza containing Hallgrímskirkja, the iconic white church tower Grey had glimpsed in the photo. The unusual saw-toothed façade of the church, reminiscent of a modern-day ziggurat, towered above the low skyline.

Though cold and damp, the air was as fresh as a national park. It was the tail end of rush hour, so the city was busy and a fair number of tourists idled about. Grey stood near a statue of Leif Erikson and scoped the crowd for signs of danger. After judging the angle from which the photo had been taken, he headed down one of the streets leading off the square.

Halfway down the block, he saw the bar Dag had entered. Grey glanced through a frost-paned window and saw dartboards, an enormous flag of Iceland draped on the wall, and a line of bowling shoes above the bar.

Grey glanced at the name and grimaced.

ÓÐINN BAR

The bar didn't open until four p.m. Once they circled back to the church, Jax yawned and said, "What's the plan?"

"I want eyes on that bar starting an hour before it opens. I saw two coffee shops, another bar, and a restaurant on the same street. Between the two of us, we can camp out and switch up enough not to draw attention."

"And if Dag doesn't show?"

"We'll go in after they close. See what we find."

Jax considered the plan, then patted his utility belt. "Gives us the morning to prepare. I need to restock."

"You have contacts here?" Grey asked.

"I never met a fence who was a stranger."

"You think they might know something about Dag?"

"I doubt it." Jax shrugged. "But we can hardly ask, can we?"

"I guess not," Grey muttered, as he debated what to do. "I should go with you," he said finally. "Just in case."

"You want a piece?"

Grey weighed the risks of getting caught with an unregistered weapon in a country with strict gun laws versus acquiring more protection against the kind of people they were facing. He cracked his knuckles, expelled a frosty breath, and patted his bulky ski jacket. "Yeah."

They decided to grab breakfast at a café fronting the church. Jax studied his contacts on his phone while he ate, stepped outside for a call, then gave a grim smile and a thumbs-up.

Grey took his coffee to go.

Jax said the fence was located at a warehouse near the harbor, about a mile away. They decided to stretch their legs, and Grey wanted to get a feel for the city. Jax led them through the center of town, and Grey was struck by the orderly streets and lack of pollution.

Most of the houses were modest affairs. Slender townhouses and bungalows made of concrete or timber, shielded from the elements by corrugated iron siding. A city of brick sidewalks, gemlike parks, cafés serving waffles and cream, pop art covering the walls of funky boutiques, quirky doorways that livened up the stoic façades. Near the end of their walk, they passed a pair of life-size papier-mâché trolls on the sidewalk.

A practical city with whimsical touches that helped alleviate its grim battle over the years against isolation and earthquakes and cataclysmic eruptions. Grey found it an honest way to live.

The sky turned leaden as they skirted a row of glass high-rises and reached the harbor district. Jax consulted his phone and led them to a street lined with grimy, low-slung warehouses. Grey breathed in the smell of fish guts and tangy salt air. The wind cut right through his coat.

He leaned on the edge of a building and watched Jax walk to the end of the street and approach a pair of locals with stringy blond hair and unkempt beards. Though Grey wanted desperately to question Jax's contact, if Dag found out Grey had followed him to Iceland, then Charlie would suffer.

The scene looked tense for a moment. The Icelanders slid their hands under their coats, until Jax said something that made them chuckle and relax. They frisked him and opened the door.

Jax disappeared inside. Grey watched both ends of the street, scanned every door and window. He didn't like how isolated the street was.

His fears receded when Jax strolled out of the warehouse, nodded to the guards, and disappeared down the block. As discussed, Grey circled around to meet him at a fish and chips restaurant they had passed.

"You get what you need?" Grey asked.

"Some of it. I'll make do."

A few minutes later, working their way back to the center via a different route, they found themselves on a deserted street fronting a handsome, leaf-strewn cemetery. Jax veered inside the gates. He found a corner shielded by birch trees and held out a holster attached to a firearm belt, along with a pistol Grey recognized as a Glock 26. An excellent handgun for concealed carry, easy to deploy and with stopping power.

"Good choice," Grey said, as he slipped the belt around his waist.

Unlike most ex-military, Grey did not have an affinity for firearms. He preferred his weapons more up close and personal.

But if he needed, he would drop a small nuclear bomb on the people who took Charlie.

———

Ten p.m.

No one Grey recognized had entered the Odin Bar all day. Jax had slipped inside to see if he noticed anything unusual, though neither of them spoke a lick of Icelandic. It was risky, but Jax was smooth and most people in the capital spoke English to varying degrees.

Grey had camped out down the street at a late night coffee bar with red carpet and wood paneling, full of students and young professionals. A tourist popped up here and there, enough that Grey didn't stand out, but it was definitely off-season.

Earlier in the day, Grey had called Viktor back on a burner cell, told him where he was, and explained the situation. The professor understood but said he had to move forward. There were other lives at stake, maybe many more.

Grey understood, too. But he was only worried about one life.

They caught each other up on recent events, discussing the virus and the players involved. After he hung up, Grey kept an eye on the Odin Bar while he did some research on Iceland's Nazi ties. Maybe he could gain some insight into Dag's motives or potential location.

Though Grey could barely believe what Viktor had told him about the Ahnenerbe, Grey's own research confirmed the Nazis had an entire division focused on political propaganda and pseudo-scientific research. Occult research. That was fact. As part of their deranged effort to prove that a Nordic master race had once ruled the world, the Ahnenerbe planned an expedition to Iceland to study the homogenous population and conduct archaeological digs. Plumb the volcanoes and crack the glaciers. Anything to serve their ends. Due to Scandinavian protest and the British occupation of Iceland, the expedition was shelved before it began.

At least that was the official statement. The mythology and remote location of Iceland possessed a strong magnetism on Himmler, and Nazi scholars had long speculated that the Ahnenerbe had continued their mission in secret, using U-boats to land on remote beachheads, sending small teams of scientists and soldiers to explore the uncharted interior.

Among other missions, such as confirmation of the ridiculous World Ice Theory, the Nazis sought the location of a magical Aryan homeland called Thule, as well as a set of tablets containing runic instructions from Odin, similar to the Ten Commandments, with instructions not to mix their blood with "inferior" races.

Grey set down his phone in disgust. He wanted to think the world had progressed, that Nazi Germany was a rip in the fabric of time, but the Wodan Society and similar organizations around the world said otherwise. Rwanda and Bosnia and Cambodia said otherwise. ISIS said otherwise. Hell, the daily news said otherwise.

12:30 a.m.

A steady trickle of people had entered and left the Odin bar. No one Grey recognized. Nor did the patrons look any different than anyone else on the street. Half looked like young professionals, half looked like Vikings with glasses and bad sweaters.

The wait gave Grey too much time to think. His guilt at losing Charlie clawed at him like a maddened bird of prey. Visions of Nya crept into his mind, those warm brown eyes so calm and collected as she fell into the abyss. He shuddered and ran a hand through his hair.

Just as Grey debated changing locations, a man exited the Odin Bar with two women. Grey froze.

The man looked familiar. He was tall and had a bundle of auburn hair tied up in a topknot. The sides of his head were shaved. It had been dark, but Grey thought he remembered him standing behind Dag on Stone Mountain.

The man shrugged into a leather jacket as he stepped into the cold, leaving it unzipped over a brown sweater. Grey had noticed that the locals dressed like they were on fall break in New York, while the tourists looked as if they were preparing to summit Mount Everest.

The two women linked arms and headed down the street. The man with the topknot walked off in the opposite direction. Grey hesitated. If he chose wrong, and it wasn't the man he had seen, he might lose another opportunity that came up.

On the other hand, this might be his only chance.

Just as the Icelander slipped out of sight, Grey grabbed his coat and hurried out the door, deciding to trust his instincts.

Shrinking into the hood of his parka, Grey shot Jax a text and rushed to the end of the street. At first he thought he had lost the man, but Grey took another gamble and turned right, into a more residential neighborhood, and saw his quarry disappearing down a dimly lit brick street.

Grey lowered his head and followed.

31

Captain Waalkamp of the Cape Town police force, the supervising officer for Robey Joubert at the time of his death, canceled his meeting with Professor Radek for undisclosed reasons. Not to be deterred, Viktor scheduled another meeting for the following day, and spent the night at a well-appointed pension in Dr. Ehlers' village.

After brunch, as Viktor headed north on the M64, straight through the lush and jagged heart of the Cape Peninsula, his thoughts turned to the impending meeting with Captain Waalkamp.

Assuming the guard they had seen was Naomi's former classmate, what was the connection between him and van Draker? What were the circumstances of Robey's death? Did he have an open casket funeral?

Naomi hadn't known whether Robey was involved in a white supremacist movement, though she described him as an outstanding athlete from a wealthy Boer family who had never been shy about his racism.

After driving through the storied Constantia Wine Valley, they passed alongside the University of Cape Town and the outer suburbs before entering the city proper. Viktor caught his breath at the sight of Table Mountain looming over the city, fog roiling like dry ice atop the colossal mesa.

It brought back a rush of memories from his youth. His father in a rare jovial mood on their visit, crowing about the modernity of the infrastructure and the perfection of the weather. His mother marveling at the chic European galleries and cafés. Young Viktor enjoying the food stands at Green Market Square, the pastel houses and cobblestone streets of the Bo-Kaap, the beautiful women with their incredible range of skin tones.

The peaks of the Twelve Apostles gazing down on a string of beaches that rivaled any in the world. Exotic flowers dripping off stone walls, the smell of tanned skin and deep ocean, a sky like crushed blueberries. His parents roaring with laughter at Viktor racing out of the water, screaming about how cold it was.

Even then, Viktor was unable to live in the moment like a normal teenager and instead struggled to understand why that week with his parents couldn't last forever and why time was an unalterable thing, who created those mountains and that glorious ocean and why some people lived in gleaming hillside mansions while others pawed through the gutter for food with sores on their feet and eyes like cave mouths.

Exiting the highway and delving into the city snapped the professor back to the present. Robey had worked out of the Central Police Station, just past the Castle of Good Hope. After his driver dropped him at the curb of a monolithic red brick building, Viktor met with Captain Waalkamp to discuss his fallen officer.

The meeting was a waste of time. The captain did not stop checking his phone, and his only comments on Robey were that he was a "good lad" and a "superb officer." He scoffed at Viktor's inquiries into Robey's involvement with extremist groups, though Viktor could tell the questions made him uncomfortable. When asked about Jans van Draker, the captain shook his head and said he had important matters to attend to.

Though it annoyed the captain, Viktor secured permission to talk to the police coroner. That was also a dead end. No irregularities with Robey's body were reported. The coroner had laughed in Viktor's face when asked if he was certain Robey was deceased. Frustrated, Viktor managed to obtain the name of the mortuary that handled Robey's funeral.

That proved more interesting.

After lunching at an upscale steakhouse near the station, Viktor ordered a cappuccino and took out his laptop. He set up a hotspot with his phone and conducted some research during the afternoon lull.

When comparing the date and time of Robey's death to the funeral, he noticed only eighteen hours had passed. A very short time. A *bizarrely* short time, for someone not Muslim or Jewish.

Viktor called the police coroner back, who said he had expedited the autopsy because of a clause in Robey's will that requested a burial within twenty-four hours if possible, at a specific mortuary: Rhodes Funeral Home.

Who designates their own funeral home, Viktor wondered? And why?

He dug deeper. Neither Robey's widow nor Captain Waalkamp claimed to know anything about his will. Through Jacques, Viktor obtained a list of officers killed in the line of duty in Cape Town over the previous five years. He researched where those officers were interred and discovered that two more deceased officers, from two different precincts, had been buried by the Rhodes Funeral home during that time.

Both men. Both white. Both buried within twenty-four hours of death.

Viktor spoke to the mortuary director, a man named Gerard Cronje, on the phone. Though he claimed no knowledge of irregularities, Viktor heard a hitch in his voice when asked about Robey and the other two officers with similar clauses in their wills.

Viktor had the strong suspicion that if he paid a nighttime visit to Plumstead Cemetery, where all three men happened to be buried, he would find a trio of empty caskets.

Chilled by the new information, Viktor left a hefty tip and texted his driver. His final stop of the day was the District Six Museum, a civil rights memorial in the heart of the city. Viktor knew he could research certain topics all day, but he would never progress unless he talked to someone with firsthand knowledge of the atrocities committed during Apartheid.

Someone with a reason to keep tabs on Jans van Draker.

Viktor's driver, a Malay man named Yusuf from the Cape Flats, drove him a few blocks over, to a street crowded with tourists, vagrants, and hipsters. Just across the street, an eerily vacant ghost town sprawled to the foot of Table Mountain. Yusuf turned left on Buitenkamp Street and pulled alongside the palm-lined entrance to the District Six Museum. "You must think I'm rather lazy," Viktor said, as Yusuf opened his door.

The driver grinned. "That's why you have me, boss."

Once a vibrant cultural hub, a middle-class stew of ethnicities and religious groups and artists, District Six had been a living testament to the peaceful co-existence of the races. Feeling threatened, the Apartheid government declared the district a whites-only zone and razed the entire neighborhood. Generations of homes and community ties were destroyed. No compensation was given, and the residents were forced into townships.

The government's plans for a new, white neighborhood never came to fruition. District Six became a scar on the face of the city, and the museum became a powerful symbol for addressing the terrible legacies of Apartheid. The stripping of both land and humanity.

As instructed when he had called, Viktor walked past the floor-size map of the district and a wall of photos, into a tiny office at the rear of the first floor. He greeted an elderly lady with a wrinkled brown face peering out of a white chador.

Fatima Benting. One of the museum's directors.

Viktor decided to be direct. The virus was spreading, van Draker knew he was being watched, and Viktor did not have time for subtlety.

"I can't disclose details," he said, "but I'm helping the authorities investigate the circumstances surrounding the gargoyle virus. I'm not here to accuse or malign anyone," he leaned forward as Fatima's eyes widened, "but I'm gathering information on Jans van Draker."

Her pleasant expression faded.

"I realize this is a strange visit," Viktor continued, "and I don't expect anything. But I know how, over the years, certain voices are . . . silenced . . . by the dominant regime. I was wondering if you had any stories to tell."

The older woman's expression grew troubled. She didn't speak for a moment, and when Viktor gently prodded her, she drew her arms deeper into the chador. "For your own protection," she said finally, "you shouldn't talk about what I am about to tell you."

Viktor waffled. "If it's something I might be able to use—"

"It's not."

"I see."

"I'm sorry to be rude, but any actual evidence of these matters is . . . you'll see."

"Shouldn't the local authorities make that decision?"

She gave him a sad smile. "They already have. After the boy's death, and just last week. When I saw the news."

"Boy—you mean Akhona?"

"No."

Viktor sat back. "You said last week—who did you contact? About what?"

"I called the police and the department of health. In the past, neither cared, and in the present, both said too much time had passed."

Viktor was getting confused. "Why don't you tell me what happened?"

She rose to close the door, returned to her seat, and took a moment to compose herself, as if struggling with the past. "In 1993, during the last gasp of Apartheid, I was a social worker in Soweto."

Viktor remembered van Draker's nickname. *The Surgeon of Soweto.*

"I was assigned a boy of fifteen who had stumbled into a shelter. A Basotho boy from a farm in Lesotho who came to Jo'burg looking for work. He contracted syphilis, visited a clinic for medicine, and the government took him off the street, under the auspices of medical care. When the boy got to us, he was . . . damaged." Her eyes tightened. "Tortured."

"I hate to ask," Viktor said, "but can you describe what was done?"

She hesitated, her eyes roving to a colorful batik on the wall depicting a lion sleeping in the long grass just outside a village.

"It might help," he said, "if the symptoms align. Please . . . if you can."

She shivered into the chador. "When he came in, the boy's skin was mottled, much of it pink and raw. As if the pigment had been stripped. There were injection marks all over, and his eyes were in a permanent state of dilation. The fingertips on his left hand had been surgically removed. He was sterilized—"

"Do you mean," Viktor began, but cut off his question when Fatima turned a haunted gaze on him.

"He had incision marks near almost every organ," she continued, "including on top of his head."

"Dear God. I assume he was reported to the authorities?"

Fatima's grim look chilled him. "The boy also had a flu when he arrived, which grew worse by the day. The hospitals turned us away. A doctor in the township came by but couldn't help. The boy grew mentally unstable and couldn't remember who or where he was. He died in three days."

Viktor sucked in a breath at the similarities to the gargoyle virus. "Did he say why he was released from the government hospital? Or did he escape?"

She nodded as if she had anticipated the question. "Someone helped him leave. As you can imagine, the boy was afraid to go to the authorities and report what had happened, for fear of being sent back. Just before he died, I managed to get him to describe the doctor who helped him flee the facility. He used a false name and wore a surgical mask, but the boy described the birthmark on his forehead."

"Van Draker," Viktor said, "releasing him into the world. Good God."

She leveled a final stare at him. "Just before he set the boy free, Jans gave him a last injection. A medicine, he told the boy, that would make him all better."

As he walked out of the museum, the beauty of the city felt soiled to Viktor, a piece of expensive jewelry covering an open sore.

The first thing he did was call Captain Waalkamp and ask about Fatima's story. "I've heard it," the captain said, with a dismissive tone. "We can hardly drag someone to the station because a deceased witness may or may not have described someone almost twenty-five years ago. In connection with something about which there is no proof."

"There's enough to question van Draker. At the very least."

"I disagree. And so did the State's attorney."

Viktor hung up on him. The captain might be right, but Viktor vowed to use the information. Involve the press if he had to. The problem, he knew, was the timetable. The progression of the virus was outstripping the investigation, and by the time Viktor got anyone to listen, he feared the damage would be done.

Maybe it already had been.

"Where to, boss?" Yusuf asked, when Viktor stepped into the car.

"Bonniecombe."

"Yessir."

As Viktor loosened his tie and stared out the window, a dark blue SUV pulled into traffic from one of the affluent neighborhoods at the base of Table Mountain. Viktor watched the SUV speed through a few traffic lights. It seemed to be pacing them.

"Yusuf, do you see that late model Fortuner behind us? A street and a half back?"

"I've had my eye on it, boss. Looks like poote to me."

"What?"

"Poote. Police."

Viktor grimaced. If the South African police wanted to talk to him about something, they would phone. His guess was Captain Waalkamp or the mortuary owner was connected to van Draker. "How are your driving skills?"

Yusuf eyed the rearview and grinned. "I used to race now and again. Before I got this job."

"You mean Motorsport? Formula One?"

Yusuf chortled. "Who you think I am, boss? A chizboy? I drag raced my auntie's Fiesta in the Flats, on the Klipfontein."

"How do you rate our prospects? Should the need arise?"

"Maybe I can lose them downtown, but they'll just call it in and send more poote. Not enough routes out of the city."

Viktor debated his options. The road back to Bonniecombe was a long one, with lots of empty highway. After debating trying another police station, he realized he had no idea how far van Draker's connections extended. "Yusuf?"

"Yeah, boss?"

"Take me to the U.S. Consulate General."

Viktor saw Yusuf's hand tighten on the wheel. "Serious, eh?"

"Maybe."

"I thought you were Czech."

"We only have the embassy in Pretoria. If we reach the Americans, our pursuers will back off. I'll decide what to do from there."

"*Jawelnofine*. Do you know where it is?"

"No."

Yusuf punched the destination into the GPS as he drove, his eyes slipping back and forth to the rearview. "Bad news, boss. It's in Constantia. In this traffic, an hour on the M3. We'll have to try to exit off the N2."

It was five o'clock, and rush hour was in full swing. Viktor swore. Why couldn't the Americans have kept a consulate in the city?

The entrance to the N2 appeared, and Viktor supposed they didn't have much choice. "Let's see how far they're willing to go. The N2, please."

Yusuf waited until the last moment, then swerved onto the multi-lane highway. At least the road to Constantia would be well-populated, compared to the wide open highways of the Western Cape.

Viktor turned and saw the SUV speed up to follow them. To make matters worse, as they approached the N2-M3 junction, Viktor saw that the M3, the road to Constantia, resembled a parking lot.

"A suggestion, boss?"

"Of course."

"A few exits up, the scenery, ya, not so good. I know those roads. If I can get to the Flats, I'll call my people, and we be fine."

Viktor wasn't sure what that meant, but they were running out of options. The SUV had drawn to within two car lengths. "Let's try your way."

As soon as the words left his mouth, Yusuf swerved into the N2 lane. The Fortuner followed. A few minutes down the road, the traffic slowed and then ground to a halt. Yusuf lurched the wheel to the right, onto the median. He blew past the traffic and sped towards an exit looming ahead.

The SUV did the same.

"Whatever I'm paying you," Viktor said, "consider it tripled."

"Ya, boss. Consider it done."

As they neared the exit, Viktor saw that Yusuf had spoken the truth. Some time back, the environs on either side of the interstate had begun a gradual change for the worse, but up ahead, the light industry and declining homes were replaced by the densely clustered shacks of a township.

"You afraid of the Flats?" Yusuf asked, as if in challenge.

"Should I be?"

He chuckled. "Ya, you should. But not with me."

The V8 engine roared as it left the N2 and accelerated into the open lane. Viktor gripped the door handle as the car whipped to the right, onto a potholed road as slender as an alley. Wooden huts and lean-tos with tarpaper roofs loomed on either side, the sky crisscrossed by low hanging wires. The SUV followed.

There was plenty of traffic, but Yusuf swerved through it like a pro. They delved deeper and deeper into the slum, the fancy sedan drawing attention from passersby. Yusuf held his phone as they drove, speaking in a rapid dialect that sounded to Viktor like a blend of Malay and Afrikaans slang.

The road turned to dirt. Yusuf dropped the phone and fishtailed to the right, onto a byway so constricted Viktor worried they would swipe the abutting shacks. Pedestrians scurried off the road, some cursing or shaking pistols at the car. One even fired into the air. Viktor looked back. The SUV had disappeared.

"Did we lose them?" Viktor asked.

"Still coming," Yusuf said. "You see that market?"

Up ahead, the road spilled into a crowded square containing a bevy of open-air stalls and a sea of black faces.

"When I tell you," Yusuf said, "get out. You'll see a chicken shack on the left. Go inside. People will help you. This is just in case."

"In case of what?" Viktor said, not liking the idea of leaving the car.

"In case I can't lose them."

The Fortuner appeared in the rear view just as Yusuf entered the congested square. He turned left and the SUV disappeared from view. "Go, boss!"

Wondering if he was doing the right thing, Viktor scooted to the left side of the car and threw the door open. The smell of diesel and frying offal hit him as soon as he left the car.

He drew plenty of stares, but the square was so crowded with cars and people that his appearance didn't cause as much commotion as he thought it would. A nest of alleyways led off from the square, and he saw the chicken shack right in front of him, a shed-like structure made of graying wooden slats and a rusty iron roof. A middle-aged black man with a potbelly tended an iron grill laid atop a wheelbarrow full of coals. A cardboard menu was nailed to the wall of the shack.

The cook met Viktor's eyes and jerked his thumb towards a carpet hanging from the doorway.

Yusuf had already sped off. Wondering how he had gotten in this situation, unsure whether he could trust these men but having little choice, Viktor swept aside the carpet. Just before he slipped inside, he caught a glimpse of the SUV crawling into the square. If they were looking his way, they would have seen him, too.

A man was breading chicken on a folding table, shooing away flies, head bobbing to a reggae tune. He jerked his thumb towards another doorway, and Viktor stumbled deeper into the shack, into a claustrophobic storage room filled with bags of flour.

As Viktor tensed in the middle of the room, wondering if his pursuers were about to burst through the door, his cell rang. He quickly silenced the ringer but saw that it was Naomi. He hesitated before answering the call in a hushed voice.

"Viktor? Where are you?"

"In a chicken shack."

"What?"

"We can talk later," he said.

"Are you all right?"

Viktor slumped against a pile of dusty flour bags. "I hope so. What do you need, Naomi?"

"Are you ready for a date?"

"A date?"

"Ten o'clock tonight, at a romantic house on a hill."

The absurdity of the situation caused Viktor to chuckle as he strained to hear sounds of pursuit above the reggae and the street noise coming from the square. A bead of nervous sweat trickled down his neck, and he loosened his tie. "I wouldn't miss it," he said, and hoped he could keep his promise.

"Great. Oh, and did you know I like men in uniform?"

32

As the snowmobile neared the glacier and failed to slow down, Charlie feared they would slam into the ice wall. Her jaw dropped when a portion of the ice levered upwards, like a giant garage door, and the line of snowmobiles sped into a cavernous chamber lit by fluorescent lights.

That was the last thing she saw before one of the guards ordered her off the snowmobile and blindfolded her. She yelled at them to tell her what was going on, but no one paid any attention.

The air was warmer than outside but still cold. It smelled like a kerosene heater. Charlie heard voices, both men and women, speaking in that strange language. She heard a few other accents, and there was even some English, discussing electrical work that needed to be done.

They hustled her forward until all she could hear was the sound of her guards' feet slapping on concrete.

"Hey!" she shouted. "Where are we?"

Someone ripped off the blindfold and gave her a shove into a small cubic chamber. The door slammed behind her.

Solid ice, streaked with blue whorls, comprised an entire wall. The rest was finished concrete. A strip of lights along the ceiling provided illumination. Charlie stood over a hole in the floor near the back wall and swallowed. The small cavity disappeared into darkness and smelled of human waste.

"Hey!" she shouted again.

Over and over and over.

Charlie was cold.

Not in-danger-of-dying cold, because she knew what that felt like, but a chill that seeped into her bones and stroked them with icy fingers.

Still, she had been here before. She could take the cold. And her captors had fed her. Decent food, even. Three times a day, pushed through a one-way section of the door.

What surprised her was that nothing had changed. No one came for her or made her do anything. No one tried to rape her.

Why were they keeping Charlie by herself? It made her nervous. Were there other children around, heads drooping and feet shuffling, put to work in some illicit mine beneath the earth?

Was this where sneakers were made?

Don't panic, she told herself. *Don't panic don't panic don't panic. See what they want and survive.*

But with each passing minute, her own advice was becoming harder to follow.

There was a lone window near the top of the door. It must be bulletproof, because Charlie couldn't crack it. Nor could she fit through. She tried to chip through the ice wall with her food tray but that was like trying to, well, cut through a glacier with a piece of plastic.

On the morning of the third or maybe the fourth day—she slept for a few hours at a time and had lost count—the door opened.

Expecting the weasel-faced man who brought her breakfast, she was stunned to see the big Viking from Atlanta carrying her tray. He set it down by the door, told her it was pancakes and orange juice, and introduced himself as Dag.

Charlie was sitting with her back against a wall. Dag squatted on his heels, a foot away from her. "Do you know why you're here?" he asked.

She glared at him.

"You have a friend, and we need a favor from him. A very important favor."

Charlie couldn't imagine who he was talking about. The only friends she had were homeless, and calling them *friends* was a stretch. "What? Who?"

"Dominic Grey."

Charlie froze. *Teach?*

It took her a moment, but then she understood. Grey must be working on a case that involved these men. She couldn't imagine what that could be, but he must have crossed someone important to go to all this trouble.

Someone real bad.

Dag clasped his hands on his knees. "Your friend, he is a very tough man."

"Damn right."

"But every man has a weakness. Do you know what Dominic's is?"

Charlie scoffed. "Teach ain't got no weakness. Well, maybe his bike. And sushi. And Reese's cups." She shook her head. "But not with fighting."

"What if I told you one of our men bested him just the other night, in a fair fight? One on one."

"With a rocket launcher?"

"Hand to hand. No tricks."

Charlie shook her head. "No way."

Dag's confident smile chilled her.

"What do you want?" Charlie muttered, her eyes lowering.

Dag took out a cell phone and pointed the screen at her. "Your friend's weakness, dear child, is you."

Charlie stared at the phone. "What're you making him do?"

"Don't worry about that. If you both do as I say—and Dominic has assured me he will—then you won't have anything to worry about."

"Don't tell me what to worry about."

Dag gave a faint smile. "I will record, and you will tell Dominic that you are fine. As long as he does what we want."

Charlie put her head in her hands and tried to buy herself time to think. She finally looked up and gave a slow, reluctant nod.

"Good," Dag said.

He counted to three and started the video. After stating the date and rattling off a number he said was the Dow Jones at the closing bell, whatever that meant, he introduced Charlie and told her to speak.

"Hi, Teach," she said, wanting so bad for Grey's familiar face and steady presence to be on the screen looking back at her, calming her down and telling her what to do.

But he wasn't. Charlie stepped closer, took a deep breath, and shouted, "Don't do it! Whatever they want, don't do it!"

Dag backhanded her. The blow was so hard and fast it rattled her head against the wall. Stunned, Charlie huddled on the floor with her face in her hands. Blood ran down the back of her neck.

When she spread her fingers and looked up, she saw Dag standing above her, expressionless, holding the phone out.

"Shall we try again?" He took a folding knife out of a pocket of his flak vest and flicked it open. "I assure you, we will get it right before I leave."

33

Keeping a safe distance, Grey followed the man with the topknot down a gently sloping street with pastel-colored houses. Shiny red lampposts arced over the road like candy canes. Rekyjavik felt like a ski village at night, soft and cozy.

A gentle rain began to patter on the bricks. The man turned right. Grey rounded the same corner and caught a glimpse of Hallgrímskirkja. The giant church looked misshapen, glowing like a stretched demonic face in the darkness.

The rain picked up. Good. People paid less attention in the rain. Halfway down the block, the man stopped in front of a boxy townhome with a pitched roof. A normal home on a normal street.

Which made it all the more unnerving.

Grey kept walking as his quarry unlocked the door, entered the house, and flicked on a light. After strolling the neighborhood at random for half an hour, Grey circled back. The light was still on. Just past the house, a footpath led to a public park squeezed between two properties. Grey slipped down the path.

The park was tiny, a courtyard with swings. After checking it for vagrants, Grey called Jax and updated him, then huddled in the rain by the swing set, popping his head around the corner every fifteen minutes to see if the light had switched off.

Freezing and wet, Grey knew breaking into the house was a risky proposition. He wasn't worried about getting caught. There wasn't a hint of traffic, and the entire street looked asleep. He worried about a confrontation with the homeowner.

Even if he killed the man or faked a robbery, Dag would suspect Grey's involvement. He couldn't afford to leave a trace.

Ten minutes later, the light switched off. Forty-five minutes after that, giving his quarry plenty of time to fall asleep, Grey approached the house.

Lock pick in hand, he pressed close to the door, giving the appearance of someone fumbling with a lock. One of Grey's areas of expertise was breaking and entering. He always carried a set of slender lock picks, and he solved the simple deadbolt in less than a minute. Holding his breath, he eased the door open and waited in a tiny foyer to let his eyes adjust to the darkness. In front of him, the man's coat was hanging from a peg. Grey checked it for a wallet.

The foyer spilled into a modest living room. Television, futon sofa, coffee table, bookshelf. A pair of low-slung chairs and a bay window with drawn curtains. On the bottom shelf of the coffee table, Grey found a chess set. Interesting. A connection to Dag?

A counter with high-backed stools separated the room from a galley kitchen. The hallway alongside the kitchen ended at a closed door. It had to be the master bedroom. He searched the living room and found a pile of magazines with a swastika on the front. After checking the kitchen and coming up empty, he let out a silent breath.

Time to make a decision. Leave empty-handed, or try the bedroom.

He knew what he had to do. After pulling on a ski mask he found in a closet by the front door, Grey crept to the end of the hallway and twisted the door as quietly as he could.

It opened without a sound. Heart fluttering, Grey took a step inside and saw the man with the topknot sleeping on his stomach on a platform bed. The back of his T-shirt depicted a green assault rifle above an inscription in Icelandic.

Grey spied a wallet, a set of keys, a smartphone, and a beer bottle on the bedside table. A desk with a laptop abutted the far wall. Above the headboard, a vintage Nazi recruitment poster hung in a glass frame.

He resisted the urge to smother the man in his sleep. After deciding that turning on the computer was too risky, he crept, step by agonizing step, to the bedside table. Halfway there, the man rolled over. Grey caught his breath. The man stirred and Grey raised his hands, ready to put him back to sleep. With a snort and a few inchoate mutters, the man rolled back over.

Surprisingly, the phone was not password protected. Lazy. He scrolled through the list of names but saw no sign of Dag. That was no surprise. If he gave out his number, it was likely a burner he made his people memorize. Instead of taking out the SIM card, which was too obvious, he knelt beside the bed and took a photo with his own phone of the list of recent calls.

A flip through the wallet revealed that the man's name was Emil Tomasson. Grey allowed himself one concession and stole a VISA card. It was easy to lose or misplace a credit card, and he thought it worth the risk. He could trace the recent transactions, then lose the card at a convenience store.

Enough. He was pushing his luck. As he turned to leave, he heard the sound of a lock turning.

Grey swore silently. It was so late he hadn't considered that Emil might not live alone. Footsteps in the foyer. Grey swiveled his head. No place to hide. Right before he resigned himself to a fight, he darted inside the master bathroom and slipped behind the shower curtain. He hated to put himself in such a vulnerable position, but he would do anything to avoid alerting Dag.

Grey heard the rustle of clothes falling away, and he had to listen to a swift, loud bout of late-night sex. What kind of a girlfriend didn't leave clothes or toiletries lying around? Must be a recent hookup. Afterwards, the couple returned to the bathroom, one at a time, forcing Grey to live in fear of a drawn shower curtain.

Half an hour later, hearing nothing but the sound of soft snoring, Grey crept out of the bathroom. After peering around the wall, he padded down the hallway, replaced the ski mask, and disappeared into the night.

Grey woke in a pension Jax had procured just off Snorrabraut Street, a short walk from Hallgrímskirkja. The two-bedroom unit had a small kitchen and a street-side exit that allowed them to avoid contact with other guests.

After pouring a cup of coffee, Grey sat across from the mercenary at the breakfast nook. A combination of rain and fog blurred the cityscape outside the window.

"Any word?" Grey asked.

"Yep."

Grey stopped reaching for the creamer. As soon as he returned to the pension, he had wakened Jax and asked him to send Emil's information to the Sensei.

Grey put his palms on the table. "Why didn't you tell me?"

"Chill. It came in five minutes ago."

"Five minutes is five minutes."

Jax bobbed a hand. "I was going to bring you coffee in bed. You beat me to it."

"And? What'd the Sensei say?"

"I'm curious: why do you think they're breaking protocol to help you? I've never had an email returned."

Not for the first time, Grey wondered about the origins of the mysterious young woman who had helped him in New York. What had made her who she was.

Judging by her appearance and her interest in Charlie's disappearance, he thought he had a clue.

"I've a feeling it's a private agenda," Grey said. As Jax mulled over the response, Grey snapped his fingers at him. "Emil?"

Jax took a sip of coffee. "He's in the business, all right. His recent call list was a who's who of high-ranking members of neo-Nazi orgs. Most of them in Iceland, a few in Europe and the States. Sensei sent us names and photos."

"Emil's helping them recruit." Grey leaned forward. "What about Dag? Do we have a number?"

Jax shook his head.

"Damn. I was hoping . . ." Grey cut off and looked away. "What about the congressman's son?"

"Nope."

"The credit card? Any suspicious transactions?"

"Define suspicious. Ammo, pharmaceuticals, call girls? Plenty of that."

"You know what I mean."

Jax pulled up an image on his phone and slid it over to Grey. It depicted a group of young, attractive patrons in fur-lined coats holding drinks and smiling as they conversed around, bizarrely, a bar made of solid ice.

Grey frowned. "What's this?"

"What's it look like?"

"A bar made out of ice."

Jax clicked his tongue. "Give this man a prize. This fine establishment is where our guy goes whenever he leaves Rekyjavik. Not counting international flights."

"Where is it?"

"It's got a really clever name: Ice Bar. It's near a town called Vik, about two and a half hours away. A village, I should say. Home to a whopping three hundred people."

"So?" Grey said. "His parents probably live there."

Jax leaned back and rapped a knuckle on the table. "That's the thing. Whenever Emil goes to Vik, he spends money in the Ice Bar for a night or two, leaves a huge tip, then disappears for a week at a time. Sometimes longer."

"What do you mean he disappears?"

"According to the records, Emil's one of those people who lives off his credit card. Uses it everyday, for everything from house bills to hookers to a bottle of water. But once he goes to Vik? He hits up the Ice Bar, puts gas in his car the next day, and doesn't use his credit card again until he returns to Rekyjavik."

"So where's he go?"

Jax spread his palms. "That's the million-dollar question."

Grey stared at the photo of the Ice Bar, thinking about Dag's last words. *Trust me when I say that you will never find her on your own.*

Dag might be a white supremacist, kidnapper, and mass murderer, but he did not strike Grey as a braggart.

Iceland was remote, but Rekyjavik was still a capital city, a prime tourist destination. A town of three hundred people in the middle of nowhere, however, combined with a mysterious credit card trail . . . .

Grey handed the phone back to Jax. "Let's go find the million-dollar answer."

34

Smoke poured out of the van Draker mansion, swirling within the beams of high-powered floodlights to create a cottony veil around the property. Her siren blaring, another patrol car and a fire truck on her tail, Sergeant Linde careened up the long driveway and parked with a wheel halfway on the curb.

She left her car and strode over to meet Jans van Draker, who was standing with Pieter, his guard, at the end of the flagstone walkway leading to his home.

Jans was fuming. Age-spotted white ankles poked out of the house slippers he had donned beneath a full-length cashmere coat. "What is the meaning of this?"

Naomi summoned her most convincing display of innocence. "What do you mean?"

"I didn't request assistance."

"Why not? It appears your house is on fire."

Van Draker's face darkened. "Vagrants from the township must have thrown smoke bombs through the windows. There's no fire."

"I'm afraid we'll have to be the judge of that," she said, as a quartet of firemen in helmets and full protective gear raced towards the manor. Naomi prayed van Draker wouldn't turn and notice that one of the firemen, even while hunched, was significantly taller than the rest. "Protocol demands that we investigate."

"You'll do no such thing. This is private property!"

"Our job is to provide for public safety. A fire could spread."

Mouth agape, his eyes turning suspicious, van Draker pointed a finger at her. "I have no central alarm system. Who told you about this?"

"We received an emergency call."

"From who?"

"An anonymous neighbor. Two, in fact. It's hardly unusual to call in a sky full of smoke."

"It's dark. I doubt anyone off the property would even notice."

Jans turned and stalked back towards his house. The firemen were clearly in view, spreading out as they approached the property. In desperation, Naomi ran up and grabbed Jans's arm.

"Doctor van Draker! I can't let you go inside." He turned and looked down as if a leper had grabbed him. She withdrew her hand. "It's for your own good," she said. "I'd be derelict in my duties otherwise."

He snarled. "You're keeping me from my own house?"

Naomi reminded herself who the police officer was. She straightened her shoulders and said, "As soon as we're given clearance, you can return inside. It shouldn't take long."

He looked at her in disbelief. "After the stunt you pulled the other day, I question the longevity of your employment. I'm calling your superior."

He took out his phone. Naomi thought quickly. She had told Viktor he would have thirty minutes to search the house, and the Captain only lived a mile away.

"At two a.m.?" she said. "I'd rather not disturb him."

He punched in a number.

Unable to think of anything else to say, Naomi started walking towards the house. She saw with a sigh of relief that the firemen had disappeared inside.

"Where are you going?" Jans shouted.

"To search the property. Those responsible might have left evidence. Or still be around."

Van Draker strode to catch up with her, the phone gripped in his hand. "You'll be going nowhere on these grounds by yourself."

Naomi's heart sank as he raised the phone to his ear. She had bought herself all of thirty seconds.

"And I've woken the captain before," he added.

The night before, Yusuf's men had proven trustworthy, no one had burst into the chicken shack, and the Malay driver had circled back later to collect the professor and bring him back to Bonniecombe. Some romantic date, Viktor thought as he slipped through the rear door of the van Draker manor, feeling awkward in the fireman's gear. At least the bar for the second date, if it ever occurred, would be exceedingly low.

He turned his head, relieved no one had followed. Nor had an alarm sounded. He was in the clear, at least for thirty minutes.

Unless, he thought, someone was waiting inside. The dense smoke limited Viktor's vision to a few feet in front of his face. With every step he took, he expected Robey or Kristof to appear right in front of him.

He forced himself not to think about that. Thanks to Thato's plan to launch homemade smoke grenades through van Draker's windows and onto his lawn, and insert Viktor into the fire department's deploying team—Thato's husband Garika was the chief of the local branch—this might be their one shot to penetrate the manor.

As someone who had been around wealthy residences his entire life, whose family castle itself possessed hidden rooms and passages, Viktor would bet good money that van Draker's manor harbored secrets. The question was whether he could find them in time.

The first place he tried was the library, remembering how Kristof's eyes had lingered on one shelf in particular. After long minutes of searching behind the books and paintings, Viktor found no evidence of a secret door.

He hurried to the second floor. There was a lot of house to cover.

Contrary to the movies, in his experience the bedrooms concealed the majority of hidden passages. Surreptitious access to a mistress.

As before, the bedrooms looked occupied. One even contained a suitcase and clothes hanging in the closet. According to Naomi, who often staked the place out, van Draker rarely had guests.

So how did his visitors arrive? Where did they park their cars?

Either the bedrooms possessed no secrets, or Viktor didn't know where to look. After swiping a set of keys from a drawer in the master bedroom, he checked his watch. This was taking too long. He picked up the pace, striding down the hallway to the billiards room. After eyeing the taxidermy, Viktor approached the stuffed gerenuk head. The deformed specimen was just the sort of thing van Draker would use, and Viktor would not be surprised if the arrogant doctor had mentioned it during their visit just to be perverse.

With an intake of breath, Viktor reached up to gently pull on the antelope's fused horns.

Nothing. Viktor pushed and tugged on different parts of the stuffed head until convinced it was the wrong choice. He quickly tried the rest of the taxidermy and checked behind the gruesome photos of the concentration camps.

Still nothing.

Frustrated, he raced through the first story, running his hands along the bottoms of the balustrades, behind the mirrors and knick-knacks, over the seams of every shortened corridor and irregular wall. He moved aside rugs and portraits and coats of arms, but still came up empty.

Ten minutes to go.

Growing desperate, knowing he might simply have missed a hidden trigger, Viktor entered the dining room. He peeked outside the window and saw another police car pull up, and a burly white-haired man step out. The captain.

Van Draker walked up to the man while Naomi stood by her car, alone.

That didn't look good.

Fearing the dining room was too close to the front door for concealed passages, Viktor gently pulled on the chandelier and searched behind the paintings. He checked the cabinets, found nothing except fine china, then walked over to stand by the creepy bear-hunting outfit. The inch-long spikes covered the entire leather suit except for openings in the eyes and mouth.

Viktor stepped forward and peered inside the orifices. Too dark to see. He slipped his finger into the mouth slit, felt nothing, and then tried the eyes.

Deep inside the mannequin's left orb, Viktor felt the smooth contour of a button. A jolt of adrenaline shot through him as he applied pressure and felt the button depress. A built-in cabinet beside the mannequin hinged open, revealing a closet-size alcove. Viktor peered inside and saw a set of stone steps winding down into darkness.

Feeling eyes on his back, he whipped around and saw Garika. The mask obscured the fire chief's face, but Naomi had given Garika and Thato the highest vote of confidence. She added that they both hated van Draker.

Outside, the smoke had mostly cleared. Van Draker, Pieter, and the police captain were approaching the manor. They would see him within seconds. With a final glance at Naomi, who couldn't see him watching, Viktor stripped off his fireman's suit, handed it to Garika, and stepped into the alcove.

Naomi was in despair. The smoke had cleared and the captain knew all of the local firemen, none of whom were an inch over six feet.

The captain offered to scour the house, but van Draker scoffed away the request, repeating that it was "a couple of blicks" from the township. After his comment, the two men chuckled in a condescending way that Naomi hated.

As the captain fawned over van Draker, three of the firemen strode onto the lawn. None were Viktor. Thato's husband removed his helmet, gave a thumbs-up to the captain as he handed over a handful of plastic coke bottles used for the smoke bombs, then returned to his truck with his men.

Naomi hurried over to pull Garika aside. "Where's the professor?"

"He found a secret passage."

Naomi caught her breath. "And?"

"And he went down it." Garika patted his backpack. "He gave me his gear, so it won't come back on us. Good man."

"Sergeant Linde!"

Elated at Viktor's find but worried for his safety, Naomi turned as the captain barked her name. Had someone noticed only three firemen had returned?

The captain was waving her over as if she were the family dog. Shoulders back, she walked over to him, and the captain jabbed a finger at her. "Don't you *ever* keep Mr. van Draker from his own house again."

"It was full of smoke. I was following protocol."

The captain snarled. "You don't get it, do you? I want you back in the station, *tonight*, filing a report. Tomorrow, you'll go to the township and find out who did this. And if you harass van Draker again, I'll suspend you."

Naomi's eyes flicked to the manor. *What was Viktor thinking, going off alone?*

Left with no choice, she gave a curt nod to the captain, breathed a sigh of relief that no one seemed to have noticed the missing fireman, and returned to her cruiser.

Inside the alcove, Viktor found a pair of switches that illuminated the staircase and caused the cabinet to swing shut. Wary but excited, he descended and found a narrow, rough-hewn stone passage at the bottom that looked as if it had stood for centuries.

The rocky floor of the passage was uneven. Every twenty feet or so, an oval stone archway reinforced the ceiling. Dim can lights, embedded at ten-foot intervals and casting a faint golden glow, supplied the only evidence of modernity.

Viktor hurried forward, having to duck beneath the archways. The passage smelled chalky. He soon reached an intersection, and then another. He also passed five sets of stairs he assumed led to different parts of the manor. It was a maze of secret corridors.

He guessed the lights were on a timer and, fearing he would get lost before they switched off, he walked as fast as he could, his long stride carrying him swiftly down the passage. In a pinch, he supposed he could use his cell phone for light. He wanted to text Naomi but the thick rock walls blocked the signal.

When he came to a much longer passage, Viktor tensed. Perhaps the entire underground level was innocuous and served as an emergency escape route to the forest, not uncommon in Europe for noble families fearing a peasant revolt. In South Africa, he imagined the same logic had applied.

But the passage didn't lead to the forest. It led, he discovered as he crept forward, to a steel door built right into the rock wall. Viktor sucked in a breath. This was why he had come.

He tried the handle. Locked. No surprise. He took out the set of keys he had stolen from van Draker's bedroom. On the second try, starting with the largest key, he was rewarded.

The deadbolt clicked.

Viktor pulled the door open.

And couldn't believe his eyes.

He had come seeking a laboratory or a medical facility, evidence that illicit experiments had been performed by van Draker. What he saw through the steel door went past that, to the edges of science and beyond, into the realm of madness.

The door opened onto an underground chamber the size of a large municipal swimming pool. The chamber had been dug at least thirty feet deep, accessible via a spiral staircase to the left of the door, and an elevator to the right.

An iron catwalk started at Viktor's feet and led to a series of interconnected walkways supported by cables bolted into the ceiling.

Interspersed throughout the chamber were a dozen circular bronze vats, standing on iron mounts and connected by thick cables and even thicker transparent glass pipes, large enough for a man to fit through. Just down the walkway, Viktor heard gurgling noises emanating from one of the vats. He also noticed a giant electronic control panel.

In the middle of the room, suspended by cables attached to the ceiling, was a metallic blue gurney fitted with leg, neck, and arm clasps. A glass tube exited onto the gurney, and thinner cables extended from the gurney to a pyramidal generator on the floor below that throbbed with green light.

Viktor scanned the rest of the floor and saw a host of silver desks and lab equipment, monitors and futuristic computer equipment, all of it connected by cables.

The floor and walls were made of stained concrete. An antiseptic smell permeated the room. Every so often, one of the cables would pulse, sizzling with an electric charge.

While Viktor absorbed the scene, a naked human form shot through the glass piping and into one of the vats.

Good God. What is van Draker doing here?

Viktor had to know. He started forward and then jerked to a halt, noticing the cameras interspersed throughout the room. Of course the lab had surveillance. He was shocked it was unoccupied, then remembered it was three in the morning.

Viktor knew he was pressing his luck. He needed to take his pictures and leave.

For a moment, he wavered. His entire life had been spent in search of answers to the mysteries of life's questions. Whatever secrets this room held, he sensed they were deep. He wanted to race along the catwalk and stare inside the vats and study the computer equipment below. Drink it all in and absorb the implications.

With a deep, shuddering breath, he realized he didn't have the scientific knowledge or the manpower. He had to take the photos and come back, with law enforcement in tow. Wait for a team of international scientists to crack van Draker's secrets.

Forcing his hand to steady, Viktor took photo after photo, still in shock at what he was seeing. He flinched when another body shot through the piping, then turned to leave just as the clammy hand of van Draker's butler gripped him by the wrist.

35

Jax rented a silver Suzuki Grand Vitara with the same fake ID. He and Grey set out before lunch. According to Jax, the bulk of Iceland's interior, ninety-eight percent or more, was an uninhabited and virtually impassable back country. Beautiful but barren. Iceland's towns and settlements were all within a stone's throw of the coast, connected via a single, eight hundred and thirty mile road called the Ring Road that encircled the island. For half the year, portions of even that road were treacherous or off limits.

"What's back there?" Grey asked. "In the interior?"

"Volcanoes, rift valleys, lava fields, a glacier bigger than Delaware. Some of the best hiking in the world, if you can get to it. Back in the day, the Icelanders used to banish convicted murderers into the interior. No handcuffs, no jail. Just *good luck in there, buddy.*"

Fifteen minutes outside of Rekyjavik, after the rain stopped and the fog lifted, the scenery on the Ring Road blew Grey's mind. To his right, a field of colored lava rocks tumbled towards a phalanx of snowcapped peaks. On the other side, a valley of smoking geysers bubbled away beneath an even more towering mountain range. The scenery changed dramatically with every bend, shifting from pockets of golden farmland to sheets of volcanic gravel, rivulets forking like serpents' tongues down jagged green cliffs, the silver spears of waterfalls arcing off plateaus.

The landscape felt Jurassic to Grey. Raw, immense, untamed. As if any moment, a tyrannosaurus might come bounding down a hillside.

"You ever consider getting some hobbies?" Jax asked.

Grey started. "What?"

"What do you do in your spare time? Besides solving crimes and killing people. Or teaching other people how to kill people."

"I have hobbies," Grey muttered.

Jax lifted his eyebrows. "When's the last time you saw a movie?"

"I love movies."

"That wasn't the question."

Grey looked out the window.

"So?" Jax said.

"I've been a little married to my work, lately."

"Have you? I did some checking around before I accepted your offer. Seems like you haven't done much of anything, since Peru."

Grey's face hardened.

"Listen. I don't mean to be insensitive. But one of the danger signs in my profession—which you're currently involved in, whether you like it or not—is personal involvement. I'm not gonna say a job has never been personal for me, because that would be a lie, but I never put myself in unwarranted danger because of a personal connection. Myself or my colleagues."

Grey looked over at him. "We have different jobs."

Jax chuckled. "There you go again. Listen, I don't care what you think of me, but I don't think you're hearing me. You bought my loyalty, true, but I won't risk my own skin *unnecessarily* for a personal vendetta that will get us both killed. And when I look in your eyes, I don't see the same caution. To be honest, and I usually am, I see someone who's gone over a cliff because of one girl, and who'll do anything in his power to save another. And I do mean anything."

Damn right, Grey wanted to say. *On both counts.*

But he needed Jax's help, and held his tongue. Instead he said, "My mind's in the right place for the job. Trust me."

"Usually when people ask me to trust them," Jax said quietly, as a volcano with snow rimming its mighty cone like gravy came into view, "I don't."

"What do you want from me?"

"Your word that I'll know what I'm getting into."

Grey met his eyes. "I'll do my best."

"Fair enough."

They stopped for fish and chips at a polka-dotted food truck near Skogafoss, a mighty waterfall just off the road that dwarfed the handful of onlookers at the bottom. Grey's arctic char tasted as if it had just been pulled out of the ocean.

After Skogafoss, the road wound around a promontory and descended into

Vik, a charming little fishing village nestled against the shore of a black sand beach. Opposite the ocean, a white church sat dramatically on a hill above town, backed by a line of stark cliffs streaked with ravines.

Jax rented a pair of rooms while Grey stayed out of sight. The tiny size of Vik made Grey nervous. Later in the day, after the Ice Bar opened and Jax headed off to scope out the scene, Grey stayed in the room until he grew hungry and then walked to the most innocuous establishment he could find: a short-order café with a few tables in the back of a gas station.

He huddled in his parka, ordered a hamburger, and stared out the window at the moss-draped cliffs of the promontory, jutting over the beach as the falling sun glowed red behind the clouds.

Grey's cell buzzed. He glanced down at the text from Jax.

–You wont believe this place. Walls, bar, floor made of ice. Tres chic–

–If you say so–

–Place is empty. Just a smoking hot bartender–

–Its offseason–

–My guess is Emil's been making booty calls here. Should I have my martini shaken or stirred?–

–Replaced with a beer–

–Don't wait up. I'll see what I can get out of her–

Grey returned to the hotel and paced deep into the night, on edge for signs of danger, constantly checking his phone.

Sometime after two a.m., he lay on his back in his bed, weighed down by depression, staring at the ceiling.

A scratching sound near the window caused him to lurch out of bed, grab his gun, and ease the front door open. Half-awake, he crept through the bushes, then stood blinking at the branch scraping against the side of the house.

Just before he returned inside, Grey looked up and saw something that took his breath away. A full canopy of stars had emerged and, even more spectacular, vivid whorls of green and pale blue light shimmied and streaked across the sky, spanning the horizon like spotlights from another dimension.

God, it was beautiful. He was so moved that he stood in dumb silence, immune to the cold, staring at the heavens until his hands turned numb.

He didn't get it. He truly didn't get it. How could such beauty coexist with a world so base, so dark and vile, that it had snuffed the life from Nya and produced a man like Dag and left little children to fend for themselves on the streets? It was beyond attributable to the cruelty of nature, beyond anything Grey could fathom. It was perverse.

When a bank of clouds drowned the stars, he returned inside and did his best to get some sleep.

He never heard back from Jax.

The next morning, Grey checked his cell, made coffee, and stepped outside for some air. The backyard had a view of three basalt columns jutting out of the ocean like fingers. His breath frosty, Grey wondered if Jax had been compromised and whether they would come for him next.

His fears proved unfounded. Jax strolled in an hour later, whistling, hair tousled. "I'll say this," he said. "I see why Emil keeps stopping by."

Grey jumped off the sofa. "Find anything?"

"Emil's name is in her phone. No wedding photos or anything, but there are signs of a man in the apartment. Clothes, toothbrush, protein shake."

"What about the Wodan Republic?"

"She's got some skinhead lit, but I don't think she's that into it. Didn't mention it to me. Then again, we were pretty busy."

Grey ran a hand through his hair and left it cupping the back of his neck. He felt like they were on the right trail, but they were running out of time. He debated going back to Rekjyavik, tying Emil up, and forcing him to reveal what he knew about Dag. That was a last resort, and . . . *no*. That could doom Charlie.

Grey had to do better.

"You following the news about the virus?" Jax asked. "It's gone, well, viral."

"Yeah. I know."

Jax looked down and shook his head. "That's not cool."

"What do you care?" Grey said. "You'd probably sell it to the highest bidder."

"No," Jax said, suddenly serious. "Not that. Moving arms for soldiers is one thing, a bioweapon that targets innocent human beings another."

"As if half the warlords you sell to don't target civilians."

Jax's jaw tightened. "I don't work for those types."

"Keep on telling yourself that."

"Are we going to argue all day, or do something about your girl?"

Grey forced himself to calm down and think. Jax was right. Arguing mercenary ethics was a displacement for Grey's frustration.

Hoping for someone important to show up at the Ice Bar might be a red herring. Then again, while Iceland felt right, Rekyjavik felt wrong. Grey thought Dag had flown in, maybe did some business in the capital, then taken Charlie to a hideout in a remote location.

He steepled his fingers against his mouth. "We'll give Emil or his buddies one more night to show. Then we split up. You watch this place, and I'll go have a chat with Emil."

"Works for me."

More waiting. Grey felt as if he were going to crawl out of his skin. Later that day, after Jax returned to the Ice Bar, Grey ventured out for a bite to eat again while the shops were still open.

Not wanting anyone to remember his face, he chose the second most unlikely restaurant he could find: a frilly café with candles in black lace sconces and Bob Dylan playing softly through the speakers. The only patrons were a pair of elderly Dutch tourists who looked like sisters.

As Grey sipped a green tea and waited on his panini, his cell buzzed. Eager to hear good news from Jax, he fumbled to take his phone out, then gripped it so hard the plastic cover crackled.

It wasn't Jax.

Grey had set up his email on the phone, and someone anonymous had sent him an image of Charlie, bound and gagged on a concrete floor, her face bruised and bloody. On her chest, an open laptop displayed the front page of the *New York Times*. With an intake of breath, Grey pulled up the Internet and went to the newspaper's home page again.

Today's headline, as he knew it would be.

A warning to work faster.

Grey's hand started to tremble. He fought the urge to overturn his table and roar at the top of his lungs. A waiter brought his sandwich and hurried away when he saw Grey's face. He stared down at the tray, uninterested in the food.

The door to the café opened, and a blast of cool air snuck in. Out of habit, Grey's eyes lifted to seek out the face of the newcomer, expecting another gray-haired tourist.

Instead he saw Emil, looking right back at Grey.

36

Kristof pulled Viktor into the passage. The sudden appearance of the butler caused the professor's heart to skip a beat. Jerking his arm away with a feeling of superstitious dread the professor thought he had left far in the past, he experienced another bout of fright when he noticed Robey in the underground passage as well, standing with crossed arms ten feet behind Kristof.

"Come," Robey said, in a voice devoid of emotion. He made a half-turn, waiting for Viktor to follow.

Kristof moved past the professor and slammed the laboratory door shut. Though his heart was about to pound out of his chest, Viktor felt relieved no one was going to drag him inside the lab and stuff him in a vat.

"Where's van Draker?" Viktor boomed, with a show of confidence he did not feel.

"I'm afraid I'm not as spry as I used to be," Jans called back, just before he materialized out of the darkness behind Robey. Van Draker's lips curled into a slow smile as he approached. "Perhaps I'll have to replace this leg one day."

Why had Jans ventured down to the sublevel, instead of waiting for Robey to bring Viktor upstairs?

The professor tore his gaze away from the insipid gray flesh of the former police officer's face. "I thought you didn't have a basement," he said to Jans.

"Didn't I tell you? The proper term is dungeon."

Viktor didn't respond, and Jans tucked a hand behind his back. "So you've seen the lab. I confess I don't understand your shock. You do realize the inspiration for Mary Shelley's novel was taken from experiments surrounding the galvanism of corpses in the late seventeen hundreds? That Giovanni Aldini actually caused the eye of a hanged criminal to open days after his death?"

"I'm aware."

"My dear professor, those experiments happened two hundred and fifty years ago. We are *way* past jolting corpses."

"Didn't you read the novel?" Viktor asked. "Why would you want to create an undead thing?"

"Oh, but the Frankenstein monster was very much alive. *Undead* is a semantic affectation. A being either possesses life, or it does not."

Viktor flicked his eyes at Robey. "You call this life?"

Van Draker stiffened. "I challenge you to prove otherwise. By any definition." He reached back to squeeze Robey's shoulder. "We have had many long and enlightening conversations, he and I."

Viktor didn't bother hiding his revulsion. "What happened to Akhona in there? Who are the others?"

Van Draker moved closer, until Viktor could see the manic intelligence burning behind his eyes. The professor heard Kristof move away from the door, and Viktor resisted the urge to whip around.

"We understand so little about the energy that animates us all," van Draker said. "Is electricity the soul? Is the soul electricity? Did you know, professor, that sharks sense fish underwater by their electrical emissions? *They* seem to know more than we do. Yet I am learning, I am learning." He bobbed his head. "And I know, like many before me, that it works."

"That what works?"

Van Draker's grin was slow and sure. "Surely you've guessed by now. Unlike my predecessors over the centuries, who could ignite life but had no way to sustain it, science has caught up with imagination. Think of it as another step in evolution. Our species is finding new ways to survive, to create the very life we have so mysteriously been given."

"How did this lead to the virus? What have you done?"

Van Draker curled a finger. "Come. I asked you to return for tea one day, and I've been a negligent host."

The professor was confused. Jans knew he had seen the laboratory, and the former surgeon had so much as admitted that he was playing with the secrets of life and death.

Yet he was inviting him upstairs for tea?

Viktor knew it wouldn't be that simple. "I'm free to leave, then?"

Van Draker spread his hands. "What power have I to stop you? Captain

Waalkamp has been informed of your trespass, and is waiting outside. Robey will have to take your cell phone—I'm afraid I've never allowed photography on the premises—but what happens after that is between you and the captain. Though I do believe if we hurry, we can sneak in that cup."

Perhaps, Viktor thought, van Draker planned to have Robey waylay him as soon as he turned his back. If so, then it was out of Viktor's control. He was no Dominic Grey.

"Rooibos or black tonight?" Jans asked, as they started walking.

"Black," Viktor said.

An hour later, in the wee hours of the morning, Viktor slumped in his bunk at the city jail. After his cup of tea, with Robey standing guard while van Draker made maddening small talk about the weather and international politics, Captain Waalkamp took Viktor into custody. When the professor requested a phone call, the captain mumbled something about the internet connection and the lateness of the hour, then promised phone access in the morning.

Viktor had no idea what due process amounted to in South Africa, but he didn't like the lack of transparency. Nor did he trust that van Draker would let him see the laboratory and walk away.

Robey had taken Viktor's cell phone away in the dungeon, so the professor hadn't had an opportunity to send Naomi or Grey a text. In the morning, Viktor would force the captain to at least contact Jacques on his behalf. It would be a violation of the Interpol treaty not to. A serious breach of international etiquette.

What were van Draker and Captain Waalkamp planning? An attack on his credibility? Since his phone had been taken and almost certainly deleted of data, Viktor had no other evidence. It would be his word against van Draker's.

Viktor was too agitated to sleep. Not only was he concerned about his predicament, but his mind kept returning to the things he had glimpsed beneath van Draker's manor.

The professor had done some research, and he knew Jans was right. Scientists were experimenting with galvanism and suspended animation and human resuscitation hundreds of years ago. A Harvard doctor had recently developed a procedure that rinsed donated human hearts of their cellular structure, regenerated them with cells grown in a lab, and used electrical pulses to restart the heart. The Chinese had already made a genetically edited super dog. An Italian neurosurgeon was seeking to conduct the first human head transplant by severing the head and spinal cord of a patient with a rare genetic disorder, and fusing it to a fresh human corpse.

As far as Viktor knew, no one had gone as far as van Draker, but God only knew what unethical foreign governments and private corporations had accomplished in past decades.

Even more chilling, his research in the last twenty-four hours had started to piece together the link between van Draker's activities and the effects of the gargoyle virus.

It all went back to the Ahnenerbe.

Historians agreed that the *Institut für Wehrwissenschaftliche Zweckforschung*, the Nazi Institute for Military Scientific Research which carried out extensive and documented human experimentation on concentration camp victims, fell under the aegis of the Ahnenerbe during World War II. As the insanity of the war progressed, so did the goals and deeds of the Ahnenerbe. Prisoners were exposed to poisons, chemicals, and deadly pathogens to develop vaccines. The effects of contagious diseases on different racial groups was studied. Identical twins, including infants, were experimented upon and dissected after death. Limbs were amputated and grafted onto other prisoners, with resuscitation attempts made on the corpses of the failures.

The Ahnenerbe was also interested in testing survival thresholds, in order to develop superhuman soldiers. Not just by selective breeding and culling, but by experimental drugs that inhibited pain receptors and granted extraordinary strength and stamina for short periods. Viktor found numerous articles confirming that Nazi soldiers made extensive use of pharmaceuticals in combat during the latter days of the war. How far those drugs had progressed, no one knew.

It went further. There were claims that American forces had raided a super-secret Nazi facility where the bodies of captured Russian soldiers were found in various stages of dissection and metal-grafting, including bones and ribs enhanced with steel prostheses. Bodies were cryogenically frozen. A rumor persisted that the Nazis had tried to revive the corpses of animals and even humans through mysterious means.

Truth: On April 28, 1945, American officers investigating a munitions factory in east-central Germany found a fake brick wall hidden in a mineshaft. After smashing through the wall, the Americans found a plethora of Nazi regalia and stolen treasure, as well as a quartet of coffins containing the skeletons of two Teutonic military heroes, Frederick the Great and Field Marshall Paul von Hindenburg, as well as von Hindenburg's wife.

The fourth coffin, though empty, bore the name of its intended future occupant.

Adolf Hitler.

How far had the Nazi's research taken them? Viktor wondered. Had it continued to this day, carried out in secret labs by the successors to the Ahnenerbe?

Was van Draker the heir apparent? What does history *not* know about the Nazis?

What does the public not know about the present?

The sound of a key turning in a lock jerked Viktor out of his thoughts. Who could that be, at four a.m.? Was someone bringing in another prisoner? Had Naomi finally heard about the arrest?

The tiny jail was in the basement of the courthouse. A block of holding cells that, come to think of it, hadn't looked very much in use. He had seen no other prisoners on the way in, or even a monitor.

Viktor had attributed the simplicity of the jail to the small size of the town, but shouldn't there be a guard posted? A sound-equipped camera in the hallway?

A door creaked open. Viktor's cell faced a hallway. If memory served, the corridor outside his cell, lit by weak fluorescent light, ran about twenty yards in either direction. He had come in from the left, down a long set of stairs.

Footsteps. Striding down the cement floor.

"Naomi?"

No answer.

The footsteps drew closer. Unnerved, Viktor backed against the rear wall of his cell. "Who's there?"

A man stepped into view, stopping right in front of Viktor's cell. A man with an ashen, rubbery face, dressed in an ankle-length black overcoat and a wide-brimmed safari hat pulled low.

"What do you want?" Viktor said.

In response, Robey took a key out of his pocket and bent to unlock the door.

37

The greatest acting job Grey ever pulled off was pretending not to notice as Emil stared at him. The Icelander's appearance had thrown Grey at first. Emil's topknot was loose and past his shoulders, broadening his face, and he had exchanged his sweater for a collared blue shirt and a sleek calfskin coat. Still, Grey rarely forgot a face, and he could feel the Icelander trying to place him. Ready to spring across the table if needed, Grey dipped his head and took a long sip of tea, shielding his face.

After a few of the longest seconds of Grey's life, Emil stepped to the counter and ordered. The attendant reached into a glass case, cut off a large slice of German chocolate cake, and placed it into a Styrofoam container. Emil made them add whipped cream.

Good god, Grey thought. The man was picking up chocolate cake for his girlfriend.

Not trusting the coincidence, Grey's eyes flicked to the window. A red Toyota Fortuna had pulled to the curb by the front entrance, engine idling. Inside, Grey saw a short blond man with a bodybuilder's chest and runic tattoos creeping out of his jacket, up the front of his neck and onto the backs of his hands.

While Emil paid, Grey texted Jax.

–Get out of there. Emil might be on way. Red Fortuna–

–His girl just invited me to a sauna tonight. With a friend . . .–

–Now–

–10-4. Will watch for his car–

Emil left the café. Buzzing with excitement, Grey finished his meal and hurried back to the rented apartment. He paced back and forth, waiting on word from Jax, wondering if Emil had swung down for the day or if something bigger was afoot.

He didn't have to wait long. Twenty minutes later, Jax sent him a mysterious text to throw everything into the backpacks. Soon after, the mercenary whipped into the parking lot.

"Get in!" he said, when Grey appeared at the door.

Grey grabbed both packs, left the key in the door, and jumped in the car. "What's up?" he asked, as Jax sped out of the driveway. Two quick turns later and they were on the Ring Road.

"Emil went in with a package and left empty-handed. I don't know what was inside—"

"Chocolate cake."

"Huh?"

"He showed up at my café. How'd you think I knew he was coming?"

After a pause, Jax said, "I don't like it." He slipped on a pair of aviators. "I suppose there aren't that many bakeries in town."

"Probably only one that makes German chocolate cake. How much of a lead does he have?"

"Five, ten minutes. He's headed away from Rekyjavik. I wasn't sure whether to stay with him or pick you up. Maybe he's turned off already, maybe he's driving all day."

"Let's find out."

Getting pulled over for speeding was not much of a threat on the Ring Road. Traffic was light, police officers almost nonexistent, and the open terrain provided visibility for miles. Jax floored the gas and took the Suzuki to a hundred and fifty kilometers an hour, slowing only when the road curved. After fifteen minutes and no sign of the Fortuna, Grey grew distressed. If they lost the trail, they might never pick it up again.

After passing a tiny settlement of turf-roofed houses nestled into a patch of farmland, they finally caught sight of a red SUV in the distance. Jax pulled close enough to ensure it was the Fortuna, then backed away and followed. Grey texted the license plate number to Sensei and breathed a sigh of relief, knowing the hard work had just begun. The isolation and sweeping vistas cut both ways. They had to follow Emil without tipping him off to the tail.

Jax proved to be an expert reconnaissance man. He kept a steady distance and used the other vehicles for cover. To allay suspicion, he even passed the Fortuna when it stopped at a roadside market, pulling into a scenic overlook until it drove by.

Grey hadn't thought it possible, but as they followed the Ring Road east along the southern coastline, sometimes paralleling the sea and sometimes veering a bit further inland, the scenery was even more startling than the route from Rekyjavik to Vik.

Silver rivers wound through blasted alluvial floodplains; mounds of silt rose like pyramids on the shores of shallow, mazelike fjords; ochre-streaked summits morphed into a boulder-strewn moonscape tucked between volcanoes. They rounded a bend and saw a sheet of immense ice curling down from unseen heights, the tongue of a monstrous glacier licking down the mountain.

It started to rain. Jax checked his cell when it buzzed. "The car belongs to Gunter Betz, a Norwegian national living in Rekyjavik. Longtime member of Vigrid."

"What's that?"

"The Nordic version of the Aryan Brotherhood. I've run across them before."

The rain stopped, and mist poured in like a fog machine. They drove through a glacial outwash plain with nothing but fierce winds and swaths of swampy black silt that extended for miles, wide rivers of muck creeping towards the ocean. The region was so bleak and lifeless that Grey felt uneasy just driving through it. The area felt dissonant, out of tune with life, cursed by its maker.

Still the Fortuna drove on. The desolation of the glacial plain ended, replaced by a vast bed of lava rocks covered in bright emerald moss. A planet-scape of giant green cauliflower stretching to the horizon.

"I've seen a lot of sights," Jax said. "But this might be the damndest."

Grey murmured his assent in a distracted voice, wondering if Charlie had passed that way.

Two hours on the road, then three. They hugged the coastline as the road wound beneath a series of onyx cliffs bursting with waterfalls. Grey was both excited and troubled by the length of the drive. Either they were getting closer to Charlie, or on a wild goose chase that could sabotage his chances of finding her in time.

What if Emil was on an unrelated mission? Visiting family, or another girlfriend in some remote town?

No. This has to be right.

A sign announced the presence of a glacial lagoon, but it was too dark to see the water. The rain got so bad and the fog so heavy that Grey didn't know how it was possible to drive much further.

And no one did.

Just after the road crossed over the lagoon on a suspension bridge, the Fortuna pulled onto a gravel drive and parked in front of an isolated dwelling. Another of the low, turf-roofed houses they had seen, built to withstand the elements. Behind the house, just visible from the road, a huge barn butted against the base of a hill.

His stomach fluttering, Grey turned to watch Emil and Gunter leave the Fortuna and approach the house.

"You think Charlie's in that barn?" Jax asked grimly.

"I don't know. But I'm going to find out. Drop me up ahead."

"Right now? Why don't we both go?"

"I'm not waiting any longer, and I'd rather you be mobile. Keep your phone ready."

As soon as the house faded from view, Jax pulled over and let Grey out. Grey stuffed his gun in the holster, zipped his waterproof jacket, and pulled the hood low. He moved off the road and stepped into the spongy, sodden vegetation. Hoping he didn't plunge into some hidden bog, he crept towards the house, pausing once he saw shadows moving in the windows.

It was time to watch and wait.

Huddled in his winter gear, Grey squatted with his back against a low mound and became still, part of the damp earth itself, breathing in the sea air and watching until the lights in the house winked out. He gave it another half hour and then circled around to the back of the barn, staying well out of sight.

He noticed a Skoda Octavia parked behind the house. The thought that Charlie might be on the other side of the barn wall caused a wave of nervous excitement to surge through him. *Please let her be alive.*

No windows on the barn. He was going to have to enter through the side door, in full view of the house. Unable to wait any longer, he took a deep breath and slipped along the wall, keeping his back against the barn. The rain had stopped. The house was still.

The door was secured with an enormous padlock. Grey took out his tools and bent over the lock, feeling as if a giant spotlight had illuminated a target on his back. When the lock came loose in his hands, he eased the door open, just enough to slip through.

Darkness. The smell of hay and diesel. Grey yearned to call Charlie's name, but he had to ensure no guards were inside. Ignoring the light switch and waiting until his eyes adjusted, he crept through the barn on cat's feet. He walked to the back of the structure and saw nothing except a Nazi flag and a pair of jeeps fitted with snow tires as tall as Grey's waist.

Disappointment burned through him.

After searching the barn, Grey returned to the road and summoned Jax. When the mercenary picked him up, Grey slumped in his seat and detailed his find. Upon reflection, the barn was much too simple a hiding place. Too unguarded, too near the road. He had let his emotions get the best of him.

Forcing himself to shake it off, Grey warmed his hands and thought about the next step. "We need to get inside that house. Tonight. In case they take those jeeps somewhere."

"You said there were two jeeps?" Jax said.

"That's right."

The mercenary patted his utility belt and gave a thin smile. "I've got a better idea."

Since they had not seen a hotel for miles and didn't want to stray too far from the tracking devices Jax had planted on the Fortuna and the two Superjeeps, they decided to grab a few hours sleep in the parking area of the glacial lagoon. Jax's mouth went slack soon after he reclined the seat, but Grey barely rested, unable to stop thinking about Charlie, jerking awake with every passing car or nighttime sound.

The next morning, as Jax started the engine and cranked the heat, Grey gazed out at a powdery black beach littered with ice crystals. Some were as big as boulders, glittering in the surf like colossal uncut diamonds. To his right, the suspension bridge spanned a natural canal that connected the ocean to a lagoon filled with calving icebergs, flopping seals, and water so blue it made Grey squint.

They didn't have to wait long for the tracking device to activate. Less than half an hour later, Jax's phone made a sharp beep, and he studied the screen. "They're on the move. It's one of the jeeps."

Grey caught his breath. "Just one?"

"Like I said," Jax said, "my guess is whoever owns the house keeps one around for himself."

"Thank God. I assume they're off the Ring Road?"

Jax watched his phone for a few moments. "I can't tell if there's a road or not, but they're going straight north. Into the interior."

Grey met Jax's eyes when he looked up. "We're going in," Grey said. "Before they get too far."

Five minutes later, Grey and Jax left the Vitara beside the Ring Road and walked down the gravel drive to the house where the Toyota Fortuna had stopped. Grey stood to the side of the front door, head lowered and hands in his pockets, as Jax knocked. The road was free of traffic.

A heavyset woman in a bomber jacket, gray hair tied in a bun, opened the door.

"Sorry to bother you," Jax said, "but our car broke down and I was wondering if we could use your phone." He held up his own phone with a sheepish grin. "No signal."

"I do not speak good English," the woman said, in a heavy Icelandic accent.

As she started to close the door, Jax grabbed her by the collar and yanked her outside. Just before Grey elbowed her in the head, dropping her like a stone, the woman managed to cry out. "Jón!"

Grey whipped his gun out and stepped through the door. Jax came in behind him, yanking the unconscious woman inside.

A huge, bare-chested man came bounding down a hallway, waving a black handgun, trying to pull up his pants as he ran. Grey stepped offline and pointed the gun at his head. "Drop it!"

"*Móðir!*" The man shrieked, when he saw the unconscious woman. He pointed the gun at Jax, who lifted the woman as a shield. Grey fired into the wall next to the Icelander, causing him to flinch and raise both hands above his head.

Quivering with rage, the distraught son looked from his mother to Grey with an expression of pure hatred.

"She's fine," Grey said, as he took the man's gun and then pistol-whipped him unconscious.

"What do we do with them?" Jax asked, after they checked the house for more occupants. "As soon as they wake up, they'll sound the alarm."

Grey mulled over the problem. Jax was right. They couldn't let them alert Dag too soon.

"I hate to say it," Jax said, pulling out his gun, "but maybe we should—"

"Put that away," Grey snapped, the harshness in his voice masking how much he wanted to do exactly what the mercenary was suggesting.

"—shoot them in the knee and tie them up."

"Just get the car, and we'll leave them in the trunks. After we get Charlie, we can call it in." He waved a hand towards the door. "Go, man."

As Jax sprinted away, Grey bound the captives with rope he found in the barn, then stuck the woman in the trunk of the Fortuna. When Jax returned, they stuffed the son in the Skoda, just as the Icelander started to stir.

After throwing open the tall front doors to the barn, they donned a pair of white-and-gray snow-camo suits with fur-lined hoods they found hanging by the door. The harder to pick out their faces, the better. Grey took the wheel as Jax checked the progress of the tracking device on his phone.

"How far away are they?" Grey asked.

"Only ten miles. It must be rough terrain."

Using a set of jeep keys he found in the kitchen, Grey cranked the engine. The vehicle rumbled to life. By the barn, a set of rutted tracks circled around the hill behind the house. Grey looked at Jax. "You ready for this?"

The mercenary laid the phone flat on the console, red dot blinking on the GPS tracker. He cracked his knuckles. "Into the breach, my man."

38

As Robey unlocked the jail cell, Viktor thought fast and hard about his options. While the professor was much larger than the other man, and Robey didn't appear to have a weapon, van Draker's henchman was a former soldier. Not only that, he had a hardness behind his eyes, visible despite the blankness in his gaze, that told Viktor he was dealing with a killer.

"You can't hold me like this," Viktor said.

The latch clicked. Robey pushed the door open.

"What do you want?" Viktor said. "Where's Captain Waalkamp?"

Robey took a step inside the cell.

"Hello!" Viktor shouted. "Is anyone out there?"

His words echoed in the empty hall.

Robey's eyes locked onto Viktor's. The professor's hand curled around the bed sheet and yanked it off. He tightened a foot-long piece of fabric between his hands, like a length of chain, and when Robey came within striking distance, Viktor tried to catch his neck with the bed sheet, planning to execute a choke Grey had taught him.

Instead of dodging the sheet, Robey stepped closer to Viktor and, like the crack of a whip, threw a punch into his gut. The air whooshed out of Viktor's stomach. As he bent double from the blow, he felt hands grasping him by the throat.

Robey's fingers felt like steel rods pressing into Viktor's flesh. The professor couldn't draw in enough air. He stopped gasping and tried to break free, but Robey was far stronger than he looked. Viktor clawed at Robey's face to break the hold, but the former soldier pushed him backwards, causing him to trip and fall on his back on the bed. Viktor recoiled at the touch of Robey's skin, which felt stronger but also spongier than it should. Unnatural.

Robey leaned over and tightened his grip, using the leverage of his standing position. Viktor inhaled his smell, the same cheap and overpowering cologne Kristof had worn.

The professor gagged and flailed, but nothing he did caused Robey to loosen his hold. *Van Draker sent him to choke me to death,* Viktor realized. *No gunshots, no blood, no evidence. Just the fingers of a dead man wrapped around my throat.*

Panic gave way to resignation. The dim light from the hallway started to recede, the strength ebbing from Viktor's limbs. He was going to die in that cell, his work unfinished, the secrets of van Draker's laboratory safe from the world.

Just before Viktor's eyes closed, a gunshot blasted through the corridor, chipping into the concrete wall.

"Get off him!"

Robey's grip lessened. It took a moment for a mouthful of oxygen to enter Viktor's system, blessed oxygen, and then he realized the voice was female.

Someone he knew.

Naomi.

Robey straightened, leaving Viktor coughing on the bed. Naomi stepped into the cell, pumped the shotgun, and pointed it at the former soldier. "Step away and hands on your head! Do it!"

Without a word, Robey came right at her. As Viktor's strength returned and he managed to sit up, Naomi shot Robey in the gut, knocking him backward. The blast rang in Viktor's ears.

Blood spilled from the wound and onto the floor of the cell. As Naomi backed away and pumped the shotgun, Robey hobbled towards the door, holding his gut with one hand.

Naomi's eyes widened. Her hands shook as she stood in the corridor, unsure what to do. Viktor could tell she wanted to shoot Robey again but felt torn. He was still an unarmed man.

"On the floor!" Naomi shouted, with the shotgun pointed at Robey. "Now!" she screamed.

The soldier swung his head towards Viktor. Robey looked confused, and blood dripped from his stomach wound. For a moment, Viktor thought he was going to attack him again, but Robey turned and looked at Naomi, hesitating a final time before bounding down the corridor holding his stomach.

"Stop!" she cried, looking shocked by the speed at which he was running.

She went after him, shotgun raised. Viktor couldn't see what happened, but a few moments later, he heard Naomi curse and pound on a door. Robey must have locked it behind him.

The sergeant returned with a grim look on her face. "Are you okay?"

Viktor gently rubbed his neck. Though painful to the touch, his windpipe seemed intact. "I believe so. You should go after him."

She helped him to his feet. "I'm not leaving you alone." They strode down the hallway together, and she aimed the shotgun at the lock on the wooden door.

As soon as Naomi and Viktor were safely inside her Land Cruiser, Naomi pulled out of the parking lot and onto the deserted main road that cut through the center of town. Her eyes were in constant motion, moving from the rearview to the street and back again. "I'm taking you home."

"What about Robey?"

"You mean the man who just took a point-blank shotgun blast to the gut and kept on going?" She glanced at Viktor, eyes rimmed with fear. "What about him?"

"He just tried to kill me. We both know where he's headed. Can't you arrest him?"

"I don't know, Viktor," she said sharply. "*Can* I arrest a dead man? Is that even possible?" She let out a deep breath, and he noticed her hands trembling. "I'm sorry," she said. "But I don't think you understand the situation."

"Maybe I do," he said quietly. When he gave her a rundown of the night's events, her face grew paler and paler.

"Christ," she said. "He's more of a monster than I imagined. We have to put a stop to this."

"That jail isn't in service anymore, is it?"

She shook her head. "I knew the captain answered to van Draker, but this . . . he allowed Robey to *murder* you."

"To attempt to murder me," Viktor corrected. "Thanks to you. How did you find me?"

"The captain was furious about tonight and made me write a report. All night, I kept trying to reach you, but you never answered. At first I figured you were hiding in the manor and unable to talk, but on my way home, I couldn't take it anymore. I decided to see if you had returned to your pension. On the way in, one of van Draker's cars passed me, a dark blue Mercedes with tinted windows. I couldn't see who was driving, but I turned and followed it to the courthouse."

"I'm alive because you did."

She reached over and squeezed his arm.

"We have to go above the captain," Viktor said finally. "To the district."

"I'll try, but you're my foremost concern. I can't protect you anymore."

Viktor knew she spoke the truth. After what he had glimpsed beneath the manor, he knew van Draker would do everything in his power to keep him quiet. And that Captain Waalkamp would help him.

"Take me to Cape Town," Viktor said.

"The captain knows too many people there. Cops. The Western Cape is a tight community. They'll trust his word over yours. And if he takes you into custody again, we both know what will happen."

"What, then?"

"Tonight? We're going to my place. Tomorrow I'll figure a way to get you out of the country."

"I'm not going anywhere."

She glanced at him again. "They'll kill you."

"They have to find me to do that. Jacques will send help, once I explain the situation."

Naomi looked doubtful, and Viktor knew it wouldn't be that easy. With the loss of his phone, he still had no evidence other than his word, and that might not be enough to go over Captain Waalkamp's head and force an investigation. Even if he made headway through the proper channels, the legal procedure could take weeks or longer, and there was no guarantee of success. He felt certain that van Draker was behind the virus, but time was running out for a cure.

Yet if he stayed, his life would be at grave risk, and he had no idea how to access the lab again.

"We'll worry about the future in the morning," Naomi said.

"Isn't your place risky? Robey saw you—what if he comes back?"

She patted the butt of the shotgun, lying on the console between them. "Next time I'll aim for the head."

As she turned onto the long gravel road that led to her homestead, Viktor eased his head against the seat rest. He was too tired to think. Once the sun rose, he would ponder his options over coffee. He doubted van Draker would come after them in broad daylight, which gave them a day to decide what to do.

"A question," Viktor said.

"Mm?"

"Do you really like men in uniform?"

She cocked her head. "What woman doesn't?"

"I don't know."

Naomi cast a sly glance his way. "I like men with family castles more."

"Oh," he said slowly. "I see."

She gave a rich laugh. "Look at where I choose to live. Do you think I care about those things?"

Viktor laughed, too. It felt good.

Five minutes later, they saw a plume of smoke staining the moonlit sky. After a moment of confused silence, Naomi whispered, "Oh no. Please no."

Viktor felt his heart sink. Instead of turning around, Naomi stepped on the gas and gripped the shotgun. The professor held on as the hardy vehicle took the bumpy road at ninety kilometers an hour.

It was just as they feared. Naomi's house was on fire. Flames licked out of the roof on the right side of the house, which contained the study. Naomi's research on van Draker.

With Max barking furiously as he trailed behind the Land Cruiser, Naomi screeched to a stop, grabbed the shotgun, and leaped out of the vehicle. Viktor shouted at her to wait, but she ran headlong towards her home. Hands shielding her face, she blew the front door open with the shotgun, and Viktor watched in horror as she plunged into the burning house. Moments after she entered, she backed out, coughing, unable to take the heat.

After following Naomi around the outside of the house, Viktor took her phone and called the fire department. She darted up the steps leading to the rooftop patio and grabbed her telescope. He took it off her hands and carried it to the Land Rover as Naomi ran in frantic circles around the property, seeing if there was another door she could enter, something else she could salvage. It quickly became apparent that the house and everything inside was lost.

"I called for help," Viktor said.

She nodded, her face white as she fought back the tears. "We can't wait around," she said, tugging on his arm. "I have to get you out of here. The station monitors those calls."

Viktor pulled her into a hug. She buried her face in his chest, shaking all over.

"I can't believe it's gone," Naomi said in monotone as they drove north out of town on a back road unfamiliar to Viktor.

"I can't imagine how it must feel," Viktor said.

"I don't own much. I don't care about the furniture. But my photographs, my research on van Draker . . ."

Viktor laid a hand on her arm and gently squeezed. From the back seat, Max looked at his mistress with mournful eyes, sensing the gravity of the moment.

They drove for some time in silence, until the dawn light illuminated a line of granite peaks glowing mauve in the morning light.

"Where are we going?" Viktor asked.

"To the only safe place I can think of."

"Thato's place?"

"No. Everyone knows we're friends." Her mouth curled into what Viktor interpreted as a guilty expression. "I have an ex I'm still close with. Not in that way," she said hastily. "He lives out of town, and I trust him with my life."

I hope so, Viktor thought.

He kept his eye on the side mirror, expecting headlights from a police car or van Draker's Mercedes to swing into view. Half an hour later, no one had accosted them as Naomi pulled onto a switchback gravel drive, and a manor sitting atop a manicured slope came into view. A perfect half-moon, white as a seashell, illuminated a sea of grapevines surrounding the estate.

"Does he know we're coming?" Viktor asked.

She shook her head. "I didn't want to risk a text."

Naomi pulled around to the back of the house, out of sight of the road, and parked. The back door opened. A handsome man in his fifties, grey hair curling at the temples, hurried outside in jeans and a windbreaker. He raised a gadget in his hand and a garage door opened. "Quick," he said. "Pull the car in."

After exchanging a look of surprise with Viktor, Naomi did as he asked. Once the garage door closed and the light flicked on, she and Viktor stepped out to meet the homeowner, who entered the three-car garage through a side door. A Range Rover and a pristine MG convertible were also parked inside.

"I don't think anyone's seen you," Daniel said, after Naomi introduced the two men. "The guest house is empty tonight. You can stay there. Max, too."

"Why are you doing this?" Naomi asked. "You haven't even asked what this is about."

Daniel gave her an odd look. "You don't know?"

Naomi frowned. "Know what?"

Daniel took out his cell phone. Viktor leaned in to look, the color draining from his face when he read the emergency alert about a foreign professor and a local police officer, both armed and dangerous, who were fleeing arrest.

39

Grey and Jax followed a worn set of tire tracks into the rugged interior, the suspension of the Superjeep bouncing like a trampoline as it clambered over rocks and streams and mossy undergrowth.

Half an hour later, they sped between two hills on the far side of the lagoon. Calving blocks of ice creaked and moaned like old men as they sloughed apart on their mournful procession to the sea. Jax checked the GPS and pointed Grey to the northeast, following a set of tracks that paralleled the hulking glacier.

As civilization fell further behind, the landscape became a mosaic of steaming geysers, boulders, gushing creeks and moss-streaked ridges, chasms, sumps, waterfalls wreathed in omnipresent mists, earth blown up and settled and then arranged by Michelangelo. Smoking hot pots and dangerous rifts littered the terrain, but Grey avoided the hazards by slowing down and keeping to the path carved out from previous journeys.

Eventually, the tire tracks disappeared, and they had to rely on the GPS. It seemed to be moving more or less in a straight line. An hour later, they approached a sight that caused Grey to grip the wheel with both hands. At first he thought the road had dead-ended at a cliff face, but then he noticed a sliver of a pass cleaving through a hundred foot tall mesa.

"The jeep just disappeared," Jax announced.

"What?"

"It stopped moving a few miles ahead, and then the signal died."

"What's that mean?"

"They found the tracker, or went somewhere that interrupted the signal."

Grey eyed the approaching mesa. The bottom third of the cliff face was white, as if wainscoted. "Then I guess we keep going," he said grimly.

Jax took out a pair of miniature binoculars. "I don't like this."

"Me neither. You still with me?"

Jax blew out a breath and shook his head. "For now."

They entered the hundred-foot wide passage. Jagged rocks stacked on either side of the tire tracks allowed only one vehicle at a time to pass through.

About a hundred yards in, Jax swore. "Sentries atop the cliffs, and a guard station up ahead."

"How many?"

"Two in the shack, two on the cliff. They've already seen us."

Grey put a hand on his gun.

"Keep calm and carry on," Jax murmured, as he lowered the binoculars. "No one seems disturbed. I think they might recognize the jeep, and two of them are wearing the same suits we are."

"They won't recognize *us*."

"Maybe they won't ask. Who could find this place?"

"If they do ask?"

Jax patted his belt. "We take out the guards, and I've got a smokescreen to confuse the sentries." He turned to Grey. "We'll have to go back, though. You know that."

Grey pursed his lips and didn't answer. If forced, he'd toss the keys to Jax and take his chances on foot.

But this place felt right, and he wasn't going back without Charlie.

The sun had emerged. Grey checked his fake tan in the mirror and slipped on his shades, which helped conceal his face. His chest tightened as they approached the guard shack, a box of wood and steel fronting a spiked iron gate that looked solid enough to withstand a tank assault. Grey stopped on a metal platform right beside the guard shack, just in front of the gate. A red laser flashed and a beep emitted from the magnetic strip attached to the inside of the jeep's dashboard. Grey had noticed the strip before, thinking it was an employee card. And maybe it was.

The massive gate slid open.

A guard waved them through.

When they passed the checkpoint, Grey unballed his fists and expelled a long breath. On the other side of the pass, the road opened up into a valley surrounded by a mountain range. The snow-topped peaks, serrated as a set of troll's teeth, looked impassable.

"Right into the lion's den," Jax muttered. "What the hell is this place?"

The road split a hundred feet ahead. To the left, it hugged the cliff face and disappeared into the distance. To the right, it wound beside a river and led to a collection of low buildings. A settlement of some sort.

Straight ahead, in the center of the valley, Grey saw a sparkling blue lake, fields of wheat and heather, horses, sheep, and bales of hay wrapped in white plastic that reminded Grey of giant marshmallows. They had dotted the pastures along the Ring Road as well.

A souped-up black golf cart sped through the intersection, heading towards the cliffs. Both people inside had on snow camo.

Jax pointed at the cliffs. "They're heading right to where the signal stopped."

Grey waited until the golf cart disappeared from view, then followed the pair. Jax trained the binoculars on the road. "Stop," he said, once they had driven a few hundred feet alongside the cliff. "Holy shit."

"What?"

"Stop the jeep."

Jax looked pale as he handed over the binoculars. Following the road, Grey saw that the golf cart had parked right in front of a wall of ice. His mouth dropped when he spied a portion of the wall levering upwards. Once it finished rising, two guards stepped out, and the man and the woman each handed over a badge.

Grey couldn't see inside the mountain. The guards scanned the badges and gave them back. The golf cart pulled through and the ice door lowered, sealing the opening.

After swallowing and lowering the binoculars, he told Jax what he had seen.

"What now?" the mercenary said. "We're not blasting our way inside that mountain."

In the distance, on the other side of the valley, Grey noticed a cell tower poking skyward. He ran a hand through his hair and did a U-turn in the middle of the road. "Let's see what else is here."

Jax gave the rearview a nervous glance. "One quick look," he muttered.

Grey returned to where the road split and continued towards the settlement. The road followed a shallow river past the lake and into a community that reminded Grey of a military base. A few dozen concrete barracks were arranged in a loose circle around a cluster of shops marked by signs in three languages: Icelandic, English, and German. They rolled through the center and saw a gas station, a commissary, a bar, a restaurant, a gymnasium, an outdoor soccer field, and a greenhouse Grey guessed was used for vegetables. There was even a bizarre wooden building that looked like a dozen pagodas stacked on top of each other, in the shape of a cheerleader's pyramid. The beautiful craftsmanship looked out of place in the compound. Grey read the sign out front.

ASATRU TEMPLE OF WODAN

Two flags flapped in the breeze above the settlement. The first bore the same insignia as the tattoo on Dag's arm. The Odin Rune. On the second, a horned red dragon curled around a pair of crossed swords set against a white background. Different runes marked each corner of the flag. The emblem of W.A.R., Grey guessed.

Plenty of people hustled about, most of them dressed in snow camo. The vehicles consisted of Superjeeps and snowmobiles and hordes of black golf carts. Everyone looked busy. No one gave Grey or Jax a second glance.

"We're *really* pushing that luck," Jax said.

"I understand if you want to go back. Just drop me somewhere out of sight."

"And you'll do what?"

"I don't know yet. Something."

Jax grimaced and didn't respond.

As they left the settlement behind, Grey felt hot and cracked the window. The air was heavy and smelled of snow. More barracks, generators, and a shooting range lined the road on the way out. A short ways past the settlement, they crossed the river and came to an airfield with two long runways, a dozen hangars arranged in a circle, and a handful of cargo planes parked on a sea of concrete.

"Good lord," Jax said. "They've got a small army out here."

"I get the feeling all this is here to protect whatever's inside that mountain."

The road ended at the cell tower they had spied from the entrance. Just past the tower, a field of jumbled, moss-covered lava rocks filled the back side of the valley.

A guard emerged from a building beside the cell tower and gave a Nazi salute. Gritting his teeth, Grey returned the gesture and turned the jeep around, hoping the guard wouldn't stop them.

The guard returned inside. Grey's heart fluttered. He knew Jax was right about their luck running out.

"I've got an idea," Jax said. "Swing by the hangars, out of sight of that guard."

Grey did what he asked and rolled to a stop behind a hangar. After ensuring no one was watching, Jax withdrew a black dot the size of a dime from his utility belt, hopped out of the jeep, and attached it to the base of the structure. He placed a rock beside it to shield it from view.

"Another tracking dot?" Grey guessed, when Jax returned. "In case we get lost?"

"That one's not for us." He clapped Grey on the shoulder. "I hate to tell you, but you're not at your best on this mission. *If* we go inside that mountain, and by some miracle make it out alive, how do you think we're getting home?"

"I hadn't thought that far ahead," Grey muttered.

"Yeah, well I did. As soon as we hit Rekyjavik. Jax's Rule the Third: always have an extraction plan in place. Especially in a neo-Nazi stronghold in the middle of the Icelandic outback."

"Who's on notice?"

"An old RAF pilot, unless he sees this place on the approach and decides it's too risky. He lives on the Isle of Skye. I'll send him the coordinates and tell him to wait offshore." Jax spread his hands. "We can call him in now, if you want. You can come back with the cops."

Grey considered the proposition. "I'm sure it's private land, and there's no proof she's inside." He shook his head. "They'd just kill her."

Jax didn't deny it.

"What was that idea you mentioned?" Grey said, as he drove back to the settlement.

"Find a place to park. As near the tavern as possible."

"What for?"

"Drunk people are easier to steal from."

Grey gave a grim nod. "The keycards?"

Jax clicked out of the side of his mouth.

Twenty yards past the tavern, Grey pulled into a parking area with a handful of golf carts and another super jeep. Jax zipped his coat, jumped out, and strolled towards the tavern.

Grey hunkered down in the seat and hoped no one parked too close. If they did, he supposed he could fake inebriation or drive away, but he wanted to be close in case Jax needed him.

Half an hour passed, and then another. Grey started the car to stay warm. He was nervous someone had spoken to Jax and realized the mercenary didn't speak Icelandic, or asked him who he was, or any of a dozen scenarios that could play out very, very badly.

He breathed a sigh of relief when Jax left the tavern with a sway in his step, as if he had had one too many. A pair of men smoking outside the tavern ignored him. Jax made his way to the jeep and hopped inside.

"Well?" Grey asked as he eyed the street, jittery with anticipation.

All signs of Jax's inebriation had disappeared. He held up a pair of silver key cards with magnetic strips on the backs. "Pickpocketing is such a nifty skill."

The two men smoking outside the bar eyed the jeep as it passed, probably wondering why Grey had been waiting outside. They didn't move or call out, but he didn't like the looks on their faces.

As soon as they were out of sight of the tavern, a light snow began to fall. They left the settlement and drove down the road hugging the cliff. When Grey saw a grooved steel platform at the base of the ice wall, big enough for the jeep to roll onto, he decelerated and glanced at Jax. "We go in there, we may not come back out."

"And?"

"You've gotten me this far. You've earned your fee."

"All of it?"

"Half of it."

Jax snorted. "You don't even have a little bit of doubt about going in there, do you?"

"It's not about me. It's about Charlie."

"Why in the world did I tell you how to contact me, when we left Egypt?"

"You probably shouldn't have."

Jax pressed his lips together, then cocked a grin as his eyes hardened. "Money talks, I don't like leaving my clients, and I'm curious as hell what's inside that glacier. If you take a risk I don't like, I'll shoot you myself. Now let's go get your girl."

As the jeep rolled to a stop on the steel platform, the magnetic strip on the dash flashed again. Something caught hold of the tires and locked the jeep in place.

Grey put the transmission in neutral and forced himself to relax.

The door of ice started rising.

The jeep lurched forward.

40

Deep within the hidden compound, Dag entered the war hall and prepared to contact the second-highest ranking member of his organization, the man they called *Herr Physician*. A brilliant man, a revered man, a visionary and a true believer who had engineered everything that was about to happen.

Well, almost everything. The one above Dag and the physician, the heir apparent, had a gift for strategy greater than any chess master Dag had ever known.

He felt a shiver of pride. W.A.R. was about to make a statement that would rewrite the history books. Reshape the cultural dynamic around the globe.

Restore the natural order.

His steel-toed boots strode across a polished onyx floor. The war hall contained a bank of computers to rival any technology company. Reams of military plans to supplement the computer models. Demographic wall maps with projected casualty percentages across the globe.

The beautiful hall, which showcased a towering ice ceiling and walls of igneous rock, contained cultural artifacts as well. Living memories of the might of their Aryan ancestors. Rune stones, bejeweled goblets, the helms and swords of kings. Not just their own relics, but priceless works of art from around the world, preserved in backlit glass frames. Nazi loot in the hands of the proper owners.

Those born to the master race didn't ask or apologize or repatriate.

They took.

At least, that was how it should be. The percentage of whites among the world population had dropped into the single digits. *Single digits.* Like any beleaguered community—like the Jews cowering in Israel—steps had to be taken to avoid extinction. While W.A.R. had chapters and soldiers worldwide, their army was tiny by any numeric measure, and they were forced to keep to the shadows. It was embarrassing. Shameful.

But that was all about to change.

As the human race had always done, as Dag knew it would always do, the strong survived and the weak perished and the world kept spinning on its axis. Despite the pampered daily life enjoyed in the wealthy homelands that he and his brothers-in-arms so cherished, Dag knew that human beings were never at rest.

Peace was an illusion. A temporal state. Mankind was perpetually locked in struggle, both evolutionary and internecine.

A grin of understanding tugged at the corners of his mouth. Three fourths of the battle was realizing that simple fact, and not being afraid to act.

After taking a few minutes to scan the latest CDC reports and the updates from W.A.R. leaders around the globe, Dag dialed South Africa on a secure satellite phone.

"Dagnar," Jans van Draker said. "Timely as always."

"Disorder is an invitation for defeat. I've just finished consulting our sources. Progress is excellent. I believe we're reaching critical mass."

"Ya, one more round of infections should suffice. Though we must be more careful than ever. The world is watching now."

"We're selecting only the most disadvantaged communities," Dag said. "Trust me, the world is not watching *them*. Whether they admit it or not, the civilized world applauds what we are doing."

"You're certain the news filters are secure?"

"The world hears what it wants to hear. What it's *told*. And once the seed is planted, it is very, very hard to discredit what one believes to be true. In a few days, none of it will matter anyway."

"Excellent," van Draker murmured.

Dag crossed his arms. "And on your end? The investigation? We've lost contact with Dominic Grey. I'm surprised to say he might have gone rogue. Not that it will do him any good."

Van Draker gave a low chuckle. "The professor has ambushed his own investigation and got himself arrested. It's only a matter of time before my people silence him."

"The girl?"

"No longer of utility."

"Understood," Dag said.

"You sent Klaus to me for further testing, as I requested?"

"He should arrive tonight. All vitals are still positive."

"I've exceeded my own expectations," van Draker said, then sighed. "Though I'd like to see more progress with the frontal lobe before we continue with the others."

"It would be advantageous to make an early statement, during the chaos. We can use the same procedures to spread fear."

"If we must," van Draker said. "I just want what's best for my . . . for the soldiers."

Dag felt a twinge of unease. One time before, he had heard *Herr Physician* refer to Klaus as his child, and it had made Dag wonder whether the South African doctor was a genius or flirting with the edge of insanity. Perhaps both.

After the W.A.R. leader ended the conversation, a frisson of excitement surged through him. Days. Mere days until the culmination of half a century's work.

No, a *thousand* years of toil.

The beginning of a new age.

A return to glory.

His blood sang with pride and eagerness. Viking ships will set sail once again, across the seas and through the skies, heralding the destruction of their enemies on wings of ancient fire. A call to arms that would put the jihadists to shame.

Dag pressed a button. One of his favorite men, a German assassin who Emil had ferried in from Rekyjavik, answered the call.

"Yes?" Gunter asked in English, the common language in the compound.

"The girl is no longer needed as insurance."

"Should I kill her?"

"Kill her?" Dag said in amusement. "I see no reason to waste a good specimen."

41

Daniel left Viktor and Naomi alone in the well-appointed guesthouse. Exhausted, they fell asleep in their clothes and woke late the next morning. When Viktor returned from the shower, he found Naomi sitting on the queen-size bed with her back against the headboard, hugging her knees and staring into space. Her hair, still damp from her own shower, splayed onto a terry cloth bathrobe Daniel had supplied.

Viktor sat beside her, clad in a matching bathrobe, troubled by the look on her face.

"I just got a text from an unlisted number," she said, eyes lowering as she passed him the phone.

As Viktor read the message, rage bubbled up inside him.

–What a terrible pity the local firemen were occupied last night.–

"He took my home," Naomi said dully. "I had so many memories there. My whole childhood . . ."

Viktor set the phone down. "I'm so very sorry."

A deep breath shuddered through her, replaced by a mouth firmed by vengeance. "What do we do? How do we stop him?"

Viktor tightened his bathrobe and began to pace. "How secure are we here?"

"As secure as anyplace in the area. Daniel sent everyone home but Rose."

"We shouldn't leave until dark, but we need to act. Tonight."

"I agree. But what?"

"Jacques has been trying to call me. Let's start there. Do you mind?" Viktor asked, reaching for Naomi's phone on the bedside table.

She opened a palm, and he started to leave the room, then realized there was nothing she couldn't hear. Not anymore.

"Thank God it's you," Jacques said, after Viktor explained who it was. "Why haven't you been answering?"

"It's a long story."

"*Oui*, of that I'm certain. Arson, burglary, fleeing arrest? Why don't you give me the condensed version for now?"

Viktor complied, and Jacques waited a few moments to speak. "That is a most . . . incredible . . . story."

"You doubt me?" Viktor asked.

"With you, professor, I've come to expect the impossible. That doesn't mean it becomes any easier to hear."

"Is there news on the virus?"

"You haven't seen the CDC statement?"

"I haven't had time to check."

"They've officially labeled the virus a communicable disease that incubates in melanocytes. Meaning it feeds and replicates within elevated concentrations of melanin. Before the immune system can catch up."

"Melanin," Viktor repeated.

"It targets people of color."

"*Do prdele*," Viktor whispered. "A true ethnic bioweapon. How does it spread?"

"Respiratory transmission. Aerosol. Like the flu."

Viktor sat on the bed. "*Do prdele*," he repeated.

"It's still unclear, but they believe the incubation period is slow, days or even weeks. But the potential for a pandemic is there. Hundreds have died, and thousands more are believed to be infected. They're trying to isolate affected communities, but new cases keep springing up."

"The Wodan Republic injected hosts in communities around the world, and it spread from there."

"There's no proof of that, but yes, I believe that to be the case."

"There's no vaccine?" Viktor asked.

"According to the CDC, they're making progress, but who knows how long it will take? Viktor, if there is anything in that lab that can help us, we need it. *Immédiatement*."

"Then assemble a team and go inside. I told you what I saw."

"What you told me, while incredible, does not appear to relate to the virus."

"There's a connection," Viktor said. "I'm sure of it. Van Draker started his work on genetic warfare during Apartheid. Over twenty years ago."

"Be that as it may, Interpol has its limits. I'm receiving unbelievable pushback from the local police, and without more to go on, the national authorities won't override them. Van Draker has connections in very high places. It doesn't help that we have no proof, and that you're a wanted man."

"Are you saying you can't help me?"

"Not as a fugitive. If you submit to the local police and give a statement, I might use your testimony to push for a warrant."

"There's a problem with that," Viktor said.

"Which is?"

"The local police are trying to kill me."

After a long pause, Jacques said, "Can you get to a border? Leave the country?"

"Probably. But we'll lose valuable time, and access to the lab."

"Do you have a way to return inside?"

"Not yet," Viktor said.

"Then what do you propose?"

"I was hoping you had an idea."

"I can't help you in South Africa, Viktor. In fact, I'm being pressured to turn you in. We shouldn't talk again while you're in the country."

When they hung up, after a stunned silence, Viktor and Naomi read the CDC's statement on his phone together and saw the panic reflected in news outlets around the world. Exhausted, the professor sank against the headboard, and Naomi laid her head in his lap and wrapped her arms around his waist.

A knock on the door startled them both.

"Coming," Naomi said. She disengaged from Viktor's lap, her hand trailing against his cheek. Attraction stirred within him, and he wished they were in a different place, with different circumstances.

When Naomi opened the door, a trim black woman in her fifties, wearing a lilac tracksuit and holding a dust cloth, smiled and gave Naomi a warm hug.

"I know none of that nonsense is true," the woman said. She gave Max a pat on the head when he padded over to sniff.

"Thanks, Rose," Naomi said, and introduced her to Viktor.

"Will you join Daniel for lunch?" Rose asked.

"When?" Naomi asked.

"Soon as you're ready."

When Viktor and Naomi arrived in the dining room, they found an elaborate spread of cheese, olives, artichoke hearts, and cured meats. A Sauvignon Blanc from Daniel's cellar complemented the meal, and Viktor sighed his approval. One must always dine in style, he believed. Even at the end of the world.

Especially at the end of the world.

Naomi sampled an olive. "Thank you for everything. We'll leave tonight."

"You'll stay as long as you need," Daniel said. He had donned a blue golf shirt and tan slacks. "And eat me out of house and home."

Viktor raised his glass. " 'A guest never forgets the host who had treated him kindly.' "

Daniel smiled. "A man of the classics, ya? Homer, if I'm not mistaken." His expression hardened. "I won't begin to speculate as to what this is about. I know that when Jans van Draker is involved, it can't be good."

"That's the understatement of the century," Naomi said.

Daniel dabbed his mouth with his napkin. "After you sought my help, I asked about construction near the van Draker estate. This morning, I got an answer."

Naomi's head jerked up. "A vineyard owner?"

"An architect. My father's best friend."

The timing was suspicious. Viktor didn't trust anyone he didn't know, but at that point, they had run out of options. "Why didn't he reply until today?"

"He's been out of the country on business. I followed up this morning, after the news hit."

Naomi leaned forward. "And?"

Daniel spread Brie on a cracker. "Soon after van Draker returned to Bonniecombe, an old water treatment plant was condemned. Slated for demolition."

"I remember that. The one near the nature reserve."

"That's right."

"Only it's still standing."

"Exactly," Daniel said. "My father's friend claims someone purchased the land from the government, but never tore the plant down."

"How would he know this?"

"He buys property himself from time to time, and had the land appraised. He made an offer but was outbid."

"By who?" Viktor asked.

"He didn't know, but I looked into it," Daniel said. "After some digging, I discovered that one of van Draker's companies had purchased the property. That's not unusual, to be honest. Land near the nature reserve could pay off handsomely in the future."

"How does any of this help us?" Naomi asked, and then sat up straight. "Wait—one of the sets of property records stolen back in 1994, the same day van Draker's were stolen, was an old water waste treatment plant. I thought it was a coincidence . . ."

Daniel took a drink of wine and leveled his gaze at her. "I asked my father's friend if he knew of any construction on or near the van Draker estate, especially underground. He did not. But he remembered from the appraisal that the water plant had an old sewage tunnel that connected to the river. It's been years, but from his recollection, the tunnel ran right past Jans's manor."

Just before seven p.m., as dusk spread down the mountains like an ink stain, Viktor and Naomi joined Daniel in the dining room for dinner. During the day, they had made preparations to visit the old water plant around midnight, once they could move about unnoticed.

"What if we find something?" Naomi asked Viktor, when Daniel left to select a bottle of wine. "At the plant?"

As the professor considered the question, he checked his remote voicemail on Naomi's phone yet again. Still nothing. "We evaluate the situation. I'm hoping we'll have help, but I'm afraid we won't."

"Help from who?"

Viktor had not heard from Grey in far too long, despite leaving a number of messages. "My partner."

Daniel returned with a bottle of estate pinotage. As he popped the cork, someone rapped on the front door.

Everyone froze.

Swung their gazes towards the hall.

"Coming," Rose called out.

"No!" Naomi said, jumping to her feet. Daniel and Viktor were right behind her as she hurried to the front door and checked the eyehole.

"Thato," Naomi said in relief. "Thank God."

When Naomi opened the door, Thato pulled her into a hug on the front stoop. "I *knew* it. I've been looking everywhere for you." Her eyes flicked to Daniel and then Viktor.

"You shouldn't have come here," Naomi said.

"I want to help. However I can."

"It's not safe to be seen with me."

"Love, please," Thato said.

Daniel interrupted them. "Why don't we return inside?"

The two women broke their embrace. Just as Viktor wondered if anyone had been watching Thato's house and followed her to Daniel's estate, he noticed a dark sedan gliding silently down the switchback drive with its headlights off.

"Inside!" Viktor roared, just before gunfire crackled through the air.

Rose screamed from inside the house. Naomi dove into Viktor, driving them both to the floor as Thato slumped on the concrete stoop, the door behind her splattered with blood.

42

After the ice door finished raising, two guards stepped out of the mountain, one on each side of the Superjeep. Grey held his breath as he and Jax handed them the stolen ID cards. What if the guards knew every face in the compound? What if Grey's disguise wasn't good enough?

The guard next to Grey inserted the chip side of the ID card into a silver handheld device that resembled a grocery store scanner. After a moment, the scanner beeped and a green dot appeared. The guard returned the ID card and Grey forced himself to appear calm, praying the guards wouldn't recognize his face beneath the disguise.

Jax cleared as well. Once the jeep had rolled fully inside, the wheels unlocked and they got a look at the cavern. Low-ceilinged but immense, with natural convex walls striated in brilliant hues of red and yellow and green, the picturesque grotto housed a fleet of Superjeeps, black golf carts, Segways, snowmobiles, and motorcycles with knobby tires fitted with snow chains.

The Segways told Grey there was a need *inside* the complex for transportation. The size of the compound could be an advantage, as long as no one recognized them.

Just to the left of the entrance, affixed to the cavern wall, Grey felt a shiver when he caught sight of a rectangular bronze plaque. He knew enough German to read it.

THIS FACILITY COMMISSIONED BY THE AHNENERBE IN 1939

Grey parked in line with the other jeeps as a group of golf carts approached from the far side of the cavern. He tensed again, but the men and women inside parked, jumped into snowmobiles, and zoomed over the grooved platform just as one of the guards pushed a button on the wall and the ice door began to lower.

After exchanging a glance, Grey followed Jax to one of the golf carts and let the mercenary drive. Grey had never played golf or ridden a Segway, and one misstep could alert the guards.

The key was in the ignition. Jax turned it to the right and, once it beeped, reversed out of the parking space. The guards were no longer paying attention. Jax pulled a handle below the seat, switching into drive, and the golf cart jumped forward. Grey swallowed. Thank God for gregarious, golf-schmoozing mercenaries.

The smell of lime and disinfectant. Voices echoing in the distance. Banks of overhead fluorescent lights providing illumination.

As they approached the far side of the cavern, three exit tunnels appeared, each with a bronze signpost listing the route choices in German, English, and Icelandic.

LOGISTICS & CONTROL

BUNKERS & ARMORY & MESS HALL

RESEARCH

Grey knew the Nazis had a love affair with secret underground bases. A fitting metaphor for the evil that lies beneath. The existence of the compound did not surprise him that much, despite the official denial of an Iceland expedition.

The current occupancy was another matter.

Each of the route choices was a wide, smooth, well-lit passage that delved deeper into the mountain as if bored out by a giant worm. Lava tubes, Grey guessed.

"This is unbelievable," Jax said in a low voice, after Grey nudged him towards the *Research* tunnel. Too many voices emanated from the *Bunker & Armory* route. *Logistics & Control* sounded like someplace Dag and a host of guards would be.

As much as Grey hated to think about the implications, *Research* was probably where they kept the prisoners.

A shudder rolled through him. *If they've harmed a hair on her head . . .*

Yet he knew they already had.

The *Research* passage, ten feet high with walls the color of chocolate syrup, bored through the earth in a gentle curve. Overhead lighting flicked on as they passed, and flicked off moments after. The passage was cold, for which Grey was grateful. Easier to stay anonymous inside the snow camo.

After passing five golf carts and a nest of unmarked side passages, they entered a grotto that branched into four smaller tunnels. The cavern had cement walls and a stippled stalactite ceiling that resembled a 3-D surface map.

The exit tunnels, each another lava tube with brilliant hues, gave more route guidance.

  RECORDS ARCHIVE
  ARTIFACTS
  LABORATORIES
  CRYOGENICS

"This is getting weirder and weirder," Jax said. "I can't believe how big this place is."

Grey felt his hands shaking at the thought of Charlie used as a guinea pig in some unholy experiment. He had to force his next words out. "Lab or Cryogenics."

Jax avoided Grey's gaze. "We don't look much like scientists."

"We'll have to take the chance."

They tried the corridor marked *Laboratories* first. A few minutes later, the passage narrowed and then dumped them in a warren of side passages with polished concrete walls and glass doors. A host of lab equipment filled the rooms behind the doors. Only one was occupied by scientists, men and women dressed in white lab coats with the W.A.R. emblem embossed on the back. None of them paid Grey or Jax any attention.

"Is it just me," Jax said as they kept driving, "or do these labs look a bit dated?"

"I was thinking the same," Grey said, remembering the high-tech equipment in the CDC.

Using a key card, they accessed a room with a windowless steel door. A blast of warmer air greeted them. They flipped on a light and found a room that resembled a cross between a torture chamber and a laboratory. Two steel cages with iron manacles attached to the wall occupied the rear corners of the room, and a pair of gurneys was affixed to a spiderlike apparatus near the left wall. The floor was stainless steel and sloped gently towards a drain in the middle. Grey didn't want to think about the fluids that had spiraled into the abyss of that drain. Human lives spent like pennies. He felt his skin crawl, and his heart started beating faster.

"I've visited a few concentration camps before," Jax said. "They gave me the same feeling, like the air is heavy. Weighed down with lost souls or something. If you believe that sort of thing."

"I don't know if I believe," Grey muttered, "but I know what you mean."

They checked every windowless room in the mazelike section. No sign of Charlie.

"It doesn't feel right here," Jax said. "If they're keeping her alive, no one's coming all the way over here to feed her."

"I agree. Let's do a quick run through the other sections."

"Very quick. I've about reached my limit."

Artifacts and Records Archive looked like Grey had imagined: another nest of tunnels and storage rooms filled with crates, desks, file cabinets, and bookshelves that looked fifty years old. The record keeping of the Nazis was legendary, and Grey had always found the unemotional ledgers of genocide and human experimentation one of the most chilling aspects of the Third Reich.

They saw two people cataloguing files. Again, the general lack of activity made Grey think they were in the wrong place. They sped back to the *Research* grotto and idled in front of the signs.

"We haven't seen a camera since the entrance," Jax said. "Why not, if they keep such good records?"

"Not sure. Maybe they don't want a visual of this place leaking out. Or maybe the cameras are hidden."

"Should we bother with *Cryogenics*, or go back to the beginning?"

"Just a glance, since we're here," Grey pushed away the thought of finding Charlie frozen, mouth agape, lost to the world. All he knew about cryonics was that some people chose to freeze their heads or their bodies just after death, in the hope science would one day know how to resurrect them. Cryonic suspension was illegal on the living.

Not that it mattered to the people down here.

They drove down a lava tube the color of unpolished gold. Two minutes later, the tunnel split in two. Another signposted intersection. The arrow pointing to the left read *Cryonic Storage, Detention,* and *Geothermal Plant.* To the right, *Cryonic Transport Facility.*

Detention. Trying to control his rage, Grey jerked his thumb to the left and tensed as Jax drove down a narrow concrete tunnel. A hundred feet away, the passage dead-ended at a steel door. Two guards with assault rifles stood at attention on either side.

Jax swore. "They'll get suspicious if we turn around," he said, in a low voice.

"Just keep going."

"And do what?"

"See if they open the door. If they don't, and we have to fight, no gunshots. It will blow our cover. Can you handle that?"

"Do Russians like vodka?"

The guards, both wearing snowsuits with three red stripes on each arm, watched them approach. One glance at their brusque demeanor told Grey they wouldn't hesitate to shoot.

Fifty feet away. Grey noticed lettering on the door, just above a small metal box jutting out of the center. Another keycard device. As they drew closer, he read the sign.

LEVEL FOUR ACCESS.

"I'm guessing that's not us," Jax said in a low voice.

"Not yet it isn't."

Jax gave him a sharp glance. "You sure about this?"

"Like you said. Too late to turn back."

The door was fifteen feet wide. Jax drove right down the middle. As the golf cart slowed, the guards watched them carefully, though they didn't raise their weapons. They clearly expected Grey or Jax to lean forward and swipe a keycard. Grey knew that if he swiped and an alarm sounded, it would be too late. The guards would shoot.

So Grey didn't wait.

"On five," he said to Jax, as the golf cart came to a stop. He counted to five in his head as he took out the key card. Instead of leaning forward to insert the chip, Grey pushed off the golf cart with his back foot, lunging towards the guard on his side. At the same time, out of the corner of his eye, Grey saw Jax take a tiny stun gun out of his belt and leap out of the golf cart.

The guard nearest Grey reared back, fumbling to bring his weapon up. Grey was too fast, and clamped down on the guard's trigger hand. It prevented a shot, but cost Grey the momentum, and the guard kneed him in the groin.

The knee hurt, but Grey pushed through and didn't release the weapon. Instead he jerked it back and forth in small increments, confusing the guard's reactions, and then stomped on the front of the guard's foot just before he slammed the butt of the weapon into the guard's face. Grey heard the crunch of a broken nose, and he followed it up with an open palm beneath the guard's chin, snapping his head back. Reeling, the guard didn't even get his hands up before Grey delivered a knockout blow to the temple with the butt of the gun.

As the guard slumped to the ground, Grey whipped around and saw the other guard convulsing on the cement floor as Jax stood over him. The mercenary put the stun gun away and gave the guard a leisurely kick to the head, soccer style, knocking him unconscious.

Grey took a black-and-silver keycard off one of the guards and then dragged him to the golf cart. "We'll lock them in the torture room."

Jax followed suit with the other guard as Grey gathered the weapons, which were true assault rifles. HK G36s with settings for semi-automatic and continuous fire. Powerful weapons.

They piled the two guards on the back of the golf cart and sped over to the laboratory section, eyes straining for enemy movement. With a sigh of relief, they locked the guards in the steel cages in the torture room; the old keys were still hanging on the walls. After that, Grey and Jax stored the rifles in the rear compartment of the golf cart and sped back to the steel door with Level 4 access. Less than five minutes had elapsed.

"Moment of truth," Jax said, as he inserted one of the black-and-silver ID cards into the chip reader.

The door retracted smoothly into the ceiling, revealing a gleaming elevator big enough to fit two golf carts.

"It can't be long before someone notices the guards missing," Jax said.

"Tell me something I don't know."

"How about that you have about half an hour of my services left before I hightail it out of Crazy Town?"

Grey grimaced and gave a curt nod.

They drove the golf cart inside and hit the only button on the control panel. The elevator whooshed downward for ten long seconds. At the bottom, Grey's eyes widened as they exited on the shore of a turquoise underground river with a thick blanket of steam rising off it. The river disappeared into the distance on both sides. A pair of flat-bottom transport barges were affixed to a steel dock.

Just outside the elevator, an arcing suspension bridge spanned the river. Grey waved Jax forward, and they sped across, encountering another signpost on the other side.

Cryonic Storage straight ahead through a circular manmade tunnel. *Detention* to the left. *Geothermal Plant* and *Mess Hall* to the right.

Three golf carts sped by without a glance, coming from *Cryonic Storage* and heading towards a line of miniature smokestacks rising out of the mist in the direction of the geothermal plant. They could see more people and golf carts in that direction.

Jax checked his watch. "It's dinner time. If we're lucky, we might have a short grace period."

Grey jerked his head towards *Detention*. As soon as they were out of sight, Jax floored the gas, and a minute later he jerked to a stop in front of a bleak concrete structure facing the river, with gray steel doors spaced ten feet apart.

"God knows who they keep down here," Jax muttered. "There's probably political prisoners from World War II."

The building extended about two hundred feet along the shore of the river. Grey counted twenty doors as he ran, and he checked each one. None were locked, half were empty, and the rest contained the same thing.

A human skeleton manacled to the wall.

"I guess I was right," Jax muttered.

Grey slammed a fist against the final door. He dragged himself back to the golf cart, his legs feeling as heavy as the cement walls of the prison, then shook off his disappointment with a snarl. There was no time for self-pity.

"That way," Grey said, pointing at the Cryonic Storage sign as they returned to the bridge.

"Really?"

"Just a glimpse. I wouldn't put it past them."

"You're right about that. What if she isn't even down here?"

"Just go."

As always, motion-sensitive ceiling lights popped on and off as they sped through a tunnel that looked like permafrost reinforced with steel beams. A short ways in, they came to another steel door and had to insert the Level 4 access card again. Grey gave the corridor behind them a furtive glance as the door retracted smoothly into the ceiling.

On the other side, they heard the distant purr of a generator. The corridor extended as far as they could see between two walls and a high ceiling, all made of ice. Instead of bright fluorescent lights, an unseen light source lit the room with an eerie blue glow, enhancing the effect of the ice.

"Jesus H. Christ," Jax said.

Grey looked to his left and saw, a few feet inside the ice, a man in a vintage Nazi uniform floating in some kind of gel within a transparent suspension tank. The sightless eyes of the soldier stared back at Grey, and the bluish-gray lips were wrapped around a black rubber tube that ran through the top of the tank and disappeared behind it, into the ice.

Grey glanced right and saw an identical sight. The steel door lowered behind them as Jax rolled slowly down the passage. Every five feet they saw a pair of cryogenically preserved soldiers on either side of the corridor, each attached to a rubber tube, on and on and on, a frozen terracotta army.

A hundred feet down the passage, they came to an intersection. An identical ice passage extended to the sides and straight ahead, all lined with preserved soldiers. Jax kept driving down the original passage. Every hundred feet they encountered a similar juncture.

"They must've built right into the glacier," Jax said. "This is insane."

Grey didn't respond. He didn't care how they did it, why they did it, when they did it. He was concerned with the living, not the dead. Or whatever these things were.

The long corridor ran into a T-intersection with another steel door. A sign above the keycard box read "Level 5 Access."

"She's not here," Grey intoned. "Turn around."

"Level Five?" Jax said. "What the hell is more secret than all *this*?" He started to reverse the golf cart, then paused. "You know there's a dispute about Hitler's death, right? The Russians never produced proof, and lots of people think the Mustache didn't die in that bunker. That body doubles took his and Eva's place."

"Turn around," Grey repeated.

"What if the Führer himself is in there? Waiting for some crazy doctor to revive him? Imagine what that knowledge could fetch on the black market?"

"What if trying a keycard without Level 5 access triggers an alarm and the door locks behind us?" Grey slammed his palm on the console. "*Turn around.*"

Jax stared at him. "All right, cuz. All right." The mercenary spun the golf cart around and drove back through the ice tunnel, across the bridge that spanned the mysterious green river, and up the elevator. Back down the long hallway and into the main cavern by the front entrance, where they had first arrived.

Except for a pair of guards by the door, the compound sat eerily empty, a military devotion to mealtime. It made Grey even more nervous, because anyone they passed would question why they weren't in a mess hall. The two guards by the door were already giving them suspicious glances.

"No way we have time for both," Jax said, looking at the signpost. "As soon as meal time's over, we're gone."

Grey chose *Logistics & Control*. Moments after they sped down the corridor, the long, low moan of a siren shattered the silence.

"Security breach," a robotic voice announced. "Intruders are inside the complex." The words repeated three times, in all three languages, followed by an admonition for all guards to return to their posts and secure the exits.

43

Viktor stared down at the bullet hole in Thato's forehead. Naomi pulled her inside, slammed the door, and took her unmoving friend's face in her hands. She checked for a pulse and let out a cry of anguish that ripped Viktor's heart from his chest. He wrapped Naomi in his arms and tried to lift her to her feet, but she wrenched away.

The professor looked out the window and saw the dark blue sedan halfway down the long driveway, its lights on high beam. "It's almost here!"

With a shudder, Naomi wiped her face with a sleeve. "Is there a place you can hide?" she said to Daniel. "They want Viktor and me, not you."

"Tell that to Thato," Daniel said grimly.

"Is there?!" she shouted.

"Yes. A secret closet in the bedroom."

"Take Rose and go. Don't call for help. After half an hour, if you don't hear anyone inside the house, get Max and leave town. Stay low until you hear from me."

Daniel nodded, and Viktor could sympathize with the unspoken question in his eyes.

What if I never hear from you?

The architect rushed off with Rose. Viktor followed Naomi as she sprinted through the back door to the guest cottage. She grabbed her keys, raced to the garage, and Viktor barely had time to shut the passenger door before the Land Cruiser reversed out of the parking space, thundered around the house, and rammed the sedan as it pulled up to the estate.

The big truck impacted the rear passenger side of the sedan, smashing the door and spinning the smaller car around. With Viktor still dazed, Naomi grabbed her shotgun, leaned out the window and shot four times, shattering windows. The shotgun clicked empty and Naomi threw the gun in Viktor's lap. "Do you know how to reload?"

"No idea!"

At first there was no movement in the sedan, which Viktor could now see was a Mercedes. His hopes rose, and then the car lurched forward. A hand holding a long-barreled pistol appeared in the window. Viktor ducked as two shots were fired, and Naomi took off again, racing past the sedan and ramping the edge of the driveway.

She barreled down the hill leading to the vineyards, bouncing over flowerbeds and through manicured hedges at forty miles an hour. Viktor hung on for dear life. He doubted the Land Cruiser had airbags, but even if it did, being trapped inside a rolled vehicle would do no good with a killer right behind.

The Mercedes careened down the hill behind them, though the lower vehicle had to avoid the hedges instead of plowing over them. Viktor tried to get a look at the driver, but it was too dark. He guessed it was Robey.

"Why didn't you shoot his tires?" Viktor asked.

"Because I wanted to shoot him in the face."

As she navigated the precipitous slope with one hand, Naomi reached under the seat, took out a box of ammunition, and reloaded the shotgun. Viktor was impressed.

The Mercedes was a hundred feet behind them, but once they hit a straightaway, the German car would overtake them. Naomi screeched to the right at the bottom of the hill, then floored it until she reached the first long row of vines. She turned left on a dirt road and accelerated alongside the vineyard. The space between the rows looked too narrow to drive through. A hundred yards down, just as lights swung onto the dirt road behind them, Naomi whipped into the vineyard between two rows spaced wider apart than the others.

Naomi killed her lights and kept driving. Fifty feet in, she stopped and killed the engine. Viktor understood. In the darkness, the narrow path was almost hidden from view, and she was hoping the other driver would fly right past it.

Viktor held his breath and turned to watch. A few seconds later, the Mercedes drove past without stopping. Naomi rolled forward without her lights. Just before they reached the end of the row, the Mercedes swung in behind them, caught them in its high beams, and accelerated.

Naomi roared out of the tractor path and onto a dirt field. She fish-tailed to the left, kicking up a cloud of dust. At the end of the field, pressing the small advantage they had gained, she continued on a dirt road that wove through a series of barns and then skirted a pond. The road wound back up the hillside on the rear of the property, heading towards the mountains.

"Where are we going?" Viktor asked.

"To see what that Mercedes can handle."

Shots rang out. Naomi ordered Viktor to take the wheel while she leaned out the window and returned fire. Her hair had fallen loose, whipped into her face by the wind. As the Mercedes drew closer, the road narrowed and curved to the left, past a row of concrete block houses with new paint. The domestic workers' quarters.

Naomi retook the wheel and kept going, climbing a steep grassy hill as the Land Rover tilted precariously to the left.

More shots from behind. One shattered the passenger-side mirror, causing Viktor to hunker down. He risked a glance through the rear view. "He's gaining!"

"Hold on," Naomi said grimly.

Rocks and unruly shrubs replaced the grass. Viktor's teeth rattled as the Land Cruiser's suspension moaned and creaked over the obstacles. The route didn't seem to faze the Mercedes. It surged forward, coming ever closer.

"Take the gun!" Naomi said, putting the shotgun in Viktor's lap. "Just put it on your shoulder and pull the trigger. Short-stroke it to reload. And don't get shot."

Viktor wondered why she had handed him the weapon about the same time he saw a flash of quicksilver caught by the Land Cruiser's high beams. It was a river, a hundred feet wide and flowing swiftly over rocks down the hillside.

Before he could question the wisdom of Naomi's plan, the Land Cruiser plunged into the shallow water, tires digging into the riverbed. Viktor leaned out the window and raised the shotgun, realizing the delay would bring the Mercedes perilously close.

The recoil was stronger than he expected, but Viktor was not a small man, and he had used firearms before. He got two shots off as the Mercedes approached, then ducked back inside when the driver returned fire.

Naomi was halfway across the stream when the Mercedes hit the water. A bullet thumped into the rear of the Land Cruiser as she steered around a boulder. The water deepened until the tires were lost from view, and then the Land Cruiser stopped moving.

The tires spun in vain. Viktor whipped around to look behind them.

"Shoot!" Naomi screamed. "Keep him in the car!"

Viktor obeyed as Naomi jerked the car into reverse. It moved a few inches. The Mercedes drew closer.

Afraid of leaning too far out, Viktor fired another shell and shattered the windshield of the Mercedes. Robey's gray face loomed behind it. He fired at Viktor, forcing the professor back inside.

The Land Cruiser's tires spun and spun. Naomi jerked the wheel back and forth, switching between forward and reverse, trying to gain traction.

Robey stopped the car and opened the door, handgun raised.

"He's coming!" Viktor yelled.

Robey took a step forward and fired, keeping Viktor at bay. He waded through the water towards Naomi's side of the vehicle, and there was nothing to stop him.

Viktor took a wild shot. Robey hunched and kept walking. Twenty feet before he reached them, the tires finally caught, and the Land Cruiser lurched forward. Robey looked back and forth between the two vehicles, trying to decide what to do. He started splashing towards them, and when Viktor risked another shot, the shotgun clicked empty.

Robey must have heard the click because he started wading faster. Viktor cursed and fumbled with the shells. He dropped them on the floor and bent down. Robey fired and took out the side mirror.

As Viktor rose up, fearing what he would see, the Land Cruiser entered shallower water and finally picked up speed. Robey tried running through the water but the Land Cruiser drew further away and he was forced to return to the Mercedes. Once Robey resumed driving and reached the midway point, the same area that had bothered Naomi's vehicle, the Mercedes stopped moving and settled into the river, up to the hood.

The Land Cruiser climbed onto the far shore and over a pile of rocks as the Mercedes sputtered and then died. A hundred yards past the river, Naomi pulled onto a dirt road that ran atop the hillside. It joined a paved road five minutes later. Not until they were twenty minutes into the mountains did Viktor dare take his eyes off the mirror.

Naomi rolled into a deserted lot behind a small office park. After escaping from Robey, they had driven through a mountain pass to reach the closest town.

When the Land Cruiser finally came to rest, Naomi gripped the wheel with both hands and stared straight ahead, into the night. Her hands started to shake, and a tear slipped from her eye.

"She was my best friend," Naomi whispered. "She came to help me."

Viktor laid a hand on her arm, providing silent support. Naomi stayed in that position for a long time.

"My parents," she said finally, "my home, and Thato."

Viktor's jaw tightened.

Naomi checked the time on her cell. The Land Cruiser did not have a clock on the dashboard. "Nine p.m.," she said, then grabbed the shotgun and a box of shells, as well as a pair of binoculars. She reached for the door. "We'd better get moving."

"Without a car?"

"I'm going to hotwire that Corolla."

"Where are we going?"

The blankness of Naomi's face spoke to the volume of her rage. "Don't you want to see the old water plant?"

"Oh," Viktor said. "I see. Yes, I very much do."

An hour later, Professor Radek and Naomi lay on their stomachs atop a low hill that offered a view of the abandoned waste water treatment plant near van Draker's manor.

Due to darkness, they couldn't see very far inside the high wall and electric fencing surrounding the sprawling industrial ruins, but they could see the trio of late-model SUVs parked beside an imposing brick building near the main entrance, on the other side of an iron gate.

They could also see the flicker of a TV coming from a guard shack, as well as a pair of armed guards who, every twenty minutes or so, stepped out for a smoke.

It appeared, Viktor thought, that the water treatment plant wasn't so abandoned after all.

44

As the siren continued to blare, Jax stomped on the brake at the next intersection.

"What are you doing?" Grey said.

"We might have a ghost of a chance if we get to the exit before it's swarmed."

Grey gripped his arm. "I'm not leaving."

Jax jerked away. "Good for you."

"Do what you have to, but we're better off hiding out somewhere and trying to sneak out later."

After a shake of his head, Jax cursed and slammed the console of the golf cart. From somewhere down the corridor, they heard shouting and the sound of speeding vehicles.

Grey scanned the signs in the five-way intersection.

    COMMANDERS' QUARTERS
    WAR ROOM
    COMMUNICATIONS
    CONFERENCE AREA
    SECURITY

A golf cart emerged from *Security* and sped towards the main entrance. Two more followed in rapid succession, all of them eyeing Grey and Jax but not stopping. The mercenary made a show of reversing the golf cart as they passed, as if getting ready to join them.

"Get us out of here," Grey said, choking on his disappointment. Going any further was suicide. They didn't even know for sure that Charlie was there.

"I'm thinking the lab area. It was the most deserted."

"Fine."

Just before Jax sped off, Grey heard a shrill cry of pain coming from the corridor labeled *Security*. He froze, his hand gripping the side of the seat, not quite believing what he had heard.

Another shriek, in the same voice.

The husky voice of a teenage girl.

Charlie.

"Go!" Grey yelled, smacking the dash.

Jax hit the accelerator. Twenty yards down the corridor, as a line of supercharged Segways sped in the opposite direction, Grey saw a familiar blond head dragging Charlie, kicking and screaming, towards a closed door.

Charlie was handcuffed and trying to dig in her heels. The man—Gunter—opened the door with one hand and smacked Charlie on the side of the head so hard she tumbled into the room. Gunter followed her inside and slammed the door.

Jax slammed to a stop. Grey had already vaulted out of the vehicle. He whipped the door open and saw Charlie lying on her stomach. Gunter had a foot on her back and was jerking on her cuffs.

The blond man turned at the sound of the door opening, just in time to catch an elbow to the face. Grey's blow rocked him a few steps back, away from Charlie.

"*Teach?*"

Before Gunter could raise his hands in defense, Grey pounced on him, a snap kick to the groin and then an uppercut and a series of elbows to the head so fast and hard Gunter didn't have time to react. Stunned and bloodied, he tried to cover up as he fell. Grey jumped on him and kept swinging, leveraging himself by leaning a knee on the prone man's stomach. Gunter's head thudded into the floor again and again as Grey rained down blows, over and over, until Jax caught his arm from behind.

"Easy, now. He's gone."

With a deep, shuddering breath, Grey pushed to his feet and wiped the blood off his knuckles. The blond man's head lolled to the side, and Grey wasn't sure if he was alive or dead.

Nor did he care.

He turned and saw Charlie staring at the neo-Nazi's prone form. The uneasy shock in her eyes made Grey feel ashamed. He shouldn't have lost control in front of her.

Charlie's eyes hardened, and after Grey found a key on Gunter and unlocked her cuffs, she threw herself into Grey's arms. He hugged her fiercely in return, pressing her head tight against his chest, then held her at arm's length. Her face was badly bruised, one eye swollen shut. "Can you walk?" he asked.

"Hell yes," she said, after a series of wracking coughs. "I'll run on hot coals to China to get out of this dump."

Grey turned to Jax. "The golf cart?"

"Will she fit?"

Grey slipped outside, laid the two assault rifles on the front floor of the golf cart, and opened the storage compartment. Jax jumped into the driver's seat as Grey helped Charlie squeeze inside. It was an extremely tight fit, but she hugged her knees and tucked her head. It wouldn't close all the way, but the cracked lid gave her some air.

Grey still thought their best option was to hide out somewhere, wait for the chaos to calm down, and make a break for it. Maybe they could follow the river to another exit point.

Before Jax had a chance to drive away, a group of Segways approached, led by a familiar face. Emil. Grey tried to turn away, but the long-haired Icelander had already recognized him. As Emil shouted a series of commands to the men behind him, Grey picked up one of the assault rifles and unleashed a volley of automatic fire. The rounds knocked Emil off his Segway, and the others jumped off and hugged the ground.

It bought them a few seconds, but Grey had no plan. As Jax flew past the next intersection, Grey saw a huge, red-bearded man speeding towards them in a golf cart, leading the charge from one of the intersecting corridors.

Grey fired. Dag swerved and kept driving.

"Any ideas?" Jax shouted, as they entered the main cavern. Grey estimated three dozen guards filled the room. The siren was still blaring and must have covered the gunshots, because the guards paid them no attention.

Grey tried to think through the surge of adrenaline. They no longer had the option to hide. He knew of only one exit, and as soon as Dag arrived and blew their cover, they would be swarmed.

"Take Charlie and go for the snow bikes," he said, forcing away thoughts of failure. Not for himself, because he had known the risks when he entered the compound, but for Charlie.

"What?" Jax said.

"She can ride well enough to get started. When the door lifts, drive the hell out of here. I'll join you if I can."

"If you can? Where are you going?"

"To raise the door. Just do it, man!"

As they entered the main cavern, full of vehicles and bright lights and swarming guards, Grey gripped the assault rifle and jumped out of the golf cart. Walking swiftly and with confidence, he strode towards the button that controlled the door.

Fifty feet from the entrance. Plenty of people carried similar assault rifles, though a few started to eye him with suspicion. In the corner of his eye, Grey saw Jax heading for the snow bikes. He had a clear path.

Grey heard shouting behind him. He glanced over his shoulder and saw Dag whisking into the grotto on his golf cart, flanked by a dozen men. He spotted Jax first and pointed him out.

"Take him!" Dag roared.

Chaos erupted. As Jax laid down a burst of cover fire and dove behind a Superjeep, letting the golf cart smack into a wall with Charlie still concealed inside, Grey sprinted for the button. Dag noticed him and yelled again.

Too soon, Grey knew. *Dag saw us too soon.*

A guard by the door leveled his weapon. Grey shot first and dropped him. Grey was steps away from the button. Without looking behind him, he threw himself forward, arm outstretched, and pressed the white sphere as a volley of gunfire peppered the wall above his head.

A familiar click of gears.

The ice door began to lift.

Grey scrambled behind a golf cart, braced the rifle against his shoulder as he turned, and sprayed gunfire over the seat. Return fire thunked into the vehicle, shredding the vinyl and blowing the tires.

He glanced to his left. A crowd of men hovered near the spot where Jax had taken cover, but the mercenary had deployed a smoke bomb and obscured the area. Automatic fire went back and forth, and Grey had no way to tell what was happening or if Charlie was safe. He couldn't do much of anything except hunker behind his golf cart and try to keep the approaching mob at bay. Left without a vehicle, Grey harbored no illusions of escaping. He would do what he could to help Jax and Charlie survive.

The door was a quarter of the way up. An inch of snow covered the ground, and more was falling. Dag and his men employed military tactics to advance on Grey, using the vehicles as shields, covering each other as they advanced. Grey estimated he had about five seconds before they overran him. At least a hundred men crowded the cavern.

Sirens wailed as the door continued to open. The stench of gunpowder fouled the air. Grey scanned the room, desperate. A dead guard clutched a rifle ten feet from Grey's position. He tried to scramble on his belly to pick it up, but someone saw him edge forward, and a burst of gunfire drove him back.

He was pinned.

Sensing victory, Dag ordered his men to rush Grey's position. Grey had room to dart under the door, but he would be exposed, shot dead in an instant. He gripped the ammo-less rifle and prepared to use it as a club, knowing it was futile.

Lying flat on his belly, he saw the booted feet of Dag's men surrounding the jeep. Just before they rushed him, two huge explosions rocked the middle of the cavern, followed by the high-pitched revs of a pair of motorcycle engines.

Screams and dense smoke filled the air. In the confusion, two snow bikes roared under the door and out of the grotto, one of them darting forward in a straight line and the other wobbling and almost pitching over before righting itself. Grey saw Charlie clutching the second bike with a white-knuckled grip. He willed her to stay upright.

Dag's men were still advancing. Grey decided to take a chance. He would rather be shot than captured by Dag. After flinging his rifle at the closest man, he darted through the entrance, head low, weaving from side to side and trying to escape in the confusion. A bullet whizzed by his head and another grazed his arm. Just when he was most exposed, certain a bullet would catch him in the back, Jax wheeled his bike around and laid down a volley of cover fire.

"Go!" Grey screamed. "Stay with her!"

They both ignored him. Charlie realized what was happening and stopped a dozen yards past Jax. As the mercenary sprayed the entrance with bullets, hiding behind his bike from the return fire, Grey sprinted with everything he had and jumped on the back of Charlie's motorcycle. A bullet plunked into her windshield, spider-webbing the glass.

As soon as Charlie and Grey drove off, Jax shot past them, veering into the lava rock field instead of taking the road. Smart move, Grey thought. It put them out of sight of the entrance for a second. Plus, the airfield was directly across the field, much closer as the crow flies than circling around on the main road. Grey could already see jeeps headed their way in the distance. Dag must have called ahead.

There was another factor. Grey heard the steady thump of a helicopter approaching in the distance, swooping towards the airfield. It might belong to W.A.R., or it could be Jax's extraction plan in play.

They had to reach the airfield to find out.

Shouts and the sounds of revving engines sounded behind them. Charlie accelerated, ramped the curb into the lava field, hit a jagged rock less than fifty yards in, and crashed the bike.

Grey did his best to curl his body to absorb the impact. He landed in a patch of spongy moss that helped cushion the fall. "Back on!" he yelled, struggling to his feet and praying Charlie hadn't hit her head. "Behind me!"

He picked up the bike as Charlie lurched to a standing position, dazed, her face scratched and bleeding. A spray of bullets spackled the rocks around them. Grey risked a glance back and saw an army of vehicles leaving the cavern. W.A.R.'s red-bearded leader was at the vanguard, bearing down on them atop a snow bike.

"Charlie!"

Dag raised his weapon. Charlie hobbled closer, and Grey helped her climb on the bike. A bullet struck a boulder beside them. Reaching a hand back to help steady Charlie, Grey cranked his wrist and shot forward, accelerating as fast as the bike would allow. She clutched his waist, and they barely hung on as he careened around a boulder the size of a car.

The lava field was akin to the world's hardest slalom course, a maze of narrow and insanely twisty paths weaving through a sea of moss-covered mounds and chest-high rock formations. All of it jagged. All of it unfamiliar terrain. Grey went as fast as he dared, making sure to speed through the stretches that exposed them to gunfire, even though he risked flipping the bike.

The terrain helped shield them from snipers, though constant bursts of gunfire popped in the air behind them. Grey kept his head low and concentrated on keeping the bike upright. He knew he could ride.

But so could Dag.

Grey's glances in the rearview told him that half of the men chasing them had already crashed their bikes, and that everyone except Dag had fallen behind. The big man took as many risks as Grey, ramping rock formations and leaning so far over on the curves his knees brushed the ground. The ride was far too treacherous to risk a shot, but unlike Grey, Dag wasn't weighed down by a second rider.

"He's gaining, Teach!"

The helicopter whipped closer. Jax's bike came in and out of view, and had almost reached the airfield. The vehicles on the main road had turned around and were racing to cut them off.

"When we hit the next blind curve," Grey said over the roar of the engine, glancing back and seeing Dag less than twenty yards behind them, "I'm leaving you."

"Say what?"

"Scoot up on the bike and make sure you've got the bars before I jump. Don't go too fast, no one's going to catch you."

"Don't do it, Teach." Grey could hear the fear in her voice. "Let's stay together."

"Dag's too close. We won't make it. You can do this, Charlie. I think that copter's ours. Jax will help you. I'll be right behind."

"Teach—"

Grey didn't give her time to finish. On the next curve, once they were out of sight, he slowed and scooted to the front of the bike, then stood and crouched on the balls of his feet.

"Take it!" he ordered.

Charlie edged forward. As soon as he saw her hands grasp the handlebars, he dove off, protecting his vitals as he crashed into a mossy mound. He thought he might have cracked a rib, but he grunted through the pain and scampered to the other side, wincing as Charlie wobbled and then gained control of the bike.

Not a second later, Dag came flying by. Grey leapt at him and just managed to grab his coat. The maneuver sent Dag and Grey crashing into another mound, the heavy bike spinning to the ground ahead of them.

Dazed by the collision, both men stumbled to their feet. Dag's gun had landed in the snow twenty feet away, across a jagged field of lava rock. Dag eyed it and knew he wouldn't reach it in time. He drew a long, serrated knife instead.

Behind him, Grey heard the whine of approaching bikes. Moments away. He had no choice but to try to end this fast.

Grey stalked forward and feinted a low kick. The bigger man bladed his body to the side, then lashed out with the knife. Fast and careful, not overextending. After another feint to judge Dag's defenses, Grey attacked fast and hard. Eyes locked onto the knife, following its every movement, he darted forward with his hands up, closing the distance and forcing Dag to react.

As soon as the red-bearded leader brought the knife up to thwart Grey's attack, Grey crossed his hands in an X and latched onto Dag's wrist. Grey stopped the knife at chest-height, locking it into place and bringing the two men almost nose-to-nose.

Dag tried to use his superior strength to free his weapon and throw Grey to the side. When Dag twisted, Grey went with the movement, bending in the same direction and using his opponent's own wrist for support. At the same time, Grey kicked him as hard as he could on the side of the foot, trying for a sweep and missing.

Dag stumbled but didn't fall. Grey's failed maneuver flowed right into his next. Once he felt his opponent's weight shift, Grey jerked backwards to keep him unbalanced, threw a snap kick to the groin to distract him, and flipped Dag's vulnerable wrist over, the one still holding the knife.

Surprising Grey with his agility, Dag flipped to avoid the wrist break, but ended up on his back on the snow. The knife fell at Grey's feet. Dag struggled to get up, but Grey kept him down by shoving a hand in his face and thrusting a knee on his chest. Grey's fingers moved lower, digging into the mandibular pressure points on either side of Dag's jaw.

The roar of the closest bikes pounded in Grey's ears. Too close for Grey to kill Dag and get back on the bike and escape.

"You do realize you came out here for nothing," Dag said.

Grey picked up the knife with his free hand.

"Don't believe me?" Dag's sinister laugh sent a chill down Grey's spine. The Icelander knew what was coming, and showed no fear. "Check your piglet's nails in the morning. They might need a good clipping."

Grey applied the pressure points so hard that Dag gagged and his eyes bulged. Grey raised the knife and pressed it against his cheek.

"Do it," Dag said, through clenched teeth.

"I'd love to, believe me. But I need a distraction."

The W.A.R. leader struggled as Grey stared into his eyes, owning him as he slowly drew the knife across his jugular. He cut deep enough so Dag would bleed out, but not so deep he would die in seconds.

Dag gasped and flopped like a suffocating fish as Grey pushed to his feet on the blood-stained snow. Shots peppered the ground. He raced to retrieve the assault rifle and then jumped on Dag's bike as the first rider came into view. The crushed front fender worried Grey, but the bike started right up.

Grey and the first rider exchanged gunfire, but as Grey weaved the bike and sped away, he glanced in the rearview and noticed the soldier stopping to attend to Dag, buying Grey the time he needed.

A quarter mile away, the helicopter descended on the airfield as a line of jeeps approached from the settlement. Charlie was waving frantically at Grey while Jax faced the approaching vehicles, laying down cover fire. He ran out of ammo and pulled Charlie towards the copter.

Grey didn't know if they would make it. He held the assault rifle in one hand and the right side of the handlebars in the other, taking risks on the uneven terrain. He cut off a few dozen yards by ramping off a flattened boulder, almost losing control when he hit the ground. He straightened out, swerved to avoid a series of obstacles, and passed a dead guard beside a mound with a hinged door flapping open. Jax must have got him.

Grey whipped into the airfield. He took the bike so fast on the straightaway the cold air brought tears to his eyes, right before he slammed on the brakes in front of the hovering copter. A ladder lowered from twenty feet up.

Bullets rained in from the approaching jeeps, smacking the ground ahead of them, just out of range. Grey fired back to slow them.

"Get her in!" he shouted.

In the corner of his eye, he saw Charlie and Jax climb the ladder and disappear inside the copter. Grey followed behind, dropping the gun once the ammo ran out. The copter started to ascend with Grey still on the ladder. Bullets whisked through the air beside him. One tore through the side of his shirt, another riffled his hair. He clutched the ladder as the wind and motion rocked him side to side. Fingers trembling from the strain, his eyes gummy from wind and cold, he finally got high enough for Jax to reach a hand out and pull him up. Grey dove inside the copter just as a pair of bullets thunked into the metal side.

The pilot took them higher, out of reach. After slapping Grey on the back, Jax let out his tension with an exultant yell. "Damn, I thought I was extreme."

Charlie tried to hug Grey, but he held her off and took her by the arm. "Show me your hand."

"What?"

"*Your hand.*"

Unnerved by his intensity, Charlie let Grey flatten her palm and examine the fingers of her left hand. He stiffened when he saw how the nails extended half an inch above the fingers and had already started tapering to a point. They felt much harder than fingernails should feel.

"Weird, huh?" Charlie said, after another bout of coughing. "This morning I woke up like this. My muscles feel weird, too."

Grey started to tremble.

45

Naomi took the binoculars back from Viktor. "So that's how they've been accessing the lab. A sewage tunnel connected to van Draker's cellar."

Viktor noticed a short enclosed walkway linking the guard shack to the large brick building with no windows they had spied earlier. "Do we try to get in? How confident are you that you can subdue the guards?"

"I'm a police officer, not James Bond," she said.

"I couldn't tell from the escape last night."

She waved a hand. "Those are just bush driving skills. What about your partner? Any word?"

"I'm afraid not."

"What if he . . . doesn't respond?"

Viktor felt his chest tighten. "I don't know. Is there another officer you trust? Someone who could help us get inside?"

"No one who would cross van Draker," she said slowly. "Especially not with a warrant out for my arrest." Naomi belly-crawled out of the bushes and pushed to her feet, leading the way back to the Corolla she had hotwired. "They'll find the Land Cruiser and be looking for this car by morning. We can't hide forever, unless we go into the bush. And that doesn't help with van Draker. We'll just be fugitives."

"I know," Viktor said, striding forward to keep up with her. "I know."

The morning sky was a forge of red light, bellows pumping fog, as dawn crept over the jagged tips of the mountains. Viktor and Naomi drove away from the nature preserve on a back road that skirted a series of ravines with muscled green slopes.

Neither Viktor nor Naomi had a plan, and the sergeant didn't know whom to trust. They were tossing ideas back and forth when a car approached from behind, blue lights flashing.

Naomi gripped the wheel. "Someone must have gone to work early in that office park."

"Every policeman in the area is probably searching for your car. What do we do?"

Naomi slowed to a stop on the side of the road and gave Viktor instructions. He felt a trickle of sweat under his collar. "Are you sure?"

"It's the only way. If it's a junior patrol officer, he might not even have a firearm." She put a hand on Viktor's thigh. "This means crossing a line. I understand if you want to stay in the car."

"I appreciate the sentiment," Viktor said, "but you're wasting time."

She met his gaze and stepped out of the car with her hands up. "I'm unarmed," she called out, and started walking towards the police car.

A young male officer exited with his pistol raised. He pointed his free hand at Viktor. "You, too."

Viktor eased out of the car, giving Naomi time to get closer.

"Stop moving, Naomi!"

"It's me, Geert. I've done nothing wrong. It's all a mistake."

Naomi had drawn to within ten feet.

Geert swiveled towards her. "Not another step!"

Viktor reached into the car and whipped out the shotgun, pointing it at the policeman. He wasn't going to shoot, but he had to sell his intent.

Geert took his eyes off Naomi and froze, the pistol pointing halfway between Viktor and Naomi. The officer knew the professor had the drop on him. Naomi approached swiftly, took Geert's weapon and phone, and locked him in the back of his own patrol car.

"Do you know what you're doing?" Geert said.

"Who do you trust," Naomi shot back, "a fellow officer or Jans van Draker?"

Geert shook his head. "I'm just doing my job, hey?"

Naomi and Viktor drove off in the Corolla, knowing it was marked but unsure where to go or what to do. They just knew they had to get off the road and find a safe haven.

The professor tried Grey again from Naomi's phone, and to his surprise, he answered. "Finally," Viktor said in relief. "Where are you?"

"On my way to you," Grey said. "Why are you using Sergeant Linde's phone?"

"What?"

"I saw the news. They might be tracing you."

"They can do that this quickly, with a cell phone?"

"They're resurrecting human beings and orchestrating a global genocide."

"Ah, yes. Good point. I'll dispose of it after we speak. What do you mean, you're on your way to me?"

Grey gave him an extremely abbreviated version of the events of the last few days, and said, "They injected Charlie, Viktor. The night before we freed her. Her nails are growing and there are other signs."

Viktor closed his eyes and put his fingertips to his temple. "*Do prdele.*"

"You said before you thought van Draker has a vaccine," Grey continued. "Is that still true?"

"If it exists. The only other place would be Iceland."

"Those labs were old, barely in use. It didn't feel right."

Viktor compressed his lips and told Grey about the secret entrance he suspected lay somewhere inside the water treatment plant.

"Can you find someplace to hole up until I get there?" Grey asked. After a pause, his voice lowered, as if he didn't want to be heard. "The sooner the better. She's changing."

Viktor thought, and an idea sprang into his head, someplace he and Naomi might be safe as long as they could arrive unnoticed. "I believe so."

"Then ditch the car and the phone, and get there as soon as you can. Use another phone and text me your location. I'll come get you. Or I can go in alone, and get you later."

"No," Viktor said quickly. "You might need me."

Grey's voice hardened. "I know there are things in that lab you want to see for yourself. But is now the time?"

"I've been in the lab and I know van Draker. You'll need help."

"Fine," Grey said, after a moment. "Now get rid of that phone. And the car."

After they hung up, Viktor held the cell phone tight in his hands, digesting the conversation. Then he took out the SIM card and lowered the window, tossed the phone, and turned towards Naomi. "I have an idea," he said.

46

"What is it with you people and underground labs?" Jax said as he drove a Nissan XTrail 4x4, rented under yet another false name, into the Cape Town city center. Grey was in the back seat, watching Charlie's condition worsen as he waited anxiously for Viktor's text.

On the flight over, Charlie's skin had turned feverish and assumed a grayish pallor. Her hair was falling out in clumps, the fingernail growth continued, and veins bulged from her engorged muscles.

In a frightened voice, she had asked Grey what was happening to her. It broke his heart, but he told her.

She took it as she always did, with a brave stoicism that a child without her experiences would never have mustered.

I'll fix this, Charlie, he vowed. *I'll fix it or die trying.*

When they reached the Isle of Skye, Grey had called Dr. Varela and asked if the vaccine was ready, and whether there was anything he could do for Charlie.

Dr. Varela said an experimental vaccine was closer but still some time away. And that he should call a priest.

Jax bartered for another flight, this one to a private airport near Cape Town. Another ten grand on Grey's dime. After a heated negotiation, Jax ate half the cost of the helicopter flight from Iceland.

They had landed near Cape Town at dusk, almost twenty-four hours after their escape from the W.A.R. stronghold. Before Viktor hung up, he had divulged the location of the old water treatment plant, in case the professor and Naomi didn't make it to a safe-house. Charlie might not last until morning, Grey knew.

As soon as midnight hit, he was going in. With or without Viktor.

"Where to?" Jax asked.

Grey had visited Cape Town once before, when he lived in Zimbabwe, but didn't know the city very well. "Any place we can hole up for a few hours?"

"How about some grub?" Charlie chimed in. She was curled into a ball, covering her clawed hands and taking in the city with wide eyes. "Do you have to starve yourself on missions?"

"You heard her," Grey said. He winked at Charlie, trying to keep her spirits high. "Burger and fries?"

"You know it."

Jax gave it some thought. "There might be a W.A.R. sympathizer in a merc joint. In the high-end places, too." Jax grinned at Charlie in the rear view. "I know just the one."

After stopping at a pharmacy for Ibuprofen, Jax took them to a bar called Rafiki on Kloofnek Street. They sat on a balcony with a view of Lion's Head peak, so close it seemed they could reach out and touch it. The clientele at the wrap-around bar resembled a pierced and tattooed United Nations meeting.

"This burger's dope," Charlie said, awkwardly trying to use her stiffened fingers to eat, "but I don't feel so hot."

Grey put a hand on her elbow. "You need some more water?"

"Nah," she mumbled, looking nauseated. "Be right back."

Grey winced as she rose to use the restroom. She had barely touched her food.

"What's the prognosis?" Jax said, after she left.

The bathroom door was in full view, and Grey kept an eye on it. "Days, at best, unless we find an antidote. And we're not sure one exists."

Jax swallowed and set his burger down. "Damn. She's a good kid."

"The best," Grey said, his voice remote.

"Would a hospital help?"

"Not really, and I can't risk her being targeted."

Jax glanced up at the proud chin thrust of Lion's Head, and then back at Grey. "Listen, I want you to know . . . whatever you need on this thing, I'm in."

Grey looked him in the eye. "I appreciate that. There's really only one more job, but it's very, very important."

"You got it, brother. What do you need?"

"A babysitter."

After dinner, they left the city on the N2. When they reached the barren lowlands near the airport, Grey noticed Charlie absorbing the rotting shacks lining the road, the slums cordoned off by trash-heaped fences that provided a physical and spiritual boundary.

"That's not cool," Charlie said, with a cough.

"No," Grey said, "it's not."

"C'mon, Viktor," Grey muttered to himself. *Hurry up and text.*

Glancing back at Charlie's drawn features, Jax veered off the N2 and took them to a coastal town called Betty's Bay. Surrounded by a bowl of sheer mountains thrusting upward like swords, kissed by the Antarctic, the teal bay at the end of the scenic drive was an awe-inspiring sight.

"First time in Africa, kid?" Jax asked Charlie, as they all left the car and followed a tourist trail skirting the edge of the rocky cove. The fishy, iodine smell of beached kelp wrinkled Grey's nose.

"Uh, first time outta New York."

"Africa is where it's at," Jax said, "if you like beauty and adventure. But it isn't for sissies." He waved a hand in dismissal. "This area's a good way to ease in. The Western Cape is like California. With cobras."

Charlie laughed. "Do you always work with Teach?"

"Jax is an entrepreneur," Grey cut in, giving the mercenary a long stare. "He helps people out sometimes."

"That's right," Jax said, with a smirk. "When people need something special, they give me a call."

"You as good as Teach is?"

"Depends on what you need done," Jax said.

"You know," Charlie threw a few air punches, "with taking care of business."

Grey had heard enough. He didn't want Jax filling her head with his bullshit philosophies. "Ever seen penguins before?" he asked, checking his phone for the hundredth time as he pointed behind Charlie.

She whipped around, gasping with delight as a pair of the tuxedoed flightless birds climbed out of the water and waddled across a rock. Charlie rushed to the railing, the conversation already forgotten.

They camped out in the parking lot until eleven p.m., after Grey had almost given up hope on Viktor. When he finally got a text from a burner phone with an address in the Cape Flats, he cocked his head in confusion, and showed it to Jax.

The mercenary took the phone. "A chicken shack?" He typed the name into his phone's GPS, then raised his eyebrows. "I'll be damned."

After a long and harrowing drive through the Cape Flats at night, a journey in which Grey thought numerous times that he and Jax were about to be carjacked—or at least attempted to be—they finally rolled through a congested slum and into a square of cracked pavement peppered with open-air stalls closed for the night. Discarded wrappers, bottles, and other urban detritus littered the streets. Groups of locals slithered into the darkness at the sight of the late-model Nissan.

Grey tensed and told Charlie to get down as half a dozen armed men emerged from behind one of the shacks lining the periphery of the square. At first, Grey thought Viktor had been compromised, but Jax kept his cool, lowered the window, and calmly told the men who they were looking for. With a nod of recognition and an almost incomprehensible accent, one of the men stepped forward and told them to park the car behind the shack and follow them inside. They gave Charlie a curious glance but said nothing.

In a tiny kitchen filled with the aroma of charcoal and caramelized chicken fat, Grey found Viktor sitting on a chair of stacked milked crates next to a tall blond woman in her forties with rugged good looks.

The professor greeted Grey and Charlie warmly, and gave Jax a nod. "Grey told me you were involved."

"Professor," Jax said, tipping his head in return. "We should stop meeting like this."

Viktor introduced Officer Linde and his driver, a ferret-like Malay man eating a chicken leg on a Styrofoam plate. Grey noticed the look of mutual respect—and attraction—that passed between Viktor and the blond officer.

After discussing a strategy to infiltrate the water treatment plant, Grey paced the room with his hands behind his head. "We've no idea what's waiting for us in there. How many guards there will be. I doubt it's a military base, but if that's where the virus is made . . ."

"You could use a distraction," Jax said. "Once you get inside."

Grey nodded.

"I could take care of that."

Grey thought about it, and discarded the idea. Not only could their enemies use Charlie as leverage if they located her, but she might need protecting from herself. "I want you with her. At all times."

Jax put his hands up. "You're the boss."

"I don't need washing, yo," Charlie said, then doubled over coughing. "I mean watching."

Though she looked fitter than ever, Charlie had lost more hair and started to slur her speech. Grey knew the muscles and other signs of advanced physicality were an illusion. The last gasp of the deadly gargoyle virus. He sensed that, if she lost her grip on her mind, even an antidote would be futile.

One of the local men stepped forward, giving Charlie a long glance before turning to Grey. "You need a distraction, is it?"

After scouting the perimeter of the water treatment plant, Grey climbed down a wooded section of the hill on the western side. The night was cool, the insects a chorus of baby rattles. Using disposable phones the owners of the chicken shack had lent them, Grey waited for Viktor to text him the go-ahead.

At 12:35 a.m., the signal came.

The guards were on a smoke break.

Grey had five minutes.

He hurried to the bottom of the eight-foot wall, jumped, and pulled himself up. Balancing on the narrow ledge, inches away from the electric fencing that topped the wall, he took four strips of black rubber out of his backpack. Old bicycle tires supplied by the men in the slum, which Grey had cut and fashioned into foot-length sections.

Four strands of taut electric fencing, each a foot apart, topped the cement portion of the wall. Grey knew the wires were live by the faint, sporadic *click-clack* sound they emitted.

Grey fitted the tire strips over the strands of electric fencing, one atop the other. He pulled on the wires to test them. No sag. Good. Cutting or touching the wires together likely would trigger an alarm.

Using the rubber as handholds and footholds, Grey climbed over the fence and dropped to the other side, noting the cameras spaced along the lower sections of the wall. If he didn't make it to the guard shack in time, the guards would spot him at once.

He took out the Glock G43 Jax's pilot had sold them and sprinted across the property, switching off the trigger safety as he ran.

He rounded a corner and saw the guard shack a hundred yards away, just visible in the darkness. He slowed and ran as silently as he could, until he saw two guards pinching off their cigarettes a few feet from the door to the shack.

Fifty yards to go.

Grey had to get closer. He gave it everything he had.

The guards dropped the butts and started for the guard shack. Grey wasn't going to make it. Left with no choice, praying no one else was in earshot, he fired above their heads.

One of the men dropped to the ground. The other whirled and darted for the guard shack. *Damn.* Grey fired at the door and missed it by a foot, but it caused the guard to freeze.

"On the ground!" Grey shouted. "Do it!"

He worried the guard would bolt inside and risk getting shot, but the man reluctantly dropped to his knees and then his stomach. Grey breathed a sigh of relief as he ran forward, keeping his gun trained on the men.

He cuffed the guards with their own handcuffs and opened the automatic gate for Viktor and Naomi. They drove down the hill and joined Grey.

The glass and steel guardhouse looked far more modern than the rest of the plant. As did the enclosed walkway connecting the guardhouse to the two-story brick building next to it.

"It appears the cameras only cover the grounds," Viktor said.

Naomi leaned forward on her palms, intent on the monitor focused on the outside of the brick building. Unlike the others, the screen of that monitor never changed. "There's something in there," she said.

Grey took a set of keys attached to one of the guard's belts. "Let's find out what it is."

One of the keys unlocked the heavy steel door at the end of the covered walkway. The door opened onto a cavernous building with age-spotted brick walls. Iron piping, catwalks, and rusting treatment equipment filled the room. The lack of windows gave it the feel of a giant cistern. Near the middle of the building, stairs led down to a slender walkway that paralleled a canal twenty feet below the surface.

Fetid water filled the canal, wrinkling Grey's nose. A modern powerboat with a long, flat, pirogue-type barge attached to the rear was anchored to the railing that ran alongside the walkway.

It's the same system as in Iceland, Grey thought. *Transport by underground canal.*

Grey herded the two guards into the building, gagged them, and chained them to separate pieces of metal piping. Grey jerked hard on the piping. It would hold.

The professor pointed down at the canal, in the direction the powerboat was facing. A hundred feet ahead, the tunnel disappeared into the gloom.

47

Grey dashed back into the guard shack and found a set of keys for the powerboat. When he returned to the building, he decided to take one of the guards with him. He chose the one who had dropped to the ground as soon as Grey fired the gun.

Naomi untethered the boat. Grey took the wheel and coaxed the boat to life. They stuck the gagged and handcuffed guard, watching with sullen eyes, on his stomach on the floor.

The boat was easy to maneuver. Grey followed the canal into a claustrophobic brick tunnel with a rounded ceiling, the water gleaming soft and oily in the headlamps. Mineral deposits had congealed on the walls and formed stalactites above their heads. The air was cold and moldy, raising the gooseflesh on Grey's arms. "How far to the lab?"

"About ten kilometers," Naomi said, "if the route is straight."

The tunnel delved deeper and deeper into the earth. Brick and silence all around, shadows on the walls, the constant fear of a spotlight flicking on. Or, worse, some monstrosity rising from the murky depths.

What other boundaries had van Draker toyed with? Grey wondered. How far had his experiments gone? Were there unnamed things gliding beneath the water, following them with lidless eyes, waiting for a chance to drag them out of the boat?

Grey was not a superstitious man, but after everything they had witnessed, the tomblike passage was getting to him. It felt as if they were drifting down the river Styx, hovering on the boundary between life and death, probing the unknown.

Just after eleven kilometers ticked by on the odometer, Naomi stood and pointed to the right, at an opening in the wall. Grey eased off the throttle. As they approached, he realized the opening was a tunnel veering gently away, like an exit off an interstate. The new passage was made of concrete and reinforced with steel at ribbed intervals.

Grey handed the wheel to Naomi, took out the Glock, and ungagged the guard on the floor of the boat. "Is this the right way?"

The guard nodded. He was short and blond, with the eyes of a snake. A survivor.

"How far is the lab?" Grey demanded.

"One kilometer."

"Are there cameras? Guards?" Grey pointed the gun at his face. "Look at me. Do you doubt I'll pull the trigger?"

A vigorous headshake.

"Then make sure you tell the truth," Grey said.

"No cameras or guards until you get inside."

"How do we get inside?"

The guard hesitated. Grey raised the gun.

"This tunnel dead-ends at a door. There's a walkway beside it, with an intercom and a fingerprint ID scanner."

"No camera?"

The guard swallowed. "Sorry. Ya. There's a camera by the scanner. It doesn't show the canal."

Grey grabbed him by the back of the head and forced the gun into his cheek. "A little girl's life is at stake. Lie to me again, and I'll make a canal between your ears. Do your prints get us inside?"

The guard gave a reluctant nod.

"How well do you know the layout of the lab?"

The guard described the interior, as well as the position of the guards on the other side of the wall. After he finished, Grey checked his watch, replaced the man's gag, and waited.

———

At the bottom of the hill leading to van Draker's manor, a dozen men from the Cape Flats poured out of a flatbed truck. Each of them carried a homemade smoke bomb in one hand, a can of Castle Lager in the other, and an assortment of homemade fireworks in their pockets and rucksacks.

The mercenary the men had nicknamed "Harrison," due to his roguish resemblance to Indiana Jones, had made the smoke bombs himself and paid for the beer and fireworks.

The men melted into the woods and fanned out in a wide circle. At precisely two a.m., they started climbing the hill. Once they reached the wall, they launched the smoke bombs, smothering the lawn with a cloud of greasy smoke. Next they released the fireworks from the safety of the trees, knowing they might get shot if they ventured too close.

Doors slammed open. Floodlights kicked on. Guards from the manor shouted across the property.

After releasing a barrage of noise and gunpowder that sounded like an advancing army, the men from the Cape Flats fled down the hillside, whooping and spilling beer, happy to have stuck a thorn into the side of the White Crocodile, a relic of Apartheid, the rich boss man infamous around the Western Cape for his cruelty to blacks.

Still, once they reached the bottom, they wasted no time hurrying into the truck and speeding away. Not only did they risk the wrath of the local police and van Draker's guards, but they feared the specter of unholy experiments that hung like a shroud above the hill.

The manor was not just a house, and they all knew it. Each of them had relatives in Khayalanga or knew of someone who did. People talked. Communities shared. Every Xhosa within a hundred miles had heard the stories, and every single one of them knew that the van Draker manor was the place where the Bad Things happened.

At five minutes after two, Naomi eased the powerboat to a stop when the canal dead-ended at a wide steel door. Viktor tied the boat to an iron stake on the platform that abutted the waterway. He eyed the place where Grey had slipped into the water and took a deep breath, trying not to think about the price of failure.

Grey knew what he was doing, the professor told himself, though he knew competence wasn't the issue at stake. The look in Grey's eyes said he would go to any lengths to get inside van Draker's complex, no matter the risk, no matter the danger.

Once the boat was secure, Naomi ungagged the guard, took off his cuffs, and leveled the shotgun at him. "I've lost my job, my house, and my best friend. Don't think I won't take it out on you."

The guard licked his lips and said nothing. Naomi wasn't as convincing as Grey, and Viktor wondered if she would really kill the guard in cold blood if he failed to perform. He rather hoped she wouldn't, but he wasn't sure.

Thankfully, Grey had a chat with the guard before he left, one that left the blond man shaken. Viktor suspected that conversation carried as much weight as the current one.

"It's time," the professor said.

Naomi nosed the shotgun towards the walkway. The guard climbed out of the boat. His shoulders slumped as he stepped up to the intercom and the fingerprint scanner jutting out of the wall, to the left of the steel door.

Naomi raised the shotgun. The guard stiffened and pressed a button on the intercom.

"Delivery," he said.

Nothing.

He pressed it twice more, repeating the command, until a voice came through. "Who's this?"

"It's Henson. Open up."

"This isn't scheduled. We've got a situation at the manor."

"I know. I have reinforcements."

"Sent by who?"

"Captain Waalkamp."

A pause. Naomi kept the shotgun aimed at the guard. Viktor could only hope he was telling the truth about the cameras not pointing at the canal. If not, then that door would never open, and Grey would never leave.

"Send them in, then," the voice over the intercom said. "Don't know what's going on, but we might need them."

As Viktor caught his breath, tensing in anticipation, Henson pressed the tips of his fingers against the face of the scanner.

Grey crouched to grasp the iron handle with both hands, ten feet deep in the cold and fetid water, his lungs straining. A manual failsafe the guard had told him about, the handle was attached to the bottom of the steel door at the end of the canal. Grey used it to hold himself in place so he wouldn't have to expend precious energy treading water.

As soon as the door rose a foot off the bottom, Grey shot under it, using the handle to propel himself forward. Once through, he used a breaststroke to traverse the length of the holding bay.

According to the captured guard, Grey had fifty feet to swim. He could see shadowy figures moving around the holding bay above him, guards opening the door and preparing for the entry. Only two or three, if they were lucky and the diversion had worked.

Despite the exertion, Grey shivered with cold. He needed more body fat for a mission like this. Spots of black filled his vision, and he stretched his fingers as far as he could, vowing not to surface until he felt the wall. Leave the water too soon and he'd be a sitting duck.

Even if things went as planned, it was going to be close.

His lungs spasming from the effort, Grey finally touched a hard surface and shot upwards. It took all of his willpower to take baby sips, and not gasp in air, when his head broke through.

He didn't have time to wait. He had to take out the guard in the control room before he could alert the rest of the compound.

His hands on the edge of the wall, Grey lifted his eyes out of the water. A glance confirmed the guard's description of the holding bay. A central basin of water surrounded by a concrete docking area full of crates and winches.

Grey risked a look behind him. The wall was up and the powerboat drifting inside, the captured guard at the helm. Per Grey's instructions, Viktor and Naomi should be lying unseen on the floor, Naomi pointing the gun into the guard's crotch.

A single guard stood on the dock watching the boat come in. *Excellent.*

Grey whipped around. The control room, which gave access to the main compound, lay twenty feet ahead. It also contained the intercoms and surveillance equipment. Grey saw a guard inside, facing the monitors, probably watching the situation unfold outside van Draker's manor.

So far, so good. Grey was lucky neither guard was facing his way. One glimpse of Grey, one push of a panic button, and the advantage was lost.

Viktor and Naomi had seconds before they were spotted. None of the weapons were waterproof models, so Grey had to leave the boat unarmed. He had also left his shoes and socks behind to streamline his swimming, and so the shoes wouldn't squeak.

He slipped silently out of the canal, a barefoot wraith from the deep. Dripping water, he walked in a crouch towards the guard room, wincing at the rustle of his wet clothes. Ten feet. Still no movement from the guard.

Five feet.

Three.

The guard turned as Grey pounced, ripping the man backward off his chair by the back of his shirt. Grey heard shouting behind him, the guard yelling for help and Naomi yelling for the guard to stand down. Would the noise reach anyone else, Grey wondered? He had ordered Naomi not to shoot unless she had to.

The powerboat rumbled to life. More shouting. Grey couldn't risk turning.

His maneuver had dazed the guard, a flaxen-haired man with ruddy cheeks and a lean but muscular build. Grey could tell he was well-trained because he didn't panic and he tucked his chin as he fell, stopping his head from bouncing off the cement floor.

The guard tried to rise but Grey put a knee on his stomach and crossed his hands in an X on his collar, applying a front choke by twisting his wrists and squeezing. The guard's bulging eyes said *no one puts on a choke that fast*. He gasped and gurgled and clawed at Grey's face. Grey head-butted him twice and choked harder.

Gunshots from behind. Viktor shouted his name.

Grey still couldn't turn.

The powerboat roared as the guard went limp in Grey's hands, finally allowing him to spin around.

The other guard was lying on his back on the dock, covered in blood and unmoving. There was no sign of the boat. The door had lowered. Naomi must have had to retreat, and shot the guard to cover Grey as the door came down.

Fine. Grey could reopen the door. He kept the choke on until sure the guard would stay asleep, then rose to survey the control room. Before he could find a switch to let the boat in, the door to his left opened. *Damn*. He was afraid of that. Someone nearby had heard gunfire and come to investigate.

A well-built man in a military uniform stepped through the door, and the flesh on Grey's arms prickled when he spied a familiar rubbery face, a blond haircut from another era, and eyes as cold as the grave.

48

At least, Grey thought, only one soldier had come to investigate the gunshot.

Unfortunately, that soldier was Klaus.

Though Grey didn't have time to reach for a weapon, he saw the Nazi a split-second before Klaus saw him. Grey used that increment of time to kick the assault rifle out of Klaus's right hand, sending it spinning into the corridor behind him.

Taken by surprise, the blond man took a step back but recovered fast enough to parry Grey's attack, a high-and-low elbow-and-shin combination. Grey's follow-up attack would have been the end of the fight for most people. An experienced opponent might have stopped two or three of Grey's five blows.

Klaus blocked them all.

Grey knew he wasn't dealing with a normal opponent. Perhaps not even with a human being at all, at least under the standard definition. He didn't know what biomechanical enhancements Klaus had acquired when van Draker revived him. The Nazi didn't react to pain in the normal manner. He probably had bones and joints reinforced by steel or some other material.

Grey couldn't rely on body mechanics, the principal weapon of jujitsu, to fight this enemy.

Still, jujitsu was born in feudal Japan. Developed by peasants fighting for their lives against the terrifying might of armed samurai. Using an enemy's strengths against him, adapting to every situation, doing anything and everything one could in the face of impossible odds: that was the essence of Grey's art.

He might not be able to rely as much on the skills he had spent a lifetime refining, but the principles and desired outcome remained the same.

Cheat.

Improvise.

Win at all costs.

Klaus took a step to the side and drew a knife. Grey disarmed that as well, chopping down on Klaus's forearm as he raised the weapon, relieved the maneuver worked. But it cost Grey the momentum, and Klaus rushed him. Grey wasn't able to avoid the maneuver in the tight quarters, and the Nazi picked him up and slammed him on the bank of monitors. Grey tightened his muscles and did his best to curl his body, taking away some of the damage, but his back screamed in pain.

He lashed out with a heel and caught Klaus under the jaw, snapping his head back. Desperate for a weapon, Grey's eyes canvassed the room as best he could while scrambling off the computers and diving out of reach. The other guard's firearm must be in a drawer somewhere.

A ring of keys. Wooden clipboards. A windbreaker Grey could use as a garrote on a normal opponent.

Klaus saw the police baton before Grey did and jerked it off the wall. Grey spun left to avoid the first blow, but Klaus caught his left shoulder with the second. Pain shot down Grey's arm. Diving backwards to avoid the next swing, knowing he stood no chance in such cramped quarters, Grey scrambled on his back out of the control station.

With an impassive expression, Klaus followed him onto the concrete loading bay, his baton echoing in the chamber as it cracked on the ground beside Grey. Once, twice, three times it missed him. Grey took a chance and leapt to his feet, the next swing missing his face by less than an inch. Instead of retreating, Grey rushed inside and caught Klaus under the jaw with a palm strike, catching him by surprise. The blond man threw Grey back, rubbed his jaw, and grinned.

Grey had seen enough. In the moment he had bought himself, he turned and ran towards the body of the dead guard, lying on the edge of the water. Klaus realized what he was after and bounded after him.

Two glints of metal caught Grey's eyes. One was a pair of handcuffs attached to the guard's belt. The other was an assault rifle two feet beside the body, half-covered in blood. He dove on the floor, fingers outstretched. The slick cement and pockets of blood and his wet clothes all carried him forward in a long slide.

Just as Grey's fingers closed on the weapon, the baton snapped down on Grey's wrist. Bone crunched. Grey screamed.

Klaus had broken his wrist.

Grey swallowed the pain and pushed to his feet. *How had Klaus gotten there so fast?*

The blond Nazi kicked the guard's corpse into the water and advanced again. His right hand limp like an injured bird's wing, Grey dodged another blow and darted to his right, towards the lever that raised the steel wall. Klaus cut him off with a smirk, knowing there was nowhere left to go.

But that isn't true, Grey thought. *There's one more choice, though I don't know what good it will do.*

Then he had an idea.

It was a crazy, foolhardy thought, one that would probably leave him floating facedown in the canal, but it was all he had left.

As Klaus closed in, raising the baton and forcing Grey against the edge of the dock, Grey stepped back, pretending to lose his balance. Klaus rushed in for the kill. Instead of trying to avoid him, Grey grabbed the Nazi around the waist and jerked backwards, kicking off the edge of the wall to gain the momentum he needed to drag the powerful man into the canal.

The maneuver caught Klaus by surprise, and when they hit the water, Grey managed to squirm away. As his opponent righted himself, Grey shot straight down, searching for the body of the guard. He spied it within moments, settling against the bottom of the concrete basin. The water was dark but not impenetrable.

He sensed Klaus behind him. Grey knew he didn't have much time. He dove straight at the dead man, fumbling for a precious moment before finding the speed release mechanism and jerking the handcuffs off his duty belt. Thank God they were steel and not reinforced plastic.

Grey turned and saw Klaus a foot behind him, arms extended. With a surge of adrenaline, Grey crouched and sprang off the dead guard, staying close to the bottom of the basin, praying Klaus had not seen what he was doing.

If the Nazi hadn't seen the handcuffs, it might even work to Grey's advantage. Klaus would assume Grey had found another weapon on the guard's body and try to drown Grey before he surfaced. For all he knew, the Nazi had iron lungs and could hold his breath for thirty minutes.

Good. Let him be confident.

Grey swam for his life. He was a good swimmer, nothing special, but he was much lighter than Klaus and didn't have far to go. He risked a glance back. Two hands, inches behind him in the water.

With a burst of effort, Grey reached his destination: the steel wall separating the loading bay from the canal. He swam a few feet to the left, still along the bottom, and felt a rush of relief when he saw the handle he had grasped onto earlier.

All the exertion had left Grey shorter of breath than usual. His lungs were on fire. Seconds remained, not minutes.

Grey turned. Klaus was right behind him. With any luck, the Nazi would think Grey had grown disoriented and swum in the wrong direction, pinning himself against the wall.

Now for the trickiest part of all.

He had to let Klaus catch him.

Kicking frantically to stir up the water, Grey hunched against the bottom of the wall. As the blond Nazi closed, Grey turned and made a show of tugging on the iron handle, as if trying to lift the door. Klaus dove straight for his throat. Grey flattened on the bottom as if trying to swim under him, drawing him lower.

The Nazi took the bait and followed him down. With his injured hand, Grey fought through the pain and threw a finger strike at Klaus's eyes, which the Nazi swiped away.

But the strike was a diversion. Grey's other hand had already clasped one end of the handcuffs onto the metal handle at the bottom of the door. As Klaus tried to jerk Grey off the bottom, he locked the other end of the handcuffs into place around Klaus's ankle, then tightened them so hard they bit into the skin.

When the Nazi felt the handcuffs constricting his ankle, he bucked and jerked like a raging bull. Grey used the distraction to turn and kick off the wall with both feet. He felt exultant until Klaus made a desperate grab for Grey's legs and caught him by the ankle.

Grey whipped around in the water, kicking to try to free himself. Klaus held fast. Starting to panic, his lungs about to explode, Grey bent double and peeled Klaus's pinky off his heel. As strong as his opponent was, Grey was able to isolate the digit and bend it backward until it snapped. Still the Nazi held on. Spots of black filled Grey's vision, and he felt his strength slipping away. In a last desperate attempt, he moved to the thumb and bent it backward as well, but he couldn't seem to break it.

Klaus reached up with his other hand, trying to snag another ankle. Grey knew if the Nazi got both hands on him, he would never get free. Just before Klaus grabbed him, Grey managed to loosen the thumb enough to slip his ankle out of Klaus's grasp. Grey threw himself backwards as Klaus thrashed and reached for him, searching in vain for another hold. Grey shot up through the water, arms pinwheeling, sucking in huge draughts of air when he surfaced.

After pulling himself out of the water as fast as he could, not trusting that Klaus wouldn't be able to snap the cuffs, Grey darted back into the corridor and retrieved the Nazi's gun. He stood over the water and waited in case he surfaced.

The mechanism above the steel wall shuddered, over and over. As if someone was trying to lift the entire thing out of the water.

Grey realized the steel barrier was more of a garage door than a true wall. The hinges controlling it might give, or the handcuffs might snap. It would require an immense amount of force, but he didn't know the blond man's limits. Grey took a step back and raised the gun. If Klaus came out of that water, Grey was going to empty the entire cartridge into his head.

It never happened. The mechanism trembled a few more times and then settled.

The ripples in the water grew still.

Just to be sure, Grey waited a few more minutes before pulling the lever. The steel door rose out of the water with Klaus still attached, dangling lifeless above the water.

Naomi gripped Viktor's arm as he steered the powerboat beneath the corpse. Grey collapsed on his back and stared up at the body of his enemy, half-expecting the dead man's hands to twitch.

While Viktor made a video of the control room with his cell phone, Naomi secured the boat and brought the captured guard inside. Grey dressed and studied the monitors, getting a better feel for the complex.

It wasn't as big as he expected. He was getting the sense that while van Draker's manor and Iceland were important pieces of the puzzle, perhaps even the nerve centers, the true strength of W.A.R. lay in its worldwide chapters, the poisonous bonds of hate that linked cities, towns, and villages.

There were forty or so rooms. Most of them small and connected by well-lit corridors. About half were laboratories of some sort. Archives. A dining hall. Sleeping quarters. Generators. A plethora of W.A.R. symbology on the doors and walls.

A few dozen guards and scientists milled about. Grey guessed some had been summoned to the manor during the distraction. Hoping another Klaus wasn't lurking inside, he had the suspicion the dead Nazi had been the prototype, a test subject for the army of preserved soldiers waiting in the ice.

One of the labs had a Biohazard designation. On another, marked as the Main Laboratory, only the door showed on the monitor. In the hallway on the other side of the principal lab, coverage resumed, and Grey saw something that stole his breath.

A line of cell blocks with children inside.

Ranging in age from seven to seventeen, they were all children of color, all huddled in fear in their cages.

Grey felt his knees buckle.

How many people had to die to slake the thirst of tyrants? How many children?

His cell phone vibrated. A text from Jax.

–Hurry. She's not faring so well.–

Grey started to shake, an involuntary tremble born of helpless rage and fear. Not fear for his own well-being, but for the futures of those imprisoned children.

Fear that the same thing would happen to Charlie on Grey's watch that had happened to Nya.

The emotion coursed through him, sapping his will but infusing him with fury, twisting him on the inside so violently spots of black entered the corners of his eyes and seeped inward.

"Grey?" Viktor said, in a worried voice.

Grey blinked until his vision cleared, forced himself to channel the emotions. He had to keep it together. *Had* to. "I'm fine," he said in a harsh voice, then pointed at the monitor.

"*Do prdele*," Viktor whispered, when he saw the imprisoned children.

Naomi stepped between them, her face draining of color. She and Grey stared at the monitor while Viktor recorded it on his cell phone.

"I'm sending this to Jacques," he said, "and requesting immediate reinforcements." As his fingers worked the keypad, he frowned. "The signal's gone. I had one when we arrived."

Grey heard a mechanical noise from the loading bay. He looked outside and saw the steel wall lowering. With an electrical whoosh, the monitors powered down, and then the lights dimmed.

"Good luck," a voice said, from the corner of the room.

Grey spun and found the captured guard standing next to an open electrical box.

49

The guard's hands were still handcuffed behind his back. Grey rushed over and saw that he had managed to flip an emergency lockdown switch with a one-hour timer. He grabbed the guard by the throat.

"You're not going to kill me," the guard rasped. "You would have by now."

Grey couldn't raise the gun fast enough. He pointed it at the guard's face, his finger on the trigger and aching for blood, when Viktor's voice rang out behind him.

"Grey! He's unarmed."

Grey snarled and took a step back, turning to eye the monitors. The screens had faded to black, but the images of the children kept flashing in his head, as if he were still seeing them. He turned and pistol-whipped the guard, hitting him so hard the man's head hit the wall behind him before he slumped, unconscious, to the ground.

"He might have been of use," Viktor said. "Cell and Internet are both down."

"We can't trust him anymore," Grey said. "And I know where we need to go."

Naomi stood over the guard. "Good riddance."

"Should we wait here, then?" Viktor asked. "Barricade the door?"

Grey eyed the timer, which showed fifty-seven minutes left. "My guess is exits on both sides are sealed. An hour delay could mean Charlie's life. I'm going for the antidote." He looked at Viktor and then Naomi. "You don't have to come, but you're probably safer with me."

Viktor opened a palm. "Lead the way."

Footsteps creeping down silent hallways lit by the dull red glow of emergency lighting. Guns raised, nerves on a razor's edge. The smell of pine-laced air freshener an unnerving contrast to the threat of menace lurking behind every closed door.

"Where is everyone?" Naomi whispered.

"Waiting for their chance," Grey said, then put a finger to his lips. He winced at the movement, though adrenaline dulled the pain of his broken wrist.

He had changed into the boots and uniform of the unconscious guard. The new clothing helped warm him up, and might give him a moment's advantage in an altercation.

Viktor was holding an assault rifle like a first-time father holds a baby. Grey held onto Klaus's assault rifle, while Naomi preferred her shotgun.

At the end of the hallway, a female guard emerged from a doorway with her weapon raised. Grey fired without hesitation, hitting her twice in the chest. Another door opened behind them. Grey spun and got that guard, too.

Naomi looked at Grey with raised eyebrows. He waved them forward, edging into the intersection.

Nothing but silence.

According to the monitors, the Biohazard area lay at the end of the corridor to the right. Grey moved forward, gun roving side to side, as Naomi walked backwards to cover their rear. Ten steps in, the shotgun made a deafening blast in the corridor. Grey spun. Naomi had taken out another guard.

He realized the lockdown had confused everyone else as much as it had them. Some of the guards were no doubt in hiding, unsure what had happened.

They reached the Biohazard area without another incident. The first door they saw was locked. Fearful of blasting through the entrance of a sensitive lab, Grey took the time to pick the lock, then moved inside in a crouch, his gun at eye level.

A group of scientists huddled behind an electron microscope in the center of the room. The lab was temperature controlled and well-lit, Grey assumed from a separate generator. "Check your phone," he told Viktor.

The professor shook his head. "Still no signal."

The room looked similar to the biohazard lab Grey had seen at the CDC. Glass cabinets, refrigeration units, complicated ductwork. A fleet of microscopes and stainless steel equipment.

None of the scientists wore Hazmat suits over their lab coats. Through a glass door in the rear of the room, Grey noticed a decontamination shower area and, beyond that, a pair of futuristic labs full of stainless steel and complex instruments.

After checking the scientists for weapons, Grey pointed his gun at their heads, one by one. Three men and three women. Grey took the one who begged for his life, a tall blond man with slicked back hair and glasses.

"Don't kill me! I just do what they tell me!"

Grey stood him up. "That's what got you here in the first place. Where's the vaccine?"

The scientist looked confused, and Grey put the gun against his cheek and started to count. "Three."

"I wouldn't take—"

"Two."

"Listen, I swear I'll—"

"One—"

"Okay!" the scientist whimpered. "Okay." He pointed at one of the refrigeration units. "In there."

"Show me."

With Grey pressing the gun into the small of his back, the scientist walked over to the largest refrigeration unit. The stainless steel container had a W.A.R. symbol etched into the side. A digital temperature box was set to 5 degrees Celsius.

"Open it," Grey said.

The scientist swallowed and obeyed with jittery hands. Shelves of small glass bottles, all labeled, filled the interior. He took one off the top row and handed it to Grey.

The label read *VAC1*.

Grey scanned the other labels. The ones on the top row were all the same. The bottles on the second row read *VAC2*, and the bottles below those bore a variety of arcane markings Grey didn't have time to parse.

"Is one a therapeutic vaccine?" he asked. He had learned from the CDC that while a traditional vaccine was a tool of prevention, therapeutic vaccines were used to treat symptoms after an infection had occurred. Antidotes, in a best case scenario.

"The one I gave you."

"Inject yourself," Grey said.

"What?"

"You heard me."

Under Grey's watchful eye, the scientist took a syringe off a shelf, broke the seal on the bottle, then filled the syringe and plunged it into his arm.

The other scientists watched in silence. No one seemed worried about the injection.

Grey waited a full minute and said, "How do I transport them? I want both."

The scientist thought for a moment, then grabbed a cold pack out of a bottom drawer. In a cabinet next to the refrigeration unit, he took out a piece of bubble wrap and a plastic container the size of a coffee can. He stuffed the cold pack inside the container, selected fresh bottles of *VAC1* and *VAC2*, then wrapped the vaccines in bubble wrap and laid them snugly inside.

"How long will it stay cold?"

The scientist handed a clean syringe and the packaged vaccines to Grey. "Six, seven hours no problem."

Grey gave the makeshift cooler to Viktor and waved his gun at the scientists. "On the floor. All of you. Stay down and pray you never see me again."

Remembering the imprisoned children, Grey wanted nothing more than to put a bullet in each of the scientist's heads. Instead he took a deep breath, checked the hallway, and rushed out of the room.

Thirty minutes to go.

"I hate to say this," Viktor whispered, "but we should think about going back."

Grey looked over. "What?"

"We have the vaccine. If we return to the control room, we can escape in the boat once power is restored."

"I'm not leaving without those kids," Grey said. "If we escape, van Draker will kill them to cover up his tracks."

"And if we fail," Viktor argued, "many lives could be lost. Thousands. We should consider the greater good."

Grey thought about it for half a second. "Fuck the greater good."

Naomi nodded her agreement. After a moment, Viktor eyed the lab again and said, "I tend to concur."

At the previous intersection, instead of heading back to the control room, they continued straight. Recalling the simple layout from his memory of the monitors, Grey turned left at the next intersection, went straight through another, and found himself staring down a long corridor with glass walls.

Shapes hovered behind the glass on either side of the dimly lit corridor, causing Grey to flinch, but he quickly realized the figures were backlit specimens of some sort, a disturbing parade of animals with extreme deformities and metal components fused onto their bodies. A two-headed alligator with the spiked back of an ankylosaurus. Squirrels fused together at the hip like Siamese twins, rubbery tentacles attached to their faces and splayed around them in an unnatural halo. A hairless vampire bat with steel incisors and wing membranes reinforced with bronze. And so on.

Cyborg taxidermy, Grey would term it. Van Draker's Believe It Or Not. A Circus of Freaks and Monsters.

Playing God with science.

Viktor was staring with grim fascination at the collection. Naomi looked as if she might be ill. Grey pressed forward to the end of the long corridor, where they encountered a door marked with the W.A.R. symbol. An ID scanner jutted out of the wall beside the door.

"This has to be van Draker's lab," Grey said. "Those kids are on the other side."

Naomi cast a nervous eye down the taxidermy hall. "If there's more guards, they must have decided to wait out the lockdown."

"Smart choice," Grey said.

Viktor related what he could remember from his prior glimpse into van Draker's laboratory. Guessing the ID scanner was either locked down or disengaged, Grey expected to have to blast the door open.

To his surprise, the steel handle on the door eased down when he applied pressure, and the door edged open.

"Do you think the lock-down disabled it?" Naomi whispered.

Grey raised his gun and toed the door open a few more inches. "I think someone wants us to come in."

The door opened onto a concrete floor stained mahogany and polished to a high sheen. Van Draker's prize laboratory sprawled before them, just as Viktor had described. A rectangular chamber as big as a high school gym, thirty-foot ceiling, a jumble of catwalks on the upper level, cables and glass piping, enormous bronze vats standing on iron tripods throughout the room.

The odor from a powerful antiseptic filled the air. Grey stepped inside, gun raised, signaling for Viktor and Naomi to wait. Straight ahead, in the center of the room, a pyramidal generator pulsed with green light. Sophisticated computers and lab equipment filled the rest of the floor.

Along the wall to his right, an elevator and a spiral staircase both led to a ledge that opened into the tunnels beneath the wine cellar.

One of the vats hiccupped, a prolonged gurgle that set Grey's teeth on edge. Even more disturbing was the body that shot through a portion of the glass piping.

He edged forward. The generator was clearly working and cameras watched their progress from all angles, which unnerved him. The lab must have a separate control room. Van Draker would want to observe his creations in private.

Was he watching them now?

Grey glanced at his watch. Fifteen minutes to go. If they didn't find the kids and get out of there, the door to the manor would open, and they would be overrun by guards.

What if, he wondered, the lab had never locked down from this side? Or van Draker had override controls and had led them into a trap?

Didn't matter. Grey wasn't leaving those kids.

He backed towards the door and spoke in a whisper. "Viktor, stay here. There's no reason to risk you. Naomi, can you cover me from the floor?"

She nodded. "Where are you going?"

He pointed at the catwalk. "Up there."

Viktor set down the cooler and raised his rifle. "I'll help her."

"Fine," Grey said, "but do it from here, so you can duck back into the hallway."

Naomi put the shotgun on her shoulder and moved into the room. Grey walked to the staircase and started climbing, pausing on every step. Fifteen feet up, the staircase drew to within four feet of one of the catwalks. Signaling to Naomi to be on her guard, Grey scanned the room again and then leaped onto the catwalk, landing in a silent crouch.

He eased to a standing position. Now he had a higher vantage point and a much better view of the room.

Still no signs of life.

Maybe they were alone after all, he thought. It made sense that van Draker would have retreated into the manor during the earlier disturbance. He was probably locked out.

Nor, after he thought about it, was Grey disturbed by the lack of guards. It was the middle of the night, and they had encountered quite a few people already. He doubted van Draker gave that many people access to his secret lab.

He passed beside one of the vats and couldn't stop his eyes from roving downward, darkly curious as to what monstrosity lay within. When he saw the naked form inside the bronze container, suspended in a pink-hued, gel-like substance, stripped of his long hair and flowing red beard, Grey took an involuntary step backwards, unnerved by the sight of someone he had known, even an enemy he hated.

They must have rushed Dag in overnight. The W.A.R. leader's eyes were open and staring up at Grey. He had no idea if the man was conscious, dead, or somewhere in between. Tearing his eyes away from the sickle-shaped wound on Dag's neck, made by Grey's own hand, he shuddered and kept moving.

Near the halfway point, he stopped again. He could see all the way to the far wall. Naomi followed beneath him. Directly across the room, he saw the steel door that led to the cells holding the children. Unable to bear the thought of those young souls trapped in that nightmare for another moment, Grey started to sprint to the door, then forced himself to proceed with caution.

An intersection of five catwalks marked the halfway point. As soon as he reached it, half a dozen armed men jumped out from behind the vats standing between Grey and the far side of the room.

He thought he had been clever, but they had read him perfectly. Guessed that he would go for the kids and for higher ground, then laid the trap and waited.

Gunfire erupted. A bullet hit him in the left shoulder and spun him around. Gasping with pain, his adrenaline spiking, Grey managed to drop to the catwalk floor and return fire, pinning two of the men against the vats, riddling them with bullets.

A muzzle flashed from below. Naomi joining the fight. More gunfire erupted from the attackers. Grey countered. Another man dropped. Grey belly-crawled out of the intersection, knowing it was a death trap. He took a risk and jumped to the next catwalk over, five feet away, pain lancing through his broken left wrist when he landed. He almost slid off the catwalk, but righted himself at the last moment.

A woman jumped in front of him, twenty feet away, and fired. Grey dropped and felt the bullet whiz just overhead. He fired back from his knees and caught her in the stomach.

Chaos and bullets all around. Grey couldn't risk looking. He knew he was cut off from the others and that his only hope was taking cover.

He took off at a dead sprint for the far side of the catwalk, shooting to the sides and the front as he ran. A woman screamed from behind him. He didn't think it was Naomi. Another burst of gunfire, then a lull in the firing. Grey was almost there. He surged forward. Viktor yelled his name just as Robey stepped out from behind a vat, the final container before Grey's stretch of catwalk ended.

The former soldier shot Grey in the chest, right in the center of his heart, before he could react. The impact sent him spinning off the catwalk, and Grey's gun slipped from nerveless fingers as he plummeted towards the floor, his body in shock and convulsing.

50

Frozen with disbelief, Viktor watched Grey fall off the catwalk and crash atop a bank of computers. He slid to the ground, twitching but not getting up. Viktor didn't understand. He remembered seeing Grey retrieve the second Kevlar vest after his underwater swim.

That didn't change the fact that Grey wasn't moving.

A shotgun roared. Robey pitched off the catwalk. His raspy scream, like his plastic skin and vacant eyes, sent a chill through Viktor.

Naomi ran up and emptied two more shells, point-blank, into Robey's head. No more screams.

Viktor didn't see anyone left standing. Naomi ran to Grey and bent over him. "He's not breathing!" she cried. "There's no pulse!"

The professor had harbored a desperate hope that Grey was feigning his death, but the alarm in Naomi's voice sounded real. Another gunshot echoed through the room, hitting the police officer in the navel and knocking her backwards. Naomi screamed and fell behind one of the vats.

Reeling, Viktor scrambled behind the closest computer bank as Jans van Draker, holding a wooden hunting rifle, stepped onto the ledge that led to the tunnels beneath the wine cellar.

From Viktor's location, he could see the lower half of Naomi's body. She wasn't moving.

Grief and despair threatened to overwhelm him. "Van Draker!" the professor roared, firing the assault rifle wildly at the ledge. "What have you done?"

"Nothing you wouldn't have done to save those you love," Jans said, stepping back into the safety of the doorway.

"Who do you love?" Viktor said. "You're a monster, trying to play God."

"Trying? I seem to be quite good at it. I wonder, have you ever considered the prospect of dissection? A brain of your age and intelligence would be useful to our studies."

"I'll destroy the vats. Everything in this room."

"You'll do nothing of the sort, and the vats are quite bulletproof. Perhaps you could destroy a few computers before I shot you, but the master files are . . . elsewhere. I'm curious, though. Did you think I harbored affection for my creations? Beyond a scientific curiosity? If you're grasping for leverage, you should know that I care about my family and my people, the survival of my race, above even my science."

"As I said. A monster."

"By my estimation, you have eight minutes before the lock-down expires and my remaining guards escort you away. I'll ask again: dissection, or a swift death?"

The professor knew Jans was right. Viktor was pinned behind the vat, his friends dead. Thinking about the situation, he was sure there was another control panel inside the room, probably near the ledge where van Draker was hiding. A way to turn on the cell and Internet from inside. Van Draker had chosen not to use it so he could tie up loose ends himself.

Viktor glanced at Grey and Naomi, and a pang shot through the professor that went deeper than he had realized it would. So deep he struggled to focus his thoughts. With a huge of effort of will, he clenched his fists and forced himself to think.

He knew that brain death—true death—occurs six minutes after the heart stops beating. There was no way anyone from the outside would reach them in time.

A movement to the left drew his attention. He whisked around, gun raised, thinking it was a guard. Instead he saw Naomi squatting behind the vat, silently reloading her shotgun, her shirt opened to expose a bulletproof vest.

Viktor sagged with relief. His elation turned to another stab of grief when he looked at Grey with hopeful eyes and saw his friend still unmoving on the floor, eyes open in the stare of death.

Grey was not in the line of fire from van Draker's ledge. If Grey was faking, he would have gotten up by now.

Let it not be, Viktor whispered.

Naomi made a series of hand gestures. Viktor forced himself to pay attention. *I'm going to walk*, Naomi mimed. *Do some talking.*

Just behind her, Viktor saw a tall, clear-walled cryogenic unit filled with detached brain stems and spinal cords in elongated jars, suspended in some type of gel. A fog of liquid nitrogen swirled inside the case.

Viktor shuddered and pushed away the horrors of the lab. "Jans!" he shouted. He had to keep him talking.

"You've decided?"

"Can you help my friends? Revive them?"

"If I so wanted? But of course," van Draker said, amused. "I can resuscitate a corpse that has been deceased for up to ninety-six hours. The longer we wait, the less brain function is recovered. But we're working on that. Making neurogenic strides every day. Brain death is not the open-and-shut case the scientific community thinks it is."

A cable pulsed beside Viktor, and Dag's body shot through the glass piping, into another vat. To his left, Naomi darted forward, hiding behind a desk.

Drawing closer to van Draker.

"Four days?" Viktor asked. "So reviving my friends would be child's play."

"In the first few hours after brain death, the Resurrector alone would suffice to revive the brain stem. Damage would be minimal, perhaps a few memories lost."

"The Resurrector?"

"The machine in the center of the room is no simple generator. It is technology of my design, built on the backs of many who came before me. The Resurrector is the beginning of eternity. Of the future of the human race."

Naomi moved again. Viktor tensed as she darted behind another vat. If van Draker was looking her way, he would have seen her.

"I won't deny your genius," Viktor said, "but what's the key to the power source? Electrolysis?"

"Suffice to say I have mastered the ion channels and the blood-brain barrier. You understand," he mused, "the war among the races is no different from any stage of evolution. It is simply survival of the fittest. The battle was predestined. Natural. I just want, as humankind has always done and as every government on earth does to this day, to ensure the survival of my people, first and foremost."

"Surely, as a scientist, you understand what a red herring the concept of race is."

"It is not a matter of biology, dear Viktor. It is a matter of culture. Values. Family. If steps are not taken, the entire human race will soon be commingled. Do you not see the barbarism in the Middle East? The destitution in the non-white world? Our organization stands for tradition, science, progress!"

Is that why you named it W.A.R.? Yet Viktor knew he could never win such a twisted argument. As a cable pulsed overhead, Naomi slid behind a third vat. Halfway to the ledge.

"What are they?" Viktor asked, grasping for another topic as the clock ran out. "Was Robey human after his revival? Klaus?"

"An excellent question. Though you present two very different examples. Klaus was a prototype of cryogenic restoration, the first of a long line of warriors for the future."

"And Robey?" Viktor asked. "Akhona? Kristof?"

Van Draker chuckled. "As you've noted, I am not God. Who's to say where life begins or ends? What does it mean to lose one's personality to Alzheimer's? Acquire new intelligence? Share intelligence with a machine or another life form? Is consciousness merely a brain function? As far as we have come, professor, I'll be the first to admit we have light-years to go."

Naomi was signaling frantically to the professor. She seemed to want him to move somewhere. Viktor analyzed their positions and understood. If van Draker stepped out, she now had a shot, but the professor would have to risk his life to draw him out.

"One minute to go," van Draker said. "A final question?"

"The gargoyle virus," Viktor said, as the seconds ticked off and Naomi continued to wave at him. Viktor had to know.

"What of it?" van Draker said.

"Did you manufacture it?"

"Of course. An intersection of my work with bioweapons, cryogenic revival, and genetic enhancement. Advances in gene splicing and immuno-suppressants were key as well. Unfortunately, I consider my work a failure. Others have redressed the issue."

Viktor didn't understand the last comment, but he was out of time. Live or die, he had to act.

"Jans?" Viktor said.

"Yes?"

"Here I come."

Viktor fired the assault rifle at the ledge as he strode across the room. Halfway to van Draker, the bullets stopped and the professor's gun clicked.

An empty magazine.

Van Draker stepped out and took aim. Before he could take the shot, Naomi rose and fired, hitting him in the chest. Jans stumbled, and Viktor feared he would slip into the doorway and lock them inside.

Naomi fired again, and again, and again. Racing towards the bottom of the platform. Screaming her fury.

Riddled with shotgun pellets, Van Draker dropped the rifle and tumbled off the ledge. Naomi bounded up the spiral staircase and finished the job with a point-blank shot to the chest.

"There must be a lock down switch!" Viktor roared. "Find it!"

Naomi whipped around as Viktor raced for the staircase. When he reached the top, he saw her fumbling with an electrical box set flush into the wall. She flipped a switch next to a timer with three seconds left on the electronic face.

Viktor heard a series of loud clicks, as if locks were engaging. The timer reset to one hour. He squeezed her shoulder and found a switch to restore the Internet connection without disabling the security. Eyeing Grey's prone form, the professor forced himself to think logically, then sent the video he had made earlier, as well as pictures of van Draker's body and the lab, to Jacques.

> –Come asap with med team. Trapped inside the lab. Cause an international incident if you have to–

The reply from Jacques was swift.

> –Stay put. Will send help–

Viktor put the phone away. Jacques knew about the secret passage and would either come through in time or he wouldn't. Right now, Viktor had a more important agenda.

He took the stairs three at a time. When he reached Grey, he jerked his shirt open and saw a bullet embedded in the Kevlar vest. Some freak accident must have occurred. Forcing his emotions away, Viktor kneeled over his friend and tried to revive him with CPR. After the first few rounds, Naomi took over, but neither of them could get Grey to respond. He was as lifeless as a piece of driftwood.

Left with no choice, Viktor picked up Grey's body and, as gently as he could, carried him to the metallic blue gurney suspended with cables above the pyramidal generator.

"At the bottom!" Viktor said. "Look for a switch!"

As Naomi scrambled to help, the professor placed his friend on the gurney, strapping him in with the leg, neck, and arm clasps. Viktor's hands were shaking and it took him a few tries to get it right. "I have it!" Naomi cried.

Viktor had a thousand questions, a thousands doubts and fears. He pushed them away and balled his fists. "Do it."

Naomi pulled a lever.

The generator hummed.

A nest of gossamer filaments popped out of the top of the pyramid, flew upwards, and attached to Grey's skull. Viktor gasped but didn't interfere. After a few moments, the green light stopped pulsing and assumed a steady glow. The hum increased in volume, the octave keening higher and higher, until the cables connecting the generator to the gurney crackled with the same green light.

Come, Viktor urged the machine. He thought he had never wished for anything so much in his entire life. *Come.*

"What's happening?" Naomi cried.

"I don't know."

Grey's hand twitched, causing Viktor's heart to lurch. He leaned down and searched for a pulse, the breath of life.

Nothing. An involuntary reaction to electrical stimuli.

Viktor could barely watch. The humming of the machine flat-lined, the green light brightened, and Grey's body stiffened as wave after wave of energy coursed through the cables and into his prone form.

The gossamer filaments quivered as if alive, pressing into his skull. Grey bucked and convulsed on the gurney, his muscles galvanized by the electricity.

Do prdele, Viktor thought. *How powerful is that current?*

The professor had no idea if the machine was helping his friend or destroying his body even further. Had Naomi done something wrong? Cranked the controls too high?

At last the cables calmed, the hum returned to a steady low thrum, and the green light began to pulse again.

As far as Viktor could tell, nothing had happened. Disappointment burned through him. He took his friend's hand in his own, not caring if he subjected himself to the energy source the machine was harnessing.

Grey's body went rigid a final time and then relaxed.

Viktor bowed his head.

When he blinked away his tears and finally looked up, sure the experiment had been a failure, Grey's eyes popped open.

51

"How is she?" Jax asked, rising from his chair in the hallway.

His shoulder bandaged and his right wrist in a splint, Grey eased the door shut behind him, not wanting to disturb Charlie's sleep. He felt an unfamiliar lump in his throat that he disguised with a gruff edge to his voice. "Doc says she's gonna make it."

They were at Groote Schuur Hospital in Cape Town, which happened to be the site of the world's first human heart transplant. Grey found it an appropriate venue after all that had happened, including his miraculous recovery.

Commotio cordis was the Latin name for the injury he had suffered. A deadly disruption of the heart's rhythm that can occur when a heavy blow—such as a gunshot from the Browning Hi-Power automatic pistol Robey was using—impacts the precordial region within the vulnerable phase of cardiac repolarisation, fifteen to thirty milliseconds before the T-wave peak.

In plain English, Grey remembered the doctor saying, the blow has to hit directly above the heart, during the one percent of the beat cycle that can cause sudden cardiac arrest.

A rare event, though not unheard of, especially for young boys playing sports. The cardiologist speculated that Grey's emaciated frame might have contributed to the incident, though *commotio cordis* had occurred over a wide age range and in a variety of situations, including police officers wearing bulletproof vests. The fatality rate was extremely high.

While poorly understood, researchers speculated that the cause of *commotio cordis* was probably related to the heart's ion channels—the same proteins that regulate the body's electrical signals, and which Viktor speculated were manipulated by van Draker's machine.

Grey could only shake his head, surprised and thankful he was alive.

Viktor and Jax had popped in and out of the hospital, but Grey hadn't left. It had been touch and go for the last forty-eight hours, ever since the vaccine had taken effect. But Charlie's vitals had gradually stabilized, and except for the hair loss, she no longer presented symptoms of the horrific virus.

"She's a tough one," Jax said.

Grey's hand lingered on the doorknob. If Charlie hadn't pulled through, he thought he might have died right there with her.

"The toughest," Grey agreed.

"Before she got too sick," Jax said, "she must have eaten twenty chicken legs in that shack. Almost cleaned them out."

Grey's laugh was the first one that had sounded genuine to his ears in months.

Jax clasped him on the shoulder. "Maybe you'll stop being such a dick to everyone, now."

Grey rolled his eyes.

"You going back to work with Viktor?" Jax asked.

"I don't know."

"Yeah, I don't really see you teaching high school. Hey, you ever need some cash, I could always use a hand . . ."

Grey pointed towards the end of the hall.

Jax spread his palms and grinned. "Good doing business with you."

He turned to leave, and Grey took him by the arm. "Thanks. For watching out for her when I couldn't."

"I'm just glad we stuck it to those assholes."

Grey's eyes hardened. "It was a real pity Dag got unplugged before the authorities arrived."

Jax chuckled and stepped away. "Listen. You let that other thing go, too. And take another shower."

Grey compressed his lips and looked away. One thing at a time.

Jax gave a mock salute and left. Grey sank into the chair in the hallway, exhausted, his mind spinning. He'd been so worried about Charlie he had not had time to process anything else.

The case, the whole incredible sequence of events, crashed over him like a freezing ocean wave. The violence. The horrors of the lab. The traumatized eyes of the children they had freed. The fear, the hate, the prejudice.

When will it stop? he wondered. *When will a few madmen stop plunging the world into madness and horror?*

Most of humanity just wanted to wake up to a beautiful sunrise, pursue their passions, enjoy their friends and family in peace.

Damn those monsters.

He shivered at the thought of his mental state after Charlie was captured, his filter gone, moral compass spinning wildly. He had wanted to take out Dag and his people as if he was picking grapes in a field, their spilled blood a balm for his soul.

And he would do it again.

Revenge solves problems, he knew. It absolutely does.

But it doesn't heal.

It was all so absurd, he thought. One tiny planet in the middle of a universe vast beyond belief, its very existence dependent on a combination of factors the probability of which is so astronomical they break the largest computers. Yet humanity can't get it together enough to work towards the common goal of survival and a better life. Instead we have politics and armies and *our country versus yours* and *our* religion and *our* race and *our* half of the valley. *Our* high school, *our* gang, *our* family.

We take, take, take. Claim, claim, claim. Kill, kill, kill.

Footsteps from the hallway. Grey looked up and saw Viktor.

After Grey reported on Charlie, the professor sank into a chair beside him. "Thank goodness she'll be fine."

They hadn't talked much since Grey had opened his eyes on the gurney and a team of special unit police officers from Cape Town had escorted them out of the manor. Reeling from his ordeal, staying awake with caffeine and willpower, Grey had made them take him straight to Charlie.

They reached her just as her mind started to slip. A few minutes longer, the doctors had said, and she might not have made it.

A cabal of worldwide W.A.R. members exposed. Chapters unearthed in South Africa, the United States, and across Western Europe. Dozens of arrests made, targeting anyone remotely linked to the virus.

The name Eric Winter, the former congressman's son, was never mentioned.

The South African government had appropriated van Draker's lab and allowed the CDC inside for immediate study. Doctor Varela had led the task force. While they found plenty of vaccine, the lack of research had been troubling. The computers were missing key data points, and van Draker's personal files had never been found. Not only that, but during the chaos of the police raid, the power core of the pyramidal apparatus that had revived Grey, The Resurrector, had gone missing. No one could figure out how to make it work again.

Grey remembered what Viktor had said about the events of that night. Some of the last words van Draker had spoken.

The master files are . . . elsewhere.

A raid by the Iceland authorities on the coordinates Grey and Jax had provided led to half a glacier buried beneath an avalanche. The avalanche looked recent, and the stress points pointed to explosives.

Even if the authorities dug it out, Grey had the feeling the preserved Nazi soldiers had been moved elsewhere. Awaiting a new master, a different age.

"There's something I haven't told you," Grey said, after he and Viktor lingered in silence. "I had an experience."

Viktor looked over.

"When I was . . . dead. I saw things. Went someplace."

"The doctors said you were brain dead for over twenty minutes. It must have occurred before then, with the neocortex still functioning."

Grey shrugged. "All I know is that it felt real. More real than anything else in my life."

Viktor tried to act nonchalant as he asked the next question, but Grey heard the underlying intensity. "What did you see? A tunnel? A bright light?"

"Nothing like that. It wasn't so much what I saw, but what I felt. For a while I was floating in deep blackness, and then there was a barrage of color, more vibrant than I've ever seen, in a space that felt multi-dimensional. Ten-dimensional, twenty. I can't . . . I can't explain it. There were mountains and cities and worlds and whole universes, Viktor. All at once. Everywhere. Then I saw images from my past, alongside images of me with people I had never seen before, as if I was seeing the future, or an alternate reality. You and Charlie were in some. Nya and my mother, too." He swallowed. "I know I'm not making sense, but the experience didn't make sense. It was like time didn't exist, the past and the present and the future all mixed together. I felt emotions so pure I almost couldn't bear them, love and terror and awe and comfort. And the thing I remember most of all—still as clear as day in my mind—is thinking, *knowing*, that the universe is way more complicated than we can ever imagine."

"That's unsurprising," the professor said wryly.

Grey shook his head. "I'm not talking about the stuff we saw in that lab or juju or the mystery of black holes. I mean *way* more complicated. I'm no scientist or theologian, but I had the overwhelming feeling that something was out there. Something vast and eternal and . . . *beyond* us. As if my mind had just been uploaded into a computer program that made what we know of reality seem like two paddles and a Ping-Pong ball."

Viktor didn't respond. When Grey finally looked over, he saw a cauldron of emotion stirring in the professor's intelligent brown eyes.

Yet the emotion that registered most of all on Viktor's face—and it took Grey a moment to realize it—was jealousy.

"I used to think human existence was like a baby abandoned on the doorstep," Grey said. "And maybe I still do. But abandoned by *what*?"

A faint smile graced Viktor's lips. "Are you telling me you've become a believer?"

"To be honest," Grey said, looking off to the side, towards the door to Charlie's room, "I don't care about that any more than I used to."

The professor leaned forward. "We should record your experience. Study it."

Grey shrugged. "It's already starting to fade. Like a dream. Wherever I was, inside my own brain or in some meta-reality, I don't think our conscious minds are capable of handling it."

"Then why tell me?" Viktor said, disappointed.

Grey looked him in the eye. "Because I wanted you to know I don't think you're searching in vain."

The professor looked at a loss for words, as if he had expected a very different response and had prepared a very different answer. "Thank you for saying that," he said slowly.

"Thanks for saving my life." Grey pushed to his feet. Only a bruise remained from the rare injury that had taken his life. A bruise and memories he would deal with later. Right now he had an agenda that overwhelmed all others.

"Where are you going?" the professor asked.

Grey yawned and blinked to stay awake. "To get some caffeine."

In the waiting room, Grey got a Coke out of a vending machine and saw the other visitors watching a news broadcast on the television. He edged closer. "Viktor! It's Dr. Varela."

Someone turned the volume up. The broadcast was from CDC headquarters, a special report declaring that a team of epidemiologists, led by Dr. Hannah Varela, had finally cracked the code to the gargoyle virus vaccine. Mass production had already begun, and shipment to destinations worldwide would start within days.

Since the CDC still did not have a handle on the transmission rate of the virus, governments planned to issue the vaccine to all people with a certain percentage of melanin, in the countries affected by the outbreaks.

"Thank God," a woman in the waiting room said.

One by one, everyone began to clap.

Grey looked over and saw an uneasy frown on Viktor's face. "What is it?" Grey said. "This is great news, right?"

The professor crossed his arms and watched the television long after the broadcast ended. "You know what we didn't find in the lab?" he said finally. "Masses and masses of the virus."

"Maybe they were relying on the transmission rate, which we still don't understand."

Viktor was still staring at the screen. "What if it isn't communicable at all?"

"Come again?"

"What if W.A.R. injected far more victims than we thought—what if they injected *all* of them? Or what if the number of victims were manipulated by the press?"

"Who would be in a position to do that?"

"I don't know."

All of a sudden, Grey's soft drink didn't taste so good.

"Van Draker was focused on the science," Viktor said, turning to face Grey. "Dag was a military man. As dangerous as they were, doesn't it feel as if there was someone missing in the W.A.R. equation? Someone who coordinated the effort worldwide?"

"I . . . what are you saying?"

"Jans said he considered his work a failure. If these people were truly waging a global war and the gargoyle virus was not communicable, and van Draker's lab didn't have the capacity to mass produce enough virus, then what does that tell you? Was it all a bluff, or did they have another agenda?"

"These people don't bluff," Grey said.

"I agree."

Grey thought about it for a moment, and then a chill spread through him, slow and sure. "It could mean the virus was manufactured somewhere else. In mass quantity."

"And?" Viktor said quietly. "What about the distribution? Using members of W.A.R. to inject every person of color in the world, one by one, isn't practical. Even if they had not been stopped."

As Grey stared at the television screen, he had a sudden thought, an epiphany about who was in a position to spread the gargoyle virus to millions. He felt his knees go weak at the knowledge, and he gripped Viktor's arm. "Get Jacques on the phone. Tell him we need a background search, right damn now."

52

The door to the master bedroom in the plush Atlanta townhome swung open. Doctor Hannah Varela stepped inside holding a wine glass. The bedroom had a white-and-silver color scheme and lots of delicate knick-knacks on the shelves. Things like colored soap and perfume bottles and blown glass figurines of opera singers and ballet dancers. A single photo graced the bedside table: Dr. Varela holding hands in a city park with a boy of eight or nine, wavy blond hair, dimples, a smile to melt a glacier.

A wrought-iron headboard climbed the wall opposite the door. To the right of the bed, the east-facing wall had a vertical window showcasing houselights sprinkling the darkness like fireflies. When Grey had arrived a few hours earlier, during the day, he had glimpsed Stone Mountain in the distance.

At first, as she kicked off her work shoes, Dr. Varela didn't notice the lean man in jeans and a motorcycle jacket standing by the window with crossed arms. When she turned on the light and saw him, she gasped and dropped the wine glass, shattering it on the wood floor.

"I admit," Grey said, "staging the attack that night behind the restaurant was a clever move."

"Thank God," Dr. Varela said, when she saw who it was. Her expression turned puzzled. "How did you get in? What are you doing here?"

"Don't bother," Grey said.

"What?"

"You would have killed millions."

"Are you feeling okay?" She dug a phone out of her purse. "I can call—"

"Put the phone and the purse on the bed. *Now.*" Grey was close enough to grab her if needed, and he knew she didn't carry a firearm to work. He was worried more about Mace.

After she complied, Grey set the phone and the purse by the window.

"I don't understand," she said, though he could tell by her roving eyes, searching for an escape, that she very much did.

"The Swedish company that manufactured the vaccine for the CDC—a company staffed by W.A.R.—produced the gargoyle virus instead," Grey said. "Millions and millions of bottles. That was the plan all along, wasn't it? Van Draker couldn't make it communicable, so you decided to whip up panic worldwide, buy yourself a few journalists and pharmaceutical regulators, and plant some fake news. You let Akhona escape to seed fear and terror, and knew the threat of a manufactured virus would only create more tension. Even when we uncovered the lab and gave the CDC the vaccine, it just moved up your timeline, gave you a reason to pretend to reverse-engineer it. Great job. The world is begging for the vaccine."

Dr. Varela edged toward the far side of the bed. "Are you feeling okay?"

"We've identified the W.A.R. sympathizers you hired at the CDC, and paid off in the customs offices of various countries. The other workers, I'm sure, just did what they were told."

"Are you listening to yourself?" she said.

"By the time anyone would have figured it out, God knows how many people would have taken the vaccine."

Hannah drew closer to the bedside table. "I need a Valium," she said, reaching for a pill bottle behind the photo of her and the child. Only two pills remained, Grey knew, so he didn't worry about an overdose.

"The FBI knows everything," he continued. "Bottles have been tested."

"And I would do such a terrible thing," she lifted her palms, "for what purpose?"

"For him," Grey said quietly, pointing at the photo.

Her eyes flashed, but he noticed her hands never shook as she opened the pill bottle and shook one out.

"Your real name is Annalena Fleischer. Your parents were both Nazis who emigrated to Mendoza to escape the war tribunals. Both prominent scientists who traveled on ratlines established by Juan Peron to bring talented German professionals into Argentina, to help improve his own country. Your parents' true identity has been known to Interpol for some time, but they died years ago, and you were never on the radar. Still, fearing scandal, you changed your name when you went to Chicago to study epidemiology. In the beginning, you wanted to escape your past, didn't you? Or at least ignore it." Grey shook his head. "Maybe you would have had a normal life, maybe not. But then they killed your boy."

Hannah's face hardened, and he could see decades of pain in her eyes, a cancer of grief and rage more deadly than any disease.

"You were a student. A single mom with no support, and you didn't live in the best area of Chicago. Two black gang members broke into your home one night and took everything you owned—including your son's life."

Her eyes flashed. "He was trying to protect me. They tied me up, and he thought they were going to do something else. He stood in front of me and refused to move and they shot him. They never even touched me." She looked away. "Why didn't they tie him up, too?"

"I don't know."

"They didn't have to kill him."

"You didn't have to kill anyone, either," Grey said. He turned towards the window, giving Hannah his back. "It was a terrible tragedy, Hannah. I'm truly sorry for your loss. But it doesn't give you the right to kill even one person who wasn't involved."

"What do you know about losing a child? That kind of pain?"

Grey heard the bedside drawer open, the sound he was waiting for. When he turned, he saw Hannah aiming a Smith & Wesson compact pistol at him.

"You should have stayed out of it," she said. "It wasn't your fight."

"You shouldn't have taken Charlie."

Police sirens sounded in the distance. Hannah's head whisked to the side.

"Those are for you," Grey said.

Hannah lowered her stance and gripped the weapon in both hands.

"You're going to kill me in cold blood?" he asked.

She cocked her head, listening to the sirens draw closer. "You give me no choice."

Hannah pulled the trigger but the weapon didn't fire. She pulled again and again until realizing it was empty.

"Damn you," she said, throwing the gun at him.

He stalked over to her, swatted away her attempt to get free, and pinned her against the wall. "I wanted to make sure you understood the stakes. That I have every reason in the world to kill you—" He took the Smith & Wesson bullets out of his jacket pocket and opened his palm "—and the means to do so and go free. A suicide, quick and easy. Someone who knew the game was up."

Fear sprang into her eyes. Grey thought of the victims who had already died horrible deaths at the hands of this woman, and untold more in waiting.

Most of all, he thought about Charlie.

Grey squeezed her throat until she gagged. "I came here to kill you."

Hannah tried to wriggle away, gasping her words. "You came here just to tell me that?"

He released her, and she collapsed at the base of the wall. "That's the only thing you deserve," he said. "Not a trial, not a sentence, not a long life as a heroine to the white prison gangs."

She stared up at him, defiant. "So do it."

"I had a realization, while I was waiting for you to come home. I realized that someone has to break the cycle. Lots of people, of course, but I can only affect what's under my control."

Her laugh came cruel and hard. "You and I are tainted. Why bother?"

"It's not us I'm doing it for." Grey stood again as footsteps pounded down the hallway, calls for someone to open the door.

"If you died here tonight," he continued, "she would know who did it." He shook his head. "I can't teach that lesson."

Sounds of the front door splintering.

Dr. Varela spat on his shoe. "I finally understood, after my son died, that my parents were right. Why they did what they did. It's us or them, and it always will be."

"There's a difference between fighting for love and fighting for hate," he said, just before the SWAT team rushed inside. "Hate never changes anything."

"Love can't bring my son back."

"No. But it can save someone else's."

53

A yellow-bellied flycatcher warbled in the distance as the pallbearers lowered Akhona's coffin into the earth. Viktor watched arm-in-arm with Naomi as the boy's mother smiled through her tears. It was a quiet joy of things remembered, a final farewell, a grieving mother's resignation that her beloved's time on earth was done. A smile that could only arise from someone who believed her child was in a better place—or perhaps from someone who had already buried him once, and realized a peaceful death was better than an unholy life.

Instead of the dusty, weed-choked cemetery for the poor in which Akhona had first lain, his new pewter casket—the most expensive money could buy—would rest beneath a jacaranda atop a hill overlooking the Langeberg mountains. Next spring, the beautiful tree's blossoms would hang above the coffin like a thousand purple bells, a clarion ode to the heavens about the boy whose rest they shaded.

A new location. A secure coffin. Van Draker dead and gone. Akhona's body, recovered from one of the bronze vats, would rest in peace permanently this time.

At least, Viktor thought, until science took another quantum leap and learned to build a new Akhona from the dust of centuries-old bones.

Would they be able to inject a soul one day, too? One preserved from the past, made in a lab, plucked from the depths of Grey's mysterious vision?

Spades of dirt settled.

Lamentations rendered to the sky.

"Come," Viktor said to Naomi, when the onlookers started to disperse.

As they walked back to their car, a woman's voice called out to them from behind, in a heavy Xhosa accent.

"Professor, please wait!"

Viktor started. For a moment, he thought he had seen Kristof's gray face and angular frame in the distance, watching from deeper within the cemetery, slipping behind a headstone just as Viktor turned.

It was probably just a caretaker. Van Draker's butler had never surfaced, and the professor had wondered at his fate. Had Kristof taken van Draker's research and disappeared? Perhaps to begin the experiments anew?

Instead of the sallow-faced butler, Viktor saw Akhona's mother running towards him, tears streaming down her face. She clasped her arms around his waist and buried her head in his chest. "Thank you," she sobbed. "Thank you for this."

Viktor embraced her in return, feeling awkward at the public display. Behind her, standing by the grave, her husband tipped his head at Viktor.

On the way back to the town car, Naomi took Viktor's hand as a breeze riffled through the treetops in the lovely cemetery. She said, "You paid for the funeral, didn't you?"

Viktor tried to conceal his embarrassment. In his circles, such things were not discussed. "I, ah, might have helped defray the cost."

"All of it?"

His silence spoke for itself.

She squeezed his hand harder. "You're a good man, Viktor Radek."

He accepted the compliment, though he wasn't sure he agreed. Viktor knew he was someone who cared far too much about the secrets of life and death that haunted mankind. Someone who elevated knowledge too high above simple pleasure, who had willingly put other lives at risk to gain the answers he craved.

Yusuf opened the door, and Viktor followed Naomi inside the town car. The professor forced away the disturbing memories of Kristof and Robey. "Where to?" he asked. "Lunch? A stroll on the beach?"

"To the hotel, please," Naomi called out to Yusuf. She put a hand on Viktor's thigh and leaned close to whisper in his ear. "I have some things to thank you for, too."

Grey slid the wrestling mats onto the concrete floor, creating a makeshift dojo in the basement of the Washington Heights homeless shelter. The sweat-stained, green-and-white mats were coming apart at the seams. Grey hung his oldest black belt, frayed and faded with age, on a peg above the mats. Jujitsu was not overly concerned with tradition, and every school differed. Some kept photos of old masters on the wall, some displayed certificates of rank, some had a favorite piece of Japanese art or a miniature bonsai garden or scrolls of haikus. Most had charts of pressure points and a rack of practice weapons.

Grey kept it simple. Just the mats, his old belt, and a framed yin-yang poster. He knew it wasn't much.

But there was no place he'd rather be.

He was especially excited that morning, since it was the first day Charlie was due to return. She would go light, practice her strikes and toe-up a few throws.

Before anyone arrived, Grey adopted a simple child's pose on the mat, taking a moment to center himself and regulate his breathing.

He was worried about what came next for Charlie. He knew the bleak statistics for homeless kids. In nearly all cases, the damage had been done, and most never left the streets.

He believed about the only thing that mattered, the one difference maker, was a personal connection to a loving, responsible adult. Something most of these kids had never had.

Grey wasn't the parental type, and Charlie had been clear she didn't want a foster family. The horror stories from some of the other kids terrified her. She had told Grey that she had a family once, and that was enough.

Grey understood. When he had been on the streets, he had felt the same. While he yearned for a normal family, he didn't want someone else's. He wanted his own. He wanted his father to change and his mother not to be dead.

So while Grey had no illusions as to how much Charlie could be helped, the one thing he could do was be there for her. Watch her back and hold her accountable and provide a blueprint, as best he could, on how to live.

Charlie swooped into the dojo ten minutes early, interrupting his thoughts.

"Yo, Teach!"

"Good morning."

"Whatcha doing down there? Is that some new way to kill someone in three seconds?"

"Um, no. It's Child's Pose."

Charlie's face screwed up. "Huh?"

"A breathing technique, like Qi-Gong. We're going to start using more of it in class."

Charlie gave him a palm. "Whatever."

She set down an old backpack held together with safety pins. When she opened it to take out her *gi*—Grey purchased the traditional cloth uniform for any student who stayed longer than a month—he spotted the top of a book. Not a novel, but a paperback or textbook of some sort.

"What's that?"

Charlie looked both embarrassed and proud. "Oh yeah. I was gonna tell you sometime."

"How about right now?"

She hesitated, then pulled out a worn GED study guide. "I found it in the free bin at Goodwill."

"Charlie, that's fantastic!" They had discussed getting her GED before, but she had never shown much interest.

She shuffled her feet. "After everything that happened . . . I been doing a lot of thinking. I know it's weird and don't you dare tell anyone else because I'll never live it down, but I think . . . I think I wanna be a cop one day. Like you, Teach. You'll help me, right?"

That mysterious lump in his throat had returned. "I'd be honored," he said softly.

"I can come over and study sometimes?"

"Anytime."

"Not in any weird way, either. You old, Teach. Hands off the goods. But somebody gotta help me pass that test."

"We'll get you another book. A new edition."

"Listen," she said. "There's something else you're gonna do for me. And I don't want no excuses."

"Is that right?"

"You're going back to work for Viktor."

Grey's grin faded. "I haven't decided about that yet, Charlie."

"Yeah? I have. And I'm serious. If you don't go back, then those bastards win. Them and everyone like them."

"There are lots of people fighting on our side out there, Charlie."

"So?"

He didn't have an answer for that.

"It's nice and all you're showing us a few moves in the basement," her eyes turned uncharacteristically serious, "but people out there need you. People like me. Other victims."

Grey averted his gaze, staring at his old black belt and thinking about the origins of jujitsu and how the world had not really changed that much in all those centuries. There were still serfs and lords, villagers and samurai, the privileged and the lost. Only the names and battlefields had changed. His eyes shifted to the yin yang poster and he wondered if there was really any balance in the world, if the old philosophers hadn't gotten it all wrong and there should be a speck of white in the center of the symbol, swallowed by a sea of darkness. A spark, nothing more. It made him feel as worn and tattered as the cloth of his old *gi*.

"Don't think that I don't know why you been moping around, either. I know 'bout your girlfriend. Think you have nothing to live for and all that."

When he didn't respond, she poked him in the chest. "All of us here lost big in life, Teach. If life was a bowling alley, we rolled a pair of gutter balls. But you *do* have something to live for. The most important thing in the world, maybe even in the whole—what do they call that thing in the comics?" She snapped her fingers. "The mul-ti-verse. That's right, the whole multiverse."

"And what is that?" Grey said quietly.

Charlie grinned and held up the study guide. "Me."

54

A few nights later, kicking back with a beer on his futon, thinking about everything and trying to decide what to do, Grey remembered a conversation he had once had with Nya about the afterlife. Whether death meant oblivion or something else.

Do you believe in God? she had asked him one night after dinner, sitting on her patio in Harare with a glass of pinotage and the insects of the bushveld singing to the night.

I don't know, he had said, *and I don't care. Sorry to disappoint.*

She fingered her wine stem. *I do.*

Why? he asked finally, after seeing her disappointed look when he didn't respond. He sensed she needed to get something off her chest.

I don't know. It's not an argument, it's a feeling. That something more than empty space is out there.

Thinking about your parents?

She looked down and took her bottom lip between her teeth. Both her parents were dead, her father the victim of a violent murder.

You know what I think God is? Grey said. *If He exists?*

What's that, my love?

Justice.

Nya slowly raised her eyes.

He could tell she liked his answer.

After finishing his lager, Grey kicked his feet off the couch, sighed, and reached for his phone. He dialed Viktor's number.

"It's good to hear from you," Professor Radek boomed.

"Where are you? I hear an ocean."

"Ah. Yes. I decided to take a few days to relax."

"I didn't know the Czech Republic had a beach."

"It's, ah, I'm actually still in Cape Town. With Naomi."

"Oh yeah?"

"Did you want something?" Viktor said, rather hastily.

"I'm not sure how to say this, so I'll just come out with it. I'm in debt sixty thousand dollars."

"Oh?"

"On your credit card."

Silence on the phone. "I see," Viktor said.

"I can't even afford the interest."

"Is that how you paid Jax?"

"Yeah," Grey mumbled. "Sorry. I didn't see another option."

"You could have come to me."

"I know you would have said yes. But I still couldn't take the chance."

More silence. Grey shuffled his feet, wondering if he had enough equity in his loft to sell it and pay off the professor. Probably not.

"In that case," Viktor said slowly, and Grey thought he detected a note of satisfaction in his tone, "I suppose you'll have to get back to work."

Author's Note

I wish I had made all of this up.

Though I research heavily for the Dominic Grey novels (I probably shorted out an FBI server during the research for *The Resurrector*), I don't usually include research notes because I think truth in fiction comes from how the words make you feel, rather than a reference to the facts behind them. That being said, with this book, I'd like to point out a few resources that might help illuminate certain issues for those who are interested.

The number of books that have been written on the weird beliefs of the Nazis and the quasi-occult forces that helped shaped them are legion. One in particular I recommend, which takes a scholarly approach to the topic, is *Hammer of the Gods* by David Luhrssen (Potomac Books, 2012). I left countless bizarre factoids out of *The Resurrector* because I felt they were too fantastical for the novel. Oh, the irony! Also, consider these eerie lines from a poem written by Adolf Hitler himself:

> *I often go on bitter nights*
> *To Wodan's oak in the quiet glade*
> *With dark powers to weave a union*
> *The runic letters the moon makes with its magic spell*
> —Adolf Hitler

As uniquely horrific as the Nazi and Apartheid eras were, the world has a long history of genocide and ethnic cleansing, including eugenics legislation and the colonization of the Americas. In modern times, the number of hate groups in the United States and worldwide appears to be growing, rather than dying out. Recruitment drives have moved online, making it easier for members to join anonymously and for allegiances to span borders. I hate to say it, but it's my belief the only reason an ethnic bioweapon has never been used on a mass scale before is because the technology was not present. In a way, all genocides are ethnic weapons of mass destruction. The only difference between an army that uses clubs, spears, or guns versus one which employs an advanced bioweapon is the degree to which science impacts the battle. Along these lines, see this chilling 1970 article from the *Military Review*, where the potential of developing weapons that target specific ethnicities is discussed:

www.usa-anti-communist.com/pdf/Military_Review_November_1970_Complete.pdf

Here is a more modern article on the topic:

io9.gizmodo.com/5883245/will-the-battles-of-tomorrow-be-fought-with-gene-warfare

For anyone who thinks mishaps never occur within an organization as critical to the Public Health as the CDC, I direct you to the six vials of forgotten smallpox at a government lab, and boxes full of other less lethal materials. During testimony at a House hearing, Thomas Frieden, former director of the CDC, admitted to a pattern of safety lapses that included mishandling anthrax and flu and shipping active and potentially dangerous samples to other labs.

www.gpo.gov/fdsys/pkg/CHRG-113hhrg92323/html/CHRG-113hhrg92323.htm

My research on molecular biophysics, gene editing, and recombinant DNA was particularly eye-opening. CRISPR is real and unnerving to read about. The future has already arrived. For those unfamiliar with the topic, a good place to start is this *Wired* article:

www.wired.com/2015/07/crispr-dna-editing-2

Finally, along with my own research and visits to homeless shelters and townships, I utilized Heather Parker Lewis's powerful account of her social work with South African street kids in *Also God's Children?* (Ihilihili Press, 2007).

Acknowledgements

Thanks to Richard Marek for another amazing edit. Ryan McLemore, Rusty Dalferes, John Strout and my wife also immeasurably improved the book. Lisa Weinberg, Maria Morris, and Bill Burdick are invaluable supporters and early readers. Jaye Manus is a book formatter and all around problem solver who I could not do without. Gary Chidarikire, my brother-in-law and *bon vivant*, has always been a font of information on South African life, culture, and politics. Dan Ozdowski, IT expert extraordinaire, ensures the technology in my novels is germane to the twenty-first century. A special thanks to Dr. Han Kim, cardiologist with Duke University, for advice on medical issues and his patience with my persistent line of inquiry beginning with "but *could* it happen?"

LAYTON GREEN is a bestselling author who writes across a number of genres, including mystery & thriller, suspense, horror, and fantasy. He is the author of the Dominic Grey series, the Genesis Trilogy, the Blackwood Saga, and other works of fiction. His novels have been optioned for film, translated into multiple languages, and nominated for many awards (including a rare three-time finalist for an International Thriller Writers award).

Word of mouth is crucial to the success of any author. If you enjoyed the book, please consider leaving an honest review on Amazon, Goodreads, or another book site, even if it's only a line or two.

Finally, if you are new to the world of Layton Green, please visit him on Goodreads, Facebook, and at www.laytongreen.com. for additional information on the author, his works, and more.

Printed in Great Britain
by Amazon